.

The Brothers of Uterica

SOUTHWEST LIFE AND LETTERS

A series designed to publish outstanding new fiction and non-fiction about Texas and the American Southwest and to present classic works of the region in handsome new editions.

General Editors: Tom Pilkington, Tarleton State University; Suzanne Comer, Southern Methodist University Press.

THE
Brothers of Uterica

Benjamin Capps

With a new Preface by BENJAMIN CAPPS

and an Afterword by C. L. SONNICHSEN

Southern Methodist University Press

DALLAS

Library of Congress Cataloging-in-Publication Data

Capps, Benjamin, 1922–
      The brothers of Uterica.
      (Southwest life & letters)
      I. Title.   II. Series.
PS3553.A59B76   1988   813′.54   87-23387
ISBN 0-87074-257-4
ISBN 0-87074-258-2 (pbk.)

PREFACE

IN the spring of 1952 my wife, two children, and I moved to an area on the western edge of Dallas called La Réunion. It was the site of a colony settled in 1855 by European socialists, intellectuals, impractical dreamers. They had intended to set up an ideal society, but failed. That brief contact with a site of historical significance whetted my interest so that in the next dozen years I read about and thought about varieties of socialism back through the centuries and on the American frontier.

One of the earliest proposals for an ideal society is Plato's *Republic*, written in the fourth century B.C. Another, equally well-known today, is Thomas More's *Utopia*, published in 1516. (More was hanged some twenty years later, though not for writing this book.) Both proposals assume that human life can be well ordered by human reason. No such proposal has solved the problem of whose reason shall be used and how leaders should be selected.

Two aspects of *Utopia* seem notable to me. First, More sets his ideal society in the New World. Out there somewhere was virgin land, not tainted by the old problems of wealth and privilege and custom, a place where reasonable people of good will could start over. All America was the West at the time, and parts of it would remain the West for four hundred years.

One study of pre–Civil War communal colonies in America shows that about three-quarters of them were located on the frontiers of their day. A more recent study lists sixty-two west of the Mississippi between 1860 and 1919. These included colonies at Aurora, Oregon; Orderville, Utah; Greeley, Colorado; and Llano, California. Some were secular; some had religious ideals. All seemed to be caught in the lure of westering, the appeal of new, pure wilderness.

The second notable aspect of More's *Utopia* has to do with the education of those who are setting up the ideal society. People in the city would go out to the farms, More wrote, "to be instructed and taught by those who have been there a year already, and are therefore expert and skilled in the care and cultivation of the land. And they the next year shall teach the others." Such an attitude is citified intellectual arrogance; any country bumpkin knows that it takes a lifetime to understand the vagaries of weather and insects and stock breeding.

In my own homeland of Northwest Texas one group of colonists came in the 1840s and tried to locate at a site between present-day Fort Worth and Denton. Calling themselves Icarians, pledged to a life of communism, they were totally unprepared for the realities of the frontier. Some died of malnutrition, some of fatigue, some of malaria. Their one medical doctor went mad. As if a jealous god watched them, one man was struck and killed by lightning. Their French leader hastily decided to get his followers off the dangerous Texas frontier, and he led them to a site in Illinois, where they failed again.

Fiction has not been kind to utopias. One thinks of *The Blithedale Romance*, by Nathaniel Hawthorne; *Brave New World*, by Aldous Huxley; and *Nineteen Eighty-Four*, by George Orwell. Perhaps it is the duty, at least the tendency, of fiction to dig beyond right reason and uncover the less rational aspects of human nature.

In my own work I have been interested in comparing

the whites on the frontier with the Native Americans. In *The Brothers of Uterica* the Indians represent two things. First, adaptation, for surely the different native groups knew by experience what the European intruders did not. Second, the unknown, mysterious, even dangerous consequences that await thinkers who learn too much from each other and not enough from nature.

I am of two minds about American utopias, admiring the idealistic intellectuals but at the same time admiring the more practical frontier folk who sometimes cooperated with each other and sometimes showed stubborn individualism. The whole subject has hardly been treated in fiction of the American West.

One might wonder how different the world would be today if Marx and Engels and Lenin had been at Icaria in Northwest Texas in 1848.

Benjamin Capps
Grand Prairie, Texas

The Brothers of Uterica

CHAPTER

1

THE wagons creaked to the patient pull of the ox teams, and the wheels clonked from side to side as they turned against the bumpy, roadless land, marking it with the first wheel tracks it had felt since the beginning of time. From somewhere toward the rear of the caravan came the occasional short, shrill whistle of a German boy, who used that sound along with a switch to urge his oxen on, and walking just ahead of me one of the American employees sometimes shouted, "Hup!ah! Hup!ah!" at his team. At the head of the column went the massive wagons belonging to the freighters from Shreveport. In days past they had become aggravated with the clumsy wagon-handling of some of the colonists, and now they would lead off each morning, never looking behind them unless they were halted by someone in authority, expecting us to bring our lighter wagons wherever they could take their heavier ones.

Out to the left I could see our herds of horses and milk cows, separate, each driven by three horsemen, and farther back the sheep, coming like a lumpy, gray carpet dragged along the land. They were herded by more than a dozen women and children on foot and one dog. The women wore simple long dresses and bonnets they had fashioned as protection against the sun. Except for a half dozen colonists who were sick, none of them rode; they herded loose stock or goaded oxen and trailed wagons, ready to push. Ironically, now that we neared our destination, we were becoming an efficient caravan.

I can hardly put into words how I felt, looking at the land ahead. It was promising country with gentle hills rising all around, but with long, fine slopes for farming, some of these covered with tall, dry buffalo grass. On this spring afternoon, it lay under a brilliant sun, vivid, almost sparkling. The post oak trees which covered a quarter of the hilly expanse still carried some old leaves of the year before in dusty tan clumps, mostly low down where the wind had been unable to dislodge them. Other trees were completely bare. But in certain protected sunny spots tender new grass was pushing up, also the bright, fragile flowers of early spring. It was as if the life in the earth was eager to burst through the gray remnants of winter. But those kinds of things happen also in a civilized land. There was more here. This was vast, strange, uncertain. We had left the settlements far behind. What lay ahead was extensive and grand, as august as the oceans, as colossal, also as mysterious; it set us a challenge, but also suggested faintly some tragic possibility. It seemed a young land, yet the solitude that lay over it seemed as old as anything on earth.

The oaks out there looked peculiar, half bare of their leaves, with blackish, heavy trunks and short, crooked limbs that quickly diminished in size to a fringe of twigs, as if each tree had changed its ambitions in the middle of its growth. They were impressive trees, seeming self-contained because they grew little wood away from their dark centers, and their outer reaches were thin, brittle-looking. They were strong but crabby and reluctant trees, like something which has seen trouble and adjusted itself.

The lead wagon stuck in a small gulley, and the freighters broke out picks and shovels to free the wagon and improve the small crossing. One of the American employees walked up to see whether any help was needed, and he and I and one of the freighters stood talking during the short delay. The freighter was a rough fellow with untrimmed beard and floppy hat, with the insolent self-assurance of a man who knows his job and accepts no other responsibilities.

"I saw you holding a lot of parley-voo with that little Frenchy last night," the employee said. "What's he doing? Converting you to socialism?"

"Naw," the freighter said. "We talked about painters."

"Painters?"

"Yeah."

"What does he know about painters?"

"He don't know nothing. Calls 'em panthers. Asked me did I ever hear one scream."

"Did you?"

"I told him they sound like a woman wailing, only worse." He grinned.

"Did you ever hear one?" I asked him.

"Can't say as I did, but I lived in painter country all my life, and anybody knows that's the way they sound, like a woman wailing, only worse. They say you can hear one three, four miles."

The employee asked, "What did the little Frenchy say to that?"

"Et it up. Hell, I told him about horn snakes, too, how they got that poison horn in their tail and all. You think he never et that up. Hell, might as well tell 'em the worst, I say, let 'em know what they're up against out here." He was half serious, half joking.

"You been out here before?" the employee asked.

"Naw, and I ain't staying out here this time a minute more than I can help. I get that load off that wagon, I'm long gone, I tell you."

The employee winked at me. "Damned if I don't think he's scared of this country."

"Scared of greenhorns, you mean," the freighter said. He looked around to see who was in hearing distance, then confided, "This here is the queerest crew of people, taken all in all, I ever run up against. You ever see the like?" He shook his head in wonderment, then, not waiting for an answer to his question, walked toward the front of the caravan.

The employee laughed. The freighter had not realized that I was a colonist. How much more than that he had failed to realize! The working people all over the country—how little they understood what was about to be born out here. That through our efforts it might be someday true that they, the hewers of wood and drawers of water, the plowmen and factory workers and miners, might find themselves the social and economic equals of anyone on earth. I didn't mind the "queer." We were more queer than such a man as the freighter could believe. A half dozen of the queer greenhorns among the colonists had been professors in the great universities of Europe, others doctors, lawyers, writers, government officials. How could he understand?

There in the wagons, in the trunks and boxes and purses, in the places where keepsakes and letters and private treasures were kept, each of us colonists preserved a single sheet of paper. It was printed in small type with this heading: "Goals of Our Common Faith." But we called it the Covenant. It listed these points:

1. All those forms of private ownership which lead to inequality and special privilege are to be abolished.
2. Every form of honest toil is ennobling, and each colonist shall take his turn at physical labor.
3. Universal suffrage shall be observed. Every male and female colonist old enough to do the work of an

adult shall have the privilege and responsibility of voting.

4. Every person shall have a portion of leisure. Intellectual pursuits as well as all the arts will be encouraged.

5. Education is the birthright of every person. We shall establish free public education for adults and children. Poetry or legend teaching old irrational beliefs will not be taught. Teachers shall devise stories which teach virtue.

6. There shall be no title based on pride and privilege. Titles may be used only to designate the occupation of the holder.

7. Money as a private holding and in any dealing between colonists shall be considered valueless.

8. Everyone shall have complete religious liberty and the liberty of his own conscience.

9. Every colonist shall take from the common storehouse according to his desires without restraint, and there shall be no locks on any doors.

10. Governmental and legal procedures shall not have such contrived intricacy as to delay and thwart justice, but shall be so simple that every person may be his own lawyer.

11. We seek a life ordered by reason and good will; we expect to find such life amid the beauties and common virtues of nature.

12. Care in old age or ill health or misfortune is the right of every human being.

13. English shall be the official language of the colony; but it is our faith that every nationality and race of man is equal.

14. The rewards of toil should go not to those who inherit wealth, but to those who toil.

15. We denounce the kind of pleasure which comes from observing the discomforts and miseries of less for-

tunate people, but we believe in human happiness and recreation. We shall have music, enjoyment of nature, wholesome conversation, lectures, and games, some of which shall be devised so as to teach to children the rewards of virtue.

16. At the end of five years or at such time as the New Socialist Colonization Company shall be reimbursed for its investment, all the property derived from the Company shall be the property of each and all of the citizens of the colony.

After the wagons were rolling again, we came shortly to a vantage point of high ground, and some of the men began to point to our right. I could see, several miles out there, a hill or ridge which stood higher than the others and had a flattish top. It was the landmark Brother Bossereau had told us about. An air of expectancy came over us. I could hear it in the voices of the colonists as they called out to one another, though the words might be French or Swiss or German. We had agreed to speak English, but they fell back on their native languages when they were angry or frustrated, as they had been more than once on this trip, or, as now, when they were full of agreeable anticipation. Some of their words were frivolous as they embraced each other or slapped each other on the back.

During the next two hours, the train of wagons became a jumble. The more lightly loaded ones toward the rear pulled out of line to find their own roads and thus prevent being held back. As they bunched up, some of them found it necessary to take routes that were rough. There was much tilting of loads and rattling of chains and straining and creaking of the wagons. I understood their eagerness. It seemed that we would never cover those last miles.

We came to a rounding crest and everyone knew that our destination was in sight. The wagons fanned out and stopped.

Before us the hill broke away in white limestone outcrops down to a broad, shallow valley. Through it wound a small stream that forked straight out ahead of us, and this creek and its tributary had tall timber along it. The grass grew lushly in the bottoms. A mile away, at a place where the stream ran straight, the afternoon sun sparkled on the water. Down to our left, in a marshy spot, pale-yellow flowers speckled the darker ground.

They looked at it a while. I think a vast sigh went up from the Europeans and that they spoke a common silent exclamation: "At last! Thank God!" It had been a hard trek for them, more difficult than we Americans could easily understand, for they had suffered the long ocean crossing and were farther from home. It was now more than three months since they had sailed from Antwerp, and, having gathered there from all over western Europe, some of them must have been as much as half a year in preparation and travel. After they had looked in silence a few minutes, they began to shift their eyes from the land to one another and talk. I heard the name "Brother Bossereau," "*Monsieur* Bossereau," and, from some of the older men, "Jean Charles."

Miss Harriet Edwards came along the straggling crowd calling, "Brother Bossereau! Where is that man? Bossereau! Brother Langly, have you seen him?"

I told her that he was down toward the end. He had been pushing on a heavily loaded wagon at the rear of the caravan the last time I had seen him. She swung along, calling his name, bringing a string of colonists behind her. In a minute they brought the man they sought toward the center in front of the resting oxen, and the people gathered toward him—we three hundred colonists, the few permanent employees, and even the freighters from Shreveport.

Jean Charles Bossereau was about sixty years old, a man of medium build in cheap, loose clothing and still wearing the crude wooden shoes that many of the colonists had worn as a symbol of humility but which the others had long since changed for good boots. He had left his hat somewhere, probably on the wagon he had been pushing, and his head was showing sunburn. He had a high and shiny bald path down his head, surrounded at the back and sides by crumpled and matted gray hair. He had the kind of complexion that does not tan but turns red in spots—at the tip of the thin, sensitive nose, at the earlobes, at the sides of the nostrils, at places on the loose skin of the cheeks. I had noticed that his skin was tender, for when he had freshly shaved, his face always showed scraped and irritated spots. His spectacles, which he took off frequently, pinched the bridge of his nose and left red marks. In sum, he seemed tender to the minor pains and itches of existence, but this did not add up to the impression he made. One could not be in his presence without being aware of the force of his opinion; one could not look at him without being aware of a great mind working behind the high forehead.

"Brothers and Sisters, I have no speech prepared," he said. He spoke English well and had little accent. "This is the place, as you know by now. The line is not located, but we stand about at the edge of the Company land.

"You must know that my heart is full of strong feeling. This occurs to me, for instance: that Louis Napoleon Bonaparte, the so-called president of the Second Republic, cannot touch me here. But the safety of one man is not important. Nothing that Bonaparte represents can penetrate here. A year ago when I saw this land, I stopped my horse and sat and looked at this valley and penned a few notes in my journal. Perhaps you will permit me to read them to you now."

He took a notebook from his pocket and leafed through it. All was quiet except for small sounds the oxen and horses made. Even the children watched him and waited. He read: "Oh, Texas! Land of commencement! Beautiful Texas! How many uncounted human comrades have suffered a limited and arduous life with never the opportunity that is here! How many have travailed through the long years of their lives without this chance! To start over, escape the old iniquity, the old anxiety, resentment, aversion, abolish the old encrustations! To have liberty! To be human spirits and not the slaves of an arbitrary past! See how she presents her hospitality! Promised land! Consecrated land! Land of realization!"

They cheered and applauded these flowery remarks. Partly his effectiveness came from our knowing what he had been: a delegate to the French Constitutional Assembly and a writer and editor of note. He had been the inspiration for the formation of the New Socialist Colonization Company, now some years old, the temporary director and definitely the spiritual leader of those from Europe, and had been quickly accepted as the leader of us who joined them in New Orleans. But his influence rested on more than what he had been. I thought of it as a kind of human magnetism. He had a power to make people feel that dreams might be caused to come true, that man's will itself is a part of Providence, that fond hopes are not absurd, or, to put it in the Christian manner, that the Word might become flesh and actually dwell among men. I could not have said how he convinced me of these things; it involved the idea that certain things must have a chance of being true because they are worthy of being true.

When he had put his notebook away, he went on in a more conversational tone. "My brothers and sisters, socialism is not an automatic system, and an ideal society is not easily established. We face difficult labor before our intentions will be realized. Allow me to propose something. We have our Covenant of sixteen points agreed upon. Let me propose number seventeen, that we might accept at this moment, in our hearts if not on paper: to renounce the past, to forgive it and turn away from it; to turn our backs on its symbols and influence as we turn our faces toward tomorrow. This number seventeen, unwritten, is the essence of the others. Will you all say, each deep in his soul, that the past is no more? That its evils and sorrows and resentments are no more? At this moment in time, looking ahead at our new home, its insidious mastery over us is finished, and we are newborn people.

"I had an argument with Mr. Finch in Louisiana and we have had some words since. I'd like to shake his hand at this time, for I hold no ill will toward him and believe we are very fortunate that he is with us."

William Finch stood back some distance in the crowd, and they parted to let him come forward. He was embarrassed, but it was not the kind of invitation one could refuse. He was a large, competent man of about fifty, who had been employed as supervisor of agriculture. As such he was my boss, for I had the fancy title of assistant supervisor of agriculture, and I had come to like him. His appearance set him apart. He wore heavy boots and a large hat such as many Texans wore farther south. Words such as "ideal society" and "slaves of an arbitrary past" were meaningless to him, but he was a man who could get things done; except for him, we would have been still stuck in the mud a hundred miles east. He was smiling and, I believe, blushing under his tan as he vigorously pumped Brother Bossereau's hand. Clearly there was no ill will between them, but I thought there would have been none with Finch; he was blunt-spoken but did not seem to bear grudges.

The French leader then began to call one of his countrymen, Dominique Henri, and when he had spotted him, said, "Where is the young American you argued with about the ox? Find him and shake his hand. Brother York it was, young York."

It was Andrew York, who, like his brother Jim, was a colonist. They had shown themselves, unlike many of the others, to be good workers. But one morning Andrew had taken a burning stick out of a cook fire and had carried it with him to use in prodding a certain fat, lazy black ox. Dominique

Henri, a man small in stature, with a heavy moustache and weak chin, had been horrified at the cruelty of it, had knocked the brand from Andrew's hand, protesting passionately. They had come near to blows. Andrew had been pulled away by his brother Jim, but had shouted these words: "You can find fault, damn you! Let's see you do something to keep the wagons rolling!"

When those two had been brought together and had shaken hands, the meeting there on the rise broke down into a confusion of handshaking and chatter. Brother Bossereau's grown daughter, Jeannette, a pretty dark-haired girl, came to him and embraced him. The idea of the importance of friendliness had taken hold of them all. If good will of the moment could have built anything by itself, we might have built a city that afternoon. Brother Bossereau was shaking hands with all who crowded near him. Everyone seemed to be congratulating everyone else. I heard Miss Harriet Edwards' voice. "If I can speak for the fair sex..." Her clear laughter rang out as she spoke these words. She was the most distinguished and well known of us American colonists, who made up about a fourth of the total number. She was making some kind of small speech, but did not have the audience that the French leader had engaged.

Mr. Finch came to me with orders. "Leave the German with that wagon you were on," he said. "He can get it the last mile by himself. I want you to catch a horse and go ahead and find a place to water the stock." He pointed. "We'll camp just between that clump of trees and the creek. There's a good place to get drinking water right in the bend yonder. See?"

"Yes, sir."

"Go downstream from there and find a good place where the stock can get down to the water. Then ride herd on all these people and see that they don't let the stock tromp up our drinking water. We can't put up with that here like we did on the move."

"Yes, sir."

After I had saddled my horse, he called to me, "Langly, take your rifle. You might scare up a deer."

I was glad to take it. We were out of fresh meat. An hour later I had located the spot for watering stock in a clearing where a sand bar sloped down to the clear stream. The trees near the water were elm, pecan, sycamore, cottonwood, hackberry, hickory, and live oak, and under them were many smaller bushes and vines, among which I saw plum bushes and grapevine runners. The elms, some of them tall, majestic trees, were blooming their profusion of tiny flowers, which were green and fading red in color when examined closely, but appeared like a yellow-brown mist sprayed over the branches when seen at a distance. I could smell them, faintly pleasant, like decaying apples, and saw small black bees plying among them. Other trees along the creek were bare, hung only with dark clumps of mistletoe or squirrel nests or a few lone pecan burrs still clinging. I spent the next two hours directing colonists to the two water holes, then, about sunset, crossed the stream and rode up the fringe of trees on the other side. A buck and three does flushed just ahead of my horse. I jumped down, got a bead on the rear doe on the run, and dropped her with a lucky shot.

We had hindquarters of venison at the employees' cook fire that night. Jim and Andrew York and I, though colonists, had got in the habit of camping with the employees, not so much because they were Americans as that we worked with them a good part of the time. We sat and sprawled around on the ground as the fire died away. Mr. Finch sat on the wagon tongue with his hat pushed back on his head, picking his teeth with a stick he had whittled down, saying little. Someone said, "This is a pretty place for a settlement." Someone else said, ". . . if that creek don't dry up in the fall." Another said, "Old Bossereau is a talker, ain't he?" "Yeah, puts me in mind of a preacher we used to have back home." "Well, he's a friendly cuss; you can say that for him." We had run out of talk and were each about ready to hunt a place on the ground to sleep when Mr. Finch finally broke his silence. "They won't make it by talking friendly," he said. "Here it's past the middle of March and not a grain of corn in the ground."

The corn planting was what Brother Bossereau and Mr. Finch had argued about. Mr. Finch had wanted to bring a small party on ahead to begin plowing and planting, had insisted that it was necessary. Brother Bossereau had been equally insistent that the primary task was to locate the colonists on the site so that they could work and also learn how to work, and that all of them had a need and a right to be part of turning the virgin soil. The Frenchman had proved more stubborn, in his humble way, than one would have guessed, and Mr. Finch had stayed with the caravan.

The journey had been a rough initiation for them. They were intellectuals and the kinds of artisans that work in civilized countries. There was not a jack-of-all-trades among them. These gentlemen had found themselves faced with an adversary so simple, so elemental, so difficult, that it was agonizing: mud. The land of east Texas looked beautiful if you didn't touch it; when it felt the weight of a loaded wagon, it became an enemy. So we had pushed and tugged and pried and cursed in several languages, sometimes using three ox teams for one wagon. The prairies of blackland had been the worst; the soil gripped the wheels like a vise and it was bottomless. Those who wore their wooden shoes had a pitiful time of it, for the shoes kept coming off ten inches underground. Some of them had brought sickness from the lowlands, too—ague, diarrhea, boils on the feet.

Their introduction to Texas had been a cruel contrast: on the one hand a virgin prairie that grew flowers as early as February; on the other, mud and boils on the feet.

CHAPTER

2

AT dawn the next day Mr. Finch set out with grubbing
hoe, spade, and broadax and one helper to examine the
soil and plan where the fields might be located. A meeting of
the colony assembly was set for that morning, and he told me
to attend. I was to speak for him if necessary and note down
any instructions that were intended for him.

There was confusion in getting the meeting underway, for
no one seemed to know when it was to be held or where, or
even who was to take part. The camp sprawled over two or
three hundred yards of ground, and the colonists went about
the chores of camping, cooking, carrying water, stretching up
canvas shelters which they had not been able to raise the night
before. Finally, Brother Bossereau got ten or twelve of them
together, and I followed them up away from the wagons.
They chatted as they walked, did not seem to be going to
any particular spot, but walked more and more casually until
they seemed to stop by common consent. When Brother Bossereau spoke, they shuffled around into a rough half-circle in
front of him.

"Well, this is appropriate for our first assembly. We start
from nothing. Only the earth under our feet and God's clear
sky above."

They smiled assent to his words. Miss Harriet Edwards laughed aloud. She had a way of laughing that was charming and proper to nearly any situation. It seemed an awkward place to conduct a meeting, standing there in the open in the damp grass. The sun was less than an hour high. Brother Bossereau held his two hands in front of him, palms up, one cupped in the other.

"Now," he said, "I think it's time that we take our heads from the clouds. We have a great deal of organizing and planning and building to do. The sooner we begin, the better. We'll make errors, but we'll correct them. The point is that we must be practical and push ahead."

His eyes lit on me and he asked, "Where's Mr. Finch?"

"He went out to look at the soil."

"Look at the soil? What do you mean?"

"To decide where the fields can be planted."

"He should be present."

"Well, he asked me to be here and note down anything he needed to know."

"But he should be present. I don't understand why he's not. This meeting is all-important. We have to consider these things." His exasperation showed in his face.

I didn't know what to say. "He didn't understand that it was necessary," I said. "He thought it was more important to—"

"But he should be present. We want his advice about agriculture, and we want him to understand our plans. This is of grave concern. Why...it could be...some day there may be a great building here, and it could be that they will point at this spot and say that here was the very first assembly. We find it hard to imagine, but this could be of historical significance. What is it? What does he say? Is he provoked with me for some reason?"

"No, sir, I'm sure it's nothing like that."

"Please go and tell him his presence is required. We'll wait until he comes."

As I turned to go, he added, "I regret giving you this trouble, Brother Langly, but you understand. Of course, we'll want you here, too."

I walked out in the direction Mr. Finch had taken to a point where I could see a good distance, but, seeing nothing, returned to where my horse was hobbled near camp, saddled him, and rode in a great circle out around the mott of oaks east of the creek. I found Mr. Finch more than a mile from camp and, as I rode toward him, noticed at two different places tall stakes he had mounted in the ground. He and his helper were busily digging. As I dismounted, he had a clod of dirt in his hand, breaking it, tasting of it. He asked, "Meeting over?"

"No, sir, they haven't started yet. Brother Bossereau says they need you there."

"How come?"

"Well, he says they have a lot of things to go over. He sent me to get you."

"What kind of things?"

"I don't know. He said they had to talk about organizing and planning and building. He seemed to think the first assembly is real important and you should be there. He said it's important to get started and push ahead." The words didn't sound the same as they had coming from the French leader.

He reached into the bottom of the little hole, took out some more clods, and squatted, appraising them. "That's good dirt. Just right to break. Another week or so and it'll be too dry. We ought to have some plows in the ground by this evening, tomorrow morning at the latest."

"He said they would wait for you."

He looked up at me and laughed a little as he said, "I don't believe I'll go."

He was serious. He had a way of saying exactly what he

meant, softening the fact with the expression on his face or a little laugh. I couldn't keep from laughing in return as I told him, "I don't think Brother Bossereau is going to like it."

"What do you reckon he really wants with me?"

"Maybe he thinks you might have some important advice about agriculture."

"Get the corn in right now. That's my advice. Tell him that."

"What I mean . . . well . . . I think he wants to talk it all over."

"That's about the size of it, all right."

"Well, then maybe everyone would understand each other's ideas about what ought to be done. Maybe it's not such a bad idea."

"I'm not part of all that," he said. "Don't want anything to do with it." He spoke to the bareheaded young man helping him. "We'll make this line straight through here just below that rock outcrop. Miss all the rocks we can. We'll get fifty acres in this patch."

To me, he suddenly said, "You think I'm going to plan this farm with that bitch Harriet Edwards?"

The words were a shock to me and I thought less of him for it. I said, "It puts me in a bad position. I'm afraid I won't be able to explain what you mean."

"Don't worry about it. Tell Bossereau I said, 'Let's get the corn in.' And I'm ready for any plain orders that have to do with crops or livestock. But I've heard their talk before. This is more important."

I could not help but believe that he was too hasty. He had made a quick judgment that nothing which could concern him would happen at the meeting. I mounted and started back, thinking how peculiar it was that the two men could be so different and each so convincing in his own way. Out here on the prairie I had a strong impression of natural things, the loneliness, the spaces—these marked by a man who as yet had set up only two far-spaced stakes in the land and had dug a few holes, but who was deliberately tasting the soil, crumbling it in his hand, and noting rocky areas which were to be avoided, and, above all, who was moving straight ahead toward the use of the soil without any soul-searching or uncertainty. How different this was from confusion of the camp area and the disorganized assembly meeting where Brother Bossereau spoke of planning and building and pushing ahead. Of the two men, Mr. Finch was the more convincing, with his plain-spoken assurance, his kind of single-minded arrogance. But what a pity to be so sure of a simple thing that one could not hope for greater things. Surely Brother Bossereau and the rest did not need to apologize for their humility, or even uncertainty, in the face of what they planned. Maybe it was proper to talk little about planting corn and to talk at length about planting a new kind of human society in the wilderness.

I found them standing where I had left them, chatting in groups of three or four. I had determined not to take any side in the matter, to be merely a messenger, but could not help trying to make it as pleasant as possible. I said, "Mr. Finch said he thought he should go ahead with his work and he begs to be excused. He thought maybe you could go ahead with the... matters that don't concern him and then he could get any instructions you have about agricultural matters later on."

"That's odd, to say the least," one of them said.

Another said, "It seems quite rude to me."

Brother Bossereau asked, "Did you explain to him that I wanted him present?"

"Well, yes, sir. He believes that it's very urgent to get the land broken and he doesn't want to... be a part of the assembly."

Dr. Valentin, a slender, hard-faced man, who had been the treasurer of the New Socialist Colonization Company until he decided to be an actual member of the colony itself and who still in some way represented the financing of the colony, spoke to Brother Bossereau. "This is nonsense. If you have a reason why he should be here, then merely order him to come. He'll obey orders or be discharged. It's that simple. Why do you want him here?"

"I'm a stockholder, too," someone said. "I think he ought to obey orders and do exactly as he is told."

"Why is it necessary that he be here?" Dr. Valentin demanded.

Brother Bossereau spread his hands in a gesture of helpless frustration. "How do I know? He is the expert on agriculture and it seemed that he should be present. If he judges that he should do something else, perhaps he's correct. How am I to say?"

"Did he actually refuse to come?" someone asked.

"Did he act rudely?" another one asked.

"No," I told them. "He just . . . it wasn't like that."

Dr. Valentin had a slightly nasal voice and he could be devastatingly casual when he tried. He was an American of French blood, coming originally from St. Louis, I believe, but he had lived in France for a decade or more and had wide contacts in Europe, so that we thought of him as one of the Europeans. Though now he addressed Brother Bossereau, the implication was that he spoke to the company, to some extent that he spoke for the assembled company. "It would seem to me that the logical thing is *not* to invite Mr. Finch here unless we have some need of him. We are the policy-making authority. Suppose we get on with the business of the colony, the most urgent of which, it seems to me, is our financial position."

Brother Bossereau seemed unsatisfied, but he took up the stance he had taken an hour before, feet slightly spread, his two hands in front of him, one cupped in the other. "Well, I think we could proceed and discuss any urgent issue. We have no particular agenda, but I desire to bring up the question of assembly membership. Are we properly constituted ... this assembly? Our leadership as established by the Company was for the purpose of bringing us here; now we are responsible for making certain that we govern by the will of the people. We'll have an election with universal suffrage as soon as it can be arranged, of course."

Several of them began to talk at once. I led my horse a little distance to a good patch of grass, ground-tied him, and came back to stand, not among them but near enough to hear all that was said. One of them was protesting to Brother Bossereau: "Jean Charles, there is no question of your standing for election. All of us have taken you for the director from the first. It is understood. I'm sure the elections should not include the director."

"Thank you," he said. "It's only that I wondered about the assembly, whether there is any faction that isn't represented sufficiently for the present, for the temporary business."

"I don't see any reason for objection," someone said. "We are all here. We are the ones who have acted as leaders. I certainly don't know of anyone who would object to us."

They had an air about them of willingness to be fair, of inviting any suggestions, but of not expecting any challenge. They may have been slightly embarrassed, for it was obvious that none of them would challenge himself and that those who might presumably challenge were not present. They looked from one to the other. Miss Harriet Edwards laughed in her free manner and said, "If I may speak for the fair sex, I'm sure that the gentlemen here are the most wise and distinguished we could hope for." Why she invariably laughed when she mentioned speaking for the "fair sex" was not clear. I think it was her apology lest she seem to be calling herself "fair." She went on, "I have an important matter to remind the assembly about when we're through with the urgent questions."

"As for the membership," someone said, "we don't need to feel presumptuous at assuming authority. In any case, some nonelected authority would be needed to set up the elections."

Dr. Valentin said, "It's clear that we are the assembly. Let's get on with a decision as to what we will do about finances. Perhaps, Jean Charles, you would want to make an accounting."

"I'm willing to proceed with any subject," Brother Bossereau said, "but I don't understand that the money question is urgent."

"Indeed! We must be nine thousand dollars out of our budget, if my rough approximations are correct. That seems urgent to me."

Some of them spoke up defending Brother Bossereau.

"The money went for transportation. Isn't that the only expense we've had?"

"Yes, transportation. And delays. And the food that spoiled. What else could we do?"

Brother Bossereau asked, "Does anyone object to any particular expenditure? What action could we possibly take now, or what is it that we must do now because it is urgent?"

Dr. Valentin said, "I feel obliged to let the company people in France know the facts, and, knowing their point of view, I expect they will want to know what is being done to make up the deficit or at least what is being done to prevent this kind of thing in the future."

"Do you object to any expenditure?" Brother Bossereau asked.

"I could hardly object when I don't even know the expenditures. But I feel obliged to report these things. They would want to know and have a right to know."

"Perhaps you could explain to them in your letter that we encountered a few unexpected expenses which were unavoidable, as they were, and explain to them that we do not expect any more emergencies of that kind. I think there is no cause for pessimism, Brother Valentin. Surely our main troubles are behind us. We are here. That's the principal thing."

"And yet if we spend, with no accounting, outside our budget, and if this were to continue, that may develop to be the principal thing."

"Yes," Brother Bossereau said. "But we are spending nothing now. We are on the land now."

"We keep nine employees. Do they expect no pay?"

"Well, that's within our proposals and understood by everyone. When we're established here, there will be no further need for them. Do you have some definite proposal to submit to this assembly concerning the employees?"

"I'm simply not satisfied, Jean Charles, to see the money go out as it has. It's a dangerous precedent that no one has seen fit to worry about."

Brother Dominique Henri, who had not spoken before, interrupted. "Pardon me, but in regard to employees, I know a little matter. The freighters from Shreveport, they say they require help to unload their wagons, for they will not remain but one day."

All of them looked toward the wagons, and someone said, "They've not touched them. Why are they so stubborn about it?"

Brother Bossereau asked me, "Could they not be expected to unload their own wagons, Brother Langly? Or perhaps we don't understand the customs of the country."

"If they're left alone, they'll unload them," I said, "but they may not be as careful as they should be. They need someone to show them where to put things and maybe to help with the lifting."

"Will you manage that for us, Brother Langly?" he said. "I'm sure you know better how to do it than any of us. You can take care of it this afternoon, can't you?"

"Well, yes, sir. Would you be able to assign me three or four men? It will only take a few hours, I guess."

He agreed to assign the men for the job. It occurred to me that it was not exactly a suitable task for the assistant supervisor of agriculture and that they, the colonists, were about as unorganized as they had been on most of the journey. Mr. Finch had, no doubt, foreseen more clearly than I the possible results of attending the assembly, but I determined to be as cooperative as possible.

Brother Bossereau's eyes fell on Dr. Valentin for a moment and he frowned, then said, "As for any financial problems, why don't we presume this for the time being: it shall be our policy to consider all expenditures carefully and to save our financial resources as much as possible? But I would repeat that I feel nothing but optimism."

Someone said, "I think one of our main purposes is to get away from so much quibbling about money."

Dr. Valentin did not appear to be satisfied, but he must have been unwilling to press it further.

For a while the meeting broke down into more informal talk. Somehow it came out that one of them was keeping a journal or diary of these days; then another confessed to the same thing. They began to call around to one another, "Are you keeping a journal? Not you, too?" It developed that each of them was carefully recording daily events and impressions. It seemed to them a delightful joke.

I did not mention that I too had been infested with the journal-keeping disease. What was happening here, that is, our entire effort, had seemed to me worthy of keeping a record about, as evidently it had to each of them. I was reluctant to join in the general confession because, for one thing, some of them were noted as writers and, for another thing, my entries were not faithfully kept each day as I had planned when I started my journal in New Orleans.

Brother Bossereau and Dr. Sockwell, an untidy-appearing

man, an American who was a colonist, talked about problems
of sickness and sanitation in the new camp. The doctor, unlike Dr. Valentin, had assumed some responsibility for the
health of the colonists and was evidently treating several of
them. He wanted a crew of men to build sanitary facilities.
From his request grew a general discussion of the organization of work crews. We already had a dozen men who had
been designated "work leaders," some of whom were present
at the assembly. It was not yet clear what work leaders would
be needed or how the colonists should be divided and assigned
to their work. After many suggestions, Brother Bossereau
took out his notebook and began assigning each of those
present, with their permission, either as general work leaders
or planners, noting this in his book. Some were assigned more
than once. There were planners for government, culture,
education, and recreation, but it was agreed that these matters
would be given only a minimum of attention until things were
more settled. The planners for town layout, architecture,
farm layout, common dining facilities, sanitary facilities, and
water supply would have priority at first. The assembly itself
would take care of overall planning.

They had talked past midmorning and there was mention
of adjourning; then someone remembered that Miss Harriet
Edwards, who had been assigned as planner of culture, had
said that she had an item of business. They gave her their
attention. She had, as always, an air about her of unaffected
good taste, which seemed to me surprising and very pleasant
in these crude surroundings. I could not help thinking of
Finch's words, "That bitch Harriet Edwards," and how inaccurate they were. Her manner was gracious but uninhibited
as she spoke. "What I have to say isn't urgent, but I believe
it's important. I mean it needs to be said now. I noticed the
women this morning, carrying water, cooking, scraping pots,
washing dishes. I don't need to remind anyone that we agreed
that we would have no servants in the colony. If a woman

does a certain chore it should be because she does it better than anyone else and not because it is woman's work. We ought to keep our commitments in mind from the very first."

"Sister Edwards, you're perfectly right," Brother Bossereau said. "Of course we do what we do now primarily for convenience. We are not established."

She laughed. She was a handsome woman with large, pleasant features. In her voice was the slightest note of irritation. "The danger is that we will begin doing what is convenient and it will never be convenient to change. The principle of equality ought to be before us in all our planning, especially at first." She laughed a little again and went on. "I mean to be a nuisance about it, if I must."

"You will be an agreeable nuisance," Brother Bossereau said gallantly. "Thank you for reminding us of this important point."

His remarks seemed to satisfy her, and again the meeting broke down into conversations between individuals. Shortly afterward the French leader dismissed them with the promise that the assembly would meet again within a day or two, when the camp was more settled. As the others headed toward the wagons, I started to catch my horse and was surprised to see that Brother Bossereau followed me. I paused, and he came up to me frowning.

"Brother Langly," he said, "what about Mr. Finch? I'm not satisfied with the way we left it. What do you think?"

"I guess I told you about all I can," I said.

"He was not angry?"

"No, sir, I don't think so. I wouldn't say he was."

"He just refused to come?"

"Well... yes, sir."

"It's the misunderstanding I don't like. Possibly the best thing to do in an instance like this is go directly to the man and clear up the matter, but I hardly know how to approach him. I thought we had settled any difference. You're an

American and understand him better than I; what would his reaction be if I go to him and question him about it?"

"Well, I don't know," I said. "He seems like a friendly man all in all." I couldn't see exactly what might be gained by pressing any questions, but it could be that I didn't understand the importance of it as did Brother Bossereau.

He thought a minute, then said, as if he had been reading my mind, "It's very important. Let's find him."

I led my horse and we walked up through the oaks toward the clear slopes where I had left Mr. Finch. Brother Bossereau was silent and serious. I pondered the question whether being an American and understanding Mr. Finch implied that I did not understand the European I was with, but came to no conclusion other than that I had rather be his guide than carry messages between the two. We found Mr. Finch and his helper some distance from where I had left them, their arms loaded with freshly cut stakes. They laid down their burdens and waited for us.

Brother Bossereau was winded from the walk. He said, "I see you are working."

"Yes, sir," Mr. Finch said. "We're hard at it."

"We've been discussing some of the problems of getting settled here," Brother Bossereau said, "and wanted you to meet with us. I think maybe you didn't understand. I was expecting that you would meet with the first assembly, and we would have the benefit of your experience in agriculture."

"Get some seed in the ground. That's my advice."

"Well, that's abrupt advice, wouldn't you say? It seems to me that we have a lack of communication here for some reason. What else do you have to say about it? We were expecting some further conferring on the general problems of agriculture and the way they would relate to our getting settled and establishing ourselves here. Surely 'get some seed in the ground' is not all you have to say. Is it?"

"Yes, sir. That's about it, right now."

"Why, Mr. Finch, surely you see what I mean. We have a difficult problem of authority here. There's no question that you are employed by the assembly, which is the policy-making organ of the colony, and are subject to the orders of the assembly and the director. Is there?"

"No question about it."

"On the other hand, you were recommended to us as a man of good judgment in all matters of agriculture, and we employed you, even though we already have some among us who are familiar with agriculture, as one whose knowledge might be of value in this particular part of the world. Isn't that your understanding?"

"Yes, sir, that's about it. And I aim to do the best job for you I can."

At these words, Brother Bossereau seemed to be stymied for a minute. He stood frowning, then finally said, "I just don't comprehend you. Why don't you wish to talk? I can get so far with you and no farther."

"Talk? What do you figure I ought to say?"

"That's just it. Just that. At this moment you stand there as if you knew something that I don't know. You know that you have a point of view that I don't comprehend, yet your answer to me is to ask what I think you ought to say. What benefit is it for me to put words in your mouth? Surely in our positions it would be better if we understood each other. I cannot conceive of what you think. Why do you desire not to talk?"

"Because I don't see what you're getting at. I don't see anything hard to understand about what I've been saying."

"It may not seem hard to you, but it seems impossible to me. I beg you for information and your answer tells me nothing, but infers that you would prefer to end the conversation. Why do you not desire to talk? What is it? Tell me about corn. What is it in your estimation that makes corn

more important than any other single thing right now? Why
is this your point of view? I would appreciate it if you would
go into detail and explain it to me and not be concerned that
you will insult my intelligence. My problem is to persuade
you to talk."

Mr. Finch grinned, said, "Well, I don't know..." and
lifted up his hat to scratch his head a little. His sandy hair was
plastered to his temples from his sweat and the pressure of his
hat. He began to speak as if launching himself with great
effort. "I raised corn in Missouri and Louisiana both. I made
some fair crops. Nobody knows this country right in here
too well, especially west of here, so I don't guarantee anything. It's kind of guesswork, but I've got something to go
on when I guess. I've been down to San Antonio and along
the Gulf; then I've been out of Westport twice to Santa Fe.
You got to estimate what it's like this far south of Missouri
and this far north of San Antonio. Then this here is the edge
of the Cross Timbers, you see. It's kind of the edge of a
desert. A little like that. I look at the size of the rivers and
creeks; you can't go on spring rains. And plants. Yesterday
and today I saw prickly pears and bear grass. Prickly pear
grows in the desert. They look kind of sickly here, but they're
here. Bear grass, that's kin to yucca.

"I won't go into it all, but what I'm trying to say is you
can raise corn here if you do it right. You could raise cotton.
You don't have to own slaves to raise cotton, like some of you
all thought. But I didn't object, because cotton is a cash crop,
and it would be a long haul to put it on the river. But corn,
that's different. It's the best thing you can raise to get along on
away out this way. Mr. Bossereau, you've almost got to have
it."

This was by far the longest talk I had heard from Mr.
Finch. He went on. "It's guesswork, but I say we've got to
crowd the cold weather now because the hot weather is going
to crowd us in June. If the leaves burn up before the corn

is made, you won't get a thing but nubbins with a few little scraggly grains on them. Well, you might have meat and vegetables this summer, but I would say, comes about December, Mr. Bossereau, and all this crowd to feed, and no corn, you would be in a bad way."

The French leader seemed to be encouraged. "Now, I can comprehend all that, and I appreciate your explaining it. Now, don't you believe that if I can comprehend it, so could the others of the assembly? This is the crucial point. Accepting the truth of all you say, how can you be sure, even so, that planting corn is the most important task that faces the colony?"

"I didn't say that. You asked me my viewpoint. I'm the boss of agriculture. That's stock and crops. If we don't let the stock stray off, they can make out. The most important thing is to get the corn in."

"I'm confused again. Don't you believe my point that the entire project of instituting a society based on new ideas is complicated, and to assume that one practical consideration is above all other matters? ... Amiability, for instance. Friendliness. The importance of friendliness. It's only an example, but I mentioned its importance before. Just that, friendly cooperation, may make the difference in whether we can work out our difficulties. Do you see what I mean?"

Mr. Finch did not see. He said, "I don't reckon I ever thought about friendliness as something you did on purpose, unless you were trying to get to somebody. Then, this fall, who's going to be friendly if they need corn and don't have any?"

"You continue to insist on 'this fall,' 'next December.' That's ten months, Mr. Finch. I assure you that if we have accomplished nothing but raising a large corn crop during the next ten months, our project will be a thorough failure. And I assure you, too, that friendliness, though I meant it only as an example, is all-important. We must have an atmosphere of friendly, tolerant cooperation. I'm not applying this to you. I offer it as an example of an issue that is as important as corn. Do you understand at all what I'm saying?"

"Well, maybe you ought to have a supervisor of friendliness. But you didn't hire me on for that."

Brother Bossereau reddened slightly, but seemed determined to pursue his intention of a meeting of the minds. "Suppose we had a supervisor of friendliness; is there any reason why he should not attend the assembly and explain his ideas and consider along with the leaders the best means of getting his ideas into effect?"

"No, sir, I reckon not."

"Then as supervisor of·corn, why can't you do the same?"

"Well, I guess I could as far as that goes. There's really not much working out to it. You just know what to do and you do it. Get it in the ground. I figured it would save time all around if you just gave me orders. There's not much in it to talk about."

"But, to the contrary, there is much in it to talk about. All of our lives will be affected by agriculture. This colony is to be supported by agriculture until we can construct some manufacturing facilities. If anything is the business of the assembly, this is. Here we come to the crux of this conversation. I comprehend you to a certain extent and no further. You are reluctant. You do not intend that I understand you. And the difficulty lies in the issue of merely discussing agriculture in the assembly. I regret to put it this way, Mr. Finch, but it's almost as if you are determined that we not comprehend each other."

"Well, I don't reckon we're getting anywhere, Mr. Bossereau, and that's a fact. All I can say is, long as you want me to hold down this job, I'll do my best."

"But I insist!" the French leader said. His manner seemed to imply that he was ready to use physical force if necessary, an ironic implication in the face of his obvious inability to force Mr. Finch to do anything. "Why must you conceal yourself behind gratuitous pleasantries? Why are you reluctant to meet with the assembly? That question is surely plain enough. If your time is so precious, the assembly might meet after dark to accommodate you. I'd like an answer to my question. Why are you reluctant to meet with the assembly?"

Mr. Finch stood still a moment, gathering his thoughts, serious, but not so obviously involved as the other man. "You've got me more or less backed against the wall. I guess it's like this business of getting your wagon train out here. You hired me on to boss the agriculture. Why didn't you hire you a wagon master, too?"

"Are you still resentful about that? Is that it?"

"No, sir."

"Then why do you mention it?"

"I figure you'll have more things like that. And worse. To put it bluntly, Mr. Bossereau, you've got a big idea. But it's your big idea. Not mine. I wish you good luck at it, but I don't aim to stand good for any and every thing that comes up that you and your friends didn't think of. No offense, of course."

"That implies a severe criticism. Is it your opinion that we are a group of children playing with ideas?"

"No, sir."

"I'd appreciate it if you'd explain a little further. What do you mean about things that come up that we didn't think of? Are you able to predict difficulties that we cannot?"

"No, sir, but, like I say, it's your big idea, not mine. It's beyond me. I'm a practical man. But I know enough not to take on the job of setting everything to rights so this whole bunch can live away out here in the wilderness, when there are big ideas around that are beyond me, and me not in on them. Mr. Bossereau, you got people, grown men, in your bunch that would die out here if you just turned them loose.

I don't want it where you have all the ideas, and I get all the work done. I want to be in charge of the stock and crops and that's all."

"Perhaps you would do me the favor of being more specific about the other work you desire to avoid."

"Well, it's not for me to tell you, but what about houses? Then what about Indians around here? How are you going to get along with them? But more than things like that, you've got a big system of some kind worked out. It's your system, not mine. You've been working on it a long time. What may come out of that I don't have any more idea than the man in the moon."

"Then isn't it accurate to say that you are not sympathetic to our basic program? Isn't that the entire problem, after all?"

"No, sir. Like I say, I wish you luck in it."

"You are just concerned that you have no part in it except agriculture. Is that it?"

"That's about the size of it."

"And isn't it true that you are being overly modest when you say that our ideas are beyond you? Isn't the truth rather this: that you comprehend the basic ideas of socialism and disagree with them and don't believe in their value? Isn't that the truth?"

"No, sir. I don't see how they can work, and that's a fact. But like I say, I wish you luck. It's just a job to me, and that's the way you put it to me when you hired me on."

"This doesn't answer my question. Why are you reluctant to meet with the assembly? We didn't employ you to actually do the agricultural labor, but rather to see that it is done properly by others. Why is it that you are so reluctant to meet with the leaders of the people and discuss with us the problems that relate to agriculture?"

"I can't take orders from a dozen people."

"Perhaps you couldn't, but perhaps a consensus would develop that would amount to only one order, and you would have some part in formulating the policies that you would administer. It appears to me that it is finally a matter of your sympathies after all. I'm not convinced that you can divide yourself in the manner that you believe. Are the practical and the ideal in reality two things? Is the food a man puts in his stomach one thing and the idea he carries in his spirit another? I don't really see how you can be in charge of agriculture and handle it properly and at the same time be no more deeply involved than you seem to desire." Brother Bossereau's voice trailed off. He seemed to see no productive way to probe further.

Mr. Finch said, "All I can say is, I'll do the best I can. I don't guarantee anything, but I think I can handle it as well as the next man."

Brother Bossereau did not answer. He looked at me, back toward camp, down at the ground. He held us there for what was a long minute, during which time he did not seem to be thinking so much as merely to be lost in reverie. I began to think that it would be embarrassing to break away from him, but then he took his notebook from an inside coat pocket, wrote on a page, tore it out, and handed it to Mr. Finch. When he spoke, his voice was low, calm, businesslike. "These are the leaders of the working crews. Some of them will report to you each day with a group of workers." Then he turned and strode back toward camp.

As I started to follow, Mr. Finch asked me, "They come up with any orders for me at the assembly?"

"No. I don't guess they did."

"You looking for something to do?"

I told him I had to see to the freighters' loads.

"Tell Andy and Jim York to catch up about six head of steers and break out one of the steel plows. Right after dinner I'd like to see what we can do with this sod."

I mounted and rode after Brother Bossereau to remind him to assign me some men to help unload the wagons.

Their disagreement, or I should say lack of agreement, or even inability to get in touch with one another, troubled me, though it really was not my concern. I saw that each of them had a legitimate position, and the idea plagued me that they both, after all, lived in the same world, and that it is impossible for two real positions to be legitimate and beyond reconciliation.

I had no doubts about the colony. It was a magnificent experiment, with a good chance of success. Yet in some subtle way Mr. Finch's ability to ignore its possibilities was a threat to it, or a threat to its conception, for he was not a wealthy man or an aristocrat or any kind of person who would automatically be against our great experiment. In fact, if one believes there are two great classes, the rich and the poor, it would have been hard to place him in either; he seemed not to fit. His having a legitimate point of view suggested to me that we would need all of the tolerance and friendliness and humility and flexibility that we expected to employ. I would have given anything to have heard Brother Bossereau utter a few short, positive statements that would have cut the ground from under Mr. Finch completely and left him dangling with no justification for his attitude.

The rest of that day and into the night the matter nagged at me, not so much that I tried to reason my way through it, but that it dominated my feelings. I tried to imagine the big building that Brother Bossereau had suggested might rise where the leaders had assembled, but could hardly see it, nor a thriving town here. It did occur to me that this many people would build something here without a doubt, since we firmly intended to, and if I could not imagine anything, it was a failure of my imagination.

As for the difference between the two men, I could not help thinking that Mr. Finch might have done better. His position was unassailable as long as he held to it, as long as he felt no need to study it in the light of another man's ideas.

He was limited in his thinking and safe because of that. Worse, he did not have the will to see the views reconciled, as the French leader certainly did. The difference between them seemed to me thus: one was a simple man who could afford to be self-assured because he thought only of corn; one was a tortured man who was forced sometimes to appear pitiful or ridiculous because he thought about the thousand twistings and turnings of these mortal coils. I couldn't deny that Mr. Finch was a likable man, but resolved in the future not to respect him any more than he deserved.

CHAPTER

3

SINCE I had not been able to get any instructions about where the freight wagons should be unloaded, I had supervised their unloading at the places where they were first parked, freeing the freighters to set out on their return journey. But on the second full day of our stay Brother Bossereau consulted with one and another of the leading colonists and they began to develop a plan of the layout of the new village. It would be centered on a rise a few hundred yards above our temporary camp, and I was given the job of moving the stacks of materials and supplies. These consisted of lumber to use along with the native logs in building, kegs of nails, cypress shakes, crates of window glass packed in sawdust; tools, including four large breaking plows which were not yet in use, cradle scythes, various axes and hand instruments; boxes of grape cuttings and seeds of all kinds; a forage and anvil and two pedal-operated grinding stones; stones for an ox-drawn gristmill; and barrels of flour, lard, sorghum, dry peas, salt, sugar, and rice. Two crates held nothing but books, some four hundred volumes which were to form the nucleus of our public library. There had been also crates of chickens, but the pitiful, long-cooped birds had been freed and were now being loose-herded near camp, as were

the sheep and other stock. Other materials, whether private
property or common, which had been brought in our own
wagons, were to be taken care of by the individual colonists,
and I would not have to worry about them.

I set two of my helpers to moving the building materials in
a wagon, while I, with Andrew and Jim York, selected some
of the heavier lumber and built a stoneboat for moving such
items as the barrels of food. I was lucky to have been assigned these two young men, for they were not only good at
such work, but also good-natured, and though they, like myself, did not talk about it much, both dedicated colonists.

That morning Andy and I were teasing Jim unmercifully
about his attraction to Jeannette Bossereau. She had been
the center of attention of several young men, and this not
because she was the French leader's daughter, but rather because she was a pretty and delightful girl. She was dark-
haired and slender, somewhat intent, and seemed to be only
now, that is, since the gathering of the colonists, breaking out
of a reserve that had evidently restricted her before, though
she had lived in a cosmopolitan atmosphere and spoke perfect
English. She was about eighteen, some two years younger
than Jim, and I had the idea that the active, informal life of
traveling with the group and setting up the colony was good
for her, that she felt perhaps freer and more a part of things
than she ever had before. To use a common metaphor, she
was blooming. The attentions she received seemed to feed the
bloom as spring sunshine and spring showers feed literal
blooms. And it did, indeed, seem that Jim York was her
favorite among the young men.

"I see he's thinking about that girl again," Andy said as we
began to load the barrels. "We'll not get any work out of
him today."

"I guess not," I said. "He's smitten. Ruined. He'll never be
the same again."

Jim responded with a big grin but no answer. Later, when

a barrel slipped from our grasp and rolled off our low sledge, Andy said to me, "See, he's weak as a pissant. Comes from mooning about Jeannette Bossereau." We could not get him to answer our teasing, but, though he tried, he could not help grinning.

The two brothers had grown up on a farm in Ohio, the only children of a hard-working farmer and his wife. I had been working and living with them long enough to know a good many facts about their lives which they had told me, and to have drawn inferences on my own. Evidently their father had been a very stern taskmaster of the type that believes children should earn their keep and that young men should stay with their fathers several years after they are grown to pay for the expense and trouble of their own rearing. One bright spot in their secluded, hard-working childhoods had been an aunt, a schoolteacher who had given them books and lent them books and perhaps encouraged them to be rebellious. Andy was some seven years older than Jim, but they each had passed through the same stages at different times: growing affection for the aunt, learning to work hard from their strict father, reading ever more advanced books up to and including translations of Rousseau and Fourier, growing rebellion against their father, finally leaving home to escape the life and work of the farm.

Andy had left home at the age of twenty, going to Pittsburgh, where he had evidently stayed about two years, then on to New York. Though not forgiven by his father for his ingratitude, he had sometimes written letters home. When Jim was seventeen he followed his brother to the big city, and they had been together since. They had worked in a dairy, as teamsters, as laborers, as mason's helpers, and had found time to attend night classes and lyceum lectures. Whereas they had been too far apart in age for much comradeship when they were children, they found much in common in their new life.

Doubtless Jim had been strongly dependent on his older brother when he first began city life, a green youngster from a farm, and I could see some of the effects remaining. At times Andy, as if forgetting himself, would give advice or instructions almost as if speaking to a child, but a snort of disgust from Jim would cut him off short. I suppose at some time, possibly not long before, they had argued the matter out and had agreed that Jim was now his own man. They usually got along well together.

It is a fact that hard physical work is pleasant when done in good-humored company. I think Jim didn't mind our teasing; from his response, he enjoyed it. He did not answer any of it until about midday, when a crate had tilted and nearly fallen from our stoneboat and Andy said that the fault was that one of us was only half there, and that the present half was extremely weak.

"I don't know about you two idiots," Jim said, "but I'm weak because I'm hungry. When are we going to eat?"

"It can't be true love," Andy said, "or he wouldn't worry about eating."

Jim said, "If you two clowns weren't so busy being funny, you'd know that Mr. Finch's men came in half an hour ago."

I told them we would haul what we had loaded, then eat. We moved out up the hill with Andy leading the single yoke of oxen and Jim and I on either side of the load, steadying it. Jim stopped, for what purpose I did not notice at first, since I was busy at that instant preventing a box from shifting. I shouted to Andy, "Hold up!" and looked around. Jeannette Bossereau was coming toward us, was already near enough to be saying hello to Jim. I stepped down the hill toward them. She said to me, a little breathless from hurrying after us, "My father wonders whether you can spare a worker for a while to help unload some boxes for us?"

I had hardly opened my mouth to say, "Sure," when Jim said, "I'll go."

There had been a recognition on her part as she approached and spoke to me that I was supposed to be a leader supervising the work of the other two, but with his "I'll go" and my "Sure," she, as quickly as Jim, accepted that it was settled. I did not have time to agree or even think about it before she said, "Thank you, Brother Langly," and they were walking away.

Andy came around to me and said, "I'll be damned!" and we laughed. I think he had already been a little surprised at his younger brother's initiative in courting the girl. Now, after our having assumed the upper hand by teasing him all morning, he had walked off as neat as you please and left us to handle the loaded sledge. We got it up the hill and unhooked the oxen; then, since it was a warm day, took them to water before going to eat.

When one of the employees asked, "Where's Jimmy?" Andy answered, "He's helping Brother Bossereau a while." When someone said, "He's sweet on that Bossereau gal, ain't he?" Andy only chuckled and said nothing. It was one thing to tease the youngster to his face and another thing to talk about him when he was absent or to encourage others to tease him.

Jim did not show up when it was time to go back to work, and I observed that he had probably eaten with the Bossereaus. Brother Bossereau, who was a widower, had none of his kin with him except his daughter, and the two ate first with one family, then with another.

Andy said, "The way everybody wines and dines Brother Bossereau, I guess Jim did better than we did."

It was midafternoon before the younger brother came back to work with us. Andy told him, "Well, it's sure nice of you to decide to give us a little help."

"That's all right," he said, grinning. "I don't mind helping you."

"Did you get on the good side of Brother Bossereau?" I asked.

"He didn't hardly know I was around. So many people always coming to talk to him."

Andy asked, "Did Jeannette know you were around?"

"I didn't let her forget. In fact, she and I are the ones that did all the work."

It was some time later that Andy told him, "I figured you'd be bragging about what a good meal you had."

I happened to glance up at exactly the right instant to see a frown, of the kind one may show when trying to understand another—that replaced by a start of realization, and that erased by a deliberate concealment. I knew only a split second after Jim realized—that he had not had any lunch at all. He had been too early at one place, too late at the other. "I did all right," he said.

Andy hadn't seen the brief look on his face, but he must have been more sensitive than I to his brother's nuances. In a minute he asked, "Did you eat with them?"

"I did all right."

"It's worse than we thought," Andy said. "He hasn't had a bite to eat. Admit it, you haven't had a bite to eat."

"If you want to try to tend to your own business, I'll try to tend to mine," he said.

"I bet she's not missing any meals over you. I know these girls."

When Jim answered, all the argument had gone out of his manner and he was talking to himself as much as to us. He said, "You don't know her. There's never been another one like her." It sounded so naïve, seemed to leave him so wide open, that it was as if he had thrown off his armor and said, "You can't touch me." It silenced our humor. I'd never known anyone who was such a delightful and pitiful example. He actually had not realized that he had missed the noon meal until we waked him up.

The ridiculous youngster picked at his food at the evening meal as if he could take it or leave it; if he had missed supper too, he would hardly have noticed. I didn't see him around as we spread our beds out on the ground. Ragged clouds covered most of the sky and silently battled with a half-moon that was overhead, sometimes shutting off its light, sometimes letting it filter through a thin spot. I suppose the rest of them were already asleep when the moon broke through in the clear for a while, and I, lying on my back, saw him out there fifty steps from where we lay, standing, leaning against the wheel of a wagon, alone. The night was rather quiet except for the myriad voices of thousands of frogs in the lowland down toward the creek. I started to call to him that it was bedtime, but thought better of it.

By the fifth day Mr. Finch had all eight of the breaking plows at work, and he had determined that six yokes of oxen were needed for each plow. Some of the soil was chocolate-brown; in other places it turned up as black as coal and gummy. Few rocks or tree roots hindered the plow, but the black soil seemed extremely heavy, and it was all a team could do to move a plow through it by bowing their heads and leaning into the chains. Because the load was enough to slow their natural plodding, the beasts did not always pull together; some would halt or try to turn out; they were difficult to control.

Six of the plows were of iron; two, of steel. Those of steel proved superior in that the soil did not gum up on them so often. This sticky nature of the dirt slowed the work more than any other thing. When the plow became so balled up that it could not cut and turn the sod, it had to be pulled out of the earth and scraped off; and the pulling out was itself a task, since six yokes of oxen cannot easily be backed up. Two men would rock the plow from side to side until it came free, then scrape it completely clean. When the shiny moldboard slid back into the soil it would cut beautifully at first, the grass roots ripping cleanly before it, then it would gather thin layers of soil on it and soon become balled up again, as difficult to drag through the ground as a rough log might be.

The York brothers were able to handle one of the steel plows by themselves. The others were manned by crews of one employee and three or four colonists. It was a slow and difficult process, but progress was evident in the growing strips of dark broken soil that stood out against the prairies. The strips looked out of place, like textured rugs unrolled on the virgin land.

Brother Bossereau had been engaged in constant planning and consultation. On the afternoon of the fifth day he came to me where I was working with a crew clearing brush near the creek and making a road so that we could get down with our water-hauling wagon to a clear deep pool.

"Brother Langly," he said, "can these men continue without you?"

"Well, yes, sir. I think so. We have it pretty well laid out."

"I want you to locate Mr. Finch and carry a message to him. We are determined to stop the plowing." This assertion was such a surprise to me that for the moment I couldn't think of anything to say. He went on: "It has occurred to us that we've done almost nothing in planning the fields, and one of our chief tenets is careful planning. The intelligent thing to do is stop the plowing."

"What if Mr. Finch objects? I mean, what should I tell him?"

"I think my instructions are clear enough: stop plowing. If he wants a reason, you may tell him what I've just said . . . or send him to me."

Seeing my reluctance, he smiled and said, "Brother Langly, don't be concerned about Mr. Finch. It's just an order and you can just present it to him and not explain it at all. Frankly, a day will come when he will be discharged—fired, as you say. He doesn't wish to be involved. He works for the money and that's all. He admits it. So we'll pay him his substantial salary and we'll use him and we'll fire him. It was my hope that when the employees understood our intentions here, they might join us. But we have enemies, Brother Langly, and there are others who are indifferent. Don't let this trouble you. We have simply invested too much of our lives and our hopes in this project to surrender our prerogatives to someone who doesn't wish to be involved."

I said, "Couldn't we send someone else?"

"Well...I just thought that since you, too, are an American..."

"That's just it, Brother Bossereau. If it is just an order, it won't require someone of the same nationality. It's a difficult thing for me. Maybe...if you have time, I could help you find him."

He thought a while, pursing his lips and pulling at his cheeks between thumb and fingers. He was facing the sun and it glared from his spectacles so that I couldn't see his eyes. He finally said, "Very well. I don't want to appear to think that I'm too important to go to him."

I suggested catching two horses and riding out toward the fields, but Brother Bossereau declined with the remark that he enjoyed walking and that he thought when a man walked he was closer to nature. In this he was the opposite of Mr. Finch, who rode horseback if he had only half a mile to go.

We set out walking and when we had come up to a point where we could see some of the plowing teams and their crews, we saw Mr. Finch ride up to one of them and dismount. We headed in that direction. It was a sunny afternoon, just warm enough to make walking pleasant. I was impressed with the fair sweep of the terrain, the clean look of the plowed land, the industry. I said, "Brother Bossereau, it seems to me like a perfect location here."

We slowed our walking as he talked. "It has an unreal quality about it. Can it possibly be that our ideas have produced

fruit? After the long years of desire? After the frustration
piled on frustration? How many years has it been that we
have written about what might be? Has it actually come to
pass? But, of course, the answer is that it has. It's sobering as
well as unreal. I must keep it constantly in my thoughts that
it's here, now, not in some distant tomorrow, but now; if I
forget a single moment, then when it appears to me, I'm surprised like a child who is suddenly given a gift.

"They, especially the young ones, don't know what it de-
notes to me. How could they comprehend? But they are wonderful. I would almost say beautiful.

"Brother Langly, the land is so novel! So new! So pure!
That's the central fact of it, its purity. Over the countries of
Europe lies a somber blanket, an oppressive mass of privilege,
class, wealth, custom. It suffocates the human spirit. It frus-
trates the aspirations of decent men. It perverts the ideals of
the reformer and leaves him in despair. But this! I do believe
this country, this land, is as pure and unencumbered as God
made it. We have a grave responsibility, Brother Langly.
What a solemn and glorious responsibility it is! I feel as if
God Himself had placed it upon us."

Before we were halfway to Mr. Finch, he had remounted
and was riding toward another plowing team a half mile distant. We changed our course, crossing one of the strips of
heavy new clods, and again before we had come up to him,
he had remounted. But this time he saw us and guided his
horse in our direction. He rode naturally and easily as if he
belonged on the horse. When he was in speaking distance, he
called, "Hello, gentlemen," and I was afraid that he was not
going to dismount; but he swung down, smiling, and said,
"Out looking it over, are you?"

Brother Bossereau said, "We have decided to stop the plowing, Mr. Finch."

The American's smile did not fade, but he said, "I don't
understand."

Brother Bossereau then explained to him, somewhat as he had to me, that the location and size of the fields, as well as the crop that was to be planted in each, was to be planned and approved by the leaders of the colony. It might take several days, since it would be necessary to make drawings. All colony lands were to be surveyed and everything, including village and fields, drawn on maps. His manner of speaking left little room for argument.

Mr. Finch said, "I guess you all thought about—"

"We are prepared to risk the corn, Mr. Finch."

"Well, can I make a suggestion?"

"Certainly. That's what you're employed for."

"Did you want to use these men that are plowing for something else?"

"Not necessarily."

"Well, then, couldn't we go on with it? You can break a patch of land and still not plant it. Or you can plant a patch one year and let it go back to grass the next. This won't mess up your planning. And some of these men that haven't done this kind of work before, they're learning to handle the work. Then, in case you all decided some of my locations are all right, we would be that much ahead."

These words were so straightforward and logical that I wondered why I had not thought of it in that way myself. Brother Bossereau went into one of his periods of noncommittal musing, and Mr. Finch went on.

"If you all agree with me about planting as early as we can, you could give us the go-ahead on these locations right away. The surveying and such can be done anytime. Even if the planning made some changes, we would still be ahead to keep on plowing."

Brother Bossereau was quiet, and I was anxious as to how he would defend his position, but when he finally answered, it occurred to me that he was showing true humility in changing his mind and also that he had placed himself on a plane where he felt no need to contend with Mr. Finch. He said, "I believe you may continue with the plowing, at least until I consult the others. But do not plant anything until you have instructions."

As Mr. Finch rode away, the French leader said to me, "You know, I am surprised at that man. I thought he would be difficult again. But he was quite agreeable."

"I think he's real friendly when you get to know him," I said.

"How does one get to know him? He's strange. I find it impossible to fit him into my thinking and I cannot help but wonder whether he purposely makes himself obscure. Is he aristocracy, bourgeoisie, proletariat? He certainly is not an intellectual with proletarian sympathies. I had the thought that he might be considered a sort of coarse, primitive aristocrat, yet he serves for wages and seems to be happy at it.

"I've thought about this before, Brother Langly, and I believe we have two basic visions in our philosophy. The first is the vision of injustice. I have seen the children in the mines and the factories and the jails—thin, stunted, with narrow faces and big eyes, with no expectation for education or decent attention in sickness, no future but toil and weariness and hunger in squalid, brutish surroundings, and an early death. And this is not the exception; it has been the rule for the masses throughout history. Everywhere man is born free, and everywhere he is in chains. How can a person not see? Or not care? I don't comprehend a man who is not moved by the pitiful things that exist before his eyes. The other vision is that of the justice that might be. It's not necessary to explain that to you, for you comprehend it as well as I. My question is this: How can a person be oblivious to either vision? Why haven't men long before this ceased the superficial business of the world and put themselves to this great problem and solved it? Sometimes I question myself about a man like Finch, 'Has he no human pity? Or has he no human reason?' "

I couldn't offer him any help in these speculations. Before I left him to go back to my work, he said, "I hope I made it clear to him that there is to be no planting until the leadership gives the instructions."

"Yes, sir," I said. "You did."

"We shall choose the best slopes for grapes, I think," he said. "We are optimistic about grapes."

My journal suffered from my lack of discipline in keeping it. I would fairly describe one day in it, then skip two days, then jot down only a few desultory notes on the fourth day. Many days it was simply not convenient to touch it. The fact that we had noted writers among us, such as Brother Bossereau and Miss Harriet Edwards, seemed to inhibit me at one time and inspire me to flights of flowery prose at another. I consoled myself with the idea that I could write sketches or impressions, dated but not intended to be any complete record of events, and so my journal became a hodgepodge, reflecting whatever seemed interesting to me at the times when writing was convenient. Sometimes I held the conceit that I might at a later date write poetry, and some of my entries were notes intended to remind me of poetic ideas that had crossed my mind. One Sunday afternoon I wrote this entry, a brief essay or sketch, which will serve to illustrate how far my journal had departed from a record of events:

On Sheep

The poet, considering sheep, needs to find the proper distance. He can hardly station himself too far away, as long as the distance contains no intruding body to distract him and as long as he can see his poetic object without much eyestrain. It is best to look down upon them in a vale, in an open glade framed by trees. They seem like miniature clouds, curiously self-contained, yet drawn one to the other, to make patterns like larger clouds from the closeness of their bodies. They exude contentment. They observe a gentle communion with the earth, moving over it, spreading, contracting, weaving. Sometimes across the distance may come the plaintive *ba-a-a* of a lamb, sad and beautiful, a small momentary suggestion inviting sympathy. And the soul of the poet incorporates faint sorrow into the contentment. It is all Nature.

If he waits patiently in his post he may see the small figures of the herders coming after their charges to take them to their fold. While the body of the flock streams toward home in the evening light, some spirited ones turn out this way and that, teasing; caught in their devilment, they bound back into the stream. The herders, gentle, patient, themselves exuding contentment, can be imagined to sing songs or whistle simple tunes. They have interrupted the peace of the glade, have introduced greater motion, more specific movement. But is beauty static? Is Nature static? The human song, the teasing frolic, the rhythm of life between glade and fold, these are food for the mouth in the poet's mind and, chewed, will add something, as the cry of the lamb added sadness to the beauty. The flock, its herders skipping beside it, dissolves into the trees and the dusk. And so, the poet to his pen and white paper. (Sheep and sleep. Too obvious a rhyme?)

If the herders do not come? The flock will not go to safety of itself. It will wander contentedly out of the glade in another direction, toward the darkening hills, where the coyote prowls, and the panther, and the wolf, and the bobcat. Here is dubious food for the poet. Innocence. Violence. Stupidity?

And what if he is not permitted his distance? What a terrible trick if the poet be forced into some practical position where he must make some individual sheep do something which that single stubborn sheep does not intend to do, where he must lay hands on it, grab it, wrestle it! He has already seen, having come too near, that the small cloud is not white, but has the tincture of mud about it, is caught with filth and cockleburs. Now, with his hands, he finds a more disgusting thing. Down inside the cloud is a damned bony dog with a distended belly, a graceless, skinny, kicking creature neither beautiful nor contented.

But this is a libel against the dog, a responsive animal with a sense of humor. A dog may fawn on a bad master, but if he is kicked he will go off and lie down and think about it. A sheep knows nothing but to whine and pity itself and shield itself from harm by the bodies of its own kind.

Why in the hell did we bring these obnoxious beasts into our wilderness heaven?

CHAPTER

4

THE assembly named our colony Uterica. There had been
sentiment to call it Utopia, but some people objected that
such a name implied goals that lay beyond human reach, and
above all else we desired to be practical. The Europeans were
strongly conscious of living in America, with its newness and
its promise, not in the land of Thomas More's dream, but in
the America of actuality. And so the composite name was
devised and adopted to symbolize, as one of the assemblymen
said, "Utopia in actuality."

In the second week of living in Uterica we had unexpected
visitors. It was noon and most of the men were in camp, waiting for food, eating, or taking a short rest after having eaten.
Our attention became attracted to two youngsters who had
been out with the herders and came racing toward camp
screaming some unintelligible news. They passed the group
where I was standing, and it was only then that I realized they
were yelling, "Indians!" When they had stopped a hundred
yards farther on at their family's wagon, they pointed and
all of us looked toward the creek.

A group of eleven Indian men had come out from the trees
into the open. They stood talking, looking toward us. I was
relieved to note that they were all dressed in the clothing of

white people, some with straw or felt hats on their heads, and thus must have had contact with civilization. I could see that three of them carried rifles, but not in any threatening manner.

Mr. Finch said to those nearby, "If you can get to your rifle without them seeing you, load it but don't show it." Andy York and another man walked around behind a wagon and followed his advice.

The Indians had evidently placed themselves in clear view purposely. They had been watching us longer than we had been watching them. They seemed to be consulting, perhaps arguing, and I would not have been surprised to see them turn and hurry away, but suddenly they started walking toward us, all together, though one or two in the rear seemed more reluctant than the others.

The one in the lead was broad and fat. His hat, which seemed too small, sat straight on his head and was held by a string under his heavy chin. His black hair, like that of the others, was long and plaited, falling down in front of his shoulders. He wore dark trousers and was the only one of them who wore a coat, this buttoned tightly across his broad front, showing bare skin in the gaps between the buttons. His manner was expansive, friendly. He smiled as he came, making little waving gestures at us and calling out a kind of half grunt that must have been a greeting. These actions seemed natural and sincere. I took him to be, if not their leader, at least their chief diplomat.

The others wore colorful shirts of red or blue, wrinkled and dirty, and some wore colored sashes at the waist. Their shoes were crude, of unstained leather. The three with guns carried them carelessly, pointed at the ground. They followed the lead of the friendly fat one, nodding and smiling, with one exception that I noted. The one in the rear was more stoic. His leathery face was wrinkled and his large mouth was drawn down at the corners as if molded by ancient trouble. Though he followed the others, this visit was not his idea.

As they passed nearby, I saw him looking straight at me and his dark eyes were an enigma. I wondered if he was thinking about what he saw, or whether his thoughts took some old, strange pattern I would not understand if I knew.

It may have been that they had spied on our camp before, for they went straight to the open, canvas-covered shelter where Brother Bossereau often worked at a table covered with maps and papers. He was nearby, about to be served the noon meal, and he came around toward the headquarters shelter, followed by those who had been about to eat with him.

The heavy Indian approached the French leader with open arms and embraced him with such enthusiasm that he knocked his own hat to the back of his head, meanwhile speaking his unintelligible tongue. Brother Bossereau responded first with a little hesitation, then warmly, embracing the heavy body of the Indian in return, and I could hear him say, "Welcome, my friends! Welcome!" He shook the hand of each of the others.

The situation seemed to be becoming awkward as they greeted each other again and again. Brother Bossereau said, "Very pleased to see you. Very pleased. We desire to be friends. Friends. Peace." The Indians nodded and grinned, made sounds and gestures. They seemed to be getting nowhere, nor did they seem about to leave. Then Brother Bossereau led them around to the makeshift table where he had been ready to eat and had them each served on a tin plate what appeared from a distance to be broiled mutton.

Mr. Finch said, "Those fellows could talk some English if they wanted to."

Someone asked him, "What kind of Indians are they?"

"I don't know," he said, "but they're not horse Indians. They could talk English."

From what I could see, the only colonist who ate with them was Brother Bossereau, who seemed to have a rib bone or such in his hand. No doubt, since we ate in fairly small groups, the Indians had been given all the food that had been prepared. Some of them squatted on their haunches as they ate, some stood; the three who carried rifles did not lay them down. When they had eaten, they seemed to have completed their visit. The fat one embraced Brother Bossereau again, and with more smiles and motions and words that we could not understand, they began to leave in the direction from which they came.

The older one, the stoic who had not smiled, had impressed me so much that I looked for him again as they passed by. I could hardly imagine his eating our food, yet all of them had. He was not in the rear as he had been before, and I was mystified for a moment at not locating him among them; he had been so distinctive. Then, when the group was even with me, I saw him at their front, walking beside the fat one. The two were talking fiercely to one another in a monotone. The older one was jerking his head in an emphatic way as he spoke and his dark eyes flashed; the fat one, evidently not realizing that he was still observed by white eyes, was no longer smiling.

The Indians I had seen before had been somewhat like these, except that they, being in a more settled part of the country, had seemed the ones who did not belong, while these here in this wild country might be more at home than we were and they seemed more a force to be reckoned with. I could draw no conclusions from their presence in the area or their visit; it left me uneasy. But if we Americans were uncertain, the Europeans were much more so. Some of them had read the novels of Cooper, and others had read or heard stories in which all Indians were fierce and cruel barbarians. Some of them expressed surprise that the Indians were dirty, forgetting that we, ourselves, were dirty. Not a few of them were afraid.

Much of the opinion was summed up in two remarks I heard that afternoon. Miss Harriet Edwards said, "They're as simple and friendly as babies. Why anyone would be afraid of them, I don't know."

But someone asked Dr. Valentin what he thought of the visit and he said, "They looked like bloody pirates to me, for all their smiles."

Evidently the question was talked over at length in an assembly meeting held that afternoon, for the next morning Brother Bossereau assigned me the task of locating the Indian camp and finding out what I could of them. I was to take Andy York with me.

When Mr. Finch saw us saddling up and heard our task, he asked, "Which way you heading?"

"West, I guess," I told him. "They were afoot, so it couldn't be too far."

"There's a man lives a mile or two down the creek," he said. "Man named Myers. I ran into him last Sunday. He's been out in these parts a year or so. I believe he would know."

I decided to take his advice. When Andy and I had mounted, Mr. Finch offered some more. "Langly, they're probably harmless. But if you find their village, stay on your horse." It was exactly what I'd been planning myself.

Down the creek not much farther than I had been before, we found the log cabin of Mr. Myers. It sat back only a few steps from a bluff bank of the stream under large elm trees and behind it was a tangle of smaller trees and vines. The building was small, with a rock-and-mud fireplace on one end, hardly disturbing the natural aspect of the place. On the end wall were tacked two bear skins, flesh side out. In front of it a man sat in a homemade chair woven of willows.

He got up when we dismounted and shook hands with us, grinning pleasantly. "Myers," he said. "Harney Myers. Proud to meet you. Don't see too many fellers out this way. You all work for them socialist people up at the forks, don't you?"

I admitted that we did without explaining that we were ourselves socialist people.

"One of you can set down," he said, laughing as he offered his chair, and when we declined, he sat back down himself. He was a heavy man, sloppily dressed and with a matted brown beard. His feet were bare; his shoes sat on the ground beside the chair. He had been whittling on a long piece of white wood, evidently making an ax handle, and he went ahead with it.

"How do you all make out with them socialist people?" he asked.

He was not looking at us but sighting down his handle. I grinned at Andy and he winked at me. "So-so," I said. "What do you think about their experiment out in this part of the country?"

"Well, I'll tell you for sure what I think," he said, cutting long shavings as he talked. "If they can do it...I ain't saying they can, but if they could, why in the hell would anybody want to? It's beyond me! Why in the hell would you live right in the midst of a bunch of people and everything you do is their business? And whatever they do, you're in it, too. Why, I wouldn't live that way at all. Couldn't stand it! What if some feller ain't worth a hoot for nothing? Can't do a thing! You got to share with him! Suppose he's lazy. You got to share with him! Suppose I'm lazy! I think a man's laziness ought to be his own business and nobody else's. Me, when I want to wander in the woods, then that's what I want to do. Somebody says to me, 'You looking for meat or honey or do you just aim to waste time?' I says to them, 'None of your damned business, I may not know myself. You take care of your business, and I'll take care of mine.' That's the way I am, and that's the way it ought to be, as I see it. Them people are a bunch of crackpots. Course, no offense. But they been living in them foreign countries too long."

I was surprised about then to see a child of six or seven peering out the door of the cabin, holding aside the weathered canvas that hung over the door. I had thought of the man as a recluse, living alone. The child had uncut blond hair and was dressed in what appeared to be a flour sack, so that I could not guess whether it was a boy or a girl. It ducked back upon seeing my eyes upon it.

Obviously Harney Myers loved to talk, but I thought we had better get any information from him we could and be on our way. I told him about the Indian visit and asked whether he knew where they lived.

"Right up Loco Crick," he said. "Maybe eight mile past your socialist people. Maybe ten. Right on the crick. I seen their place, but I don't have nothing to do with them. They keep away from me and I keep away from them."

"We just wanted to find out about them. Whether they are dangerous or anything."

"They're scum. Just scum. They's a breed with them, red-headed feller, and I told him, I says, 'I don't have nothing against you, but I don't want them Injuns around.' I've got me a shotgun and I'll wad her full of bacon rind and let them have a charge right in the tail. That's what I'll do."

I asked him, "Loco Creek, is that the north fork?" We had been calling them North Creek and West Creek.

"That's her. The main branch. Maybe eight, ten mile. You can't miss it. You don't want to swap that bay horse, do you?"

I assured him that I didn't and said that we had to go.

"Stay to dinner if you got time," he said. "The old lady will stir up a mess of something after while.

I declined and thanked him. We rode back up the creek, joking when we were out of hearing of Harney Myers about being crackpots. Andy became serious. "That man's wrong," he said. "He doesn't understand. But, Mr. Langly, I'm worried. It's not that they're crackpots; I don't mean that. It's not even so much that they don't know how to work, but so many of them don't see the importance of learning. They don't seem to understand what work is. I can't explain it, but you've got to make a living first, you know; you've got to be men first and then socialists. I don't see how they can even appreciate our big chance out here unless they understand about work; that's the main part. It looks like we would succeed or fail on our work, and also I think the importance of work is behind all our goals." He said these things in a serious manner, and while he was saying them, seemed as young as his younger brother. I told him that I agreed with him.

We crossed the creek and headed northwest in order to get away from the thicker growth along the watercourse. The main branch angled west a few miles above the colony site. When we came on a rise we could see its course far ahead of us. We rode to it and up its windings until past noon and I judged that we surely had come far enough. Then Andy pulled up and said he heard something.

There were a lot of birds—mockingbirds, redbirds, jays, wrens, nest-building and mating in the trees, and I thought the faint sound came from them at first. Then, as happens with far-off sounds, some distinctive note carried to us and we knew what it was. Children were laughing and playing.

We moved forward carefully to a point where we could see them through the trees. A dozen or more children were playing in a shallow pond of the creek and along a gravelly clearing at the water's edge. They were splashing and chasing and crying out to one another, boys and girls from the age that can barely walk up to eight or ten, all completely naked. A few of them were digging in the mud; the others seemed to be playing a game that had to do with splashing water. Their little brown bodies were so nimble and they frolicked with such innocent abandon that it was a delight to watch.

Just past their playing area, a hundred yards from Andy and me, adults were working, bending over in a patch of reeds, partially hidden from us. Three of them straightened up, and we saw that they were women, bare of clothes from the waist up. Around their lower bodies they wore skirts of what appeared to be coarse cloth. Their bare shoulders and breasts were as brown as their faces, and I had no doubt that they were in their usual dress. They seemed to be gathering reeds; I saw one of them hold up a bundle while another bound it with a string of grass.

Beyond the women was a large structure of some kind that we could not make out. I motioned to Andy and we turned our mounts and retraced our steps to a place where it was safe to talk.

"One of those women is a beauty," he said.

"You want me to introduce you to her?" I asked.

"I don't believe so. I'm a little leery. We're not going up there, are we?"

I told him I wanted to get a look at the place from another direction. We rode back downstream to an animal crossing, crossed the creek, then rode straight away from it a half mile to the higher ground. We stayed somewhat concealed by the scattered post oaks as we rode in a rough half-circle toward a point above where we had been. We reached a vantage point where we could look down upon the Indian village. It was no more than a quarter of a mile away and larger than I had expected.

The most impressive part of it was the scattered dome-shaped grass houses, some twenty feet high and twenty-five feet in diameter. Beside these, here and there, were smaller structures of limbs and cane and grass, some enclosed and with sloping roofs, others open-sided arbors that seemed designed merely for shade. The houses lay on both sides of the creek. Here and there the inhabitants could be seen walking along the paths, standing, talking, sitting on mats doing some kind of work. The women and children were dressed—or un-dressed—like those we had first seen; the men wore only a breechclout pulled through a belt and falling as low as their knees. Nowhere did we see anyone dressed as those had been who came to the colony site.

Several grown ones and children, perhaps ten in all, came

from the trees beyond and entered one of the larger houses. It occurred to me that a large family or even two or three families might live in each.

I asked Andy, "How many big huts do you make it?"

In a moment he said, "I count twenty-eight."

I asked him then, "How many people would you say live there altogether?"

"It's hard to say."

"Take a guess."

"Two or three hundred. Maybe more."

I agreed with him. We could see a dozen or so men and women walking along a flat lowland space with sticks in their hands, jabbing the ground, and we both realized at the same time what we were watching.

Andy said, "My God, do you know what they're doing?"

"That's corn if I ever saw any," I said. I could see the little broadleaf plants in regular hills, some of it already six inches high. They were cutting weeds with sharpened sticks. We saw another patch of it farther up, and, after some studying, figured out that they were much better farmers than we would have guessed. Levees about three feet high had been thrown up between the fields and the creek, evidently as protection against high water, and what seemed to be irrigation ditches led into the fields from upstream.

We looked at the peaceful village for half an hour, but could discover nothing more that would be worth reporting to Brother Bossereau. We headed back, and had not been seen by the Indians as far as we could tell.

I thought that I had fulfilled my mission well enough, but I could not resolve some questions about it in my own mind. The place had seemed so idyllic, so natural, full of such simple and lighthearted people that I was impressed; but somehow it was too perfect that way. We had seen no sign of a gun or weapon of any kind or even any evidence that they could defend themselves. We had seen no white man's clothes, nor anything that showed any contact with whites. Our visitors had had guns and clothes both; it made one wonder whether they had come from the village we had spied on. But surely they had; their appearance the day before must have been what they thought proper for a diplomatic visit. Thinking of Mr. Finch's suspicions as to the danger from Indians, I could not help noting that the evidence showed him very wrong. On the other hand, it must be that he was right about the need to plant corn early here. And I was not convinced even that the Indians were harmless, not enough to have placed myself at their mercy.

We got back to the colony site about sundown. Though we were hungry as bears, I hunted up Brother Bossereau before eating and reported it all to him. Like me, he was uncertain, but believed that we could only watch them and suspend judgment, hoping for the best. He hoped that they might turn out to be a type of primitive idealistic society, from which no harm could come and from which, indeed, we might some day learn something.

Mr. Finch thought differently of it. When I told him as much as I knew, he said, "I don't like it. If they're good Indians, all right. If they're not, then what? We ought to have a plan."

I asked him, "What kind of a plan?"

"I'd form a militia. Train them, have them scout, stand guard, keep mounts ready. If Bossereau had seen what I've seen on the Santa Fe Trail, he wouldn't trust to luck on a thing like this."

Jim York and I drove the cows in toward their lot early one evening. Some of the girls were going to learn to milk. Whether it was intended that they take over that chore or whether the point was merely to teach them a useful rural skill so that they might some day do it, I did not know. Most of them were city-bred young women who had not been around animals much.

The cows were well fed, the grass in the vicinity now being so plentiful and rich that they could lie down half the day, chewing their cuds, and still come in stuffed at night. They did not object to being driven in early, but proceeded at their own pace in a lazy and deliberate manner, and the bull went along gently, as if he were one of them. Jim cut a switch to hurry them. They paid no more attention to it than to the swarm of gnats that followed, at which they swung their tails in a kind of automatic languor, but plodded toward home, chewing, belching, sometimes stretching their necks to answer the calves that waited in the pens.

The girls were escorted by Brother Adams, a skinny, serious-minded man from New England and, I believe, a Unitarian. They had been to the creek to rinse out the milk pails and bring water to wash the cows' udders. The girls were chattering and laughing. As we came around the herd toward the gate, one of them called out to Jim, "Are you the teacher? Look, Jimmy's the milking teacher and he has a switch."

"Yes, and he'll switch you with it if you don't behave," another said. "Right on the bare legs."

Among them were Jeannette Bossereau and Dr. Sockwell's chubby daughter Wilma, altogether eight or nine girls, a lively and agreeable sight in their colored cotton dresses. They seemed gay, willing to act younger than their ages, and little daunted by Brother Adams.

I opened the gate and Jim, grinning a little self-consciously in the presence of the girls, helped drive in the lead cow. He patiently guided her stubborn slowness with motions of his outspread hands; then, when she put her head in and moved willingly toward the lower calf pen, he shouted, "Go in, you old chunk of wolf bait!"

They thought it was funny. A German girl of about sixteen had the tendency to giggle, and she infected the others.

They thought it all great fun. Wilma Sockwell shouted at
the cow, "You big lump of dough!" They made an incongruous, if somewhat delightful, impression, nubile, of womanly form beneath their light dresses. They could be ladylike
when they chose, but were now caught up in a zestful spirit
and dominated by the most lighthearted and youngest among
them. The milk cows stared at the girls out of large, solemn
eyes.

We let the calf in with its mother, and Jim demonstrated
how she could be milked, competing with the greedy calf.
He made the calf go around to the left side, sat himself on
a small stool on the right, and deftly shifted the calf's head
from one teat to another.

"The first is blue John and the last is cream," Brother
Adams pointed out. "Don't let the calf get more than half
the cream." But the girls paid him little attention.

Jim rinsed the cow's udder and began to squeeze two sing-
ing streams of milk into the bucket. He seemed to be making
a point of acting the serious instructor and of not noticing
Jeannette any more than any of the other girls. The milk
quickly covered the bottom of the bucket. The alternating
streams hissed into it, foaming. He suddenly stopped and
asked, smiling at them, "Who wants to try?"

They shoved at one another, and Jeannette was pushed toward him, blushing slightly. She submitted, taking it as a serious duty to learn, but still half in the influence of their playful
nonsense. Tucking her skirt modestly beneath her, she sat on
the stool, grasped the teats, and began to make what appeared
to be the same kind of effort he had made. No milk issued.

She looked at him in surprise. "How did you do it? Make
them stop laughing."

He showed her again. She tried once more without success.

"It won't do it," she said, having trouble maintaining her
serious mien. "I must be too weak."

"No, you're not," he said, and putting his hands over hers,

after some clumsy squeezing, began to produce milk once more. She cooperated, her face, and particularly her mouth, alternately showing concentration and a near surrender to the laughter of the girls.

"Don't watch Jimmy!" Wilma ordered her. "Watch the tits!"

"Oh, Wilma!" another girl squealed.

"What's the matter? A tit is a tit. You can't be squeamish if you want to be a milkmaid."

Jim suddenly seemed to become conscious of the youthful female body of the girl he was against and of their audience. He backed up slightly, still kneeling, and allowed her to try alone. She did well enough until the calf took one of the teats from her hand, and he came to her aid. Then he, too, succumbed to the laughing. "He can't take it if you won't give it up," he told her. "Here, saw, bossy, saw. Get over there where you belong, young fellow. Saw."

Together they took command of the situation again, laughing at the eager single-mindedness of the calf. She asked, "Is it a fight with the poor calf every time?"

"Well, if he's big, you tie him off."

Some of the other girls had watched long enough and were ready to try for themselves. We brought in another cow and her calf. Brother Adams, commanding the attention of some of the girls, said, "When you approach a cow, put your hand on her hip, thus, and say 'saw' or some other soft word." But they were not ready to yield to his dignity. Wilma went up to the cow and recited inanely, "Saw, hammer, and tongs!" as if it were a password.

We brought in other cows and their calves, in most cases letting the calf suck only long enough to satisfy its mother, then tying it off with a short length of rope to a rail of the fence. The girls went diligently to work, but constantly called out to the placid cows and one another.

"Let down your milk, bossy!"

"Nice cowsy. If you won't bite me, I won't bite you. Why does she look around at me?"

"She's never seen the likes before!"

"Come back here, cow! I'm not going to follow you all over. Please. Come on. Pretty please."

"Whoa! Nice bossy."

"Don't say 'whoa.' It makes her think she's a horse."

"*Ee-ee-ee!* He's sucking my finger! You calf-slobbering silly!"

"Look at him! What a pig! He ought to be ashamed!"

"He's just a baby."

"I'll baby him! He's trying to get all the cream."

"Keep your tail to yourself, you big milk pitcher!"

They learned that if a teat were turned up, a stream of milk could be shot in the direction of another girl. This brought screams and protests about getting dresses dirty, also a frown from Brother Adams. It was stopped.

Of them all, Wilma Sockwell, who was attractive though chubby, seemed to be the favorite and the spark of their foolishness. But I think it was Jeannette whom they most highly regarded. The French leader's daughter responded to their spirit and was a part of it, but also clearly represented that other part of their natures—that they were not children, but young women. At such a time as this, her manner seemed to say, "Now, we must be serious and do our best," which she would do for some moments, until the good humor burst through again.

She had dark-brown hair and a sprinkle of freckles on her cheeks and nose, these seeming somewhat out of place, because her eyes were dark, almost Italian, with heavy, eloquent eyebrows. Her mouth was expressive. I had the impression that she had been around adults a great deal as a child and had heard much serious talk, and that the companionship of the past few months had been a surprising boon to her. It was the combination of lightheartedness and the streak of seriousness that had caused the others to push her forward to be the first to milk, and that had caused her to agree to it. Altogether she was an attractive girl. I could not blame Jim York for his response to her.

About sundown the three women and two men who usually helped Brother Adams milk came to assist us, and we completed the job shortly afterward. We carried fourteen full pails of warm, sweet-smelling milk up to the camp as darkness came on.

When Mr. Finch had completed the plowing, they would not allow him to begin planting. He built drags out of logs to use in breaking up the heavy clods the plows had turned up, but after these had been pulled over the fields two times, the leaders of the colony still had not completed their plans as to what would be planted in each plot. He took his crews out of the fields and began to build fences.

He believed firmly, not only that the seed should be in the ground, but that this beautiful spring weather was the ideal time for getting some work done. Sometimes six men were assigned to him, sometimes more. As these crews cut rails, they also produced some good building logs, and he secured permission to begin the building of a large house that would serve as living quarters for the employees. These logs began to pile up on the spot which the planners designated, and the employees worked trimming and notching them in their spare time.

Mr. Finch did not complain about the delay in planting but went about supervising the rail cutting and some sheep shearing that had to be done; he had a grim aspect and did not joke with the men.

It began to rain on the same day that the plans were completed. The surveying had been done and several drawings made of the entire colony lands as well as the proposed village and the town it was expected to grow into. The field locations were those which had been laid out by Mr. Finch, and in each was shown in fine lettering the crops that would be planted the first year. Brother Bossereau showed me the drawings in the afternoon and it was raining lightly on his canvas shelter as we talked. He said, "You may inform Mr. Finch to begin planting in the morning if it doesn't rain too much."

Shortly afterward the rain began to come down heavily enough that the work crews quit and sought shelter. It rained intermittently the rest of the day, misting out of high gray clouds between the showers. We went about with shoulders hunched, doing the chores that needed doing: milking, cooking, gathering wood, covering things to keep them dry, improving our shelters. Night came unnaturally early because of the dark sky. In the last light of day we could see an increased movement in the clouds; they rushed wildly in the sky. The wind gusted; trees bent and jerked before it. Willows that could be dimly seen down along the creek doubled toward the ground. Water came down in large drops, in flurries, as if it were flung out of the clouds. Then the night closed down; there was utter darkness except for the flashes of lightning, and we were left with the sounds of erratic thunder, the rushing wind, and water falling in sheets and splatters all around us.

I slept under a wagon with the York brothers and one of the employees. We had a tarpaulin fastened between the wagon box and the ground on the west side, which kept out most of the wind and water. I was a long time falling asleep as the elemental forces pounded about us, and then my sleep was fitful.

I was awakened suddenly during the night with such an unusual feeling that it led me later to try to describe it in my journal. When the description was completed in a few days, it read thus:

Premonition in an Instant at Night

The last thing I remember being aware of was the strident sound of the rain. Also, I was tired and cramped, I think. Rainy weather seems to do that. A person strains to be out from under a drip or away from a puddle; or maybe, only standing still, he shrinks to hold his legs in the center of his soaked trousers. Or he holds himself in an unnatural position to avoid being against other wet human bodies. Perhaps, too, the dampness itself creeps into one's bones.

I must have been in a deep sleep and not dreaming at all. Then, what followed, what transpired during some short period of time, I can only attempt to reconstruct, for I was conscious, but hardly in any way sensible. Cold water was suddenly in my face, with no explanation. Sounds and lights raged about me, these with no meaning, no definition, no arrangement. Most distressing of all, I could not orient myself, could not understand whether I were standing or sitting or lying; to be truthful, I must have believed I was in the act of rising from a chair or such and that one of my legs was giving way, for I thrust with it and lurched. The top of my head came in contact with what must have been the fifth wheel of the wagon, though I did not know what it might be at that instant. I actually did not know the location of the earth, or which way I should reach out to feel myself on solid ground.

The feeling of being utterly lost may have lasted a second or a minute. Time made no sense. The end of it came when I thought or cried out, "What's happening?"

Then I knew where I was, under the wagon, and that I was in the middle of a thunderstorm. The tarpaulin had flapped in such a way as to toss a collection of water in my face. Though my situation had taken on some meaning, the world about me was shaken with such violence that my existence seemed precarious. The night was as dark as can be imagined, this shattered frequently by lightning flashes so bright that I could see nothing but the intense light itself. The light was as impenetrable as the darkness. Lightning must have been coming to earth right in the confines of our camp. The sound resolved itself into the heavy crackling of thunder, the hissing of wind, and the rattling of hail on the wagon box above me. The storm, immediately over us, or all around us, shook the ground. I felt lonely, isolated.

Then the premonition struck me. It came in the form of a question: What in the name of God are we doing out here in this place?

It was as if the storm were not natural, but made of giant spirits that fought around us and might trample us out at a whim. Having never experienced the strength of the weather in this far-out part of the world, how could I, or any of us, be sure that it did not have unexampled violence? The forces that could make the rumbling and booming and snarling sounds I was hearing could surely strike us dead.

But the threat—for a threat it appeared to me in those moments—had more to it than the possibility of an accident in a storm. I feared that our being here, the colony, Uterica, all of it, was a supreme audacity. We had presumed too much, had dared too much, had thought too much of ourselves, and had thrust out into a place where we had no right. We would be terribly punished. It was not reasonable, this conviction that had seized me, but a kind of elemental belief that could not be qualified by reason. We had rashly overstepped a bound. We had made a foolhardy challenge.

My thoughts went to our neighbors, the Indians, who live in this land. I imagined them cringing, fearful in their shelters. But immediately it occurred to me that they might better be considered a part of it all. Whether they are as simple as some think or a hundred times as complex as we can imagine, they belong. They have permission to be here. They appeared to me to be a part of the larger, mysterious thing, of which the storm was also a part.

The premonition was strong and persistent, though, again, I cannot say how long it dominated me. For a time, I thought of awakening my companions, who seemed miles away, though they were within reach of my hand, in order to have someone to talk to. But as the more severe part of the storm passed over, my feeling dissipated. I settled down, found the most comfortable position I could for my cramped limbs, and finally went back to sleep.

The writing of this piece gave me some satisfaction because, if for no other reason, it put into words what had been a wordless experience, difficult of explanation. The words were somewhat inaccurate, as when one tries to tell a dream, but the best I could manage.

As for the implication in it, the threat, I took it for nothing. It was impossible to dismiss it, not that it overpowered me, but that it all had not enough body in it to dismiss. How does one dismiss a vague feeling? Surely a man should not dignify such a thing by making an issue of it even in his own mind, and this regardless of any tenuous connection my feelings or my journal writings might be seen to have with later events, for no one deserves to be judged on his attitude about the future—by a judge who sees it all in the past. And if I had taken it seriously, what could I have done? Sometimes I am not satisfied with my own behavior and am able to see, upon careful consideration, that I might have done differently with better results, but on this point, what could I have done? Had I shown it to someone else, what could he have done, other than laugh? And so my thought about it at the time was that it was a reasonably faithful, if extravagant, piece of writing about a peculiar experience, and I considered that the beginning and end of it.

The storm that night was the beginning of sixteen solid days of rain. It poured down, rushed in sheets this way and that along the ground. It made shallow lakes in every low place and the water surface was pitted and rough from the falling drops. At times the air was so full of rain that everything was seen through an angling veil. The whole world seemed half water. Then for hours it sprinkled and misted.

Sometimes a patch of blue sky showed, but a new bank of clouds would scurry across to cover it.

We did some little work herding and cutting rails, but mostly we endured the rain and waited. Clothes hung up in a shelter would not dry. Our fires, when they would burn at all, gave out a profusion of smoke from the wet wood. In our camp area the grass was all destroyed; we tramped it underground or picked it up in the gobs of mud that clung to our shoes. The place became like a pig pen. The water edged under our shelters and wet our bedding. I heard here and there among the colonists evidence of short tempers and fussing that the leaders had chosen the colony site in such a rainy climate, but also I noted the comradely good humor that comes when people endure hardships together.

When finally it ceased, we let the ground dry three days, then planted corn. Mr. Finch said it was six weeks late.

CHAPTER

5

THERE were fifty-four families in the colony and twenty-one single men and nine single women who were not members of a family, though the single women were mostly nieces or cousins of some family member. The young men and women associated together freely, usually in groups. Jim York and Jeannette Bossereau were the exception. They were in the company of each other every time Jim could manage it, whether working or strolling through the trees around camp or sitting by a fire at night, and she came to be as forward as he in arranging the opportunity for them to be together. If they went with a dozen young people for a picnic along the creek or to pick flowers, as the girls were fond of doing, the two unabashedly held hands. The other young people accepted that they were sweethearts.

To Andy York it was a joke at first. He teased his younger brother with great good humor, and I believe he thought it was a passing thing, but after some weeks he became quiet about it and I began to detect even a note of resentment in him. He had a strong streak of seriousness deep in his nature and had seen more difficult times than his brother, and I think he had engaged himself thoroughly in two things: the ideals of the colony, though he didn't discuss it much, and hard work, in which he took pride. I was not alone in recognizing the two brothers as the best workers among us; it became understood that if a work leader had the York brothers assigned to his crew, he could accomplish his assigned work. After Jim began to spend so much of his time with Jeannette Bossereau, Andy would sometimes speak sharply to him as they worked, as if impatient of his slowness or ineptitude—a ridiculous attitude, for if Andy was the most productive worker in the colony, his love-sick kid brother was the second most. But Jim was not letting sharp words or anyone's irritation bother him in those days.

One Sunday afternoon Andy and I were helping Mr. Finch and the employees notch and mount logs on the building that was to be their living quarters. They had, during the rainy spell and during spare time, cut and dragged up all the logs that would be needed and, probably because no one was required to work on the building unless he wanted to, the construction seemed more a lark than a task. Andy and I worked with ax and adz and left the heaving of the green logs to the others. We were surprised to look up from our work and see Brother Bossereau approaching us with three boys ten or twelve years old at his heels.

"There is trouble about the milk cows," he said. "I regret to disturb you on Sunday, but I see you're working anyway."

"What's the trouble?" I asked.

"They say they have gone into the barley field."

"And the bull, too," one of the boys said.

"Isn't there a man out there herding with them?"

"Brother Henri," Brother Bossereau said. "But I suppose he sent these boys for help."

"We were told to keep the sheep in front of the field," one of the boys said, "but the cows came and won't go out."

Another one said, "They're eating the barley, too."

"I don't think it's important," Brother Bossereau said. "A

few milk cows couldn't do much damage. Dominique probably has them out by now. Still, he sent for help."

"We'll walk out that way," I said.

Andy and I put away our tools and headed for the field,
followed by the boys, still explaining the trouble.

Andy asked them, "Is Dominique Henri afraid of the milk
cows?"

"He's afraid of the bull."

"And the cows, too."

"But not the sheep."

We found the colony's seventeen milk cows and one bull
standing in the middle of the barley field, a long patch of
about forty acres. A few of them browsed at the barley,
which was three or four inches high, but most of them were
merely standing, chewing their cuds and swinging their tails
at the gnats. A long stone's throw from them stood Dominique Henri and three more boys about the age of those with
us. They were throwing clods of dirt at the cows. Some bits
of clod went as far as the cows, but did not disturb them as
much as the gnats. As we came up to Dominique Henri, he
began to throw with greater vigor and to shout, "Go out!
Out of the place! Shoo! Shoo! *Fuera!*" He turned his excited face to us and said, "*Mince alors!* We may have to use
horsemen. They charged us once already." He seemed so
serious and ludicrous that I could think of nothing to say to
him, but it occurred to me that he was a poor example to put
with a group of boys who were supposed to be learning about
livestock.

We went past him and up to the cows and set them moving to leave the field by the shortest way. The lazy bull and
the older cows plodded straight away, but the younger ones
darted this way and that in a spritely, stubborn manner as they
will when they are well fed on spring grass. Andy and I had
to run to keep them together. The boys quickly changed their
understanding and began to help us, running one way and

another to head the cows that tried to turn away. Dominique Henri followed behind us, doing nothing, obviously ill at ease.

As we came to the edge of the field, one of the boys yelled, "The sheep, Brother Langly! The sheep are coming now!"

They were, all three hundred or so of them. They had come half the length of the barley patch, spread out as if purposely trying to trample it all. Andy, who had been running until he was short of breath, shouted at Dominique Henri, "Don't you see the sheep? Are you afraid of the sheep?"

"I wash my hands," the little Frenchman said. "You are so active, you proceed."

"You're assigned to it, you idiot!" Andy yelled. "Get the damned sheep out of the field! Can't you do anything?"

Dominique Henri walked away from the sheep toward the trees, saying in an agitated voice, "I'm a wine worker. I wash my hands. I'm a wine worker and a watchmaker. You Americans are so competent."

I took the boys to drive out the sheep, and Andy came with us, still angry. The cows had done little damage, but the sharp hooves of the sheep had cut up half the field. I left the boys with the flock, which they could obviously handle, and told them to stay with them until someone came to help drive them back to the pen where we put them at night. The cows would give no more trouble; they were now drifting toward the lot where the calves were penned in the daytime and where their full udders would be relieved by the evening milking.

Going back toward camp, Andy and I saw Dominique Henri sitting alone at the edge of the field. "That damned idiot!" Andy said. "Half this field's to be planted over."

"I feel a little sorry for him," I said.

Andy said quickly, "I don't feel a bit sorry for him. If he and some of the others didn't think they were so good, it would be different. He's got a nice, tender conscience to judge other people with, but he can't do a damned thing himself."

I could see that he was still angry and it would be useless to defend the Frenchman to him.

He went on, "I've had this before with that man. He wants to have all the morals and let somebody else do all the work. I jab a fat steer a few times to make him pull his part of the load and he raises a big stink to Bossereau and everybody about how cruel I am. But he couldn't do any work then and he hasn't done one day's work since he's been here . . . only mess up. We had a good stand of barley there. Why should we have the trouble of doing all that work over?"

I thought of pointing out that we had been present when the sheep did the damage and we might share a little blame. I said, "He's not a good model to put with those boys."

"I'm sick of him. This colony's too important to put up with people like him. We can build something here. But I don't see how we can if we've got to carry a bunch of parasites."

He went with me as I went and reported the matter to Brother Bossereau. As tactfully as I could I let the French leader know that Dominique Henri was completely incompetent as a herder and at every other work we had tried him at.

"Well," he said, "it's my hope that we will all be excellent farmers at the end of a year. Some of us are certainly not at this time."

Though Andy said nothing and made no outward sign, I could feel his strong tendency to object to such glossing over of the trouble and to condemn Dominique Henri, but I knew too that he had great respect, even awe, for the French leader.

I said, "Perhaps it would be better if he were not put with

the boys at herding. They would learn more with someone else."

"Well," Brother Bossereau said, "perhaps. I'll mention it when we arrange the work crews for next week. We all must toil at something, of course."

I left it at that. Andy entered a sullen silence and did not break it even as we ate the evening meal.

Jim came in about sunset. He was ebullient, with nothing in particular to say, but with much good humor. He ran quickly against the sullen manner of his brother; the two were sensitive to each other's moods. He said, "What's eating you?"

"Nothing's eating me," Andy said. "What's eating you?"

"Looks to me like you got a bellyache." To me he said, "What's the matter with him?"

I told him about Dominique Henri and his herding adventures in a light vein. He laughed and said, "That man's a character."

Andy said, "It's real funny. It'll cost a whole crew of us a day's hard work to sow that patch again. Then another day's hard work to drag the seed under. And no telling whether it'll come up to a good stand like it was."

"A little hard work never hurt anybody," Jim said.

"It won't hurt that Dominique Henri or a lot of these other colonists because they never do any. Seems to me like some people take it pretty lightly. Like it was all a joke."

"Well, some people sit around and brood about it too. Which does no good. It's all in the way you look at it. I asked you to come with us this afternoon and have a little fun, but you wouldn't. You're getting to be an old grouch."

I had a foolish impulse to try to stop their bickering, I suppose because they were among my best friends and because it had seemed they always got on so well together. I said, "Some of us find all the girls taken up and we're left out. That Jeannette Bossereau, for instance; she's monopolized all the time."

Jim laughed a little. Andy was sitting on an upturned keg, staring into the gathering darkness. He said, "Girls are a dime a dozen."

I was surprised at this unexplained remark and wished I had not brought in the connection between Jeannette and the younger brother. Andy's ill temper extended further than I had guessed.

"What do you mean by that?" Jim demanded.

"I mean just what I say."

"If I was an old sourpuss like you, I'd knock you right off that keg."

"You could try it, young fellow," Andy said. "I remember it wasn't too long ago you used to wet your britches; now you're going to start knocking me around. You must think you've grown up fast."

"I'm old enough not to slur people I don't even know. You've got no reason to make a crack like that."

Evidently Andy wished to turn the argument away from the girl. As he answered he sounded serious but more reasonable. "They can't handle a team. They can't plow. They can't split rails. They can't watch sheep. All I wonder is why I should work like a mule for people like Dominique Henri."

"What's that got to do with the girls?"

"Because of that girl you're blind to what's going on. There's about seventy men here besides the employees, and about ten of them are doing more than half the work. I'm not in this thing for fun. I thought we'd build something worthwhile out here. How are we going to do it with ten men carrying sixty others on their back?"

Jim seemed to be glad the argument had turned away from the harsh personal note. He said, "Me and Langly will help you. Won't we?"

I laughed. Andy did not laugh, but he had no more to say about it at the time.

After the long period of rain the leaves and grass had come out with new vigor, and as the days grew warmer, even hot in the afternoons, the foliage grew lush, ever thicker and heavier. What had been a network of limbs and bare vines along the creek turned into a jungle growth that could hardly be penetrated except along worn paths, and every growing thing seemed to compete for the sunlight, determined to spread over the earth. In low places thistles and sunflowers and other weeds as well as a dozen grasses flourished. The oaks and elms scattered over the rolling hills came into full leaf.

We were greatly isolated from the rest of the world. Twice that spring we sent wagons back to Jones' Mill, a small trading point forty miles southeast, once to sell wool, the second time to replace some flour and other supplies that had spoiled from getting wet, both times to receive and post mail. It was a five-day round trip, and each one added to our sense of being away from civilization rather than reducing it. I would not say that we felt at home or at ease in our location; the sense of our having thrust ourselves out into a wilderness remained; yet the place became more familiar and we felt more as if we belonged as we began to see the result of some of our labor, even though that labor was not so productive as we had hoped.

Our ideas about work were hard to reconcile. We believed that everyone should do some physical toil for the good of his health and also so that he should understand better those who do physical toil and also so that he should be brought closer to nature. Then we believed that there can be joy in work of any kind and this enhanced if the worker is able to follow his own choice of vocation. Then we had the practical problem of trying to assign workers to that for which they were specially suited or trained, though few were suited for the work available. Brother Bossereau was well aware that we did not have the answer to these problems but believed we should experiment until we found a system that fulfilled most of our wishes. The men, and to some extent the women and children, were assigned to work leaders who were assigned certain tasks, but it was necessary daily to make adjustments. Brother Bossereau and a committee out of the assembly made the tentative assignments. Then the work leaders might, for any reason, request that their crews be given different work or that they be given smaller or larger crews, and these requests were usually honored; sometimes it was simply that they had completed the job the day before and sometimes it was a difference of opinion about what should be done. Then the individual worker had the right to ask that he be assigned to a certain crew or to certain work within that crew or even that he be excused for the day; these appeals were made to the work leader or a member of the committee, and they were often granted.

As it might be supposed, these arrangements did not produce as much work as others might have, but we hoped that through their flexibility a system would develop that would suit many of our ideals, and we had not established Uterica to be stern taskmasters to one another but in the hope that the will of the worker would produce its own just and effective regulation. There was this understanding, too: that goods and services are not the only end of human industry, that we spend one half or more of our lives working, that work must give satisfaction or even joy to the one doing it, and that in older systems so much is lost through ostentation and unequal distribution that we should have no trouble producing enough basic goods and services for everyone. These were the prevailing ideas, though there were some among us who had entered the colony through family ties and did not particularly believe in our ideals, and among the leadership were some who believed we should have more strict regimentation until we were better established.

We had several large projects which were being planned or considered by the leadership. Among these were an irrigation system, a gristmill, and a sawmill—all of which would depend upon our creek—a brick kiln, a lime plant to produce the material used in mortar, a basket factory, and a winery, the latter encouraged by the great number of wild grapes along the creek already loaded with tiny fruit. The project which had progressed farthest was the field crops, mainly because of the drive of Mr. Finch, though he maintained that he was not satisfied with them. Two projects which pleaded their own causes were building and fencing. Of the latter we needed a great deal, to prevent the stock from straying off and to keep them out of the crops and gardens. Buildings we obviously needed, since we were living halfway in the open, and though we had trees all around us, it was necessary to do a good bit of searching and long hauling to get logs that were large enough.

Our village was to center along a broad main street. "Sunshine in every street" was a motto of our city planners. They looked ahead to a time when our population would be many times expanded and we would have multistoried buildings, and they wanted no dim narrow alleys such as the poor live in elsewhere. But, for now, their plan was more practical. The street would lead from the top of the rise where we camped down toward the flatter land near the creek, a distance of some two hundred yards. The buildings would face each other across this broad street and each would be connected to those beside it with rail fences. With the ends fenced, we would have a large common garden area in the middle, more like a compound than a street. This arrangement would be used until we were established and prosperous and were ready to take in more colonists.

The corn looked good as it came up. We had altogether,

in seven different fields, about three hundred acres in this crop. When it was a foot high, it was badly infested with weeds about the same height. Although I did not serve regularly as a work leader, I agreed at Mr. Finch's insistence to take charge of a large hoeing crew of about twenty men to work in the corn. On the morning when we were to begin this task, I went early to the makeshift blacksmith shop to see to the sharpening of the hoes. I saw two or three men up at the headquarters area posting the work assignments on the board, and of them, one, Dr. Valentin, came down where I was busy over a grindstone.

He had the ability to appear like a serious gentleman on a city street even there at dawn. He said, "Langly, may I see you a minute?"

I stepped aside with him out of the hearing of the two I had been working with.

He said, "There will be an important assembly tomorrow. I hope you plan to attend."

I told him about my intention to head the crews in the cornfield and that the job would take more than a week.

"You'll have two work leaders under you. Let them handle it," he said.

"Well, Mr. Finch thought I should see to it."

"I'll come to the point," he said. "I hope we can have some evaluation of our progress in the assembly tomorrow. No one seems to know exactly where we are, nor where we're going. Frankly, there has been some criticism of Jean Charles Bossereau, not entirely without justification. There is a feeling that our organization is too slack and irregular. If you have any criticism along this line, I think you should make it known."

He was a man who could stare another right in the face and give no hint of wanting to communicate, yet in his skinny face now seemed a question beyond his words. Who did he mean was criticizing? I had heard complaints of one

kind and another but no particular criticism of Brother Bossereau. Something in his manner put me on my guard.

"I guess I don't have any special suggestions," I said.

"It's not so much suggestions that are wanted as the truth
about our progress. You are the ranking colonist in agriculture. If our irresponsible, slipshod way of operating has an
ill effect on agriculture, you should so state. If you cannot be
present at the assembly tomorrow, you should have someone
else speak for you."

I felt that he was trying to browbeat me. Thinking of
Andrew York, I said, "We might devise some kind of special
recognition for the best workers. That's the only suggestion
I would have."

He might as well not have heard me for all that he responded. He said, "I hope you'll think over what I've said
and consider whether you should attend," then turned and
walked away.

Shortly afterward the two work leaders reported to me and
I led the crew of twenty men to the field where we began
hoeing, but my mind was on the question raised by Dr.
Valentin. He had seemed to be part of a conspiracy. He
wanted to know where I stood. He had not been merely
asking whether I had any criticism, but had been requesting
that I produce some. I wondered how serious he was, what
his intentions were, and how many among the leaders agreed
with him. For myself, I could not conceive of our following
any leadership in the long run other than Brother Bossereau.
The assembly, or parts of it, had been meeting almost daily,
but I had not been attending though I had been frequently
invited. I honestly did not want to be one of the leaders who
set policy, but I decided to be present on the following day if
it would not interfere too much with my work, as much out
of curiosity as anything else.

It was a clear day and quickly became warm. The two
work leaders and I did not take a hoe, for while some of

the men knew as much about the work as we did, others were as ignorant as babes about it and required careful supervision. We went downfield, turned, and made our way back to the starting end. I kept so busy going from one to another of the workmen that I did not notice until almost upon them that a group of women and children awaited us in the trees at the end of the row. When I noted Brother Bossereau among them, I quit and went to him.

He was smiling broadly as he said, "You will desire to murder me, Brother Langly. I've brought you more workers."

"I'm afraid we don't have hoes for them," I said.

"I hope you'll allow us to interrupt you anyway," he said, and somehow managed to compound a frown of seriousness in with the smile on his face. "I wish so fervently for these women and children to have the pleasure of field work and know how hard it is and understand it. I know it's not convenient."

He had brought about as many would-be workers as were already in the field, not to take over the job for the day but to try it. It was a kind of lark to them. The two work leaders and I set about making the change. Most of the men who had been working sat down under the trees; one, Jim York, quickly made himself instructor and helper, but instructed and helped hardly anyone except the French leader's daughter.

Our tools were gooseneck hoes, and the weeds fell easily before them. The thing that was difficult was to accept that the beautiful young corn must be thinned. To some of the women, it seemed almost cruel, but since Mr. Finch was certain our biggest problem was enough moisture, I determined that the plants should be well spaced. I kept getting questions such as this: "Brother Langly, these aren't too thick, are they?" and answering, "Yes, much too thick." Sometimes the questions were foolish: "Should I cut out the big one in the center, Brother Langly, or leave it and take the small ones beside it?" I would answer with a big smile, "Take them all out. All three."

I came up to Jim and Jeannette, who were working side by side and having a great deal of fun over something. Jim was saying, "Do you think there'll be a next time?"

"Oh, sure," Jeannette said. "Miss Edwards is nice. She'll forgive us."

Jim said to me, "Don't expect us to work too hard. We're crippled, you know. Our hands are burned. Show him."

Both of them laughed and turned the palms of their hands up for my inspection. I saw nothing wrong, unless it was a slight redness.

"We burned them pulling hot taffy last night," he said.

"But it was in a good cause," she said.

"That's right. We did it entirely for the benefit of the children."

"After they were asleep," she said. "They didn't even know how we suffered for them."

I gathered from them, mixed up with a good bit of laughing, that the young people had had a party the night before. That Miss Harriet Edwards had secured out of the supplies two gallons of sorghum molasses, from which they had set out to make candy for the children of the colony.

"But that silly Wilma and the others," Jim said, "they started eating it as fast as it was made."

"But not us," Jeannette said.

"No, sir, not us. We didn't eat ours till after we dropped it and it was too unsanitary for children."

"No one can be blamed for dropping hot candy," Jeannette pointed out. "It was greasy with butter, too. It's very easy to drop."

"I found it easy," he said.

"Do you think we looked suspicious? I dropped my end as accidentally as I could."

"Me, too. If Miss Edwards won't forgive us, next time

we'll have Brother Langly get some molasses for us. He has lots of influence."

I left them to themselves.

Brother Bossereau did not ask questions nor give advice but went doggedly down his row, with great vigor at first, then slowing to a pace he could maintain. Some of the women wasted time calling to their children or chatting with the others, but most of them began to give a real account of themselves. A half-grown boy who had the row beside Brother Bossereau left to go to the toilet and I took up his hoe. He did not return. I carried on his work without any feeling of aggravation, for I'd done about as much instructing as would help any of them. It did not require much learning; those who would do it well would do it well, and the others perhaps would do passably. Beyond a certain point, it took only patience and endurance.

I could not work beside Brother Bossereau without being conscious of him. He worked with regular motions and without becoming careless. At times he paused briefly to remove his glasses and hat and sop the sweat from his high forehead with his shirt sleeve; then he would look ahead at the row and start on. He no longer wore the wooden shoes, but more sensible leather ones. He and I—all of us, including the women in their cotton dresses—were dripping with sweat by the time we had gone one full round. He looked at me with a simple smile and asked, almost like a child, "May we continue? I think we're doing well."

We took new rows and went ahead. I paid little attention to the work of the others, except for that of Brother Bossereau beside me, and that not only because of his identity but because he seemed to have an almost religious dedication to what he did.

Even though I was used to hard work, my shoulders and arms became tired from the constant motion, and then I fell into a slow rhythm that seemed to allow the heat of the sun to draw the soreness out as it came. The swinging of the hoe became almost automatic; it cut and raised and began to descend almost before I had chosen the spot to apply it next, and it seemed almost as if the weed or tuft of grass or excess corn plant moved to meet the blade. The footing in the clods was uncertain, and this was a petty annoyance at first, but only if one allowed it to be; it was like the sweat that dripped from our chins and ran down our bodies inside our clothing, like the bits of dirt that got in our shoes, like the gnats that buzzed at our necks—things that could be fought by an idle person, allowed to occupy his time, but need not be fought or accepted as anything other than another small fact of existence, and, if borne, would then be seen as surprisingly bearable. If the clods cocked our ankles, the heat sucked the soreness out, and as one progressed over the poor footing, the movement of the legs, like the arms, became nearly automatic: one foot came forward and found its hold, the other came forward and found its different hold, each suitable. But these feelings were not so definite and specific; it was more as if one gave himself up to a slow dance with the soil as a partner, meanwhile bathed in the heat of the sun, or as if one submitted to a benevolent hypnotism. I felt it and observed it in particular because of my awareness of Brother Bossereau.

I wondered whether he thought about some idealistic problem or whether he analyzed his own sensations or whether his mind was deliberately empty. This unimportant irony occurred to me: that such work as we were doing did not require one to be a farmer, that one might enjoy it and do well at it without any knowledge of managing a farm.

He stayed with me through the morning, and in the afternoon I had barely saved enough workers to man all our hoes. Some of the men and some of the later group of women and children had made excuses or had wandered off without saying anything. Brother Bossereau stayed with me through the long, hot afternoon, and his dedication to the work did not flag.

At sundown we put our hoes on our shoulders and headed home, walking slowly. He said to me, "I've proven a thing to myself today."

"What's that, sir?"

"I've caused disruption in your plans, Brother Langly, but we've accomplished a day's work, haven't we?"

"We certainly have."

"There are more important things than proper organization. Out of disruption can come progress. We search for a way of life, and our quest is certain to involve trial and error. Much error. But our principle of toil on the land is not in error. I'm speaking of our covenant. I could plan to work a day a week or six days a week at farm work and be pleased at the prospect. And as we remain near the soil, all of us will come to accept it."

His words brought to my mind Dr. Valentin's criticism about "slack and irregular" organization.

"I believe you comprehend my views, Brother Langly," he said, "and I appreciate it. Some of the assemblymen are critical. They are people of good will, but they are afraid. Their past experiences have affected them. But they will develop; all of us will develop. I have faith. These are the important things: spirit and brotherhood and tolerance. All the rest will be added."

I took his hoe as we entered the area of the compound and said good-night to him. It was dusk as I took our two implements to stack them near the makeshift blacksmith shop.

A group of people strolled by and from them Miss Harriet Edwards detached herself and came toward me, smiling. "My!" she said, "you've done a full day's work, haven't you."

"I guess so," I said. "Enough for one day, anyway."

"How is your work proceeding? Satisfactorily, I hope."

"About as well as we could expect."

"Someone mentioned that you might attend the assembly, Brother Langly, and I just want to extend my invitation to you. You might be interested in some of the issues." The smile briefly left her face as she added, "Frankly, there has been some criticism of Jean Charles Bossereau, not entirely without justification."

I told her that I intended to be present. As she walked away from me in the gathering darkness, it struck me that, as well as I could remember, she had used the identical words Dr. Valentin had used about criticism of the French leader, "not entirely without justification." It seemed likely that the two of them, possibly in the company of others, had speculated about Brother Bossereau's shortcomings and the attitude I might take toward them.

CHAPTER

6

THE following day I helped to set the crews to work in the fields, then hurried back to the new building, which had been planned as a dining hall and was now used for meetings. The log work on it was finished, and the roof, but the eight windows and two doors were not set in their openings. The floor was dirt; there was as yet some uncertainty as to where our diminishing supply of lumber should be used. I need not have hurried, for the assembly had not begun.

A dozen people were there and half of them were busily moving the long table from the side down to the end. I learned that this was for the benefit of an artist, a Belgian man with a great beard, who wanted the morning light through two windows and a door to fall on those who would sit at the table. He was going to make a sketch as the meeting proceeded. He arranged the cane-bottom chairs all on one side and the ends, but two or three of the less cooperative assemblymen moved the ones they took to place their backs toward the artist. He moved about looking at the scene from different angles and speaking to them officiously as if the sketch were the purpose of the assembly, but not insulted by those who ignored him.

In a minute I realized they were waiting for something.

Brother Bossereau was absent. Dr. Sockwell came in, and they turned to him as if he knew the answer. He ambled heavily to an empty chair and plopped down.

Someone asked, "Is it serious? Is he coming?"

He said, "My diagnosis is that Jean Charles Bossereau is about twenty years older than he thinks he is. He has strained every muscle in his body."

"Will he be here?"

"He says he will. Between moans. His daughter is rubbing liniment on him." He grinned. In his sloppy, careless frame a puck was poorly hidden.

They asked me and I had to admit that Brother Bossereau had been working with me the day before.

"This is the kind of stupid thing that is happening," said Dr. Valentin sourly. "With a hundred problems needing the attention of the director, Jean Charles goes into the field like a peasant."

I took a chair at the end away from the door. The group was quiet, restrained by Dr. Valentin's obvious bad humor. Beside me sat a man about whom I did not know much and who had not been attending assembly meetings; at least he was not considered one of the leaders. His name was Deveraux. He was clean-shaven, had a rough Roman nose, and his stringy black hair lay slick back on his head. His face had a blank look that was both hard and youthful. Someone had told me, whether as rumor or fact I could not remember, that he had once been condemned to death for a conspiracy. He sat stiffly and stared at the others.

Dr. Sockwell was fussing with his large briar pipe, which he seemed always to be knocking out or lighting or cleaning. He asked of no one in particular, "What is the agenda of this little picnic, anyway?"

Dr. Valentin answered immediately, "The agenda is to attempt a candid assessment of our situation and to try to convince Jean Charles Bossereau that matters cannot go on as they have. The agenda being what it is—"

The painter leaned over him and asked in a low voice whether he would mind turning more to the light. Dr. Valentin snapped, "Yes, I would!" The painter shrugged and went back to his easel.

Dr. Valentin gazed at us a moment, his thin, dignified face flustered, then went on. "Since Jean Charles is absent through his own fault, I think we could go ahead and consider some of the problems that must be settled. I know that some besides myself realize that he is leading us down the wrong route. Something must be done."

"But not behind his back," someone said.

"Why not!" Valentin said. "Why is this behind his back? This is the proper time and place. Whose fault is it if he's not here? I tell you that I hope some of you are ready to voice your dissatisfaction. As the American gamblers say, it's time for a showdown."

The man beside me, Deveraux, asked in a harsh, plain voice, "Why was I requested to attend this meeting?"

Valentin was not pleased at this question, which was not responsive to his talk. "Who asked you?"

"Bossereau."

"Then I would suppose you could get that information from him."

Dr. Valentin's contempt was clear to Deveraux. While the doctor went ahead, the strange man beside me regarded him with a cool, mirthless smile. The others around the table seemed uncomfortable.

"My point is that there comes a time when we are not doing our duty if we merely defer to Jean Charles. We are headed for trouble. The time to speak frankly is now."

Miss Harriet Edwards said, "Well, I've spoken out many times. I think I've been frank. I find myself, as the director of culture and recreation and the temporary director of education and the supervisor of young women's activities, without any facilities and nothing to direct. I want a recreation building and a young women's barracks. I feel that we're wasting time."

"Whose fault do you suppose that is, Sister Edwards?" Dr. Valentin asked.

"I don't know. I just know that I'm not in charge of building buildings."

"It all goes back to our slack organization under our great director. We absolutely must impose a strict discipline upon ourselves, and that goes for everyone in the colony."

Deveraux asked, still smiling, "A what?"

Valentin frowned. "What do you mean?"

"We must absolutely impose on ourselves?"

"Strict discipline! Strict discipline!"

The painter had been going from his easel to one and another vantage point, sometimes approaching near to the table and looking at us with squinting eyes, his head cocked or thrown back, unconsciously thrusting out his beard. Valentin, though he kept his back in that direction, caught sight of him and said, "In the name of heaven, man! This is no show! Why don't you put that stuff away and report to your work leader and do an honest day's work?" The artist smiled innocently and went ahead as he had been doing.

Valentin turned back as if to talk again to us at the table, but at that time Deveraux rose and said, "Attention! I pose." He stood in a ridiculous manner with one foot on his chair and one hand on his hip.

Dr. Sockwell chuckled. The others seemed embarrassed. The man's impudent action silenced Valentin's attempt to start a serious discussion.

We were silent until Brother Bossereau came in. He shuffled along, leaning heavily on Jeannette, whose arm was clasping him firmly around the waist. As he came to his chair and settled into it, he made little grunting sounds with each movement. In answer to our greetings, he grinned in a hang-dog manner. Jeannette leaned over and whispered to him. I believe she asked him whether he would be all right. He patted her arm and nodded. She left.

"Please excuse my tardiness," he said.

Valentin, straight across the table from him, demanded, "Are you able to take part in this meeting, or shall we post-pone it?"

"Please give it no thought," he said, though he winced with every small shift of his weight in his chair. He waved pain-fully at the artist, who was at that time sizing him up.

I expected Deveraux, who had sat down decorously when the French leader entered, to again ask why he had been invited to the meeting, but he did not.

"Jean Charles," Valentin said, "we understand that this is to be a frank and straightforward assessment of our problems, our entire situation. I'd like to ask you first for an accurate accounting of the money of the colony. That seems to me basic. Perhaps if you don't have your books here, you would want to send for them."

"I believe I can assure you that our financial condition is satisfactory," Brother Bossereau said. "We have little money, but with prudence it will suffice until our income increases."

"That's all right for the rest of the colonists, but this is the assembly," Valentin said. "We want a complete and precise account of the money that belongs to the colony."

"For that you would require an accountant." Brother Bos-sereau raised his glasses and rubbed his eyes. "As for my own transactions, I actually did not expect that the assembly would require a complete account."

The others were interested in Valentin's questions, but now they murmured, "I don't think we should require that," "I think we should trust the director on that."

"How much money do you have?" Valentin demanded.

"What particular money?"

"Any money that belongs to the colony. Do you have any colony money in your strongbox? If so, how much is it, Jean Charles?"

"Well, any money that I have belongs to the colony, Brother Valentin. I have no private property at all. Everything I have belongs to the colony. And I'm pleased to discuss it if you consider it useful. I believe I have twelve hundred American dollars. And four hundred five-franc thaler. And then I believe eight hundred reales. And—"

Valentin interrupted, "The French and Spanish money comes to less than five hundred dollars." He was scribbling in a notebook.

Brother Bossereau said, "I haven't figured it. And there is, I believe, seventeen dollars owing us for the wool. The man at Jones' Mill did not have in stock some of the supplies we traded for. Then I believe there might be some among the colonists who have a small amount of money, who, in the future, will want to give it into the common fund. In addition, we have friends around the world; I intend to write letters to them and I'm quite optimistic about their response, if we become seriously short of money."

"I think I can enlighten you about some of our friends, Jean Charles. Those who put money into the Company expect an accounting. Can we ask them for more money without telling them what we have done with the first they supplied? What shall we tell them?"

"I think we shall tell them that we are alive and reasonably healthy and are located on the land. And we are beginning to bring into reality some of their oldest and most cherished dreams."

"That won't be good enough, in my opinion. We don't have enough money to pay the employees for the year as we planned. Isn't that correct?"

Someone said, "The employees are taking too much money. I think we should discharge them."

"Discharge them and we'll never get anything done," Valentin said. "They are doing half the work."

Several of them objected to this as an exaggeration. Dr. Sockwell said, "We've built all the sanitary facilities without any help from the employees."

Valentin returned to his inquisition of the French leader. "We have no sawmill and we have no money to buy lumber for flooring and doors and such. Is that correct? Yet we still continue to plan buildings that require lumber."

Brother Bossereau grimaced as he shifted in his chair. "Are you approaching a particular point, Brother Valentin?"

"My point is that we need a complete reorganization. We need to face facts instead of floating in the clouds. We are bankrupt! I say let everyone in authority accept a definite job and let him answer strictly for the accomplishment of that job. Let every man, woman, and child work six days a week with no excuses." He turned to glare briefly at the artist. "Now half the people do not work. The other half work whenever they wish and however they wish. We are going to have strict discipline or ruin. Mark my word!"

Deveraux spoke up. "Why was I invited to this meeting?"

Brother Bossereau seemed only now to see him. "Brother Deveraux! I'm pleased that you could attend. I hope that you will bring any suggestions you have to the assembly."

"Why did you tell me to come?"

"You have been talking to people. You have criticism. This is the place for it. As you observe, we speak frankly. Actually we are not so difficult with one another as we may sound. We are all good friends. But this is the place to make criticism instead of telling people who might not comprehend and might be agitated."

"They require to be agitated! We're soft! Not revolutionary! We bring too many old rules and old morals. I've served in jail for talking previously, and I don't mean to quit in the future."

"Yes," Brother Bossereau said. "We hope you will attend the assembly and speak about your criticism here. We expect criticism."

Miss Harriet Edwards said, "Brother Bossereau, if I could just raise a point. Whom would he represent? I have the feeling sometimes that we have too many topics already before the assembly and that certain issues in which I am interested and which are set forth in our covenant are not really given adequate consideration."

Deveraux said, "*Bagasse!* Who the hell do you represent?"

Her face hardened as if she had been slapped, but she did not hesitate long with her answer. "I presume you are one of those who believe women should keep their places and don't deserve any representation, but this colony is not founded on that premise."

"You damned sure don't represent women that I've talked to," he said. "Director of culture! Very humorous! An American dame is the director of culture!"

Valentin said, "The truth is that he's an anarchist and represents no one. He merely wants to cause trouble and waste our time."

Brother Bossereau said, "We have various . . . we are not all of one mind."

"I don't deny that I'm an anarchist," Deveraux said. "A pernicious disease takes a radical cure. I don't intend to cease talking."

"Jean Charles, before this man interrupted, we were trying to analyze the disorganized mess that this colony has become. Now, quite a few of us have some legitimate criticism, and I think we should seriously consider making some changes."

Brother Bossereau frowned in thought as he began speaking. "Allow me to discuss that. And pardon me if I repeat what I've said before. I believe the day of our arrival here I said that socialism would not be easily established. We attempt to unravel injustices and wrongs that have tangled together for centuries. We have difficulties, but we are not children. We're the pioneers, or even martyrs, if you will. Some people don't approve of the food. We must do the best we can and endure what we must with good humor and good-will."

"Jean Charles, we agree with all that. But some of us believe we need to be more definite. More businesslike. More strict. More orderly."

Deveraux snorted and leaned back in his chair with his eyes half closed.

"Well, yes," Brother Bossereau said. "I want to comment on some of the things you say. I believe we are taking the scientific approach. Try all things; hold fast that which is good. We are doubtless doing things at this time which we will change in the months to come. We know what our goals are. We will approach some of them sooner than others. But I believe our people need to have considerable freedom at this time, that we should not establish definite patterns until such time as trial and error, a sort of scientific willingness to observe and be patient, begins to indicate what route will lead us toward our goals and what will not. Tolerance . . . tolerance and patience.

"Then, too, I am concerned about money. But I don't be-lieve we should attempt to plan ahead in any definite manner, that is, too far ahead. We may find ourselves anxious about matters which might happen in a year, when we would be better advised to think about the present. Sometimes the future arranges itself.

"But we should remember, too, that one of our goals is to abolish money. It seems basic to me." He smiled. "I may be guilty of oversimplification, but, in general, when we have abolished money, we need not worry about money.

"We have accomplished much. Soon we'll be having many types of vegetables. The fields are in excellent condition. I had a little experience with them yesterday and I suppose I overextended myself, but I assert that in spite of my own immoderation, I have complete confidence that great spiritual and moral benefits will come out of our agricultural basis for Uterica. I'd be pleased for Brother Langly to give us a brief assessment of our crops, since we're observing our progress in this meeting. Not any complete account of the work, but just a judgment about the condition of the crops."

I felt very much like an observer rather than a participant in the meeting and hoped that I would not be drawn into any argument. "The crops were planted rather late," I said, "but Mr. Finch believes they will do well if the rains come right."

Dr. Sockwell asked through a cloud of pipe smoke, "What do you believe?"

"I would agree with him. They look good now, and it depends on the rain."

I intended to report that I knew of some dissatisfaction because some colonists were doing more work than others, but I was interrupted, and as the discussion progressed, several assembly members mentioned the point. Brother Bossereau agreed and said that when we had become better established we could work out a system of honoring those who worked hardest. He hoped our colony would eventually prove that work is its own reward.

None of the assemblymen was satisfied with our progress. Each of them felt that we needed more supplies for some project that he was particularly interested in, but, though they addressed their complaints to Brother Bossereau, it became clear that they were not willing to turn away from his leadership and make a reorganization sponsored by Valentin. At each complaint Brother Bossereau turned their attention away from the narrow difficulty and toward our general goals and hopes.

They responded to him differently. Miss Harriet Edwards held the dignified silence she had entered when Deveraux spoke insultingly to her. She kept her handsome head erect, paid polite attention, and said nothing. If she had been a part of any plan, definite or indefinite, to try to change our organization, her support of the plan had been stifled because of the presence of Deveraux. I thought she believed that disagreements, legitimate and necessary, must always be handled on a certain level of propriety. Or it may have been that her personality simply would not let her speak after she had been insulted.

Brother Adams was Brother Bossereau's unconscious aid, for he was always the first to respond to the French leader's words. After some difficulty had been presented as a serious matter that needed immediate attention, Brother Bossereau would begin to speak his soothing and inspiring words, and Brother Adams would soon begin to nod and murmur, "That's true," "I agree," "That's right," "Yes." As for the others, they did not respond with the tolerance and goodwill and patience that Brother Bossereau asked for, but they seemed led by his words to continue without any radical changes.

One event marred the latter part of the meeting. Deveraux rose and, without a "By your leave," or "Go to hell," walked out of the building. There followed a discussion upon which all agreed: that his manners were terrible.

Brother Bossereau terminated the meeting by asking that we all do what we could to reduce and answer the critical private conversations in the colony. He knew that it was easy to find fault with the food and lodgings and to engage in malicious gossip against one another, but we were all brothers and sisters with noble ideals in common. He believed in absolute freedom of speech, but everyone should use that freedom wisely, particularly because we were undergoing hardships which would be made easier by solidarity and harmony. He realized that some in the colony did not definitely share our political and economic ideals but had come because of family ties, but these people would share in the common happiness and gains as much as anyone, and they, also, should be encouraged not to grumble.

When they rose from the table, several went to the artist's sketch to see what he had done. They exclaimed over it. Brother Bossereau labored toward the door, grunting, and Jeannette came in quickly to support him; she had been waiting, I do not know how long, outside the door. Although it was near noon, I went out to see how my field crew was doing.

I had not known before this meeting how much difference of opinion and willingness to dispute existed in the assembly. It was clear that Brother Bossereau had met a serious challenge to his leadership by Valentin and had won for the time being, but the victory had come more from lack of agreement on any alternative than from support of Brother Bossereau. I felt uncomfortable about the reservations and unsolved problems that they carried away from the meeting.

CHAPTER

7

DURING the third month we finished the common kitchen and dining hall. The kitchen was crowded with two large iron stoves and two smaller ones, storage cabinets and bins, several worktables, tubs and vats for washing dishes. The women who were assigned there found that cooking for a family and cooking for three hundred people are quite different things. They would not cook enough to last through the third table. They solved the dilemma partly by cooking what could be boiled in large kettles and pots: mush, soup, stew. There was seldom enough bread.

Rumor had it that the cooks and dishwashers and vegetable peelers and milk handlers were putting pressure on Brother Bossereau for more room. When he asked them to be patient and do their best, they demanded that all of the work of the colony cease and everyone get busy building a kitchen that was large enough. I did not know what the outcome had been, but rumor had it that some of the women said the food would be poor until they had a decent working area.

The dining hall seated about one hundred, and so we ate in shifts on a schedule: breakfast at five, five thirty, and six; lunch at eleven thirty, twelve, and twelve thirty; supper at six, six thirty, and seven.

The system did not work well at first; even so it seemed an improvement to me. I had eaten with the employees and we had taken turns at playing cook. Some of them were not such good cooks, for which I could hardly blame them. The food at the common dining hall seemed high enough in quality to them; it was only when it was lacking in quantity that they complained.

On the Sunday following the week when the dining hall opened, the employees intended to sweep out their new quarters and move in. We went for the last breakfast shift but found ourselves thirty minutes early, since it had been decided to allow everyone to sleep thirty minutes extra on Sunday and postpone breakfast by that amount of time. I sat waiting with the employees on the rail fence that tied into the dining hall.

One of them asked suddenly, "What the hell are them women doing?"

"What women? The cooks?"

"Naw, down yonder. They went in our bunkhouse with a tub of dirty dishes."

"You're seeing things," someone told him.

"No, I'm not. I saw it."

"I ain't bunking with no dirty dishes," another said.

"I guess they aim for you to wash them in your spare time," someone told him.

After breakfast I went down to the new bunkhouse with Mr. Finch and some of the others. It was true that some women had brought in dirty dishes. There were a half dozen women in the room. They were busily arranging a worktable and sacks and kegs and crocks of things from the kitchen, using the racks we had built in for beds as storage space. They showed no inclination to move out or even stop their work at the objections of the employees. The place was an auxiliary kitchen and laundry. Brother Bossereau had given them permission.

One of the men said, "Why, I'll hook me a team to this place and jerk it right down level with the ground before I'll be hornswoggled out of it this way!" But the women simply paid no attention to him. They had their sleeves rolled up and were already sweating at their work.

Outside, Mr. Finch told them, "Take it easy. I'll go talk to Bossereau."

I walked along with him and said, "I'm sure there's some explanation." When we came to the French leader's quarters, I asked, "Do you want me to go in with you?"

"Why? All I want to know is whether he means to keep his promise to us or not."

I waited. He stayed inside for half an hour and I wished I had not come with him. I considered knocking on the door and going in and I considered walking off, either of which seemed awkward. When the door opened, Brother Bossereau was talking to him in a low voice. Mr. Finch came directly out without answering him.

As we walked away, he grinned sourly and shook his head. "That's the damnedest man there ever was. It's sure hard to get a straight answer out of him."

"He's got a lot on his mind," I said, "and a lot of pressure on him."

"He doesn't know much about handling a crew of workmen. You've get to keep your word. If you don't, a lot of gab won't smooth it over."

"What did he say?"

"Aw...flexibility...good humor...the women have got to have room to cook. They screwed up on planning buildings and don't have enough lumber for doors and windows and such. Be patient. Tolerance. Faith, hope and charity."

He did not seem really angry, but merely surprised, halfway amused. He said suddenly, "Can you imagine having the gall to tell a bunch of men they can build them a house on their own time, then, when they get it done, giving it to someone else? Men have been killed for less than that."

"Maybe they really did have to have it for cooking."

"Maybe if he'd come to us and put it to us straight, we'd have given it up on our own."

"Well, maybe he had about a dozen things to do besides that."

"He just made a mistake, Langly. The employees are not going to build another house on their own. And they've got sense enough not to stay the winter here in the open. They'll just leave when they get ready, without notice. And they won't ever trust another word he says."

I decided not to press my defense of Brother Bossereau any further; the chances were that I would only ruin the employees' opinion of me. My view of the justice of the matter was influenced by one thing which was so obvious that it did not need to be argued, though they may not have seen it: they were out here doing what they were doing for pay, while the colonists had given up luxuries and come into the wilderness through a faith in high principles. The difference in motives was so great as to make a meeting of the minds almost impossible.

The employees accepted it but did not like it. Mr. Finch's halfway-amused attitude doubtlessly prevented any of them from doing any more than gripe about it. One of them said, "If it was a bunch of men, I'd say let's go over there and throw 'em out. But what the hell can you do with a bunch of women?"

That afternoon was when the Indians came back. They did not seem like a diplomatic mission this time, but a good-natured and neighborly people bent on trading and visiting. They began to appear leaning on the rail fences of the compound, looking over at us, grinning, calling out what must have been greetings in their unintelligible tongue. A short time later they began to perch on the top rails of the fences like so many big friendly birds.

Excitement ran through our budding village, surprise, apprehension, then relief as we saw the manner of our visitors. They dropped off the fences into the compound carrying baskets of squash, strings of dried gourds, cured pelts, mats woven of reeds, but no weapons. Their clothing was less formal than it had been before; many of them wore a breech-clout pulled through a string or colored sash at the waist along with some item of white man's clothing, a hat or red shirt; a few of them wore trousers. It was as if the eleven men who had come previously had divided the clothing they had worn among these three dozen or so.

Brother Bossereau came out and spoke to them with a broad smile, but they did not gravitate to him as they had before. Most of the compound was planted in garden. On either side a path ran along in front of the doors, and a number of cross paths cut from one side to the other. What would someday be a broad street was now a promising garden surrounded and divided by paths. Our chickens ran loose here; it was hoped that they would do more good eating insects than they would do harm pecking vegetables. Along the paths, the Indians scattered, chattering and smiling and making signs. Among them was one woman, a heavyset female past her prime, with a skirt of faded blue cloth wrapped from waist to ankles. Her wrinkled, pendulous breasts were bare. The women of the colony who came out saw her and hurried back inside; some of them called their children in. The Indian woman carried a few mats and acted exactly as did the men, evidently unconscious that her bare breasts made her a startling exception.

I was sitting under a canvas shade toward the lower end of the compound with Andy York and a few of the employees, who had been moody since losing their bunkhouse. One of them said, "I wish I had me some beads and a few mirrors. I'd trade them out of those pelts."

Another one said, "Look at that squaw! That's enough to make a man swear off women, ain't it?"

Andy and I walked up into the garden to see what was going on at closer range. They were making it clear by pointing and motioning that they wished to trade for everything they saw. I saw a few trades take place: a pencil for a dried gourd, a handkerchief for a small woven mat, a pocket comb for a yellow crookneck squash. Then they began to get interested in the chickens. I don't know how the first trade took place, whether a colonist did not understand what he was doing or whether he traded to keep from offending an Indian. Within a few minutes a dozen Indians were chasing chickens through the garden, dragging the squawking birds by feet and neck and wing out from under the pea vines. The trading got out of hand. It was impossible to tell whether a particular Indian was dodging down a row after an old hen because he thought it was already his property or because he intended to try to trade for it.

I saw Brother Bossereau frowning nervously except when he had to smile in response to a friendly Indian greeting, and I heard him say twice, "I don't believe we should trade the chickens." His soft voice had no effect.

There was about it a kind of carnival air. And a strangeness. They kept speaking their meaningless words long after they had obviously greeted every colonist who was present. They spoke obligingly and at length as they were consummating a trade, ignoring the fact that we couldn't understand a word. They responded not at all to our language.

I thought about our other contact with them, and this present scene did not follow. Nowhere was the old man with the hard face and the dark, enigmatic eyes, and one could hardly imagine his being one of these people. I thought of the simple, idyllic village I had spied upon; these Indians hardly seemed to come from such a place. They should be quieter, more timid, less forward. I had the impression that they had been spying on us and studying us and had planned this visit in detail.

One of them squatted where two paths crossed and laid out in front of himself a kind of game or gambling device. Into a thick mat he would insert pegs in a pattern. These he would cover with the halves of small dried gourds, six of them, which he would quickly and nimbly move here and there on the mat. Two Indians squatted in front of him, sometimes pointing at a gourd half, which he would lift; then they would exclaim gleefully. When several colonists gathered around to watch, the Indians by motion persuaded them to point at gourd halves. The pegs did not seem to stay in their old patterns after they were covered. Whether the colonists involved knew the point of the game on the mat I do not know, but it appeared to me that the Indians, for all their mirth, took it seriously as a gambling game. The stakes were our chickens.

I headed for Brother Bossereau, thinking that he should stop the game, even if it caused trouble, but I found that he was hunting me for what he considered a more serious problem. He said, "They say some Indian boys are chasing the sheep, Brother Langly. Across the creek. Would you ride your horse over there and investigate?"

I hurried to get Andy York to go with me; it would be awkward to ask one of the employees in their present mood. Then it occurred to me that Dominique Henri might be one of the sheepherders, and he and Andy did not get along. Jim York was doubtless somewhere occupied with Jeannette Bossereau. I resigned myself to going alone, but even so I had a problem: my saddle horse was out with the colony horse band perhaps a mile or two away, and the only horses nearby were a half dozen staked near the creek belonging to the employees. I went to Mr. Finch and briefly explained it to him and asked whether I could use his horse.

"Get your rifle and a bridle," he said. "We'll catch a couple of horses and go bareback."

I don't know what I'd expected from him; maybe I'd forgotten what manner of man he was when some action was needed without procrastination. I'd felt guilty approaching him, and then found myself almost running to keep up with him as we headed for the creek.

We caught horses, crossed the small stream, and kicked them into a lope up toward a low ridge. We paused there to scan the country. Farther along the ridge grew a lone clump of oaks and under one of them we spotted a man sitting.

It was Dominique Henri. He rose as we rode toward him, a forlorn figure standing with his hands clasped behind him.

"*Bigre!*" he said. "They got them! It's over with the sheep! They're slaughtered for pleasure, I imagine."

"Which way did they go?" Mr. Finch asked.

"All over. All scattered. It's the finish of the sheep. The boys departed, and I only stayed to comfort one creature while it died."

"Did some Indian boys come?" I asked.

"*Mais oui!* The demons! They are maniacs! They laughed!"

He pointed and we saw one sheep dead in some tall grass a hundred feet away. We dismounted and looked at it. It had been shot in the stomach with an arrow, which had penetrated almost through.

We could get little information from Dominique, except that when he insisted the sheep had "scattered all over," he pointed generally west. We rode in that direction in a lope, slowing to a walk on the higher points of the rolling prairie to look at the land ahead. In no more than three miles we saw them, first one bunch huddled in a woolly clot in a draw, then two other bunches stringing out toward each other to join in a common herd among scattered trees. No Indian boys could be seen. The sheep had been through a good run, for none of them were grazing, but they did not seem to have been

harmed. It is impossible to count sheep in the open; our esti-
mates, however, showed that we had found them all.

"What was it?" I asked Mr. Finch. "Just a bunch of wild
boys, you think?"

"I guess so. If they'd wanted the sheep, they wouldn't have
quit here."

"Maybe they didn't even know they belonged to anybody.
You know, maybe it was just wild animals to them."

"They know the difference in sheep and deer," he said. He
slouched on the horse's back and mused a minute. "It's hard
to make out. All those Indians are a queer bunch. They've
come from farther east. Some of them could talk English if
they would. I know it."

We began the difficult task of driving the sheep back. They
did not want to run but were flighty and stubborn, shying
this way and that, putting their heads together and standing.
We got off and back on our horses a dozen times, pushing
and worrying the herd a mile's distance; then, seeing that we
would not get home by dark, Mr. Finch sent me ahead to ask
Brother Bossereau to send several colonists out on foot to
drive the creatures to their pen. I brought them, and Mr.
Finch and I left the footmen to take care of the tedious job.

The Indians in the village had left before dark. They had
taken with them the pelts they brought, evidently having
found no need to barter them, and all our chickens except
three or four of the fastest runners. The chickens had been
a source of contention in the colony. Some had belonged to
certain families; some had been common property; yet they
were all mixed together. One or two stubborn women had
insisted that they could identify their own hens' eggs. All the
chickens had laid no more than twenty eggs a day, these
dropped here and there on the prairie or hidden in some
clump of grass. There was no way to divide the eggs, nor
serve them fairly to three hundred hungry people. A tentative solution had been accepted: the eggs would be saved for

hatching and the flock built up. But now the Indians had taken care of the matter. We had no chicken problem left.

As for the items they had traded, the mats woven of reeds or grass had seemed legitimate items of trade at first, but on second thought we realized that they were as worthless as the dried round gourds they had been so willing to trade. The colony had profited by enough squash for one mess, but this was not even enough to pay for our own vegetable plants the Indians had trampled.

It seemed to me ludicrous. We had been taken in.

The colonists generally felt relieved. The visit appeared to prove that our Indian neighbors were friendly, simple, sociable. I heard suggestions of two kinds, not thought to be contradictory, that we might learn from them some knowledge of living in conformity and symmetry with nature, that we might teach them the principles of the science of society.

Sometimes I saw Deveraux talking to a small group of men, always serious, never laughing, though sometimes a listener might laugh at his sarcasm. He would gesture with the edges of his hands as he talked, chopping down with one, then the other, destroying some idea or situation he was opposed to; and his bold, youthful face would hardly change expression, though one knew without listening that he proposed a "radical cure for a pernicious disease" in everything he did not like. If the man worked, I didn't see him.

There continued to be talk, too, among the leaders, but it was quite different, more responsible, though its purpose was a change that would set us on some firmer course toward secure communal living. This, I'm sure, was not apprehended by the average colonist. I knew about it because I spoke more with the leaders and had attended a few assemblies.

One day after lunch Dr. Sockwell asked me to walk with him down to the springhouse which was then in construction and being supervised by him. At the base of a high bank of the creek we had found a clear trickle of water from the limestone, had dug into the rocks and made a catch basin, so that we had a fair spring. Around this and also around a dipping basin in the bed of the stream, he was building a stone house to assure us a source of clean water.

He stopped at a turn in the path, looked all around, and drew from one baggy back pocket a glass flask which would hold about half a pint. He began to twist on the cork and asked, "Would you care for a small sip of brandy?"

"I don't believe so," I said. I had not known of any colonist drinking any kind of liquor before, but there was no rule against it.

He put it to his lips, took a swallow, and said, savoring it, "I sometimes take a little after a meal to settle my stomach." He took another swallow, patted the cork back in with the palm of his hand, and dropped the flask into his pocket again.

"I keep a stock of brandy and wine for medical purposes," he said. "They mix well with certain medicines and fortify them. They relax the nerves. Wine, of course, is a tonic, and for certain chills and related symptoms I prescribe brandy and hot water."

I had supposed that he might intend to talk about the work on the stone house, but he led me aside a little distance from it. He began to work on his pipe, reaming it out with his pocketknife, then asked abruptly, "If the assembly were to vote on removing Bossereau as director, how would you vote?"

He had a kind of sloppy directness about him that could hardly offend a person. I told him, "I wouldn't expect to vote."

"You ought to."

"Why?"

"Well, you're a levelheaded fellow."

I asked, "You think the assembly is short on levelheaded fellows?"

"No. I admire the French. But sometimes they seem to take off in all directions at once. I think you ought to consider yourself a regular assemblyman."

"You think they will actually vote on removing Brother Bossereau?"

"It'll come to that before long. They're afraid of him, but they're hunting for something definite to accuse him of. They'll conspire behind his back till they work up the courage."

"How would you vote?" I asked.

He chuckled. "You know why I'd hate to vote against him? I wouldn't want to hurt his feelings. Isn't that a hell of a reason to keep a man in a spot like that?"

"Then you wouldn't vote against him?"

"I don't know. I'm trying to make up my mind. I do know they're going to press it. Valentin insists there's money missing. The way some of them talk they'd like nothing better than to find proof that Bossereau stole it. Then they'd have a clear case. They're hard up for certainties."

"You think he's capable of it?"

"Valentin's capable of anything."

"No," I said, "Brother Bossereau. Is he . . . ?"

"Stealing? Bossereau?" He laughed through a cloud of smoke and spit into the weeds. "He might have lost it or given it away or frittered it away, but stealing? Never. They don't know their man."

I told myself that Dr. Sockwell was a fair judge of character.

"The troubles are hard to put your finger on," he said. "So many of them we might have expected, no matter who was director. It's confused. Sister Harriet says we've made no progress at all in anything, but it's not clear what she expects."

"Do you think she and Valentin . . . ? Do they plan together against Brother Bossereau's leadership?"

"Sure they do! They plot and plan and conspire and intrigue. Those two are the ringleaders. But they haven't got a damned thing in common. They just haven't got around to finding out about their differences. All they know is that they both don't like the way things are going. Sister Harriet is a woman with energy and willpower, and I don't believe she's going to agree with Valentin in the long run. What she really wants is something to do, but it's got to be something she wants to do. This life is a comedown for her."

He stuck his finger in his pipe, evidently burned it, jerked it out and looked at it, frowning, then said, "How do we actually stand on the crops?"

"I can't add much to what I said. It depends on the rain. They're late, especially the corn."

"Is that serious?"

"It can be."

"Was it Bossereau's fault?"

"Yes, I guess it was. More or less."

After a moment, he mused, "I don't know what I expect you to tell me, but I thought you might help me make up my mind. It's hard to talk to some of the assemblymen."

"I'm sorry," I said. "I'd hate to see them offend Brother Bossereau."

He laughed and began violently beating his pipe against his palm to empty it. "That's what I meant. But I may vote to offend him." I thought he was about to end the interview when he said suddenly, "You know Finch pretty well, don't you?"

"Not too well. What do you mean?"

"I mean what he would do and what he wouldn't."

"I guess I know him as well as anyone does."

"What would be the chances, say, over a few months' time, of converting him to socialism and putting him in as director of the colony?"

It was my turn to laugh.

"It was just an idea," he said.

I had first seen the York brothers as much alike—capable, youthful, good-humored men, stamped with their country rearing but drawn to and appreciative of ideas. The longer I knew them, the clearer it became that Andy was not merely an older version of Jim, and what he thought of his younger brother was not what his younger brother thought of him. I guess the assumption that a debtor recognizes his debt and is thankful is superficial; maybe he rarely recognizes it unless it's a sum of money; maybe it's the lender who is pulled into the relationship deeply, who feels the dependence, who wishes to hide his investment at the same time he guards it. Jim had been a naïve youngster when he left home and went to his brother. He had been able to make the break with the past, learn about the wide world, sow a few modest wild oats, all in the companionship of a tolerant but responsible kind of parent-brother; probably he thought everyone has such friends. For Andy it must have been all different. When he had made the break a few years before from a stubborn and narrow-minded father, it had been into a world larger than he could have guessed, with no familiar object in it. At a certain age a youth can appear to be an adult on the surface while underneath he is a turmoil of uncertainty and oversensitivity. He must have wished many lonely times that he could go home to familiar people and things. And then he must have cursed himself for his weakness. The impersonal city must have seemed at times like a noisy, confused, hostile world, and he must have remembered simpler, quieter scenes, more pleasing in retrospect than they had been in fact. And then, when he had mastered the new life enough to bear it, came an unexpected reprieve. The brother he had thought of as a child was suddenly a man, representing the past and understanding it, but needing the wider world and a guide in it. So he had seized upon his younger brother, supported him, protected him as much as would be permitted, aided him, taught him, having discovered the value of comradeship in a hard way. He had invested himself in a person who had little way of knowing that an investment had been made. It could have nothing but ill effect; a certain kind of ingratitude is almost intolerable.

Part of this I came to know about them. Part of it I guessed. I could have been wrong. They could have been different at birth. All I was certain of was that they were not the same, that Jim was the normal one, free and easy and uninhibited, understandably attracted to a pretty girl, able to take the difficulties of our life in stride; while Andy took every slight trouble as a personal frustration, fumed that he could not make his brother agree with him, felt unadmitted jealousy that the younger no longer needed his friendship.

One afternoon Andy did not show up at the dining hall for supper, and after we had eaten, Jim and I found him down at our shelter area sitting on an upturned bucket, staring into the distance. We sat down, expecting him to offer some explanation, but he didn't offer any.

"You sick?" Jim said.

"Yeah."

After a minute I said, "Why don't you go see Dr. Sockwell?"

"Sick of that slop they mix up in the kitchen. And sick of everything else around here. I'm going to do something about it, too."

Jim asked him, "What's happened?"

"I don't know what you mean, 'What's happened.'"

"Something must have happened. You're gripier than usual even."

"I just finally got a bellyful. That's what's happened. Only now I'm going to do something about it."

I intended to stay out of it if I could because it would certainly end in an argument. Finally Jim asked, "What are you going to do? Hit somebody?"

"You're real smart."

"I just thought I'd stay out of your way if you're going to get wild."

"You're real smart."

"Well, if it's a secret what you're going to do, why did you bring it up? We're not trying to prize any secret out of you. We thought maybe you brought it up because you meant to tell us. Of course, if you're that sore . . ."

"I'm not sore."

"Naw, I can see you're not."

"Jim, you're getting to where you've got some smart answer for everything. I don't know where you get it. You didn't used to be this way. Here lately, when you're not off drooling around that girl, you've always got a smart answer. I don't know. Everything's a joke to you. Nothing's serious."

"By God, I don't sit around and mope, and let every little thing bother me."

They were silent a minute, then Jim gave in and asked, "What have you decided to do?"

"Quit."

"Quit? Leave the colony?"

"That's right. And if you don't go with me, it'll be the biggest mistake you ever made."

"What's happened?"

"Nothing's happened except the same thing that's been going on all the time. I just got a bellyful."

"Something must have happened. You were stronger on this than I was. It was the greatest idea you ever heard of. Why, we were lucky they would let us in; you said that yourself."

"You know what's been going on. I'm quitting, and if you don't go with me, you'll find out it's the biggest mistake you ever made."

I ventured to ask him, "Have you been discussing this with Deveraux?"

"No. I've listened to that son of a bitch and I don't want anything to do with him. Far as I'm concerned he's just another useless baby that I'm carrying on my back."

"Well, something must have happened," Jim said. "When did you decide to quit?"

"I just stood there with an ax in my hand and the sweat pouring off of me today and looked at the colonists that were supposed to be working—the ones that don't know how to do anything and the ones that can't do anything even when they're told and the ones that work all day to get an hour's work done and the ones that talk and wander around and sit under trees; and I saw it would always be this way, and I've had a bellyful. And I'll tell you something else, too: When we're gone a while and they think about it, they'll change their tune. They'll wish they'd stopped to think about it before it was too late. They can't run a place like this without hard work and they'll sure find it out."

"Where do you figure to go?"

"New Orleans. Anywhere but here. Some of the employees are going to quit before long, and we could throw in with them."

"We? I'm not going with you, Andy."

"Why not? If you don't, it'll be the biggest mistake you ever made in all your life."

"Well, I'm not going."

"Why not?"

"I'm just not."

"You better see what you're getting into with that girl."

"Don't start that, Andy."

"She's the reason. You can't see a thing that's going on around you and it's her fault. You're a sucker, boy."

"Don't call me 'boy.'"

"I'll tell you something: You're one of the workers, the

slaves; she belongs to a different class. She's one of the talkers and walkers-around. You're one of the class that does all the work without even a word of thanks."

"I'm not listening to you when you talk against her. You don't even know her. I don't understand why you always criticize Jeannette when you get sore."

"Don't say I didn't warn you. If you don't go with me, you'll be sorry. I've done plenty for you, and now I'm telling you for your own good."

"You were a hundred percent for this colony, Andy. Now you work hard a couple of months and you're against it. I don't understand you. Can't you give it a fair trial for a year or two?"

"No, I can't. I don't mind the work. But they don't even know anybody's working. They don't know the difference in working and not working. Like it gets done by itself. Like it didn't matter. They'll see some day when it's too late. The workers will get out of here and leave them out here with the Indians and coyotes, and then maybe they'll see. You're getting tied up to something you don't understand and the time to get out is now."

"Well, if you're set on going, go. I'm staying."

"She's not worth it."

"Dammit, Andy, I don't have to put up with that and I won't. I told you to leave her out of it. You don't know her. She's none of your business."

"I'm trying to tell you something for your own good."

"Stop telling me stuff for my own good."

After a minute Andy said, "I'm warning you. If you don't go with me..."

"Stop warning me! I heard you the first time."

Jim got to his feet at this, as if to make clear that the conversation was ended. He went to a keg of water that sat in the back of the bed of one of the wagons, drew a dipperful, sipped at it, and threw the rest out on the trampled, dusty ground. He came back to the front of the shelter and squatted down clumsily.

Andy said, "I'm not set on New Orleans especially. If we were to go to New Orleans and you didn't like it around there, we could move on—anywhere you wanted to. Or you may have a better idea than New Orleans right now. I figure we can find work. If one of us gets a job, he can split with the other, like we've always done, fifty-fifty. I'm not trying to run your life."

Jim laughed without much feeling in it and shook his head.

"If you want to stay here a month or six weeks for any reason, I'll stick it out—if you'll quit with me then."

"I don't mean to go with you at all. I mean to marry Jeannette Bossereau and live right here the rest of my life."

"That just shows how mistaken you are. She won't have you, and if she would, Mr. Bossereau would never give his consent."

"Well, I'll find that out for myself and not take your word for it."

"If she says No or Mr. Bossereau says No, will you leave with me then?"

"She won't say No. And I'm not leaving with you at all."

"Well, it's no use to argue with you about it; I can see that. Don't forget that I warned you about it. If you change your mind, you can go with me. I don't mean to beg you anymore or argue with you."

"I'm glad to hear that. I thought you were going to worry me about it from now on."

They supposedly left it at that. But that it stayed unresolved in their minds was proved to me the next day. In the early dawn Jim found the chance to ask me in private, "Do you think he'll quit?" "I don't know," I said, "but I'm inclined to think he'll stay." "I think he will, too," he said. "One good thing about the fuss: it made up my mind for me; I'm going to ask her this afternoon. What do you think? Will she say Yes?" I laughed at him.

Then at noon, as we were washing up, Andy asked me, "Do you think he'll go with me?" I said, "I doubt it." "Don't you think he'd be better off with his own brother?" I told him, "I think you're mistaken about this place."

That night Jim did not eat supper with our shift, nor did he come around our living quarters by our usual bedtime. I could hear a violin and a Spanish guitar in the trees above the upper end of the village, and I knew he, and doubtless Jeannette too, was with the couples who sometimes gathered to sing and make music. When he finally came in, I raised up, half asleep, to see who it was.

Seeing me move, he almost sprang at me, whispering huskily, "She said Yes! Are you awake? She said Yes!"

"Congratulations," I mumbled.

"We'll go east to a county seat on the next supply wagon." From his voice it was clear that he didn't remember ever having argued with anyone about anything at any time.

"What does her father say?"

"She'll ask him some day when he's in a good humor."

From one of the employees lying twenty steps away came, "Why don't you shut up and go to sleep."

From Andy, nearby, came no sign that he had heard. He had made no preparations that day for leaving, nor did he the next. He remained sullen and evidently undecided.

CHAPTER

8

OUR bulletin board stood in the open, easy of access to everyone, but, being exposed to the weather, it had a small roof or wooden awning projecting from the top. Here were posted assignments and announcements and orders from the assembly. On it appeared one day a beautifully written copy of "Goals of Our Common Faith." It was in fine, even script on good-quality paper and tacked securely to the board, obviously intended to be permanent. People commented that it looked "nice." It had been executed by Jeannette Bossereau, and I had no doubt that her father had encouraged her so that we might have the Convenant always before us. At the end of the sixteen points, which we had all agreed upon, had been added number seventeen, which he had suggested on the day of our arrival. It was worded thus: "17. We forgive the past and renounce it. We turn our backs on its symbols and influence as we turn our faces toward tomorrow."

About this time, having reflected upon the differences between the York brothers and having been reminded of goal number seventeen, I tried to write an essay in my journal under the title: "The Nature of Our Many Pasts." I never came to any firm conclusions, nor wrote anything that was satisfactory to me. My feelings about it were contradictory. I agreed with Brother Bossereau and yet at the same time could not escape the conviction that many of us as individuals were molded, or even defined, by our pasts. I think that in my attempts at the essay I was trying to find a way to reconcile the contradiction. Among some of the colonists was an unspoken agreement, almost a moral matter with them, that they would not reveal their pasts, particularly would they not talk with pride about honors or positions they might have had in the old civilization. Of course, we knew something of the distinguished career of Brother Bossereau, but of most of the colonists I knew little that was specific, thus could not seem to get my teeth into what kinds of things they brought with them out of their pasts as part of their natures and what kinds of things they might renounce. I gave up the essay.

I remember thinking that my own past was inconclusive in this respect. I was certainly not in the habit of boasting about it, nor had I concealed it; all that I had done was tell some of the leaders that I had done work in agriculture.

In my early seeking after a career I had attended a small Methodist seminary, which I later came to understand was not a very good school. I went into the ministry with private uncertainty, but the intention to do the best I could for my congregation. I found hypocrisy among them. They confused faith and certitude. About those matters of which I had uncertainty, they expected me to preach with righteous fervor, and those matters about which I was deeply sincere they thought as well left alone. My greatest frustration was that I did not have the ability to lead them. I was assigned to another local church, then another, and finally came to a small one which could hardly support a pastor. I worked part time for a local landowner and tried to serve that church the remainder of the time, but found the people ever more difficult to work with. It was also doubtlessly true that I had lost all my patience and self-confidence.

I left the ministry with a strong sense of failure and disillusionment and entered into a kind of individual monkish seclusion, making my living as a farmhand, doing little other than work and read. During this period, which lasted about eleven years, I realized that I was a skeptic in religion. It was a sad period, but I improved my education by informal application.

After that I worked as a printer, a clerk for a shipping firm, and, for six years, as a schoolteacher in several communities in Tennessee. I never married.

When the opportunity came to join the colony, I welcomed it as a change—for the congenial company, and for the way the ideas reawakened my earlier hopes. I had long before given up any idea of making a mark, had come to see myself as more of an observer than an influence, but had maintained the deep conviction that some day human reason will produce widespread reform so that people may actually live nearer their ideals. To go with these tolerant and intelligent people, to take action with them, to be of aid in their project had seemed to me a rare privilege; and if we could provide a model colony for the world, I was willing enough to renounce and forget my past in order to be a part of it.

It had been planned in a vague way that we would have organized recreation when more pressing practical affairs had been taken care of and when facilities were ready. All of us were interested in ideas. If the recreation could be instructive, so much the better. We would have lectures, attendance to be free and noncompulsory, and most of us looked forward to these as pleasing benefits that would come when we were established in our wilderness home.

The business and confusion of our lives seemed to provide poor background for such recreation, so that it was with surprise that we found Brother Bossereau scheduled to deliver a lecture. The notice on the bulletin board read: "Brother Bossereau, the director, will speak on the topic

'Modern Woman and Socialist Society' on Wednesday evening at Seven in the Main Street. Women colonists may find this lecture of particular interest."

A buzz of talk passed among the females all that day, at their work, in the dining hall, in the kitchen and garden and laundry. Some of them appeared at supper dressed in their best; it was clear that they looked on it as an important occasion.

The early summer evenings were long and pleasant. Before the sun had touched the trees out on the high ground west of the creek, the air became cool, and as much as two hours of daylight remained. Our eyes would grow accustomed to it as the light faded, so that we hardly noticed when night came on. It was usually a time of lazy talk or gossip.

That evening a small table appeared outside Brother Bossereau's quarters at the upper end of the compound. I saw Jeannette bring a pitcher of water and a glass to set upon it. The women gathered, bringing chairs and boxes and stools, even pieces of canvas for seats on the ground; they filled the open areas and spread down into the garden paths. I stood back on the outskirts of the audience, as did other men here and there. Jeannette brought out a white lacy scarf which she spread on top of the table, lifting the pitcher and glass deftly with one hand while she smoothed it with the other.

Mr. Bossereau came out exactly on time. A hush passed over them; then began a polite clatter of applause which grew into a spritely ovation. I could hear his words as he began to speak, but paid less attention to them than to their effect on the women. He was modest and gallant, and they were highly receptive.

I realized that Dr. Sockwell was beside me and said, "He has a way with an audience."

Dr. Sockwell grunted.

I said, "Looks like every woman in the colony is present."

He chuckled a little. "One exception, Langly."

"Who's that?"

"Don't you miss a certain prominent woman?"

"Well, I hadn't actually tried to count them," I said.

"I don't think Harriet Edwards will be here. She's mad as a wet hen."

I looked at him and saw that he was telling the truth, though in a half-serious manner. "What's the matter?" I asked. "What happened?"

"It's happening right now. She's supposed to be the supervisor of recreation and culture, but you can bet your life she wasn't consulted on this speech, or, worse, consulted so that she couldn't do anything but agree. And she thinks of herself as representing the women in the assembly; he's cutting the ground out from under her."

He began fussing with his pipe, and I turned my attention to the speaker. What Mr. Bossereau was saying, the actual words, was not so impressive as the effect. His sincerity came through. His statements were taken as great truths. One moment they were laughing at his reference to a person who might refer to women as the "weaker sex"; the next they were hanging on breathlessly to his explanation of what constitutes strength in a human being.

I said, "He has them in the palm of his hand."

"That's a good description of it," Dr. Sockwell said.

"Why do you say he's cutting the ground out from under Miss Harriet Edwards?"

"Well, nobody can assume she represents the women any more than he does. It's not just her; it's every assembly member who has ideas of voting Bossereau out. This is a demonstration. Bossereau knows what he's doing. This is his answer and a damned good one."

His remarks seemed cynical to me. I stopped talking to him and turned my attention to the speaker. Brother Bossereau spoke softly, but the audience remained so still that he could be heard even where I stood.

Our goals, he said, we had always before us, written down and clear, agreed upon. He hoped that we might bring them to pass within one year. The method of bringing them to pass would be scientific good-fellowship: scientific, because of our reliance on the facts of human nature, because of our willingness to experiment in locating the proper route, because of our use of right reason instead of superstition; good-fellowship, because we must have cheerfulness, courage, patience, tolerance toward one another.

Then Brother Bossereau set up a kind of Devil's Advocate, whom he called "the objector." The objector would point to this or that problem we had and would look forward pessimistically to the difficulties we were certain to meet in the future, would say that we were defeated and the colony was sure to fail. "But," Brother Bossereau said, "the objector does not comprehend the human spirit. If there is a truth I've learned from a lifetime of observing idealistic people, it is this: Expect to be surprised at how they will travail and what they will suffer to achieve what they desire. Hunger will not stop them, nor disease, nor sorrow, nor physical pain. Present them difficulties, present them a tortuous and thorny passage; then you will discover in many of them, deep in their beings, an amazing resistance and determination. The objector has underestimated human beings. They are more than he thinks.

"They are petty, yes. Not all of them are handsome. They sometimes gossip. They make errors. But these superficial faults do not describe them. They have a depth beyond the comprehension of the objector. Allow them to clearly see the corruption and injustice and exploitation in civilization, allow them through God-given reason to develop a vision, allow them to have firm faith in their vision, and what can stop them? Problems? Difficulties? Obstacles? People with faith in their convictions have not been stopped by torture, crucifixion, death! And now it is our faith that we have found the key to universal brotherhood on earth. I don't believe we'll be stopped by things enumerated by the objector.

"I would like to make very clear to you this evening my conviction in this matter. Aware of the crude life of this present time, aware that we may encounter troubles not expected, I tell you from the center of my heart that we will not fail. We will reach our goals. We have the strength that will be required of us."

There was no devised drama in his manner. He did not wave his arms, nor shout, nor purposely charge his voice with emotion. If anything, he seemed to deprecate himself with his manner. In the dim light his face beneath the high forehead had a strange mixture of gentleness and sternness. In all of it there was no ostentation or egotism. It occurred to me that if I had ever heard a man telling the truth about what he believed, it was then and there.

They felt his sincerity and were moved by it. When he had finished, I saw several places among them handkerchiefs pressed furtively to cheeks.

I remembered that not only had Dr. Sockwell attributed ulterior motives to the French leader but that I had implied as much when I said, "He has them in the palm of his hand." I turned and walked away from Dr. Sockwell, not wanting to talk to him anymore that evening.

A peculiar aura of expectation pervaded our life, or I might say, flitted about our life, providing an uncertain and changing background for everything we did. There were the various planned goals which we would bring to realization in one way or another, sooner or later, as deliberately and wisely as we could. Beyond these, we had a kind of vague expectation that we would be affected by forces we had not planned. This latter, too subtle to be understood by any two of us in exactly the same way—I would say we halfway expected the unexpected—arose out of the vast, unpopulated land and our ignorance of it.

The night following Brother Bossereau's speech the wild cattle came. I first heard the sound when most of the colonists had gone to bed and the camp had become quiet, a bellow from far out to the southwest. It sounded more than a mile away, faint but with challenge in it.

"That sounds like a bull," I said.

"He's on the warpath, too," Jim said. Andy, in one of his sullen periods, said nothing.

The distant bellow came out of the darkness a half dozen times, then ceased. A quarter of an hour later it started again, perhaps from a different spot, as if the animal had walked to another rise. It was persistent and urgent. I heard with a start what was probably inevitable: from where our milk cows were penned two hundred yards away, our fat, lazy bull answered him.

Immediately the sound from the distance changed. It became not the still challenge but the restricted and intermittent noise forced out of the great chest of a lumbering beast. It came toward us. Sometimes it dwindled to a stubborn complaining, as if the animal threaded his way among the trees; then it would rise, as if the passion that produced it surged suddenly up, and it would become so piercing and shrill that it was beyond the range of hearing; and one could sense the breath of the animal rushing fiercely and futilely out, trying to express a rage that was too strong for expression.

He came without pause, and when he must have been just beyond the creek, I began to hear other cattle, the foolish bawling of our bull in the pen and one or two milk cows, but also other strange ones out in the darkness. I got up and dressed, feeling apprehension but not knowing what could be done.

There was no moon. In the jumble of voices that started

up along the compound, I heard Mr. Finch's giving orders. In a few minutes, when I found Brother Bossereau, I learned that Mr. Finch and three of the employees had taken their rifles and gone to catch horses to do what they could. I knew that there were no more than four horses available nearby, so did not try to follow them.

From the time he was answered, the wild bull did not seem to pause. He crossed the creek and his roar became loud, ugly, threatening. I clearly heard the cracking of posts and clattering of rails in our cow pen, as if they were swept over by a heavy weight, then the moan and clack and thud of bulls fighting. At the same time came a rush of running animals along the creek and beyond. Small limbs popped in front of them and their hooves rattled against the ground like hail. It became impossible to guess what was happening out there in the darkness because of the noise of the people in the compound; men yelled to one another and women screamed for their children. Those inside stuck their heads out and shouted for information or for others to be quiet.

The running cattle passed between us and the creek, or, as we learned later from the tracks, one bunch did. Just north of our village another bunch splashed across the creek and joined them and they turned east out across our farmlands. They laid flat most of a quarter mile of fence, angling up it, and trampled some thirty acres of corn and an unfenced millet patch. I would not have been surprised from the sound they made to find that there had been thousands of them, but we guessed later that there had been a few hundred.

After it was quiet, Brother Bossereau and I agreed that nothing could be done in the darkness. I got a few hours of fitful sleep. At dawn I took Jim and Andy York and two other men out to find the horse band and catch mounts. We returned to get our saddles and eat a quick breakfast. As I had known it would be, the cow pen was destroyed. The milk cows were gone. Fortunately, their calves, which ran loose at night, had not been caught up in the stampede. In the wreckage of the milk pen sprawled the carcass of our bull, the hair of his head matted with blood, one horn shelled off, gored in a dozen places.

As my crew of men were mounting, Mr. Finch and his three men came across the prairie driving nine milk cows. They were worn out.

I and the four men with me followed the clear path made by the running cattle toward the north. We rode three or four hours and I had begun to wonder whether the search was hopeless; then we were met by six of our cows, coming single file, walking deliberately, their udders distended with milk, heading home to their calves. Andy was beginning to argue with Jim, so I sent him along with the other two men to follow the cows home, while the younger brother and I went ahead to look for the two milk cows which were still missing.

We rode till about noon, and the clear hoof-cut trail we were following began to split up. We kept on after what seemed the larger bunch, but their trail split until we were following no more than a dozen animals. We began to make a large circle to try to pick up a better trail and as we came out of a clump of trees saw about two hundred yards from us one of the wild cows.

She threw her head up stiffly and watched us. She was long in the body, swaybacked, with patchy, shedding hair that gave her a rough appearance. Her color was a dirty dun which shaded into a dark stripe along her backbone and across her shoulders. Altogether she had a crude and mean, perhaps dangerous, look. Her horns on the high-held head were keen and long. She was perfectly still as she watched us; then she bounded away in a hard run with her tail sticking out stiff behind. I had never seen so large an animal run so fast.

After we had searched a little farther, we guessed that the

two missing milk cows did not have calves back at the village and might as well be given up for lost. We rode back.

Curiously, most of the colonists never understood the nature of the wild herd that had come past us in the night, that the beasts were actually cattle descended from domestic animals lost centuries before by the Spanish, but wild in a real sense, adapted to the wilderness and no friend to man. At first many of the colonists referred to them as "buffalo." Then some of the more sophisticated explained that "buffalo" was a misnomer, that they were actually "American bison." Then others, more liberal about nomenclature, believed that though they were "American bison," the name "buffalo" had gained authority through use, so that most of them refered to it as "the night the buffalo came." I tried to explain to Brother Adams at the dinner table one day that they were actually wild cattle, and he understood me to mean that such a term would be descriptive and would avoid the difference of opinion over the other terms. I did not think it worth my trouble to set him straight.

In the week after the Indians had made their trading visit to us, we had seen some of the younger ones prowling around the village, boys fourteen to sixteen years old. Sometimes they watched us from a distance, again they might be seen playing alone, shooting at a mark with bows and arrows.

One afternoon three of the boys came up to the edge of the village and began chasing the three or four chickens we had left and which now lived half-wild in the high grass. The boys chased them with great glee and shot their arrows after them. No one paid it much attention until one of the employees came in with a wagon and the playing Indian boys caused his ox team to shy. The employee seized one of the boys, shook him, took his bow, and broke it in halves. The three boys quickly departed.

Evidently this matter was argued at length in the assembly

the following day. The outcome was that Brother Bossereau would go on a kind of peace mission to the Indian camp, take them a few presents, let them know that we remained friendly, and also try to make them understand that the Indian boys should not play around the colony village. I did not think much of the mission; although it was probably not dangerous, I did not think he would make them understand anything.

Dr. Sockwell thought it was useless, but he had not been able to push his view far in the assembly. He seemed surprised that so many of them were in favor of it, not only those who were friendly toward the Indians, but also those who usually thought they should be ignored or avoided. He asked me, "Why does Valentin want him to go? That man's a monomaniac. All he can think of is money. Now why is he suddenly interested in the Indians?" I could not suggest any answer.

I was relieved that Brother Bossereau did not ask me to go. They put a single yoke of oxen to one of the light wagons and set out after breakfast one morning, one employee and two men of the colony in addition to the French leader. The chief present they carried was a basket of sweet cookies baked for the purpose the night before. I walked with the wagon to the creek crossing to see them ford it safely. As they disappeared up the valley of the north fork, or Loco Creek, I felt admiration for the French leader, who was doing what he thought needed doing even though it was an awkward and uncertain task.

That day I had three watering crews at work, hauling water in barrels, primarily for the grape cuttings, some of which had taken root but none of which were growing as they should. Also, we would haul some for the garden. The long hauling made the water precious. We poured it by bucket at the base of each plant, scraping up little dams with hoes to keep the water from spreading and wasting.

I walked first out to the field where the grape settings were, then came back to the garden in the compound and took down some fence rails to allow the haulers to come in conveniently. They were using a hundred-gallon cask and several thirty-gallon barrels on the sledges we had constructed.

As I was about to help the two men with the unloading, my attention was drawn by a sharp, harsh voice, as in an argument, at the upper end of the compound. I looked in that direction and saw nothing except Jeannette Bossereau standing in the door of her father's quarters, a man in front of her with his back to me. I had thought I heard the word No spoken emphatically, but was persuaded for a moment that my ears had deceived me. The set of the man's hunched shoulders was familiar. I probably would have thought no more about it except that Jeannette had always given the impression of a pleasant girl, and it was hard to imagine her arguing with anyone. Then the man's voice rose and, without hearing the words, from an element of abrasion or sarcasm in the tone, I recognized him. It was Dr. Valentin. I was even more surprised. She was obedient and respectful toward the colony leaders. Yet the stance of each of them, their stiff ways of holding their bodies, and the unclear notes of voice I heard left no doubt that they violently disagreed over some matter between them. Had the place been more private and had I known him less, I would have thought he made an indecent proposition to her.

He walked away and I began to help with the work at hand. Several women, who usually did the garden work, were helping distribute the water. When we had used the first load, I stayed with them as they went ahead working with their hoes, planning to try to estimate how many loads would be required in all. I did not see her approach, but noted that Jeannette Bossereau had joined the women.

She worked silently with her eyes downcast. I would have noticed nothing wrong with her had I not studied her closely.

She was greatly disturbed. Sometimes she drew a deep breath and at the end of it her throat and chest quivered like that of a child who has been crying. I had the impression that she wanted no attention but that she needed the company of the women she was working with.

She dropped her hoe suddenly and walked quickly up one of the paths. My eyes had not been on her at the moment. She had seen something I had not.

She screamed, "Wait!"—her voice a combination of pleading and anger.

Coming to Brother Bossereau's quarters were six people, assembly members, including Dr. Valentin and Miss Harriet Edwards. They paid no heed to the girl hurrying toward them. The doctor had opened the door and they were entering by the time she came up. She appeared to try to squeeze among them, but in a moment they had gone in and closed the door, shutting her out.

She pushed on the door, beat on it with palms and fists, cried to them.

The working women around me all stood and watched. One said, "What on earth is the matter with that girl?" Another said, "What are they doing?" Still another said, "She's a spoiled young lady anyway, if you ask me."

I felt myself in an awkward position. My inclination was to go to a person who was obviously in distress, but it seemed equally clear that her distress was caused by Dr. Valentin and other assembly members. I hardly believed what I had seen, that they had entered Brother Bossereau's quarters against her strong protest. I thought surely there must be some reason for their action better than any I could think of.

I waited, uncertain, for perhaps two minutes, then walked up toward her. She was breathing deeply and trembling.

She heard my footsteps and turned. "They are searching our things!"

I said, "What is it? What's the matter?"

"They caused my father to go away on purpose! They have no right! What is he? A thief?" Her face was flushed. Her outrage made her seem adult, but at the same time her directness and single-mindedness made her seem juvenile.

"But what's the reason? What did they say?"

"They have no reason but to insult my father! It's not right! They caused him to go to the Indians on purpose! They knew he would ... show them anything ... but they wanted to insult him!"

I noticed a spot of blood on the plank door, then saw that the backs of both her hands were bleeding. She wrung them together, oblivious to the blood, smearing it. "I wouldn't search their things," she said. "A person has a right to privacy! They are malicious! Why did they come now with my father gone?"

Dr. Sockwell came striding up at the same time that the door began to open. Some piece of furniture had evidently been wedged against the door; it was pulled away, so that the door would open wide. I heard someone say, "Put the money back where it was." They began to come out.

Dr. Sockwell had heard part of what Jeannette had said. He demanded, "What's the meaning of this?"

Dr. Valentin said in a dignified manner, "The meaning is simply this: we have demanded an accounting and we have taken this means of discovering what we have a right to know!"

"You can't do a thing like this, Valentin!"

"My good doctor, we have done it."

"Well, you've gone too far! This kind of thing is not at all necessary. To go into a man's quarters ... break in! ... force your way in!"

The six of them remained dignified and not apologetic. They squinted a bit from having just come out into the sunlight. It occurred to me that they had expected to find some piece of evidence, which they had not found, and thus they were in a more defensive predicament than they had hoped for. Dr. Valentin said, "I might remind you that we have no locks in this colony. No private property. No secrets. This is a legitimate act by members of the assembly."

"No secrets!" Dr. Sockwell said. "Is that why you had this door barricaded? Is that why you favored having the director go away today? If there are no secrets, you will tell us what you were looking for and what you've found. What do you have in your hand?"

I think Dr. Valentin had been unaware that he had brought out a thick sheaf of papers bound with black lacing at the edge. He glanced at it with a start, but recovered himself quickly and said, "A journal with nothing in it but high-flown words! Meaningless fancy words!"

Jeannette stepped forward unexpectedly and snatched it from him. She clutched the papers to herself with hands on which the smeared blood was now nearly dry. Dr. Valentin gave her a faint smile, as if he were a man of utmost patience.

Dr. Sockwell asked again, "What did you find? We have no secrets, as you say."

"Nothing. Precisely nothing, and that's the point."

"Is the money there as reported by the director?"

"That's correct. It is there. But we are concerned with the money which is not there. The records of this colony are nonexistent. None have been kept. The man we have trusted as leader has spent a fortune of our money without a figure down on paper. If I had a clerk who did such a thing, I'd have him whipped."

"If I had my way," Dr. Sockwell said, "you would be whipped. All six of you. You ought to be ashamed of yourselves."

They were frowning, starting to move away, perhaps finding it hard to maintain their aspects of innocence and dignity; then Dr. Sockwell asked, "Have you taken anything else from Brother Bossereau's room?"

Dr. Valentin ignored the question as beneath him, but Miss Harriet Edwards said, "No, we took nothing." I thought that she must be aware of how the incident looked to us who had not been a part of it. Valentin undoubtedly was aware, too, but he seemed able to bluff his way past any feeling of guilt. I thought that she must feel shame and also chagrin that she had been led to take part in an act of such a questionable nature. Certainly the six of them were not now so much of one mind as they had been earlier. They went to the assembly hall.

Jeannette went in the door. I asked her whether she needed any help. She looked at me with a searching glance, her face a combination of distress and embarrassment, then said, "No, sir."

Dr. Sockwell said, "Those damned fools. I'm going to get the assembly to vote a reprimand against Valentin on this. This kind of thing will gut the colony."

I went back to the work in the garden. Jeannette Bossereau did not rejoin the women.

The incident was beyond my comprehension. My sympathy had been with Jeannette, and I would have said the things that Dr. Sockwell said if I had been a regular member of the assembly—or perhaps it was that I did not have the distinguished reputation of some of the assemblymen. I felt dissatisfied with myself that I had stood back, uncertain, wondering what to do; I simply had not felt adequate to opposing them, had not been willing to trust my impulse until it was too late. The puzzle was that they were intelligent people of good will and sensibility. Miss Harriet Edwards was the epitome of good taste and manners; how could she have been part of such a vulgar and unnecessary act? Or the others either?

The peace mission to the Indians turned out as well as we might have hoped. The redskins had not shown any anger and had accepted the modest presents. They had nodded and grinned and jabbered and had given no particular sign of understanding the English that was spoken to them.

Evidently the assembly had a long and serious discussion over the issue of a reprimand of Dr. Valentin. Ironically, Brother Bossereau himself, the injured party, played the peacemaker, and his efforts prevented any further disruptive action. The matter was declared officially closed. The French leader did not show that he bore any grudge.

CHAPTER

9

WE got on with the building and fencing, making slow
progress, and with the hundred tasks necessary to
living. As early summer came on, the sun gained a potency
which was easy to underestimate, and those who remained
outside without their heads and arms covered got a painful
sunburn. One insect of the region, the redbug or chigger,
became about this time a serious nuisance. They were tiny
creatures, hardly visible, that got on our ankles from the
grass. They would make an itching welt, then move up the
legs and all over the body to find more places to bite, favoring
spots where clothing fit tightly against the skin. When one
of the bites had been scratched until it was raw, perspiration
irritated it further. Bathing helped. We bathed in the water
holes along the creek, though the nearest one deep enough
and large enough to decently accommodate a dozen people
was a mile downstream. We also hauled water for bathing and
used it later to water the garden. Altogether the tiny bugs
caused us much petty misery and loss of time.

The assembly scheduled a trip by two wagons to Jones'
Mill and put a notice on the bulletin board so that anyone
could prepare letters to be carried to post. After supper on
the evening before the wagons would leave, half the colonists

were writing letters, but Jim York was shaving and putting on a clean shirt and pretending that he was not nervous. It seemed that he and Jeannette intended to make the trip and return as man and wife. They had not yet spoken to Brother Bossereau, but she had been hinting to her father that she was going to marry and she was now arranging an interview for her suitor.

Andy lounged on the ground in front of our weathered canvas shelter and I kept thinking that he was about to make some sarcastic remark as his younger brother tried to improve his appearance in front of a small mirror that hung on a post, but he said nothing.

We did not notice the girl come up. She said, "Jim?"

He jerked his eyes out of the mirror and turned to her, laughing, perhaps to cover embarrassment at being caught combing his hair. "Do you have him softened up for me?"

"No, I . . ."

"Oh, you promised!" he said in mock accusation. Then, more seriously: "We've got to tell him tonight. I mean, ask him."

"Jim . . ."

"What's the matter?"

She glanced at Andy and me and made a hasty decision that we were familiar enough that she did not mind our knowing what she had to say, or perhaps she even expected support from us for what she had to say. "We'll have to postpone it. I mean that we can't go tomorrow. We'll have to wait."

"So he said No."

"No."

"What did he say? Isn't it because of him?"

"Yes, but he said he wouldn't refuse. He doesn't want me to give him a thought, what he desires, or his problems. It's not that he said No."

"What *did* he say, Jeanie?"

"I want to explain it to you," she said. "He doesn't want us to be hasty. That's part of it."

"But he's known about us before now."

"Yes, but ... if he thinks it's hasty ... I don't want to turn my back to him and leave him now. He has such a charge. Everything that happens here ... he's so involved in it. I think every pain that anyone here feels, he feels it too. If a bad thing happened to the colony it would kill him."

"Well, what does that mean? How long are we supposed to wait?"

"I don't know." She looked at him anxiously and asked, "Do you understand what I mean?" When he did not answer immediately, she looked at me as if I might help.

Andy had not risen from the ground. He lay on his side, propped on one elbow. He said, "What's the matter? Does Brother Bossereau think you're too good to marry Jim?" It was not so much the tone as the abruptness of it that made him sound like Deveraux.

She was shocked, as he had meant her to be.

Jim said, "Never mind that. Do you want to walk around?"

But she ignored the insulting nature of Andy's speech. Evidently she wanted very much for her explanation to be accepted. "It would never enter his mind," she said. "Any sort of inequality. Really! Equality is a religion to him. But now he has serious problems. Some of the leaders are conspiring against him behind his back. He would give anything, labor day and night, even give his life, to help the people be happy here. He has placed all his hopes in it."

She seemed extremely anxious that we should understand. Her brown eyes searched our faces as she spoke; also, I think the very passion of her own words inspired her to go on.

"You cannot imagine how he's suffered. They have been against him always, everything he tries to do. They insisted on misinterpreting his action and trying to prove him a bad man. And he is not. If it's possible, he's loved people too much and tried too much to assist them, especially poor people. But his enemies, they insist on misinterpreting him, because he won't retreat. I just think they believe they can't permit such a man to exist.

"You should have seen him at the barricades. You can't really know him, you can't possibly, unless you saw him at the barricades. He mounted up in the very face of the police. Already he was wounded from a piece of paving stone and he had a bloody bandage on his head. I could recognize him by the bandage. It was dark and there was only the light from a building that was burning. He rose up in their very face. They were coming on horseback. And he cried out, 'Liberty! Equality! Brotherhood!' He didn't offer any resistance. Just that shout before the box inclined and he fell back. I was crying because I believed he would be killed. They were bloodthirsty, certain ones of the Paris police, worse than the army. We heard later that they had actual orders to kill some students if they got a proper excuse, to make an example.

"And my father, you know what he said about it? If they would kill a man for shouting what he did, if that cry is forgotten or forbidden, then he felt it was necessary for him to stand up and shout it and pay the price, to permit the world to know the circumstances.

"Some of these people here, they don't really know him. They think he's just an old man. They don't realize that he would surrender his life for what he believes."

She had made her passionate speech mostly to Andy, I think. But Andy made no answer. Jim said to her, "Let's walk around." It was about sundown. They walked away together, not talking.

Finally, I said to Andy, "That girl's got spunk."

"I've got nothing against her," he said. He sat up with his arms resting on his knees. "Only if she really had spunk like you say, she would get married when she gets ready and she would come along with me and Jim to New Orleans or someplace where a man can get paid for what he does and have his work appreciated."

I said, "I don't want to argue, but did it ever occur to you that this place might improve? A baby has got to crawl before it can learn to walk."

"You mean Dominique Henri, for instance? Maybe he will stop sniveling around and go to work?"

"Well, maybe he is a good wine maker."

"Half the damned grapevines are dead right now." After a moment, he said, "Jim will leave this place with me sooner or later."

Up until that time, I had been undecided about whether I personally should try to change Andy York's position in the colony. But it occurred to me now that I could understand his attitude to some extent and also that I could talk freely with Brother Bossereau, for he had several times shown himself willing to talk seriously with me in private. I concluded that I would be guilty of a sin of omission if I did not try to make the French leader understand and take some action.

I neither told my intentions to Andy, nor tried to conceal them. I walked straight up the compound to Brother Bossereau's quarters and knocked. He opened the door and I saw that he was alone. When I told him that I had an important matter to talk about, he invited me in and showed me a cane-bottom chair.

The room was lighted by two candles on a table where he had been reading, but it seemed darker generally than the dusk outside. The space was limited, some ten by ten feet. Under the single window stood a narrow bed and of other furnishings there were only a chest, some boxes which contained books, two straight-backed chairs, and the table. Some clothes hung on pegs on the wall. An open doorway at the rear led to a similar room, which I took to be the quarters of his daughter.

"I don't have a complaint, but a suggestion," I said.

He smiled in understanding of my meaning and said, "You are welcome even to complain, Brother Langly."

I told him that I knew he already understood the problem and had agreed that some rewards for good work should be set up when the colony was better established, but that I believed Andrew York should be given some kind of encouragement now; that he was disappointed at our progress and this bore heavily on his mind, but that he was an excellent worker and very competent.

Brother Bossereau took off his glasses and squeezed his eyebrows together with one hand. I thought he had probably strained his eyes reading by the poor candles. He said, "They are excellent young men, the York brothers. We need Americans who will faithfully follow our philosophy and help us develop it, for this is America and this is a cosmopolitan project. Of course we have a problem in singling out one worker to praise; it tends to violate our principle of equality. And then we are searching and waiting to find the abilities of every person, for we have faith that every person has value, and it may be that social organization in the past has not allowed it to reveal itself.

"But then certainly we must be practical. That's unnatural for some of us. But as leaders we have it placed on us. Sometimes we have to choose the expedient. Are these young men really so much superior to the average worker?"

"Yes, sir, they are. But I'm thinking of Brother Andrew York. I think he might leave the colony unless he has reason to stay."

"I'm ashamed to admit that I cannot distinguish them apart. Are they twins?"

"No, sir. Andrew is quite a bit older."

"If they are determined to leave, then there's no help for it. I've come to accept that, Brother Langly. Some will leave us. In these first few months we have all the labor of building and not the exact socialism that we will have later. Naturally it's harder to build a house than it is to live in it. Some will lose faith and go, but I believe that those with the greater spiritual strength will remain. Don't you agree?"

"Well, yes, sir, it might be. But in the case of Brother Andrew York perhaps we should choose the expedient, as you say. He's a valuable man to the colony."

"Pardon me, Brother Langly. I am uncertain. Is this the one who has been paying attention to my daughter?"

"No, sir, that's the younger one."

"How is it that one of them is a good socialist and delighted with our colony and desires to marry my daughter and the other one is disappointed in us?"

I told him that I had no explanation. He was silent a minute. No light came through the window now, and the still small candle flames hardly lighted the details of the room or even his drab clothing, so that his face with its high forehead seemed suspended alone, shining a little from the moisture of perspiration. The face was simple and sincere and intense.

He said, "I would never refuse permission when she has honestly decided to marry. If it's her decision. It must be her true and sincere wish and desire. Then I would never say No. I cannot say No to the girl. Her choice is like a command to me. I would be an unnatural father to restrain her after she had clearly made her decision.

"But I'm anxious about it—that I haven't explained it to her well enough. The girl does not know what a big step she contemplates—to join her life to another for all time. How little a young person knows! What an infant she is!

"And at this time when we are not yet on the clear route ... when there is confusion. ... She may judge wrongly. She has been bound to me through all her young life, more so than with many fathers and daughters, and the time will come when she will move away from me ... from the refuge of a father ... but it ought not to be at this time. Our lives are torn up, chaotic. I could never forgive myself if she acted impetuously because I was too willing to give her liberty.

"What does she really know of the young man? How could she believe that he will ever love her as I do? She is pure and simplehearted. How can I explain it to her?

"I desire her with me. I would be less than honest if I didn't admit it to myself—now, when the charge of the colony is crucial. This is delicate to explain. The assembly members are men of good will. They intend to do right. I respect them. But they have all lived different lives in a senseless social structure and they are molded this way and that. I contend with them, we all contend together, as friends and colleagues, but as people who observe from different points.

"But Jeannette . . . she is like a little mother to me. If I cannot find my spectacles, she gets them for me. She mends my clothes. If I forget lunch, she brings it to me. She does it out of love. It is not these acts that I desire, but what they represent. She does not contend at all, but only offers loyalty. If I were to strive with the devil, she would be my partisan, and if I were to strive with an angel, she would be my partisan if it damned her to eternal punishment.

"I desire her with me. Especially now—until the colony is established. But I don't ask her to consider my comfort or my requirement—not because I am magnanimous, but because her future is the single most precious thing in my private life. She must not act impetuously. All that I ask is that she consult her own heart. I cherish her. I would die before I would cause her pain.

"Youth is hasty, Brother Langly. She is such an infant. Her head is turned by the first young man who pays attention to her. But I am forcing my personal problems on you. I hope you'll excuse me."

I stated again to him that the York brothers were quite different, that Andrew was older and a dependable man, that he doubtless was against hasty marriages himself. "I didn't mean to emphasize that he might leave us," I said. "Actually he is a very hard worker and competent. He would be a good example to the other workers."

"What do you believe we should do? Pass a resolution in the assembly?"

"Would it be possible to give him a position of more responsibility? Make him assistant supervisor of agriculture in charge of livestock?"

"It would reduce your own authority."

"He knows as much about it as I do."

He was interested in the idea. "We have a problem in agriculture. Mr. Finch is not committed to our goals. We require more supervision in the hands of men who have socialist ideals. Do you recommend him for the specific position you mentioned?"

"Yes, sir, I do."

He agreed that it would be done.

When I went out, the moon had risen. In the garden I passed a young man and young woman walking slowly, holding hands, speaking to one another in low voices. I did not stare at them and did not find out whether it was Jim and Jeannette or another couple.

I said nothing to Andy. The following afternoon we found this simple notice on the bulletin board: "Brother Andrew York is appointed supervisor of agriculture in charge of livestock. Workers and work-crew leaders assigned to livestock will report to him and accept his instructions. Jean Charles Bossereau, for the Assembly."

He was congratulated by a number of people and accepted their words good-naturedly. To me he said, "The chickens are gone. The bull's gone. When the cows go dry, we won't be able to breed them again. A little work stock. A few saddle horses. Two average farm boys and a couple of good dogs could take care of that bunch of sheep. What the hell do they need with a supervisor?"

"Maybe the chickens and the bull wouldn't be gone if we'd had a good man in charge of them. At least you can keep Dominique Henri away from the stock now."

"This job won't keep me here when I get ready to leave," he said. But he entered into the work and I had hopes that he would take enough interest in it that he would forget the things that had disturbed him.

The assembly had argued the matter of our financial condition during several sessions, and it had become clear to all of them that we could continue to pay the employees for only a limited time. When the wagons came back from Jones' Mill and there were no letters containing donations for the colony, the leaders made up their minds that the employees must be immediately discharged and sent away, or else, if they chose, become colonists and work for nothing except our future hopes.

The last day of the month was their payday, and on the afternoon before, Brother Bossereau asked me to assemble the employees an hour before supper. They pestered me to know the purpose of the meeting, but I let them wonder until the French leader came down to where we waited among the parked wagons. He carried a handful of papers.

"Friends," he said, "I have no proper speech prepared for you. Which I regret, for the time has come for you to make a serious decision that may affect the entire course of your life. I must apologize for being poorly prepared. Brother Langly, will you please pass these out for me?"

I took the papers. It was our printed circular, "Goals of Our Common Faith." I gave one to each of the nine men. They lounged about, leaning against the wagons, squatting on the ground. Mr. Finch sat on a wagon tongue, whittling on a small stick. They paid respectful but informal attention.

"We designate this our covenant," Brother Bossereau said. "I hope you will study it this evening. We are inviting you to become colony members on an equal basis with all other members. This list of our goals is the foundation of our association together into what might be described as one large family. You may have noticed that this same list of sixteen points is permanently fixed on our bulletin board. To that list is added number seventeen, which is more a philosophical point than a tangible goal. I trust that you will understand that our efforts thus far have been toward creating a living place in the wilderness and that our life will be more pleasant when we have become organized and established."

They stared at him. One of them asked, "We getting paid tomorrow, like we s'posed to be?"

"Certainly. Those of you who prefer to be paid will be paid. The question is whether you will decide to become members of the colony on a basis of equality with all the others—after you have studied the covenant carefully, of course."

One of them said, "I thought we hired on for a year."

"I'm not here to procrastinate," Brother Bossereau said. "Frankly, we have a financial problem. If you will consider the point of view of a working colonist . . . he works for no pay, except the portion of a good life which he may expect in the future. Yet he sees you working and receiving pay each month, when that money might be spent for colony equipment or supplies. It makes an impossible situation. The consensus has developed that we have the right to expect everyone who lives in the colony to have faith in the goals and work toward them. We see only two possibilities open to you: that you become members or that you leave. I regret to say it so abruptly, but I wish to make it clear."

One of them said, "Tomorrow's payday. You got the money to pay us?"

"Certainly. Those of you who don't desire to join us may take your pay and leave. Those of you who stay will receive your food and lodging, care in sickness or old age, our common cultural advantages, educational advantages, your common share of all the property we develop. As members you will come to learn all the further advantages that may be expected.

"Notice our goal number seven. Money will be abolished. I know that this appears strange to you, but I assure you that it's possible and highly desirable. Many wise writers and thinkers have recognized that the institution of money is wasteful and artificial and provides too convenient a means of exploitation of the poor. I wish that we had time to deliver a series of lectures on the fundamentals of socialism as a humane science. Let me just say this to you as members of the working class: you are the beneficiaries. You are the people who are to gain. As for the intellectuals who are involved, may they not achieve a high place socially and economically in the decaying civilization which exists, if they are so inclined? No, the goals point toward the worker, the laborer, the poor in spirit, the meek, the downtrodden. You have a world to gain. You have nothing to lose.

"I'm confident that you will come to understand it better after you become members and come to associate with the other colonists. We will have appropriate lectures from time to time. Are there any questions?"

Mr. Finch had not spoken. He sat calmly, pushing fine shavings off his small willow stick with his keen-bladed pocket-knife. He had folded the circular twice and stuck it in his shirt pocket.

Brother Bossereau asked, "Is it clear, Mr. Finch, that is in regard to the option? Did you desire to ask any questions or perhaps make any remarks?"

"Nope. It's clear. Join up or get out."

One of them said, "I'm going to want my money tomorrow."

Brother Bossereau acted as if he had not heard. "I trust that each of you will search his conscience carefully and study our goals. If there are any questions, you may ask Brother Langly, or please don't hesitate to approach me. We are here to serve you."

He left and I hope that he was out of earshot before they began to laugh.

One of them said, "What in the hell was that Frenchman talking about?"

"He was talking about Willie, there, the weak and poor in spirit! Hey, Willie, you bastard, he was talking to you."

"He wasn't talking to me. Except about that money. You reckon when they abolish money, they would give me what they got on hand?"

"If I don't miss my guess," one of them said, "they ain't got no great amount of money on hand."

I did not laugh with them, and they did not ask me any questions. They began to talk about where they were going. None seemed to consider joining the colony. They read the printed circulars and shook their heads and laughed. I could understand how it seemed to them, but I thought, too, with a little bitterness, how it would have been if some great man out of the past had spoken to them—a Plato, a Bacon, a Voltaire, a Rousseau, a Jefferson—how if such a man had been obliged to explain his philosophy to them in a few words, they would have laughed.

I ate with the last group, and as I started to leave the dining hall, Dr. Sockwell called to me. He was sitting with Brother Bossereau and Dr. Valentin at a table in the corner. When I had sat down with them, Brother Bossereau asked, "How many employees will stay?"

My first inclination was to avoid the responsibility of making a guess, but they seemed concerned with what I would say, as if they needed to know my best assessment. I said, "I'm afraid that none will stay."

Dr. Sockwell asked, "How about Finch?"

"I don't believe he will stay."

"He must stay," Dr. Valentin said. "We've got to keep him. I knew he wouldn't stay when it was presented to him in this way. A man of his caliber will not be cowed by an ultimatum."

Brother Bossereau said, "I believe you were in agreement to the idea that we must stop paying employees."

"In agreement? Who could agree otherwise, Jean Charles? They won't accept grass or leaves for money!"

"But why is Mr. Finch the exception? Just what is it that you believe he will do for us?"

I was pleased to see the three of them consulting together. There was a tension between them, only barely visible in their outward manners, from the surreptitious search of several days before. Brother Bossereau had been the victim. Dr. Sockwell had been passionately opposed. Dr. Valentin had been the chief instigator. The assembly meeting which had settled the matter officially could hardly have failed to make it more vivid to the principals, by exposing the details and implications. Had they been less civilized men, any of the three might have felt honor bound to challenge one of the others to a duel. I think each of them had this determination: that in spite of his feelings, he would be open to cooperation, but would not lean over backward, nor fail to support his own convictions.

"We hired him in the first place because we don't understand this part of the country," Dr. Valentin said. "If I could say what he might do for us, we wouldn't need him."

Brother Bossereau said, "I hesitate to agree to the proposition that, although he has no social conscience and no ideals, he might have some unknown knowledge that would be crucial to us."

"One thing for certain," Dr. Sockwell said, "we can discharge him at any time, but when he's gone, he's gone for good."

Dr. Valentin said, "By letting the others go, we can keep

Finch a few more months. I believe we should pay him and keep him."

Dr. Sockwell had managed to get his pipe lit and had surrounded himself with a fog of smoke. He said to me, "I asked you once before and you laughed. If Finch stays, what are the chances that he will join us?"

"They don't seem good to me," I said.

"Such a man is impressed by organization and hard work," Dr. Valentin said. "If we could show him real progress and not preach to him and offer him a seat in the assembly, I just believe he might come around in a few months."

Brother Bossereau said quickly, "I would want to be quite sure that he accepts every one of our goals before he is offered a seat in the assembly."

They discussed it a few minutes further, then the French leader agreed that Mr. Finch should be paid and kept. I thought he agreed not because he felt the necessity of it but to follow his own doctrine of tolerance. They thought Mr. Finch should be approached immediately lest he began packing or making plans, so I was sent to ask him to report to them.

Later that night I found the occasion to ask him, "Are you staying?"

He chuckled briefly. "I guess so. I sort of hate to be the only man around drawing wages, but I sure wouldn't stay around and not draw any."

Aware that I would supposedly have been the chief expert on agriculture had he left, I said with sincerity, "I'm glad you're staying."

"Well, I can't figure out what they expect of me. I just said I'd do my best. Maybe it will work out."

The next day the other eight employees took their wages and began preparing to leave. For transportation the eight of them owned only four saddle horses. They wanted to borrow a wagon and leave it at Jones's Mill. Brother Bossereau would not hear of it, but finally sold them a light wagon and one yoke of steers at the same price he had paid a few months before.

The colonists in general were not informed of our financial condition. The official word was that the employees had been asked to have faith enough in the colony to become members and when they refused they had been discharged. But I think our low treasury was rumored about, for two families resigned and left with the employees—one German family which had kin in south Texas, and one American family which owned land in Arkansas. It had been understood that both the German and the American had money; if they had, evidently they loved it more than they did our plans for an improved society in Uterica.

Rumors about our finances and about those who left us did not prevail long, for on the day after that departure, on a Sunday, another event occurred, or supposedly occurred, which set tongues wagging. A group of boys and girls went swimming together at the deep hole a mile down the creek. Once I heard that they swam together without a chaperon, again that they swam together nude. It was not clear whether they were twelve- and fourteen-year-olds or grown young men and women. Some colonists thought it a harmless thing. Others were shocked and demanded more supervision of the young people. I did not ask Jim York whether he knew anything about it and he did not say.

CHAPTER

10

JULY came in hot. Each day by the middle of the morning the sun would be burning down with such intensity that it would seem that it could get no hotter. Those of us who worked with axes would become literally soaked in our perspiration. By the middle of the day every bit of shade large enough to shelter a person became precious, and to leave a shade tree near the creek and walk up through the violent sunlight to the dining hall for lunch seemed almost too great a task. It was equally hot inside; we had not enough windows in our buildings, and the cracks between the poorly fitted logs began to seem a blessing. We fanned ourselves with hats, pieces of paper or cardboard, pieces of cypress shingles.

And during the afternoons men, women, rarely a child, began to fold up from heat exhaustion. The victim would become nervous and deathly pale and so weak he could not stand. Dr. Sockwell would elevate his feet, stuff him with water and medicines, and prescribe rest in the shade for a week. The doctor was concerned. He went about the village and the colony lands, panting, red in the face, looking more sloppy than ever in his sweat-soaked clothes, like a fat hen caring for a brood. He threatened dire consequences if we did not wear hats at all times and forbade anyone to work out-of-doors between noon and three in the afternoon. We obeyed him.

I could not judge whether he was a good doctor, but he was a busy one and interested in his work. One day, resting in the shade after lunch, he offered me his pocket flask, but did not press it on me when I declined.

"It's only wine," he said, taking a deep gulp. "No one should drink heavier liquor in this weather. Brandy and rum and whiskey are heat-producing. But a little red wine is very good for the digestion at any time. Many a doctor could throw away half of his powders and pills if he would learn the proper medicinal use of wine."

He had another drink and mopped his face and said, "Half the preparations they use are quack remedies anyway. Some of them are only cayenne pepper and chalk."

He discoursed on congestive fever, erysipelas, bad liver, tertian ague, and bilious stomach, and on the curative powers of tartar emetic, ipecac, sulfate of quinine, calomel, rhubarb, magnesia, Epsom salts, castor oil, and blue pills. When he had drained his flask, he rose and waddled out into the fierce sunlight to go and tend a man who had collapsed from the heat that morning. I sat and dozed for a half hour, leaning against the shady side of the building, before I rose and braved the sun.

Unless a breeze came up, it was hard to sleep at night. Those with beds inside, which was nearly all the colonists by this time, frequently came outside with or without bedding to try to find a cooler place. Now and again griping could be heard, that the authorities of the colony had chosen our site in such a desert climate.

The soil around our buildings and in the paths toward the stock pens and the creek became pulverized by our feet to a fine dry powder. It sifted along the ground when a hot breeze stirred, rose in clouds when children ran. It settled on our sweat-damp clothes and slipped through the cracks of our houses to make a film on everything. We found our food gritty from it.

The corn crop looked poor. It had come up to a good stand, but since had grown ever slower because of lack of moisture. The center stalks had pushed up out of narrow, wilting leaves to shoulder height, where they had made skimpy tassels. Now ears had formed, as large as a man's thumb, not noticeable except for the thin spray of shiny silks that hung out of the small shucks.

I walked through two of the cornfields one afternoon with Brother Bossereau on an inspection tour. He was aware that the crop was poor. We noted here and there grasshoppers, some busily eating on the corn silks. He asked me to what extent the stunted plants were due to insects.

"Not much," I told him. "It's rain they lack."

"If it rains now, they will grow larger then?"

"Well, the corn would make, I think." I broke off one of the ears and peeled back the husks. The ear was pithy and the immature grains were so poorly developed that they hardly showed any milk when I crushed them with my thumbnail.

He asked, "Suppose we haul water. Would it help?"

Looking at the dry-weather cracks in the soil, I shook my head. "No sir, I don't think so."

"Not even if we use Mr. Finch and all the men who are building fence?"

"Well, it's the equipment," I said. "If we had more wagons and barrels and work stock, we might do something, but it's nearly impossible to haul water for a field."

Around the horizon were the kind of tall, lumpy clouds that build up in hot weather, and we talked, as farmers have always done, about the possibilities of rain. We also discussed building in some future year a gravity irrigation system, bringing the water from upstream out of North Creek.

Then he began to talk about the hot weather and how it is a part of nature and that we should not expect nature always to be gentle, that it is like a stern father who is sometimes harsh and seemingly careless of his children rather than always lovable. He said that to be children of nature would not be easy, but that good things are more clearly seen as valuable when they are dearly bought, and that in the end we would be toughened as well as made more humane by nature. He went on in this vein at length and during his talk repeated several times his conviction of the perfectability of man.

I don't know whether I seemed to him to have an understanding nature or whether I seemed like one who is harmless, or what, but it was not that I gave the impression of a stupid listener who can be used as a sounding board because he is dull-witted, for he spoke to me with such sincerity and passion that I could have no doubt he wished desperately for me to understand him and believed that I could. He had done it a number of times before. It was curious the way he spoke to me and kept doing it—not an incidental thing but a thing which must have someway seemed important and proper to him. He was not begging or ordering or even suggesting that I do anything. His words had an intimate cast, more in the way he spoke them than in the meaning I got. At times I had felt as a new-frocked priest might hearing the confessions of a bishop, and, having heard liberal theories that one who confesses does actually speak to himself and his God rather than to his confessor, I guessed that I must serve a similar neutral function, though he spoke of his convictions and not his sins. The ridiculous idea had come to me at one time that he talked to me to keep from talking to himself.

When the confidences first began, I had been flattered. My title—assistant supervisor of agriculture—actually meant little, while he was the titular and spiritual leader of the pioneering colony now and destined to be the same for the larger colony when it was formed, perhaps even the leader of some great, as yet unplanned, revolutionary nation. What man like me would not have been flattered? But when I had been his confidant a few times and the novelty had worn off, I had learned that his talking left me moody. Though my respect for him did not waver, I'd found something painful in listening to him; it might have been a matter of the high moral standards that were implicit in his talk and his assumption that his listener would measure up.

I guess it was in the cornfield that day or during our slow walk back to the village that I reached the point of planning to anticipate his talking to me in private and trying to leave him no convenient opening. But it would be a tactful avoiding; I would suffer a lot of discomfort rather than hurt his feelings.

Wild grapes were ripening along the creek. They appeared a lush bounty in contrast to the poor showing of our tame cuttings in the field on the hillside. The wild vines swarmed over trees and tangled together with other vines. Many of the grapes were beyond reach, but it appeared that we could pick a wagonboxful or ten times that many if we wanted them. We had tasted them as they began to turn and found them exceedingly sour. Brother Dominique Henri planned to make great quantities of wine, and he judged that the fruit should be dead ripe before picking.

When the grapes turned black in color and began to drop of themselves, Brother Henri lost some of his former meek demeanor. He demanded a wagon and a crew of pickers. He drove his helpers, mostly women, unmercifully during one long hot day among the junglelike growth near the creek, and they returned to the village in the evening with five barrels full of grapes and an equal amount piled loose in the wagon. The women were much scratched up, two of them with bad hives from poison ivy, and all of them irritated and cross. They were determined not to pick any more and swore that the grapes were too sour to be of any use whatever.

I had supper with the third group that evening. I kept hearing a commotion in the rear, where most of the cooking was done. After some particularly loud talking, Brother Henri was pushed through the door into the dining room by a large woman who was a work-crew leader in the kitchen. She had a German accent.

"There's no room!" she said. "Can't you understand anything?"

"I have orders to make the wine!" he said.

"Stay out!" she said. "I won't have it. I have a hundred troubles without your big mess."

She went back into the kitchen and he followed her, only to retreat immediately from her again. She was a very sweaty and determined woman.

"I'm going to tell Brother Bossereau," he said. "I have orders."

"I don't care what you tell him! You expect to eat like a hog three times a day!"

"But I require room for my work as much as anyone, and containers too."

"I don't care what you tell him!"

"My work is important!"

"I don't care what you tell him!"

Brother Henri left looking flustered and full of righteous indignation.

The next day there was further hubbub. He began to make wine in the building used for an auxiliary kitchen and storeroom and laundry. Some of the women fought him all the way, and Brother Bossereau was called in several times to mediate and decide whether the wine maker might use a particular tub or milk vat. Lunch was two hours late that day.

Two things stopped the wine making. Dominique Henri's experiments with the grape juice showed that he would need a great amount of sugar. He took as much as the cooks would let him have, demanded the remainder in store, and requested that the assembly send back to Jones' Mill after another thousand pounds.

About the same time that the assembly was deciding to stop the wine making, Dr. Sockwell was asked to come to the auxiliary kitchen. Dominique Henri and his wife and one sympathetic woman helper had picked several bushels of grapes off the stems in order to get rid of the spider webs and spoiled grapes and had washed them. He had begun to crush them in a vat with his bare feet. Then the three of them realized that the grapes contained a potent acid that burned the skin. Their hands turned red and began to sting. Dominique Henri frantically washed his feet. Dr. Sockwell could do little except apply a greasy salve and order them to stay out of the grapes. Dominique Henri could not bear to put his shoes back on. Silently and void of the confidence he had shown the past two days, he stumbled to his quarters.

The women put his grapes outside the kitchen door beside the wagon, which still had three fourths of its load untouched. There they stayed until, two days later, Brother Bossereau asked me to get rid of them. I hauled them, with the help of two men, and dumped them in a gulley a quarter of a mile from the village.

The grapes along the creek seemed hardly diminished at all by our picking. They clung in their small clusters, dark and deceptively luscious-looking. I noted bluejays and other birds sometimes pecking at them.

I had not seen our neighbor Harney Myers since the time Andy and I visited him to get information about the Indian village. One cloudy afternoon Jim and I were hauling water with a wagon for the kitchen supply and we had prodded our ox team up out of the lower part of the bottoms when we saw two strange horsemen riding up the creek. We stopped to let the oxen blow a minute. I did not recognize either of the riders until they came directly up to us; then one of them dismounted and I saw that it was Harney Myers. From his grin I supposed that he recognized me.

He pumped my hand and I introduced Jim. Harney said, with a flick of his thumb, "That's Louey," but the other rider, a red-haired man in buckskins, said nothing and did not dismount.

"You fellers are hard at it," Harney said, chuckling as if it were a joke.

"Hauling a little water," I said.

"Crick's getting low," he said. "Two years ago I seen it dry as a bone 'bout this time a year."

"You think it's going to rain?" I asked him. The sky was nearly covered, and the clouds toward the west were dark.

"Naw, it ain't going to rain. Few little thunderheads."

I remembered from seeing him before that he had a friendly manner but expressed his opinions in a positive way.

Vaguely I remembered his saying something about a "red-headed breed," and I took the man Louey to be part Indian, I suppose because he did not speak. He was a rough-looking man with coarse features, not flabby like Myers, but strong, like one who lives a difficult life. He wore buckskin moccasins, trousers and a sleeveless vest and a floppy felt hat. His red beard and hair looked peculiar with the dark-brown skin of his arms and face. He carried a rifle across the pommel of his saddle, and I noted a revolver and knife stuck in his belt.

"Lucky I run into you fellers," Harney said. I believe he mistook Jim for Andy, whom he had seen before. "I got a proposition to put to them socialist people. I reckon they're the same as anybody else when you get to know 'em, but I can talk to you fellers better than I could them foreigners."

"What's the proposition?" I asked.

"Then you could sell them on it or else tell me who to see."

"What kind of proposition?" I thought he was about to ask for a job.

"Hide and fur business. They's a fortune in it. With Louey

there I got safe passage amongst three Injun bands, maybe more. Country west of here's just itching to be trapped."

"I'm afraid these people don't know much about the hide and fur business. They're not really suited to that kind of thing."

"Don't have to know nothing. Me and Louey and the Injuns know it. They was to put up a thousand dollars' worth of trade guns and traps and poison and knives, and stand ready to do the hauling back east, they would all get rich. Coons, wolves, bears, badgers, even wild cows—this country's crawling with 'em. I don't know nothing about socialist ideas, but everybody's got to make a living some way. They's a fortune in it."

I could think of two reasons why the leaders of the colony would not be interested in such a project. First, there was an undercurrent of feeling toward animals that was associated with our goal of living near to nature; we should keep a few gentle animals and take their milk and wool. A few colonists were against eating flesh, and probably a majority would have been against slaughtering them for their skins. Second, we had no thousand dollars for any project. I did not think I could explain the first reason to Harney Myers, and did not want to reveal the second.

I said, "I'm sure they wouldn't be interested. They're planning several businesses: making bricks, weaving woolens..."

"Ain't no money in that," Harney said.

"I'm sure they wouldn't be interested in investing in anything unless they were going to do the work themselves."

He was not satisfied with my answer. I agreed to take him to Brother Bossereau. They followed the wagon up to the compound, and I found the French leader in the storeroom. He came out to talk to them, and I did not remain to hear the conversation, but noted that Louey sat on his horse as silent as ever. Harney talked to Brother Bossereau a quarter of an hour and then they left.

At supper everyone talked of rain. The wind had become gusty, and the clouds looked promising. After supper, people stood outside and looked at the sky. Women took their clothes off the lines that were strung here and there between the buildings. A freshness in the wind seemed to bathe away the heat that had lain so long over the land. About bedtime thunder was rumbling faintly, and lightning was winking in the west. I fancied I could smell rain, that sweet fragrance when the first drops spatter on dusty grass. I slept well, but in the morning we found it had not rained. The sky was clear. The sun came up in it as large and hot and cruel as ever.

Mr. Finch, the York brothers, and I had moved into the room toward the lower end of the compound which had been vacated by the German family that left with the employees. We planted two posts twelve feet in front of the door and stretched up our canvas to make an airy pavilion, where we lounged and slept.

They made acceptable, if not lively, companions. Taking responsibility for the livestock had not improved Andy's temper. It had seemed to for a while, during the time when he was trying to improve things, but now he seemed to have resigned himself to the inefficiency. At times he seethed with resentment, ready with a sharp answer; at others, he appeared to be watchfully waiting. Mr. Finch tended to be taciturn by nature. He worked with the colonists with a great amount of patience and around our quarters acted with good humor. I could never tell what he was thinking.

Andy did not fit into the young set that Jim was with all the time he was not working, or it might be more true to say that Andy had deliberately removed himself from that set through his dissatisfaction. The brief periods of time when Jim was around us he showed high spirits and expressed no bitterness at the marriage which had been delayed.

One evening after supper Andy, Mr. Finch, and I sat under

our canvas. There had been some question whether a good rain would save any of our corn, and Andy asked Mr. Finch abruptly, "Can a bunch of people go through the winter out this way without any corn?"

Mr. Finch stared toward the horizon a minute. He never directly answered the question, but in what for him was an unusually talkative mood, speaking in a leisurely way, told this story:

"My uncle went into the Santa Fe trade when it first started up in the twenties. Then he quit freighting and threw in with three other men out there to trade for furs. You had to have a permit from the Mexicans to do anything like that, and they couldn't get one, so they just packed up and went on anyway.

"Well, the first thing that happened, they lost all their grub and about half their supplies in a river. They couldn't go back because the soldiers were on the lookout for them, so they went on.

"That was in the springtime when they left Santa Fe. Fourteen months later my uncle came down the old Big Muddy into Westport, Missouri. He had cleared three thousand dollars for his share of the trapping and trading.

"He claimed he had walked forty thousand miles, most of it up and down mountains, and hadn't seen a dozen white men all that time. But he was ready to go again."

Andy seemed more interested than he had been in anything for a month. He asked, "What did they eat all that time? Game?"

Mr. Finch chuckled a little. "First time I asked my uncle that, he grinned and said, 'Yerbs. We et yerbs.' I pestered him a while about it and he said, 'Hell, boy, we lived off the fat of the land.' "

Andy asked, "Could four men do that these days?"

"I reckon they could, but they wouldn't get the beaver."

"Could they do it around here in this country?"

"They could live off the fat of the land, but they wouldn't come in with that kind of money. No beaver."

"That's what a man ought to be doing these days," Andy said, "instead of living like this and nothing to look forward to except carrying all these deadbeats on his back."

The leaders of the colony were beginning to understand that our field crops should be considered failures, and, in casting about for some farming project that might be done successfully and in some way compensate for the failure, they hit upon the idea of making hay out of some of the native grasses. Some of the grass was tall and now curing. It would have made good hay, but we did not need to cut it. Standing where it was it would feed our small numbers of animals through the winter. And it was too bulky to haul to any market. Mr. Finch agreed with me. One day I headed for the regularly scheduled assembly meeting with the intention of stopping the hay idea before planning on it had gone any further.

Customarily I avoided the assembly. Since the intensely hot weather set in, the meetings had been starting immediately after lunch, since this was a rest period, and presumably a member would be free to go to regular duties afterward; but long bickering often stretched the meeting all afternoon.

I saw Brother Bossereau and several assembly members inspecting the nearly completed barracks for young women. This project had aroused controversy among the colonists and the leaders, and I did not care to become involved. I went directly to the meeting room.

Two people were there, already seated at the table, Sister Harriet Edwards and Brother Adams. She was talking to him in an animated manner and glanced over at me just enough to identify me before she went on.

"If there is a chance to break the vicious circle of flighty-headed women and the tyranny that makes them flighty-headed, it just may be that the barracks is the place. Let them, while they're young and have vitality, express a few independent ideas in a free atmosphere among others their own age, away from the father's frown and the mother's whining. If their ideas are foolish, that's better than heads filled with the same old bourgeois nonsense about the inferiority of women."

Brother Adams was nodding slightly. He was a good listener and polite. She went on:

"I don't know whether I'm sicker of highbred women or lowbred. These kitchen biddies—they smell of dirty baby wrappings and soured milk and cheap soap and cooking cabbage, and those are the things they dwell on. Their minds smell the same way. Never a higher thought. Not one jot of time given to the higher things of life. Ask one of them what are the proper qualifications for the director of this colony or whether she thinks a woman might ever aspire to that post, and she will stare at you as if you were mad."

I felt out of place sitting there, as if I had intruded into a social situation where I did not belong, and, of course, the feeling came from the fact of her ignoring me. There was something impolite in it. A person may express ideas and have implied a consideration of his listeners, or he may deliver a harangue that hardly admits the existence of the personality of the listener. It's like whispering in public, or pointing. Or perhaps it was the implication that Brother Adams didn't amount to much, and I, even less. I'm sure she intended no slight. It was rather that she was talking about a subject on which she felt strongly. And it is doubtless true that everyone commits impoliteness at times without realizing it.

"And the highborn, the wealthy," she said, "they give all their attention to appearance, to their attractiveness, to their snobbish ideas about society. Is my dress exclusive? Is my girdle as tight as I can draw it? Is that a new wrinkle coming on my cheek? Have you heard the latest? I've seen those fine-feathered ladies parading with their escorts on the streets of New York when it looked for all the world like some sporting fellow showing off his thoroughbred mare. And the good sense of the woman would be about equal to the good sense of the mare.

"The fault lies with the men. I'm sick of women for their willingness to be what they are, but I'm sicker of men for their presumption. My position here is not easy. I know that they talk about me behind my back. I'm perfectly aware of it, and I'm going to do what I think is right regardless."

The other assembly members began to enter the room and she stopped talking.

They all found seats at the table and the issue before the meeting was evidently what they had already been discussing outside, the young women's barracks. I became aware, in fact, that this issue had been seething for some time. Considering the difficulty of building, the shortage of lumber, the cramped quarters of some families, the fact that much material and equipment was still stored outside, some members believed that the young women's barracks was a project that ought to be postponed and the space used for other purposes. There was also some implication that the barracks was a concession to the women of the colony, who had already had concessions in the matter of space for cooking and laundry. This assumption obviously nettled Sister Harriet Edwards.

One of the Americans said, "It appears to me that we need a schoolroom much more than we need such a barracks."

Dr. Valentin said, "We'd better put a stop to all excess building and devote our time to some project that might support us."

"If I may speak for the women," Harriet Edwards said, "we need a young women's barracks *and* a recreation hall *and* a schoolroom. Not one iota of concession has been made to the women of this colony because you have ceded to them space where they can slave away at their traditional tasks."

"Madam, pardon me," a Frenchman said. "A dozen times I have heard it assumed that you speak for the women. Why is this? Pardon me, but it is time to question this. What do you know of the European women? Perhaps it is the Americans that you speak for. Surely your writing encouraged some of them to join the colony."

She had spoken aggressive words to Brother Adams before they came in, but her tone had been conversational. Now her neck seemed to stiffen and she stared the Frenchman into silence.

The American who had brought up the need for a schoolroom said, "I don't believe she represents the views of the Americans. Not to be unkind, but how does she speak for a man who is the head of a family and has the responsibilities—"

"Perhaps I don't speak for anyone," she said rapidly. "Perhaps I don't represent anyone. I'm not quite sure just what the formal credentials amount to that each and every one of you have, and perhaps I just don't qualify."

"As for that," Brother Bossereau said, "I believe each represents the entire group. It is not necessary that it be an issue."

"Oh, it's an issue," she said. She gave him no gratitude for his help. "It's an issue, all right. I see twelve men here and one woman, but not one man has had to defend his seat here. Only the woman. Let's have it before us. I'm tired of insinuations, and I have a thing or two to say about it. Most of you won't like it, but it's true!

"I speak for the whole group in the same way that the rest of you do, but I speak for some also that you are afraid to speak for, or are too arrogant to speak for, or are too ignorant to speak for. Some women don't know they're human beings. How could they know? Get back in the house, woman, and

tend your chores! Tend the babies, woman! What would you
know about important things; you're just a woman!

"I speak for human beings that don't even know they need
a voice. How do you expect them to speak out? You've told
them to keep their place until they believe they have a place.
Dependent! A man's helper! A man's plaything! A man's rib
bone! You ask them and they may deny me, but I know what
their hearts say! And I know what most of you say; you say
one thing and you do something else."

She paused, as if to get her breath, and the American said,
"When we are able to hold elections, we'll all have to defend
our seats, I think. Do you expect to have all the women's
votes?"

"I expect to have the support of thoughtful people," she
said. "You imagine that you are setting up a society for the
advantage of the working class. Did you get the vote of our
employees? When their salary was stopped, they couldn't
wait to get away. If you expect the gratitude of those you
speak for, you are ignorant!"

Brother Bossereau tried to speak, but she went on. "Why is
it that all the interesting work is men's work? That's what
I want to know! Why don't you really face the issue? Or do
you intend to build a Utopia here just for men? Are you
going to let it drift and slide and let it go on as it has for
centuries, one of the biggest tyrannies and injustices in all
the world, while you go smugly on? Maybe toss a few crumbs
to the women to keep them satisfied?

"I have a message for you, sir." She addressed the Frenchman who had challenged her speaking for the women. "You
can look patient or innocent—any way you please. You can
look away. But I'm sitting here in front of this company and
you and in front of God, if there is a God, to tell you this,
plainly and simply: I'm your equal! Whether you like it or
not, I'm your equal! It's that simple. The issue's that simple.

You'll agree, but not one man in ten has the decency to act as if it is true! You can cringe from it or act innocent. I don't care! I'm your damned equal! Do you hear me? Is that plain enough for you?"

She seemed almost prepared to spring on him. Her face lost its handsome cast when she was angry.

"Whom are you addressing?" he asked.

"You. I'm speaking to you."

"I don't think you're speaking to me."

"Well, I am, sir, no matter what you think. I want to make it plain."

"Madam, perhaps you're speaking to someone else—your father, your former husband, someone. You hardly know me. I haven't harmed you. In fact, I haven't beaten my wife once in fourteen years of marriage, but if I did, it would be none of your concern."

"You think I'm speaking to someone else. You'll have it that way, will you? Have it anyway, as long as it's not on your conscience. Don't face it! Accuse me instead! If you're like the average man, you've beaten your wife regularly with a weapon worse than a club! You've made a slave of her! You've taken her mind and will away from her!"

"Sister Edwards, please," Brother Bossereau said. "This isn't like you."

She turned her glare on him.

"Please, this is not necessarily an issue. What do you require us to do?"

"Do you want to start carrying logs?" the American asked. "Is that it?"

"Why do you throw that up to me?" she said quickly. "You're not as strong as a horse. Does that make you inferior to a horse? What about intelligence and good judgment and morals and ethics and ideals? Is civilization built on brute strength? I don't ask a thing for myself. I'll carry logs, if you demand it."

"Please, Sister Harriet," Brother Bossereau said. "What would you require us to do?"

"I'll carry logs if you insist. If that's your judgment on human worth. It won't be so hard to keep up with some of you."

"But what do you desire that we do? Haven't we planned universal suffrage when we are established?"

"You'll toss a few crumbs to the dear ladies to keep them satisfied."

Brother Bossereau was sincerely pained. "But what do you desire? What can we say? What is it?"

She seemed to gather her thoughts for a moment. Then she said, "It's the same here. Can't you see it? Can't all of you see it? We give lip service to our goals, but we push them back and back. So it's the same. Or worse. What does it mean that I am the director of education and supervisor of young women's activities? It means nothing. I have a plan for the women to have art classes and make paintings, which, I might say to you who are so worried about our support, could be sold to the country people of this region, bringing brightness into bleak lives as well as giving us an opportunity to express our artistic instincts; but I can get no support for the idea. I don't know of any project in this colony that might move in the direction of enlarging the lives of the women here, with the one small exception of the barracks for young women. And yet, after planning it and agreeing to it and building it, you want to take it away. And when I begin to defend it, you are after me like hounds chasing a rabbit.

"I feel as if I've had an attack against myself and everything I stand for. I question whether all of you believe in our ideals of the equality of the sexes."

After this speech Brother Bossereau and several others protested their innocence of the charge of disloyalty toward our final goals and assured her that they valued her point of view and opinions. Those who disagreed with her kept silent. It was accepted that the barracks for young women would be used as planned.

Finally I got the opportunity to explain my opinion and the advice of Mr. Finch about the hay gathering. The assembly understood and agreed. I further stated that the area round about was good grazing country, that we ought to purchase another bull as soon as possible, and that we ought to consider stock growing in the coming years as a favorable possibility for the colony. They tentatively agreed.

As the assembly broke up, I was talking with Brother Bossereau. Outside, I started to move away from him, but he put his hand on my arm and said, "I would like to have a private conference with you when it's convenient."

I told him that I was at his command.

"Perhaps this evening?" he asked.

I agreed to come to his quarters.

After supper I went to see him, reluctantly, yet with curiosity, for I could not imagine what could be so private that we could not have talked about it standing together in the garden. It was still daylight. He asked me in and motioned to a chair. From his frown I got the vague idea that I was to be tactfully scolded for something.

"I wish I knew you better, Brother Langly," he said. "I request permission to question you, but I don't wish to be presumptuous."

"That's all right," I said.

"I can only be candid with you. And if you do not wish to answer my questions, please be candid with me."

I nodded and waited.

"Do you know any of the younger people, or older ones, either, for that matter, who indulge in this so-called free love?"

"No, sir, I don't."

"Do you know any who advocate it? Or who appear to be in agreement with it?"

"No, sir."

"Pardon me for pressing the matter, Brother Langly, but I would like to understand your attitude. Do you believe this is a private matter which I should not question?"

"No, sir, I'm sure you have good reason. I've heard only the barest rumors and really know nothing about it at all."

"Rumors, yes," he said. "I wonder if that man Deveraux is preaching free love."

"I haven't heard him, but I wouldn't be surprised."

"He is not motivated by the love of humanity but the love of disruption. We made a mistake in allowing his membership."

After a moment he said, "How I deplore this irresponsible talk! Or is it just talk?" His last question was not directed to me. Evidently he was satisfied with my answer, but he was seriously troubled. It was about the time when summer daylight begins to fade. His daughter Jeannette was nowhere to be seen. I could not help but wonder how much his concern about free love was affected by his concern for his daughter.

"Why in the name of God," he said, "isn't it possible for them to see the important course, the main course, to live together in equality and brotherhood without experimenting with every dangerous notion that every irresponsible radical has ever proposed? They do not know what they meddle with. Is marriage an arbitrary form imposed by the whim of some recent authority? Do they imagine that men and women lived in a type of perfect harmony until some tyrant devised the chains of marriage and hammered them around us? Do they see no benefit to it?

"Marriage is not a devised or imposed institution, but a useful practice developed through the ages by human beings for their own benefit. When a man and a woman enter into an intimate relationship, it is more important than they may realize. I mean to them personally, individually, to their spiritual well-being or lack of it. The relationship may ennoble or degrade either of the partners or some other person; it is one of the most affective of human relationships. It may be beautiful or ugly, but it's always of consequence. It's private, but it's far-reaching. Therefore, sanctions have been slowly produced in practice, so that such an important matter should not be ruled by accident or passion or ignorance and so that the individual does not depend entirely on his own experience, and these sanctions provide stability in a union; they aid or protect all those who may be affected by it.

"These young men and women, when they are attracted to one another, they imagine that it's the first time it has happened. The first time! As if they were Adam and Eve! It's unique! But every sigh, every gesture, every whispered word, every problem, every failure, every impulsive act, good or bad, has happened countless times in the ages before us, and people in the aggregate have distilled the wisdom into a viable institution called marriage, in which there is a balance of freedom and restraint.

"How do they know, these innocents, what they are doing when they try free love? It's like entering into a secret forest when they don't even know the extent of the forest or the demons that lie concealed in it. They are signing a contract without knowing any of its terms.

"Common-law marriage! Free love! What is it? There is the question, and they don't even realize that a question is involved. What is an innocent entering into? She doesn't comprehend. She doesn't even comprehend her own innocence. If any stupid advocate of it could define it and explain its terms and conditions, I might not even object. I might welcome it. But its nature and appeal is its uncertainty, its liberty from precondition. It is romantic nonsense! It is reluctance to face the reality of human nature. Marriage has its faults, but so does human nature. Even when an innocent girl, or rather an innocent young person, enters into marriage —and he should not at too young an age or under chaotic conditions—even then she is ignorant on many points, but at least the extent of the forest is known and some of the routes are clear and some of the pitfalls are uncovered.

"I'll oppose them at every place. I not only forbid its institution in this colony; I don't want even the presumption that it might have merit. The beautiful fine little girls of this village are not going to grow up in any such atmosphere."

He did not tell me all this for any expedient purpose. I felt, as usual, uncomfortable, and this peculiar question occurred to me: How does he know as much as he certainly knows about marriage and love? I tried to imagine what manner of woman his wife must have been and found it impossible to conceive that he had ever been married at all. He was a complicated person. I felt so strongly his knowledge of people and powers of reasoning that I could not imagine that he had ever been young or foolish; yet there was feeling under his speech; he was not a cold person.

In what he had said lay implications that were disturbing. Of course, he was in contradiction to his own point seventeen: We forgive the past and renounce it. We turn our backs on its symbols and influence as we turn our faces toward tomorrow. But it was doubtless true that he had not meant the point to be an absolute. I had the feeling that he could explain the contradiction had I not felt uncomfortable about asking him to do so, for his thinking was involved and comprehensive. What he had to say about marriage came from a very deep well within himself.

He apologized to me for taking so much of my time and explained that he was becoming worried that so many extraneous issues were constantly arising to threaten our central purpose.

It was nearly dark outside. When I had gone some thirty steps down the garden path, I noted him standing alone in the door of his quarters. The most clear sound of the night was the laughter of a group of young people out toward the creek.

CHAPTER

11

WE harvested a little barley and millet, enough to have fed a flock of chickens through the winter, but we had almost stopped even talking about the corn. Thunderheads built up on the horizon to tantalize us, sometimes bringing a day or two of relief from the heat, but they always faded without dropping rain. One day I went with Brother Bossereau and two other assembly members for a tour through the cornfields. They hoped to determine the size of the crop, though they thought it would be small. My more pessimistic hope was to set at rest any belief that we could expect a crop.

I carried a tow sack, for we did not wish to waste any good ears we pulled. We crashed through the tan-colored stalks, which had hardly any green in them even near the roots, searching for the larger ears. At first they looked to me to do the pulling, as if it required an expert hand, and they watched as I broke the shucks away from the undeveloped corn. The cobs were small, the grains hardly noticeable. The assemblymen began to aid the search by gathering and shucking, to no avail. I carried two ears in my sack for awhile; they, with a hundred like them, might have shelled out and ground enough meal for a mess of cornbread. We passed from one field to another, trying to find a patch that might have done

better, but it was the same all over. Our tour took several
hours, but it answered the question with finality: the corn
crop had completely failed.

Brother Bossereau seemed not as disappointed as I had expected him to be. As we walked back to the village, we talked
about what might be planted for a fall crop and what might
be done differently next spring. He asked me to sound out
Mr. Finch and form an opinion as to whether he would ever
be converted to our social ideas.

That same day in the late afternoon I rode with Mr. Finch
to drive a dozen oxen out to the herd and bring back another
dozen to the pen where we kept those we were working. We
spotted eight of the colony horses down the creek, and he
rode a half mile out of his way to catch the one which belonged to him. When he had rejoined me, riding the same
horse and leading the one he had caught, I asked, as much
to make conversation as out of curiosity, "What do you want
with two horses?"

He didn't answer, though I knew he heard me. We brought
the oxen back and penned them, then took the horses to stake
in some good grass not far from the stock watering hole. As
we walked toward the village, he said, "I'm pulling out,
Langly. Going to south Texas."

"Are you serious?"

"Yep."

"How come?"

He didn't answer for a minute, then grinned and said,
"This is a queer business here, I mean me drawing wages and
everybody else working for nothing. Like you, for instance,
and the York boys. Puts me in a bind. But I damned sure
won't work for nothing. Then I have a good deal down south,
I think."

We walked back to our quarters. It was half an hour before
time for us to go to supper. Andy was there. When he heard

that Mr. Finch was leaving, he was immediately full of interest and eager curiosity.

In his good-humored but laconic manner, Mr. Finch answered the questions. He had been in correspondence with two old friends who were buying land south of San Antonio, and he was going into the cattle business with them. He believed there was a good future in it.

Andy asked, "Could you use two good hands?"

Mr. Finch grinned. "We could use a couple of good hands, all right. Who did you have in mind?"

"Me and Jim."

"I'm afraid Jim won't go."

"He'll go, all right. Would you really take us if he'll go?"

"Well, we could work something out, Andy, no doubt about that. But I don't think Jim would do it."

"He'll do it."

Jim did not come in before we went to eat; then, in the dining hall, we saw him eating at a table with Jeannette Bossereau and other young people. After supper Andy fretted as he waited, but his younger brother did not come to the quarters. After dark we heard the music of a fiddle and Spanish guitar from up at the assembly meeting room. Andy got up abruptly and strode in that direction. He came back some time later, without his brother, as Mr. Finch and I were removing our shirts and shoes to go to sleep.

Mr. Finch asked me, "They having one of those assembly meetings tomorrow?"

"Yes, sir."

"Guess I ought to go and tell them I'm leaving. I hate to quit suddenly like this."

"Me and Jim will be going with you," Andy said.

I had gone to sleep when Jim came in. Then the argument began. Andy took the peculiarly unreasonable point of view that it was already decided; they would certainly leave the colony next day to go south with Mr. Finch. He interspersed his assertions of this certainty with arguments and persuasions and castigations. The leaders of the colony were fools; the corn crop was a failure and the colony broke, and we were certain to starve in the winter. A few people were doing all the work. The colony could never be a success because too many of the people didn't know how to work or wouldn't. The leaders were traitors to the goals they themselves had set up. He attempted to get Mr. Finch to affirm his arguments, but Mr. Finch remained as silent as if he had been asleep.

Jim met it sometimes with good humor, again with silence, again with sarcasm. He would not talk when the girl came into the argument. Some time past midnight they reached an impasse and became silent.

The next morning Andy did not oversee the milking as he usually did. He said to his younger brother, "Let's get everything together. Mr. Finch wants to leave this afternoon."

Jim grinned and said nothing. After breakfast he picked up his ax and headed for the blacksmith shop.

"Where are you going?" Andy demanded.

"I'm going out on the rail crew where I belong."

Andy followed him, arguing. When they got in with the gathering workers, Andy seemed to stop talking, as if biding his time, and he went out on the wagon with the work crew that his younger brother was on. I was concerned and certain that no good could come from such dogged insistence.

That morning I got two of the large breaking plows started turning under the stalks in the cornfield nearest the village. We intended to prepare it to plant turnips and peas and some other seeds for a fall garden. It was dusty, hot work. The soil did not gum up on the moldboard as it had when we first plowed it, but it had baked extremely hard in spots. The oxen did not want to knuckle down and pull in such hot weather. To control them was a constant battle for the five men on each plow.

I came in late for lunch and did not see either Andy or Jim.

Mr. Finch wanted me to go to the assembly with him, but I refused. I had not hired him nor had anything to do with his decision to quit. If he felt ill at ease going there alone, it was his problem.

In the middle of the afternoon I saw him bring his two horses up into the compound. Not wanting him to leave without our passing a final word, I left the plowmen with their work and returned to our quarters. There, with mixed emotion, I watched him pack his gear and saddle up. He had an easy, unhurried way of doing things that was deceptive; he seemed to exert little effort, yet his pack was quickly made and lashed solidly to the back of his second horse. I wondered what was on his mind, whether perhaps it had actually hurt his conscience to be the only one around who was being paid for his work, or whether he was looking into the future and thought he saw failure for the colony, or whether he perhaps saw too much eventual success for it. His easygoing manner told nothing of his thoughts.

I asked him, "Why don't you wait and get an early start in the morning?"

"Going to be another scorcher tomorrow," he said. "I'd rather ride at night and lay up in the heat of the day."

I envied him for things in his character that were rare among us whom he left: practical knowledge and ability and confidence, all natural and peculiarly unexamined by himself. He could ride up to a backwoods cabin or into a log-cabin village and be made welcome by the strangers he found, be trusted by them, be at ease among them. He had a special capability which would allow him not only to get along with people, but lead them, even understand them in some vague, unconscious way; yet this unaccompanied by any kind of social consciousness at all, it seemed. He was not committed in his life, or selfishly committed; above all, his human sympathy was particular and did not extend itself through reason to a universal love of humanity.

He mounted, holding the lead rope to his pack horse. He was a large man, and the horse he rode was large. He towered impressively higher than an ordinary man on foot. I remembered his having said once to Brother Bossereau, "You've got grown men that would die out here if you just turned them loose." How different he was from that. He could as well have been riding alone to California as to San Antonio, and with the same expectation of reaching his destination safely.

"No use to ask you to go with me, I guess," he said.

"No, sir."

He started to raise the reins and turn his horse, but paused and looked at me for a moment, then asked with a serious expression, "You're pretty strong for this business, aren't you?"

"Yes, sir, I am."

"If I was in it, Langly, I'd stand behind Bossereau. All this backbiting—they don't have a chance unless they stick together."

It occurred to me to mention that he wasn't in it, but I didn't answer him.

He said, "I hope you all get your corn in pretty quick after the first of March next year. If it doesn't sprout or if it freezes, you might try to get hold of some of that little hard Indian corn. It stands up good to dry weather."

"I'll keep it in mind," I said and some of the resentment that I was feeling surged up into my voice. I remembered Brother Bossereau's words that it was inevitable that some would leave us, and I wanted to yell, "If you're determined to go, then go!" Which feeling, of course, was illogical; he had never professed to believe in Uterica. He was no traitor to an ideal, for he had never involved himself, and had now a freedom of choice denied the rest of us.

He said, grinning, "You're not sore because I'm leaving, are you?"

"I just don't understand you," I said.

"Hell, there's nothing to understand, Langly. I just got a better deal someplace else."

"There are plenty of things I don't understand."

He dismounted and went back to check the tightness of the ropes on his pack. "Name one," he said.

I realized that I had a small hold on him for a simple, unimportant reason. He preferred to leave this place where he had spent several months with a friendly good-bye. I felt faintly vengeful toward him. I asked, "Why did you call Miss Harriet Edwards a 'bitch' that time?"

"I remember that. I just said it on the spur of the moment."

"But you did say it."

"I shouldn't have said it."

"But why did you?"

"I don't know. It just seemed like the right thing to say."

"What made it seem right?"

"I don't know. She puts herself forward. But a man really shouldn't cast a slur like that on a woman."

"What do you mean 'puts herself forward'?"

"If you don't see it yourself, I can't explain it to you."

"Did it ever occur to you that in spite of any shortcomings she may have, there are places in this world where she is highly respected? There are places where there might be a gathering of refined and cultured people, lawyers and statesmen and artists, thoughtful and educated people, and she could be a part of it; she could understand their discussions and contribute to them and be at ease among them. I wonder how you would fit into a place like that? How would you look?"

He grinned. "Like a hayseed, I imagine. I guess I better stay away from places like that."

After a moment he said, as if to show that he was not ridiculing my questioning, "They say there's some good in everybody, if you can find it."

His homely philosophy did not ease my resentment. I knew

as I went ahead that I had no justification for my pestering, but I could not resist one more approach. I said, "I guess you're leaving here with a pretty good stake?"

"Nothing to brag about. I've got nine hundred dollars."

"That's a good bit more than all these three hundred people have for supplies and things. How do you feel about taking your salary and leaving under those conditions?"

"Well, that's why I'm leaving . . . before I get to feeling too bad about it."

"Then you do feel bad about it? You've wondered whether these women and children and all might not need the nine hundred dollars for food this winter?"

"Well, if I had to take care of them, I would also have control of them. I would take them east. I would use the money I've got for transportation to send them where they belong. I'd send Miss Edwards back to those refined people you say she belongs among."

"Then you've decided the colony is a failure."

"I don't know. It's not my damned colony."

He swung back into the saddle and I saw that he was on the point of going. I had been unfair, asking about the money. I said, "I guess I'm a little grouchy today. Good luck to you."

He grinned broadly as he said, "Don't let these Frenchmen throw you."

He rode away and I was strongly aware that we had lost a valuable man. I would really have appreciated knowing what he thought about it all, but it is evidently true that some men do not wish to explain too much or perhaps they do not think of their lives at all in terms of explanations.

I had watched him disappear over the ridge before I realized that his action settled the question of Andy's and Jim's leaving, though it was not necessarily true that he had talked to them since morning. Mr. Finch had been handling all the details of the fencing work. It might be well for me to find out what all his crews were doing and at the same time hunt up either Jim or Andy to ease my worry about what might have happened between them. I caught my horse, saddled him, and rode out, following the freshest wagon tracks.

The crew Jim was on had its wagon in the woods about a mile north of the village. There I found the two brothers some distance from any other workers. Jim had just felled a tree, the trunk of which would make a good post and the limbs of which would make two or three rails. He was trimming off the smaller branches. Andy sat on a cut-and-trimmed post which lay on the ground nearby. Evidently he was doing no work, but work habits were so irregular that probably no one had noticed. They were not talking when I rode up and dismounted.

Jim paused, wiped his sleeve across his forehead, and asked, "Is Mr. Finch about ready to leave?"

"He's gone," I said.

"Thank goodness! Now maybe this leech will turn loose and let me alone." To Andy he said, "You've probably got some work to do with the stock. You can go on now, whenever you're ready. No use to mope around me any longer."

When Andy spoke, I was surprised at his voice. There is a voice that wheedles, one that argues rationally, one that releases passion in words, but it was none of these. It was cold and simple, and behind it, even in the face of this ridiculous situation, seemed to lie a determination which would have its way even at great cost. He said, "Finch leaving has got nothing to do with it."

Jim whirled toward him. "Nothing to do with it! My God! What have you been talking about for two days?"

"This thing's going to be settled whether Finch goes to San Antonio or to hell."

"Andy, sometimes I think you're crazy."

"I may be crazy, but this thing's going to be settled."

"It is settled. I won't do any of the crazy things you've

been talking about. I know you don't like it around here. You've made it plain. That's your business. What you can't get through your thick head is that some things are your business and some things are my business. I like it here, and I'm going to stay. I'm going to get married. That's my business. So it's settled. I won't do what you say, and you can't make me. So all that leaves for you to do is start taking care of your own business any way you please, and that settles it." To me he said, "Wouldn't you say that just about settles it?"

I did not intend to answer, but Andy quickly asked me, "What did you want? Are you the big cheese now, the one that goes around to check on everybody?"

"You're in charge of the stock," I said. "I don't guess anyone checks on you except the assembly." I smiled at him, but he did not return it. I felt enough concern about their words and moods that I did not want to go on and leave them.

Andy said to Jim, "If you're not going to do anything to settle it, I'm going to Bossereau myself."

"Well, if you're determined to make a fool out of yourself, go do it. I don't know what good you think you'll do talking to Brother Bossereau."

"I'll do something nobody else has got the guts to do. I'll talk up to him. With you it's 'Yes, sir, Brother Bossereau; no, sir, Brother Bossereau.' Brother! Brother, by God! This place was supposed to be a place where the workingman was equal. It didn't matter who your father was or how much money you had. Work was supposed to be appreciated. Just work. That was enough. But now it's just the opposite and anybody with eyes in his head can see it."

To me, Jim said, "He's told me that a dozen times."

But Andy went on, "You're not good enough to marry Jeannette Bossereau. You're low-class. If you sit around and talk big, you amount to something, but if you're one of the damned few that does a decent day's work, you're not in it. This colony's the biggest hoax ever put out. I'm going to speak right up to the son of a bitch. That's what I can do with Brother Bossereau. He may not do what I want him to, but he's damned well not going around grinning like a jackass with the idea that I can't see through his hoaxes and lies."

"You're sure getting in a good decent day's work today," Jim said.

"I'm going to the girl, too. When I say I'm going to have it settled, that's what I mean. You can say everything I've done for you doesn't matter and this is none of my business, but I don't mean to let it be that way. You came to me, boy. You don't know what all I've done for you, and you're the one that came to me, not the other way round. When I did a thousand things for you it was damned well my business. I'm going to Bossereau and that girl both."

Jim had been half leaning on his ax, ready to be sarcastic, quite aware of my presence, and not so tensely involved as his brother, but at the first mention of the girl he went back to trimming branches. It was clear that he didn't like it.

"I'm going to talk up to her too. She may not believe me, but she's going to hear what I've got to say. She's just like her old man."

Jim was swinging the ax carelessly, growing angry. He said, "I've told you about that, Andy!"

"She's part of the whole damned hoax. She's flighty-headed and young and childish."

Jim swung the ax hard with one hand, setting it solidly in the wood, and strode toward where his brother sat. He stood over him. "You're fixing to get the hell beat out of you!"

"If she wasn't so flighty-headed and childish, she'd quit this place and go with you." Andy was looking up at him coldly, not retreating at all from the threat.

Jim struck him full in the face with what was half a push, half a blow. Andy fell backward, then scrambled up. They moved immediately toward each other, almost eagerly, it seemed, and began mauling furiously. Neither ducked much nor feinted nor fought cleverly, but threw punishing blows into body and head. As much alike as they were physically, they seemed entirely different, for Jim's was a kind of hot, incensed anger into which he had been goaded, and Andy's was ruthless, even calculating.

They fought silently, stumbling over the post and in the high bunch grass, the only sound being the thud of fists striking and grunts of pain and savage effort. My horse shied back and I let him, for he would not go far with the reins down. I not only felt that it would be undiplomatic to try to stop the fight, but had some vague idea that it might serve as a purge of their ill feeling.

They fought through the scattered trees, in and out of their shade, sometimes threshing into their lower limbs. The ground on which they tramped had short and tall grass, some green, some drying, and low ground plants and bare places with rotted leaves a year old. Of all their surroundings they were oblivious, paying single-minded attention to giving pain with their fist. I was struck with amazement at how hard they worked at it, how fast they sometimes moved, how each pressed in upon the other.

Andy had suffered a bloodied nose with the first blow, and his younger brother soon took a cut high on the cheek from which blood ran down and was smeared. The sleeves of their shirts were torn, and their hair stood up in disarray. Their deep breaths hissed through set teeth. Their faces were contorted, Jim's angry, Andy's brutal, both ugly in their single-mindedness.

Jim stumbled on the uneven footing of the grass and fell backward. Andy, lunging with a blow, followed him to the ground. They rolled a moment, pawing and flailing, then rose, seeking each other with hard blows again even before they had gained their feet. The bare parts of their skins and their sweaty clothes were stuck over with loose grass and dirt and rotted leaves. Their breaths came in hoarse gasps.

I don't know how long it went on before I saw the change in Jim. He was not beaten. He had taken no more punishment than his older brother. But he had had enough. He had fought out the resentment that he had built up from Andy's words during the day and from what he had taken as an insult to the girl, and he was ready to stop. But there was no way to stop. He did not leap forward as he had, but he tried to keep from retreating; his blows turned to pushes and shoves. Andy, though clumsy with fatigue, did not alter his determination at all.

They had moved in a circle through the trees and back to where the fight began. I was thinking about trying to stop it, for I did not like the look on Andy's face. They were beyond the felled tree from me.

Jim's foot evidently struck a limb on the ground. He fell backward. Andy dropped deliberately upon him. I could see the older brother's upper body, his bloodied face, his gritted teeth. There was a struggle, but Andy remained on top, his shoulders tensed, his arms down. I ran around to see.

Andy's hands were locked on his brother's throat. Jim was writhing and clawing weakly.

"Andy!" I screamed.

I pulled at his arm. "Andy!"

I grabbed his arm with both hands and jerked back with all my might. He came free and tumbled back.

Jim's face was dark. He breathed rapidly and shallowly. I said, "Are you all right? Jim, are you all right?" He began to move and I helped him to a sitting position. Andy had disappeared without a word into the woods.

Jim spit out phlegm with a little blood in it and put both hands to his throat. He raised troubled eyes to me and asked, "What's the matter with him?" His voice was as husky and constricted as that of a man with a bad cold.

"He got carried away. Lost his head."

"He wasn't ever this way before. What's got into him?"

I had no answer. He expected to rest a few minutes and go back to work, but I persuaded him to ride back to the village behind my saddle and let Dr. Sockwell look at his throat. The doctor found no permanent damage and tactfully refrained from asking questions.

Andy had come to our quarters and got his rifle and gone. We did not think he had followed Mr. Finch, for mine was the only horse near camp, and it would have been difficult for him to have caught one of the loose horses down the creek. He did not show up that night nor the next morning, but was present at the evening meal. When we met at our quarters after supper, he said nothing about where he had been or about the fight.

I had, several weeks before this, begun to write in my journal a kind of essay under the title "On Associating with Evil," from what I had thought to be a general impulse to moralize. After the fight between the York brothers I recognized with amazement that my scribblings might be applied to Andy, that I had doubtless been studying him without admitting it to myself. Now I returned to the writing, at which I had been stymied, worked at it as time and company permitted, and finished it so that the whole read as follows:

On Associating with Evil

It is a basic Christian teaching that sin is not a matter of action but rather intention, not a matter of flesh but rather spirit, not a matter of body but of mind. On the surface this seems like nonsense. Who could hurt another by thinking harmfully? What does it matter that a man has bad intentions if he never brings them to actuality?

First, it should be noted that harm can be caused to one being by another without evil being an issue. When a large fish gulps a small one, the smaller is put to a proper and natural use. The smaller is harmed, indeed disintegrated, but the larger could not even exist unless he went about eating his normal food, and it is not evil which has overtaken the smaller, but rather neutral fate. This example may be extended so that even if one man kills another, it need not be evil. If two companions go out to hunt and one kills the other entirely by mistake, he may be blamed for carelessness, but not for an evil deed. The question hinges on whether the act is entirely accidental. If a man goes to rob another with a gun and the gun discharges and kills the robbery victim, then the man may protest all he wishes that it was an accident, may even convince himself of its accidental nature, may scream like a child, "I didn't mean to!" Yet the gun in his hand was a damning symbol of what was in his spirit. He has done an evil murder. It is not the gun that is evil, as it was not in the case of the careless hunter. Nor is it the needless death; the victim of the hunter is as dead as the victim of the robber. The question of what is accidental and what is not is a subtle one; yet in these clear examples it is manifest that we believe that a man may associate with evil on what might be called the spiritual level.

We may not condemn the man until his association matures into objective harm, but when it does, we do not condemn him for the harm but for the evil he either welcomed or permitted inside himself, the evil with which he traveled, a thing not a part of the physical world.

The question remains as to whether evil thoughts must have repercussions in any objective world. Should evil be defined as a factor which might cause harm, or one which will probably cause harm, or one which must cause harm? The harm might be to the sinner as well as to the sinned against. Altogether a difficult question.

These ideas are not mere theory and abstraction. We are all approached by evil, tempted. All succumb in one small measure or another. Yet it does seem that sometimes a man gives up more to it, accepts it, comes to live with it as if it were a companion. He receives some slight or some frustration and allows it to rankle in him; he does not or cannot throw it off and renounce it, but accepts it as a friend, so to speak, and agrees to bitterness as a way of life.

One could hardly give a single name to the inner companion of Andrew York. Of the seven sins, he is guilty of Pride and Envy, and these straightway led him to a third, Anger. He was proud of his skill and knowledge in the kind of work we had before us, and, whereas he might have taken humble joy in his work, he chose to resent the lack of skill in others instead. And if in the others' lack was even some degree of prideful ignorance, he might have chosen to look at the good in them rather than the bad, but he chose malice toward them instead. He had envy toward his younger brother, though he certainly must have told himself it was based on love, must even have believed it; evil will not be an equal with a man; it will come to blind and dominate him so that he is finally pushed to this kind of inhuman conclusion: I love you, therefore I will choke you to death with my bare hands! The envy was not direct and simple. Surely he never analyzed it, but he might have put it thus: You cannot be that innocent and find happiness in it! The world is harsher than that! I have seen it and learned! Why should you find joy, never having paid the price of it? It will not be permitted in the course of things! And so, with his arrogant knowledge, he has given up learning what the world is and what man is. He already knows and only waits for his preconception to manifest itself, ready, if necessary, to aid it. In addition to pride and envy and arrogance, he is filled, too, with self-righteousness. No wicked man agrees that he is wicked. Though evil dominate him so that he is void of kindness and completely miserable, he tells himself that he is in the right. No one else agrees. He is alone. Thus is added self-pity, which binds up all the other sins into a single strong force and tends to extend indefinitely the association with evil.

Andrew York is not a weak person. He is young enough to be full of energy and old enough to have all the potential for hate. He seems somewhat like a drunkard who has found a kind of acid which he drinks and who has taught his stomach to tolerate it. He continues to drink it because he started to drink it. The acid stimulates the making of bile in him and other body juices, and these, tainted with the noxious nature of the acid, flow out through all the members of his body. Like a drunkard, he may believe that he is brilliant or jovial or shrewd or perfectly normal, but he is a man with a mixture of acid instead of bile and blood, and his closest friend will cry out, "What's got into him?" His demeanor may appear rational to an acquaintance, but his brother knows that something hideous is wrong, and it is also clear to an observing friend with whom he lives—all too clear.

The question as to whether evil, when it exists, must come out of the realm of spirit and thought and produce objective harm has no answer. It is a matter of degree and opinion. The evil in Andrew York already harms Andrew, the sinner, though he has been prevented from a crime against another man. He surely is never happy or at peace. Regardless of any reason he may have had for his original resentments, he, in his present attitude, is sensitive to every trifling injury and must magnify it. In every word he must find a sly insult. So his evil harms himself, and he is to be pitied more than he knows.

But his condition seems unlikely to change of itself or through his will. The acid boils through him and seethes in his mind and soul. What can stop it other than violence carried through to some sad conclusion? His condition promises hurt to anyone around him or to all of us. He is like a tragedy waiting for its time to occur, a nemesis planning a dark surprise.

When I had written this essay and read it over, I decided it was too fanciful, even pompous. I had overemphasized and overdramatized, had got carried away by my own verbosity. The irony of it was that at the end of all the high-flown presumption of wisdom, in the last sentence, I had made a prediction that I should have taken seriously, in the words "...a tragedy waiting...a dark surprise."

Why I did not want Dr. Sockwell to know what had happened, I do not know. Sometimes I think I have a kind of character disorder that makes me hesitate to act, that prevents me from making a firm decision until it is too late.

One thought about the essay impressed me strongly—how necessary it was that neither Jim nor Andy see it. To describe a man you live with in such a manner is a great impropriety.

After this we three lived together in a social situation that was highly artificial. Everything that Andy said was insincere. He seemed at times to be daring us to bring the fight into the open for discussion, as if he were ready to overwhelm us with sarcasm. He quit doing any kind of work. Being supposedly in charge of the livestock, he was never assigned to a work crew, but he allowed the sheepherders and milkers to carry on however they were able and he paid no attention to where our few oxen and horses roamed. He passed his time wandering alone in the woods and on the prairie or lying on his back inside our room staring at the ceiling.

CHAPTER

12

THE hot weather eased and we got two showers of rain a week apart. I think this made everyone feel better. We regained some of our optimism of the spring. But at the same time a kind of nervous appraisal of how the colony was faring passed among the colonists, and I became aware that the intrigues among the leadership continued.

One evening at supper Dr. Sockwell asked me whether I would come to the assembly tomorrow. I asked him why and said I hadn't planned to. He looked at the eaters around us, and though they did not seem to be listening, said he would talk to me later.

We strolled in the dusk down toward the springhouse, his pet project and now nearly completed. He offered me a drink from his flask, as he had done several times before, and when I refused, took one himself. "Our stock of wine is exhausted," he said, "but I find brandy more suitable for most medical purposes anyway." When he had dropped the flask back into his pocket, he told me his reason for our talk: the assembly was about to vote on removing Bossereau from his position as director. If I wished to vote, I should attend.

"Who is doing it?" I asked. "Will they actually vote on removing him?"

"Valentin is behind it as much as anyone. I'm sure they'll vote on it tomorrow."

"But they can't do it, can they? I mean, how are the votes divided? Or do you know?"

"I would think they could very likely do it. Some votes are doubtful. You might attend and vote for Bossereau. Then you might change my vote if you give me some good reason."

"Then you expect to vote against him?"

"I expect to."

"Why?"

"Well, Langly, we're not operating successfully. We need to cut out the quibbling and get our government in good shape. If we can make it through the winter and begin next year with an efficient work system, we have a chance. It takes time to set up a workable administration, and the sooner we take the painful step of removing Bossereau, the better."

"Who is the alternative?" I asked. "Would you take the post?"

"They wouldn't have me." He beat his pipe in the palm of his chubby hand and said reflectively, "I can tell it—since those idiots made that useless search. They're ashamed of themselves but they resent what I said about it. But, regardless, I'm ready to vote to remove Bossereau, even though I respect him more than any other man here."

After a minute, he went on. "Don't let me influence you. But I think you ought to attend the assembly. The more practical points of view represented, the better."

He chuckled and said, "There's a ridiculous problem connected with it that may not have occurred to Valentin. If Bossereau doesn't like the outcome, he may press for an election in the colony. For a director and an assembly both. Bossereau might come out of that with the directorship and a new assembly. They're not ready to risk an election. Most of them think we have enough of a confused mess already without an election."

Dr. Sockwell had made up his mind about how he was going to vote, though he was none too happy about the decision. I could not make up my mind at all, but knew that I ought to attend the meeting. Actually I did not know enough about what was going on among the leaders.

When I entered the assembly room the next day after lunch, I soon noted a mood among those present. They were not talking. Each came to his seat and took it silently. The only greetings they passed were nods. It seemed that all of them, perhaps with the exception of the director himself, had in mind what Dr. Sockwell had called the "painful step."

Dr. Valentin's eyes had flicked around as if counting them, and no sooner had Brother Bossereau settled into his chair than he said, "Jean Charles, we have a consensus as regards the first order of business today. We don't believe there should be any delay in taking up a particular matter."

"Then let us not delay," Brother Bossereau said.

"There is sentiment for vacating the office of director of the colony. We believe that this important matter should be put to a vote here in the assembly."

It was impossible to tell whether Brother Bossereau was surprised or chagrined. He looked calmly at all of us and asked, "Would it be preferable to discuss the matter or do you wish to vote immediately?"

His manner was innocent, even though his words implied the question: Had we already decided it in secret? Perhaps some of them had agreed that discussion was not useful, but others, as if to deny the implication said, "Let's have open discussion." "Yes, of course." "... if anyone wants to speak."

Brother Adams said, "Perhaps Brother Bossereau should certainly have time to comment, if he wants to." Some of them nodded, uncertain.

Brother Bossereau rubbed his high forehead with one hand, both elbows on the table, then looked around at us with a ridiculous little smile. He said, "Brothers and Sisters, I'm really not much inclined to defend myself. I comprehend you perfectly. You are all rebels. The reason that I understand you is that I am a rebel too."

He paused and it seemed for a minute that he was finished, but he went on. "I ask no titles from you, and no authority. 'Brother' is the greatest title I have ever had. I have never had deeper satisfaction than in being in this place, being your brother, and laboring in this cause.

"It is difficult to be a leader. It has taken corrupt men centuries to bring civilization into the noxious state in which we now find it; yet we propose to set up a state of justice and equality in only a little time. We have so many things we desire to do. So many plans and intentions and ideas. I've found it easier to criticize than to take the responsibility for progress."

He turned the naïve smile on us briefly and said, "Something within me desires that you relieve me and select another director, for I want to be a rebel, too, a gentle rebel, I hope, but a rebel nevertheless. Something within me desires to play the gadfly.

"But what I really shall do is serve however you wish— whatever you desire. If we have not done as efficiently as we might in our colony to date, it is my fault, for you believed in me and put the responsibility on my shoulders, and I have failed you. But I trust your judgment and I say with great sincerity that I prefer to follow your will. If you believe I should work in the kitchen washing the dishes, there I shall go.

"My primary concern as director has been with good fellowship and it still is. This is important. I believe that we will have spiritual community—I imply nothing about religion— spiritual community or nothing. I believe that it's possible to have so much a sense of common high purpose, so much a sense of family, that tolerance and unanimity and good judgment flow out of it like sweet water from a spring. Excuse me for appearing to give advice, but I would like to try to say something to express what is to me vital and central in connection with all our goals. And what I would say is part of the philosophy of the Jew, Jesus of Nazareth. Love one another. Find accord. Find singleness of heart. For these things are the key to all the others.

"But I've said too much. Do you require me to leave the room?" He half rose, questioning, suddenly cooperative to the process, whatever it was to be. "Is there a bill of particulars or anything? I wouldn't want to answer any charges; I'm sure they're true."

I was sorry and faintly angry at the rest of them at that moment, for he was ridiculous, too eager to please, awkward, without the dignified appearance he deserved. He appeared to be acting, which he certainly was not.

Valentin asked, "You don't wish to say any more?"

"No, Brother Valentin, pardon me for saying too much already. Shall I leave?"

"As you wish, Jean Charles. This is an open proceeding. Go or stay."

I could not read their temper. His speech had been so humble as to be almost sarcastic, but he had been sincere. I thought, that if they had been near evenly divided, then he had pulled it off; for certainly what he had said moved me so that I could not vote against him. But then I had not sat in the many meetings that they had sat in with him.

They observed a moment of silence, properly giving anyone a chance; then Valentin took the vote. They voted by raising the hands. Brother Bossereau did not vote, nor Brother Adams, nor did I. The vote was ten in favor of vacating the director's position, none opposed, three abstaining. Brother Bossereau gave no apparent reaction, though he must have been surprised at a vote so strongly against him.

Dr. Valentin said, "I believe we should proceed immediately toward a reorganization that will give us a stricter, more effective, government and productive system."

"Pardon me," Dr. Sockwell said. "I'd like to point out that the vote we have just taken did not make Dr. Valentin director."

Valentin looked at him through narrowed eyes and said, "I'm growing a little weary of that kind of insinuation. What you say is obvious. Perhaps you would like to explain why you felt it necessary to say it."

"I thought it a pertinent observation."

"I thought it a gratuitous insult. Because I try to introduce a little common sense into our proceedings, you intend to make an ogre out of me. You try to cast me in the role of the devil. As I say, I grow a little weary of it. I don't quite understand why some of you are not willing to consider my viewpoint on an intelligent basis rather than imply that I am a devil trying to assume power. I presume your votes just now meant something. What did they mean?"

He sat back and folded his arms. The silence did not last long before it came home to us all that we were like the crew of a ship which has just lowered its sails and thrown its helm overboard, presumably for a purpose and in expectation of some further action. While Valentin had no mandate, as the prime agitator behind the removal he was the logical person to be given attention.

Dr. Sockwell, not as much taken aback as some persons might have been at the rebuke, said, "If you have specific proposals, let's hear them."

"Do you object," Dr. Valentin said, "to my saying what I have to say in my own way? I have a few observations to make before I come to specific proposals."

Dr. Sockwell shrugged and the others appeared to pay him close attention.

"There is a certain basic minimum status which does not depend on any goals," he said, "nor devolve from them. It is simply that you cannot exist at all without this status. Its elements are food, clothing, and shelter, and a minimum degree of order and a certain degree of foresight in regard to these minimum elements. These matters are in issue today, and as long as they are, they transcend our goals. We are simply going to pay them our primary attention, or we are going to be dead socialists.

"What are our plans should this village catch on fire? I presume we plan to do this: all scream and run in opposite directions.

"What are our plans should the Indians prove to be not at all what we assume? Suppose they make a savage attack; what are our plans? I presume they are the same: all scream and run in opposite directions.

"This kind of planning conforms very well to the rest of our planning. We have a hundred ways in which we intend to use lumber. Now, what lumber is this? We have no money to buy lumber, no sawmill, no money to buy a sawmill. We have a good supply of beautiful ideals. I would say we have a surplus of ideas and theories and notions and whims and high-flown language, but these won't get you a single god-damned plank of lumber! You must buy it or make it. You cannot talk it into existence.

"We are not as well off today as we were the day we came here. We must have efficient industry, agricultural and other-wise, to provide not only that basic minimum status, but a material basis for a more complicated society. When you have done that within a framework of order and foresight, then you will have alternatives, and not until. Why should social-ists expect to behave like spoiled children? Why cannot they submit themselves to discipline?

"I propose that we put all authority in one man for at least one year, and let him be responsible for the welfare of the people and the preservation of the colony. Let everyone sub-mit himself to that authority. The assembly should meet only once a month and act only in an advisory capacity. Any authority might be delegated as the leader saw fit. This is the crux of my proposal, though I realize that all of us might want to know in more detail what such a single leader intended to do."

He paused and Dr. Sockwell observed, "Of course we just had a single leader and we just got rid of him."

"You seem addicted to saying the obvious, Mr. Sockwell. Jean Charles Bossereau did not do, and had no intention of doing, the kind of thing I say must be done. He has been the gentle leader of a benevolent anarchy."

Dr. Sockwell grinned. "I'm stating the obvious and you're beating around the bush. Exactly what do you mean to do if we hand over all authority to Michel Valentin for one year?"

He was not embarrassed, but launched immediately into his proposals. "I would have two kinds of organization, one based on citizenship and the other on production. The first would be made up of a group which might be called the "guard," which would be ready to act in any emergency. Each member of the guard would have assigned to his care or protection ten or twenty colonists, and he would provide liaison between the leadership and the people. The guard would be the means of organization of the colony outside of working hours. If the leader, or governor, decided that a certain regulation was necessary, usually after consulting the assembly, each member of the guard would be expected to let his people know about it and to make certain they understood it.

"The other organization would be based on work leaders as we have it now, except that our work could be much more efficient. The governor would decide priorities and have the last word in planning. Our greatest problem is that we have too many idlers and too much careless work. For the first few years everyone should be assigned to the work where he is needed and to that which he can do best for the common good, not that which he would prefer. I see no reason why we should treat ourselves like spoiled children."

Miss Harriet Edwards said, "I think we would like to hear some more details about that."

"About what?"

"Who are the spoiled children? Do you advocate assigning the assembly members without regard to their preferences?"

"I believe everyone must give up his cherished ideas and projects temporarily for the common good. The assembly would meet once a month and act in an advisory capacity."

"To what work would you assign me? I notice that when you spoke of one person in sole authority you made the usual assumption that it would be a man. I'd like to know where you would assign me."

"I'm not trying to make it sound easy, Miss Edwards. It seems apparent to me that the time has come when every citizen must make some direct and tangible contribution."

Into her face came a momentary revelation of strong feeling. I remembered Dr. Sockwell's having said that, though she and Valentin were the chief conspirators, they actually had little in common. She surely must have known before that they had differences, but I think she came to believe in that moment that he was her enemy. She paused during two breaths, as if to compose herself, and asked, "Would you please answer my question?"

"I would assign you where you were needed—as I would any worker."

"Well, if you don't choose to answer my question, I'll tell you where I shall assign you if I am made governor. I shall assign you to the kitchen."

Dr. Valentin turned his eyes away from her and said calmly, "Anyone who found the work unbearable could leave. I see no reason why we should not be willing to submit ourselves to the discipline and sacrifice that are necessary."

The others entered into the discussion. They were interested in Dr. Valentin's proposals, but some were suspicious and all were reluctant to make such drastic changes without much further study. The meeting became confused, with various people talking at once and frequent interruptions. Dr. Sockwell proposed that a temporary chairman of the assembly be elected. Sister Harriet Edwards nominated Brother Adams, who was soon elected by voice vote with no "nays" audible. This seemed to mean that the assembly had no intention of implementing Dr. Valentin's plans at an early date.

Finally they set up three committees: for Effective Government, for Effective Production, and for Finance. Dr. Valentin was made chairman of the latter but was not a member of the others. It was not clear what changes would follow from our action against the French leader.

It occurred to me to wonder whether the influence Brother Bossereau held could be voted away from him by his colleagues. There was ironically little immediate tangible change, no gavel to hand over, no accounts or records to surrender. The only official things we had on paper were our Compact and a few lists of colonists and work assignments, all of which had belonged as much to any member of the assembly as to the ousted director. No one mentioned a possible colony election. That extent of democracy was a luxury we could not yet afford.

It was agreed that our financial condition was crucial. Several planned buildings—school, recreation hall, various shops —were held up because we were not able to buy flooring and trim lumber and window glass and shingles. Some assembly members thought our lack of a printing press was a problem of emergency proportions. There was no doubt that we needed money to buy food. The Finance Committee was instructed to consider whether our next year's crop might be mortgaged and to draw up a proposal that the New Socialist Colonization Company sell more stock. All of us were instructed to contact our liberal friends in the outside world and let them know that donations could be used and would be appreciated.

During the long months of autumn the weather was pleasant with occasional showers. The temperature was mild, day and night. Often the sky was soft with a thin high veil of clouds. I heard no more complaining that we had located in a desert country, but some about gnats that pestered us by day and mosquitoes that stung us in the evening.

Brother Bossereau planned to deliver a speech to the colonists, rousing a controversy in the assembly. Dr. Sockwell reported it to me. The colonists had not been told about vacating the position of director, and it was believed that if Brother Bossereau were to speak, it should be made clear that he did not speak for the entire leadership. Some of them demanded that he submit his speech to the assembly for prior approval; he countered this by assuring them that he would use no prepared text or notes and so had nothing to submit, that they knew his views and knew they were not subversive to our goals. The truth was that the assembly had no system of discipline that could prevent his speaking, even if they had all been in agreement about it. Dr. Sockwell saw it as the opening guns of a campaign by Brother Bossereau that would lead to his popular election to a post even stronger than he had held before.

Rumor among the leaders had it that Harriet Edwards was waiting to see what happened, that, if the ex-director made an old-fashioned, romantic appeal for the loyalty of the women, she herself would schedule a speech that would wake up every woman in the colony and anger every man.

The notice on the bulletin board read: "To all interested Colonists. Brother Jean Charles Bossereau will speak in the Main Street on Wednesday Evening at 6:30. His subject is Socialist Goals, Our Present Situation."

They gathered as they had before, some of them dressed for the occasion, except that the men did not hang back on the outskirts. The women in the kitchen left their work, and of the three hundred colonists probably no more than half a dozen were absent. They crowded the compound—standing, squatting, sitting on boxes, chairs, kegs, buckets.

I was impressed as Brother Bossereau began, as I had been at other times, with the way he gained rapport with his listeners through an unpretentious, conversational beginning. He spoke simple things about our everyday life, but his quiet dignity made us understand that these simple things held meaning, and there was suspense concerning his trend of thought, for everyone knew that he would proceed to speak of more than simple things; we knew his command of words. He went on to talk about the difficulty of seeing the greatness in our present humble situation. He said that it is one thing to live in harmony with nature and another to wrest a living place out of the wilderness, that we had been doing the latter, which was difficult but unavoidable in the beginning, but that our efforts led us surely toward the former, the harmony, toward a natural paradise. And that these two, the difficulty and the harmony, were symbolic of our total situation today and our expectations for tomorrow. "A true life," he said, "though it aims beyond the highest star, is redolent of the healthy earth. The lowing of cattle can be sweet accompaniment to the melody of the human spirit. We shall find the harmony. Difficulties in these early days are like the thin vapors of the dawn which precede, but do not prevent, the rising of the sun."

He spoke of the great character of our intentions. "Our presumptions are glorious," he said. "Our goals are founded on nothing short of faith in the universal man as he comes fresh out of the hands of his Creator. How daring it is that we should be true to our natures as men and women! But these are not merely dreams as they may sometimes appear to us in these primitive surroundings. Even now we can see the faint light, the first glitter of the dawn of a new era for humanity. Already social science begins to verify the prophecy of moral vision."

No notes were before him, but I had the impression that he had planned his lecture carefully. He returned to his less fanciful manner to explain certain advanced understandings and discoveries that had been gained in the area of finance. The creation of money in the form of credit is a social function, he said, and generation after generation of mankind pays a tribute in the form of interest for this function, which ought to be free, since it is generated by society and not by bankers. Also, the rich and powerful have the ability to tamper with the evaluation of money, to create monopolies and control the market by holding goods off the market. Thus by little effort the rich get richer, while the poor, shackled by the money system, can never get a decent living from their hard labor. Not only this, but the rental value of land is a social creation and ought to belong to the people; they have been robbed of it by lies and manipulation.

"There is no more certain indicator of our success," he said, "than in the area of finance. For not only are we determined to do justice to the laborer for his real value, but we shall eliminate the flagrant waste that continually accompanies ruthless financial competition, and we shall do it by abolishing money. The rich man may say this piece of paper is money and it has a certain value, but value does not inhere in money, nor even in coin. Value comes from agreement. If we abolish money, what can he do? And then consider the great piece of land on which we sit. All of its rental value, its certain increase in value, its certain increase in usefulness, all shall belong to us, the people. We know that we stand on sure and solid ground. If we adhere to our goals, and in the light of what every thoughtful, unselfish student of economics can clearly observe, I do not believe we could fail in this colony even if we desired.

"And we believe that the society we create here will serve as an example. The world waits to be taught, not comprehending how much it has to learn. When man is denied a crust of bread for his child, then a higher law sends him to steal it; then civilization provides a policeman, a magistrate, countless lawyers, a jailer, perhaps a hangman, and all these trappings of what civilization has called justice. What a useless, tragic process! They are blind to the primary truth of it: no one else can own what a man truly needs. He could not steal the crust, for it was already his! And not merely the crust, but abundance! The way to stop a man from stealing a crust is to give him the ten loaves that nature intended him to have.

"We serve as an example, but I would not imply that we are alone. The aspirations and the spirit of the best of humanity are with us. For they believe that our demonstration will be accepted by the world by reason of the genuine advantages that it will procure for all classes, through reconciling all interests in unity and harmony. They study us, for they believe that our accomplishments will bless humanity with ages of abundance and joy above the most visionary hopes.

"I have written a letter for the next posting to a man whom I count a friend and of whom you have heard, Albert Brisbane. I've asked him to use his generous influence to procure money for supplies and materials for us so that our project can move forward. I'm sure that he will respond. This is an act that many of you can do, each at his own initiative, for we do not apply merely to the great or wealthy, but to anyone of goodwill who might desire to be a part, by proxy, as it were, in our great project. It would be possible to send fifty such letters with our next wagon to Jones' Mill. Will you search your conscience and act on this matter—each of you?"

They sat attentive to him as dark came on, slapping at mosquitoes that swarmed among us, but missing no word of what he said. It occurred to me that he had proved the other leaders wrong in their suspicion that he spoke merely to increase his personal prestige among the colonists, for he had not handled the money question like a demagogue. Without frightening anyone about our shortage of money, he had asked them to help. And he proceeded even further along the same line.

He said that our goal, the abolishment of money in our dealings with one another, was unlike other goals in that it did not need a long period of waiting, but was a question of personal conscience and faith, that any colonist who had money might donate it to the colony, affirming as he did so that it was worthless to himself as an individual but of value to our common efforts, affirming also confidence in our certain success. And while there would be deep satisfaction in donating money now, a year from now, when the colony prospered, one might feel ashamed to donate money which one had hidden back. He believed that it was difficult sometimes to give up things, that we were all influenced by ideas taught us in a corrupt civilization, but finally the law of mine and thine would be shown to be incidental in human character. And the sooner each of us could throw off this artificial idea, the better.

He drew from his pocket some objects that I could not identify from where I stood. Holding them cupped in his hand before him, he said, "Here is a gold ring that was worn by my wife many years ago and a watch with a gold case which I have carried for some years. This evening I shall present them to Brother Michel Valentin, who is the chairman of our Committee on Finance for the colony. They are not of great value in money, I believe, but I give them as a symbol. Gold is ostentatious and of no use to us as individuals."

Without begging, but with great dignity, he asked that each of them consider giving up any money or object of value into the coffers of the colony. Any such gifts might be brought to the assembly room and placed on the long table. He received a rousing applause when he had finished his speech, and in the confusion, as the crowd rose and began to move, I saw that many of them were following along with and behind him as he walked toward the assembly room.

I talked to Dr. Sockwell and two other assembly members in the darkness of the compound. Their opinions of the speech were favorable. The ex-director had perhaps exceeded his authority by proclaiming the abolition of money without action by the assembly, but it was, as he had said, a matter of individual conscience, and the action might add something to the colony treasury.

I went an hour later with the doctor to the assembly room, which had by this time cleared of the influx of people. Dr. Valentin sat between two large candles at the table with an open notebook, wherein he had obviously been listing the additions to the treasury. On the table were thirty or forty pieces of gold or silver, rings, watches, brooches, earrings, as well as a smattering of smaller coins.

Dr. Valentin ignored us, but when someone made an optimistic remark about the evening's developments, he looked around and, seeing no one present but me and two or three assemblymen, said, "This may indicate enthusiasm by a percentage of the colony members, but it certainly is no solution to our financial problems." I had the impression, though he sounded fussy, that he got satisfaction from the itemizing and evaluating and totaling, even though the total might be small.

A week later the assembly came up with a plan which I did not care to take part in but which I could not deny was sound and advisable. We would determine whether our Indian neighbors had raised a good corn crop, and if they had a surplus, we would attempt to trade for some. There was concern among the leaders that we treat the Indians fairly and probably an even more important concern that mutual understanding underlie any trading.

They decided that a dollar per bushel was a fair evaluation for corn. If possible, we should see their supply before we made any trades. If they had a large supply, we might trade a wagon and a yoke of oxen. We would begin the negotiations by trying to trade some pieces of the colony's jewelry.

I was drawn into the project and did not have the heart to refuse, since Brother Bossereau had agreed to take part in it. He had been to the Indian camp before and would be in charge of negotiations. I respected him for his willingness; he might have told them that he was no longer the director and they could find someone else to do the difficult tasks.

We set out with a light wagon early one morning, Brother Bossereau, Brother Adams, and I, with Jim York and several other men aiding us over the creek ford, where the water was now wagonbox-deep. The countryside seemed more gentle now with the rains and cooler weather. New weeds and grass were sprouting out of the ground foliage which had dried out in the summer. We walked beside the oxen, taking our time.

When we came in view of some of the swelling, cone-shaped huts, a quarter of a mile from them, we paused. My rifle, which I had brought in hopes of some game rather than for protection, I laid in the wagon and covered with a dozen burlap bags we had brought. Brother Bossereau said that we should approach in the open, away from the trees along the creek, and should not pause when they began to come out to meet us unless the chief came, but should proceed on to the center of their village. Brother Adams was nervous, but Brother Bossereau seemed not at all so. I believe he had concluded that these people were simple, sometimes mischievous, but never to be feared.

We moved on and were surprised that they did not come out. We paused again about a hundred feet from the first house. Not a sound could be heard. I called out, "Hello! Hello, there!"

We prodded the oxen and circled down among the trees to

the center of the village. Not a soul could be seen, nor a sound heard. Brother Bossereau suggested that perhaps they did not recognize us, and we walked around the wagon a couple of times. We stared at the dark holes which were the doors of the grass-covered houses. I called out again and again.

"I don't comprehend," Brother Bossereau said. "Something has occurred to make them afraid of us."

Brother Adams said, "We're not welcome. That's plain enough. I think we should go."

The houses were not crowded together but scattered through the trees. Well-beaten paths crisscrossed between them, and the earth was packed and worn bare around each one. I looked at the scene two or three minutes before it struck me: not a footprint had been made on the ground since the rain nearly a week before.

We went into one of the abandoned houses, moving cautiously, all somewhat nervous. It was more spacious than one would have guessed. Its framework, not covered on the inside, was an intricate arrangement of curved poles. The floor was completely bare. The emptiness left an eerie impression.

The poles were peeled willow. Near the ground they had been worn and polished, as if many a hand had grasped them. Faintly I could smell the odor of human beings of another kind, who have a different diet and different ways of living. The sense of the strange, absent people was strong in the hut. All three of us felt it; we stood silently pondering a long moment.

I asked, "Why do you suppose they moved?"

"I haven't the slightest idea," Brother Bossereau said.

Brother Adams suggested again that we go home. We looked in several other houses, all of which were bare, and peered at the cornfields across the creek. After getting Brother Bossereau's concurrence, I waded the stream at a place where it was knee-deep and made a tour out through the fields. Their corn had been gathered. Though the dry stalks were no taller than those in our own fields, each had had an ear pulled from it, and I could not find a single ear, immature or otherwise, remaining. I waded back across the creek and we turned our wagon for home.

We talked about it, whether they might have gone because of the founding of the colony nearby. Or whether they might have moved to a better farmland. Or whether they had moved for the winter, or had gone on an extended hunt and would return. All the colonists speculated about it. Some even wondered whether our neighbors, those children of nature, had discovered a danger here of which we were unaware.

CHAPTER

13

OUR turnips came up well, took hold, and grew as the wild plants around us had done in the spring. The fields of greens, lush and thick and new, were an encouraging sight. While the turnips were not yet half grown, we began to dig them to cook with the greens, for it was obvious that here was some of the abundance of nature that we had hoped for.

About this same time, other food being scarce, we began to slaughter four sheep a week, usually two at a time. We did not like to deplete our wool flock, but it was necessary to keep food on the table.

Living with Jim and Andy was difficult. I felt the tension in each of them and the complicated tension that always stretched between them. I might have felt at ease with Jim alone, I think, for though he existed in a frustrating uncertainty about which he could do little, he was always ready to be agreeable. He made a good hand in any crew he worked in, pressed his courtship by spending all the time he could with the girl, and in our quarters made tentative, friend-seeking small talk. He would say, "Looks like it might rain, doesn't it?" or, "Isn't that mutton-and-turnip stew awful?"

I stood as a kind of buffer between them and also as a potential bridge. The younger brother could speak to me without compromising his pride, and almost everything he said when the three of us were present betrayed his willingness to reconcile with his older brother.

I don't know whether Jim analyzed his predicament. Evidently the girl remained as eager as he to marry, yet she was unwilling to forsake all others. In fact, her ties to her father and her concern for him were so strong that she was unable to even probe into his obscure, dubious objections. Evidently Brother Bossereau passed over the situation as a settled matter, if he thought of it at all. His daughter would not press him on it, but waited, trusting him. Possibly she thought the wait would only be for a short time, until the colony was on its feet and running smoothly, but how she reconciled this with her knowledge of the trouble among the leadership I do not know.

And so the three of them, the father, Jeannette, and Jim, were caught in a web of loyalty and misunderstanding and desire. Brother Bossereau had said, "Youth is hasty," and this disposed of it in a sense, for he implied "too hasty," as if it were a thing they would understand better later on; but there was a question whether he appreciated the express truth in "Youth is hasty." It was no tragedy, but it was awkward and perhaps unnecessary.

As for the rumors about free love, I doubted that Jim and Jeannette had done anything they would have been ashamed of. I never knew what the younger set was doing. It's quite possible for older people to be surprised at what a younger generation is doing, but it's also possible for cynics to be surprised at the innocence and purity of such as Jim York and his sweetheart.

Andy York was not recognizable as the same young man who had come to the colony site a few months before. He had contempt for the girl because she would not marry without consent, contempt for Brother Bossereau because he would not give consent, contempt for Jim because he wanted to marry the girl, and contempt for the affairs of the colony because effective work was not credited. His manner said that he had done his best to make matters proceed as he knew they should and now all of it was beneath him. His impenetrable contempt was expressed usually by silence, sometimes by a sarcastic statement, which he would make as he was walking away so that Jim and I would know he was not trying to start a conversation. He did not work for the colony, but walked or rode out into the countryside with his rifle without explanation. I was glad that the assembly had not seen fit to give me the title Finch had held, supervisor of agriculture, since I might have felt obliged to do something about Andy.

Pecans were falling out of their husks in the tall trees along the creek. They were small with hard shells. The meat was tasty, but the job of picking it out was tedious. The nuts varied from tree to tree—some round, some long, with differences in size and thickness of shell, and anyone gathering them, seeing more and more trees up or down the creek, tended to move on and on in the hope of finding a better quality. We thought of them as a food, but the truth was that a person might sit with a hammer and stone cracking and eating them eight hours a day and starve to death.

The pecan trees seemed to stretch without end along Loco Creek and its western branch. The leaders thought it worthwhile to search several miles for better pecans, and if they were found, to bring in a good load. The nights were becoming chilly; winter would be upon us before long; the nuts were a food that would keep well. When it appeared that more than half the nuts had fallen, they planned a one-day expedition and put me in charge of it. I was not optimistic about finding superior pecans, but thought we might find a bee tree or some game.

We set out with a wagon one morning following up the

west branch of the creek. The party was made up of three young couples, including Jim and Jeannette, a half dozen older men and women, including Brother Henri, and several children. It seemed to all of them as much an outing or picnic as a work crew.

It was a pleasant day. Thin high clouds filmed the sky, but now and then the sun broke through. The leaves at this time of autumn were undecided; from some trees half of them had fallen; on others they were coloring or turning brown; on others they were dark green. The oaks had dropped leaves so that they were ankle-deep around them, but I saw one here and there which held them and they were crimson orange. The large cottonwood leaves, fluttered by the wind, were half tender green, half yellow. The fine leaves of the willows seemed small yellow flames when the sun came suddenly on them. Some of the vines carried a spray of red berries.

The oxen and wagon made a great rustling in the leaves and dry grass as we skirted the small stream, and we twenty people made even more noise walking, kicking and crushing dry leaves. Squirrels were thick in the trees; they seemed to put on an acrobatic show for us. The only other wild creatures we saw were blackbirds in huge flocks, rising and swinging through the sky, settling onto the prairie or into the trees.

We sampled the fallen pecans at several places and, though they seemed no better than those nearer home, picked up a couple of bushels. At noon we found a low clearing where we stopped. The women had brought baked bread, now precious to us because of the shortage of flour, and a pot of cold stew, which they wanted to warm up. We started building a fire. A boy of about twelve was climbing a tree toward a thatch of dead sticks, probably a squirrel's nest.

No one had paid attention to the boy until he yelled, "I see our Indians! Brother Langly, I see our Indians!"

I walked toward the tree he was in and asked, "Are you sure?"

"Yes, sir, they have horses now."

"Which way?"

He pointed northwest.

"Come down," I said. "Come straight down."

Some of my party had heard and some had not. I ran to Jim York and grabbed his arm and said, "Get the fire out. Without smoke. Pull it apart. Keep everybody quiet."

I pushed into the undergrowth to the stream, forded its cracked limestone bed, and scrambled up a bank into the vines on the other side, wondering whether I should have brought my rifle from the wagon and whether I should have taken my cue from the boy and climbed a tree. But out of the trees on the north side of the creek rose a small ridge, and five minutes after I left the others I had gained this vantage point.

A half mile away I saw a hundred mounted Indians, riding south. I crouched down and watched them. They would strike the creek a quarter of a mile above us. Their horses' trotting feet raised a low stream of dust. The animals were nearly all spotted brown and white. I could make out little about the riders except that they were certainly Indians, some of them with feathers, others with a heavy headdress on their heads. They rode at ease, but the steady gait of the horses and the hunkering posture of the riders produced an effect of deliberate and ominous intent.

As well as I could see, they carried in their hands what might be guns or bows. The tails of the horses were bobbed, or perhaps it was that they were bound up. All the riders seemed to be grown men.

As soon as they entered a mott of trees near the creek, I sprang up and hurriedly made my way back to where the others waited. Some of them were badly frightened, others unconcerned and busily eating our treasure of bread. I wished that I had never brought such a group so far from the village. Jim and another young man had taken the two rifles from the wagon. I told them that if the Indians turned down the creek,

I would walk a little way to meet them, and they should cover me with the guns. After a quarter hour of nervous waiting, we saw the horsemen emerge onto higher ground, still riding deliberately south. They had passed us by.

Brother Henri said, "I think we must go home."

Someone else said, "It's nothing to send us home. Those people are like children."

I did not suppose that the Indians would turn around and find us, but they had impressed on me how defenseless we were. Had we been men, well mounted, it would have been different. Against several objections, I turned the party back for our village.

On the way home and later, while reporting to the colony leaders, I thought about how little we knew of the natives who inhabited this land with us. When Brother Bossereau asked why I believed these were different Indians, I could only say that Mr. Finch had once said the others were not horse Indians and we had never seen them with horses, whereas these seemed to ride as if they were grown to their horses' backs. On the other hand, I could not dispute with any certainty what some of the colonists believed, that they were all one tribe.

It occurred to me that our first Indians might have found it necessary to move because these—perhaps their enemies and more warlike—had come into the area. But it also occurred to me that it was all speculation with little foundation, that there are mysteries, upon which each man has his opinion, which mysteries are never delivered out into the clear light to be examined and handled and agreed upon, and so must be tolerated as part of the uncertain condition of life.

Dr. Sockwell put it in a similar fashion after supper, as we loitered briefly in the dining room. "It's like medicine," he said. "I'm a traitor to medicine to say this, but I've learned to live with my own ignorance. Sometimes I think the ancient science of medicine has more ignorance than it has knowledge.

You learn to live with it, but you never learn to like it."

During these days I wrote some impressions which, after much striking through and rewriting, and after much thought toward a title, I completed in this form in my journal:

The Maze of Growing Things

Along the creek in places grows a profusion of trees and shrubs and brambles of many kinds. This was a single thing, a mass of foliage, but now, with the leaves fallen, the bare limbs exposed, it is a multiplicity, a maze, a horde of dark-gray skeletons lying in confusion with fingerbones and hair thrust up and out in every direction.

Looking into it one sees every kind of crook, bend, angle, fork, bow, and cross, lines going in a fantastic random variety; every kind of size and erratic sweep—knobby limbs, smooth limbs, rubbing, clinging, crisscrossing, defying any pattern. A single limb—why should it rise at that place rather than another and twist over just there and turn out to the side? Did some conglomeration of forces mold it to its shape? Stopping it, guiding it, urging it, defining its existence so that it could be nothing else? And if one, all the seemingly endless others? They become too much for the human mind.

Inside each limb are the minute details and arrangements of vegetable life, but these are smaller than the layman sees. He sees the maze, or perhaps more often only feels some sense of the profusion. It is one thing, a unity with vague borders. And the impression of unity may have some legitimate basis in nature—plant life gathering in the lower places along the creek to seek water in a semiarid land, each individual struggling against its neighbor for a share of air and sunlight, these actions a part of a pattern which justifies the existence of the maze if not its particulars.

If he has the tendency to observe things and wonder at them, a man gets a similar impression from the swarms of blackbirds in this country. They come as thick as insects, sometimes flying over in a long, straggling train, miles long, each fluttering black speck an infinitesimal atom in a far-flung motion; one of them, somewhere, knows where they are going, or is it the whole of them that knows? Again they come feeding and they are like a blanket of connected dots, waving down onto the wild field. There the blanket ripples and moves, its edges fluttering. Then an edge lifts and, as if it were truly one thing, it billows up into the sky and wings away toward another field.

The effect of the maze here comes from the variety of movement. To the observer the individuals seem indistinguishable. One is a cruel little beak, a pair of bright eyes, tiny muscles covered with shiny feathers. In profusion they are something else, again one great thing with vague borders.

Sometimes they soar in the chilly wind as if with no purpose, as if they take part in a mystic rite. They labor into the high reaches, holding together, with no stragglers. They turn and fall in a swift glide, sweeping across the gray sky, using the wind. When they turn, the sky is darkened with their outstretched wings. They wheel and cavort in a strange unison as if exulting in the cold, gusty, empty spaces they inhabit, as if celebrating the cruel necessities of their high, bleak home. The flock expands and curls and draws together, surrenders to the wind and fights it in a single mad communion.

The insights that one may have of such matters are sporadic, now of the whole, now of the detail. One sees them as one saw fireflies along the creek in balmier weather, winking here and there in the dusk. The tiny sparks of light, always coming from an unexpected spot, add to the mystery rather than illuminate it.

I have felt it in the city, the maze of growing things, on a busy street where the carriages and buggies and commercial wagons clatter in either direction and the throngs of people go. They saunter or hurry or walk deliberately, moved by a thousand purposes, in them the clutter of crisscrossed branches and the wheeling and flutter of the blackbirds. There are partial patterns in it, yonder a factory from which people spill into the street, yonder a bridge toward which the traffic converges, these like the moisture in lowlands or the crowding for sunlight or the food in wild fields. All of it has, too, the ability to impress as a whole and raise the question whether all the people do something that none in particular does, whether they curl and cavort in any strange, purposeless unison.

The mind seeks order and imposes order. My impressions don't find a place in the patterns known by many a wiser man, but I would hope that we never shut the doors of Uterica to a poet or anyone who senses a mystery, for there seems to be kinds of truth dark to reason, so intricate that only quiet guesses might penetrate at all.

What I found out about Brother Bossereau's taking Jeannette out of the young women's barracks I found out mostly through secondhand and thirdhand gossip. He had not offered any pressing reason; he was not in the best of health and his daughter would be able to help him in one way or another; but primarily it was just a matter of his wanting her in the quarters with him, and he was her father, and he saw no reason why it should be otherwise.

Evidently, when Jeannette began to move her belongings out of the barracks, where ten other young women lived, she had considerable words with Sister Harriet Edwards. Dr. Sockwell described it as an "argument." I could imagine Miss Edwards engaging in argument with someone, for though she had dignity and good taste, she also held firm opinions. But Jeannette never seemed like a person who would engage in such an opposition with an older person. She may have pleaded for understanding. Certainly she would have felt bound to follow her father's wishes.

Anyway, the girl moved back into the room adjoining Brother Bossereau's. Rumor said that the real reason was that much immoral conduct was taking place in the slackly disciplined colony, and he wanted his daughter where he could keep a close eye on her.

All I got firsthand about it was what I heard one day

before an assembly meeting. I wanted a firewood crew to begin working full time and thought the assembly should consider it. When I got to the assembly room, Sister Edwards and Brother Adams were already there, talking, as I had found them once before.

She was saying, "But the way that York boy moons over her, I don't know whether to laugh or cry. I guess laughing is more suitable. She is just not developed as a real woman. She has no womanly nature at all that I've seen. These men, how they judge! If a female child has breasts, she's a woman!"

Brother Adams clearly blushed.

She went on. "What she needs is to be out from under the thick protective wing of her father. That's a good metaphor. Without being disrespectful, Brother Bossereau *is* rather like an old clucking mother hen. What she needs is experience and the training to respect herself as a person. Travel. Nothing would improve her like travel. That's impossible, of course, but any sensible person can understand that it's more broadening to live with other young people, where she can discuss advanced ideas, than to live cooped up with a reactionary old man.

"It's nothing short of scandalous that he insists on having her beside him all the time. Sick! He's no sicker than I am! I have pains that I don't tell the world about, back pains and others. I just don't make it public news, nor use it for an excuse.

"This is a question for the assembly to vote on, whether he can take her out of the barracks, where she is supposed to be. What is he? Some special case? He ought to set an example for the others."

She stopped talking when the others began to enter, but lifted up a sheaf of papers which I had not noticed before and placed them on the table. She sat in a kind of determined silence until most of them were seated, then, looking only at Brother Adams, she asked, "May I take up the matter at once?"

He seemed surprised, but nodded assent.

She looked at her papers and did not seem at ease as she began talking. "I have a number of things to say. In all candor, I do not believe that I have ever had a fair hearing in this assembly, and I'm sincere when I say that I mean to have it now—even if someone is offended. There are those who say that there are minimum essentials that transcend other things and others who say that certain things must wait until we are better established, but I say we have ignored essentials from the very first day, that our true goals here are not even understood except in the most superficial manner, and that certain facts cry out for expression and must be spoken."

She paused for a breath, and Dr. Valentin asked, "Mr. Chairman, what's the issue?"

"Well..."

She said, "I move that the barracks be compulsory for all unmarried females of the colony above sixteen years of age. I have the floor right now to speak on it."

All of them seemed somewhat surprised at her determination.

She went on. "I don't wish to be argumentative. I do not mean to be insulted. But I do mean to speak... and have a fair hearing. I'm sorry to say that I have decided that if I don't have a truly adequate opportunity to address this governing body, I mean to address the women of the colony. Jean Charles Bossereau does not ask permission from the assembly to speak, and neither shall I. Also, if I must, I intend to organize the women into discussion groups... if I must, that is.

"I would like to read to you some descriptive words that many writers and thinkers have used to distinguish the characters of men and women. I hope you won't be offended. Surely you've read the same things many times. Men are called tough, crude, aggressive, and nomadic; women are called gentle, helpful, refined, and pure. Men are described as cruel and selfish—witness the sly trickery of male lawyers and merchants; whereas women are said to be unselfish, to love justice, to be superior in morals. While some think that men are more logical, they admit that women are more flexible and subtle in their thinking, more quick in their understanding and perception, having a finer intuition. Men are like brutes, with hair on their faces and bodies; women are said to be more graceful of body and soul, and certain scientific investigations indicate that the female nervous system is more delicately developed."

"My God A'mighty!" Dr. Sockwell said.

She colored and continued. "There is a body of modern opinion, gaining more recognition daily, that woman is superior to man in every one of the most humane faculties. I do not maintain this. What I do say is that, in the face of many wise opinions, we should not fail to agree that woman is the equal of man—and act on that agreement as if it were really true. If we expect to make any worthwhile reform of society, how can we fail to appeal to those womanly qualities that have been recognized and try to bring them to bear?"

Dr. Valentin said, "Miss Edwards, isn't this superfluous? Don't we know your point of view? Haven't you said it or inferred it a hundred times?"

"I'm not half through," she said. "I presume you may make a statement when your time comes."

"I didn't say you were out of order. But haven't you said this a hundred times?"

"I haven't been heard once. What I have to say goes straight to the heart of socialism. And I've stated what I mean to do if I cannot get a hearing in this governing body."

Brother Bossereau was listening to her in patient silence.

Another man asked, "Are you asking that the women have half the votes in this assembly and the men have half? And you cast all the women's votes? Is that what you want?"

"I want you to listen," she said. She seemed to be holding her resolve not to be insulted. "It's not easy for me to do this. I know what some of you think. I mean to speak out anyway.

What I have to say now is the hardest of all for me. I want to try to explain something, and I use myself as an example, not because it hasn't happened to a thousand others, but because I can testify personally to the facts.

"When I was a child, I worshiped my father. I thought he could do no wrong. He was moral, philanthropic, what the world calls a good man. I worshiped him. He seemed an ideal of goodness and strength and seemed to be worthy of any devotion paid him. When I was twenty years old, he said these words to me: 'Oh, if you had only been a son!' I don't know what the words meant to him. As for me, I wished he had plunged a knife into my breast instead of saying them. This world doesn't require a man, even a good man, to understand. I was a living, breathing human being, just as he. I had feelings, just as he. His esteem would have been precious to me. But I was just a woman. This was his response to my whole being: 'If you had only been something else!'

"I don't want you to think I'm asking for sympathy. I'm trying to get you to understand how a terrible and hateful insult to the dignity and the very existence of a human being can be delivered blindly by one whom the world calls a good man.

"I attended the London antislavery convention in 1840, at great expense to myself financially, and I know that we women who went as delegates had nothing but the most altruistic motives and nothing but the sincere desire to work toward reform. Some of you know how we were received. We had to fight hard even to be seated; then we had to sit in the balcony. What was our sin? We were the wrong sex.

"I attended a teachers' convention in New York City where, though two thirds of the delegates were women, every scheduled speech was by a man. When I stood up on the floor to speak out, a number of men had the impoliteness and arrogance to get up and leave. This world is full of men who pretend they want reform, but who would rather see all the corruption continue than see women escape from the place they have assigned to them.

"At the heart of the problem is sex, or lust. I know that a woman is not expected to speak about any such thing, but you tell me why the word 'obey' is used in the standard marriage ceremony. When women are equal, they will own their own bodies. When one man attacks another man, society has a means to stop it or impose punishment. But what about the plight of the poor wife and mother who is mistreated by a drunken brute of a husband? She has no legal recourse. She belongs to him, and he may do whatever he pleases with her, no matter how cruel. The truth is that many men oppose equality for women because they are afraid it will bring restrictions on their sensual indulgences."

The members had evidently given up any thought of opposing her or stopping her. They listened in various attitudes, some slightly ill at ease, some with condescension, some seeming to study what she said, and others to study the woman herself.

"I must tell you," she said, "in all candor, that I have never heard an intelligent analysis of socialism from anyone who is a part of this colony, nothing but a superficial, almost childlike, understanding of it. The lecture which was delivered here titled 'Modern Woman and Socialist Society' did not in any sense whatever relate to the deeper meaning implied in the title. If we see no connection between public education and universal suffrage and common ownership of property and the social position of women, then I say we are playing with a large question which we do not understand. We make much of this idea of 'private' and 'public.' But what is truly private is not, and should not be, the concern of anyone else. The difficulty is that when some people who imagine themselves to be intellectuals say 'private,' they should have said 'family.' One who is against public education does not really expect private education, for no child can educate itself; what he expects is that the family will take care of it. And the problem of economic security is not handled as a private matter in the civilization you pretend to rebel against; it is a family matter. This is the heart of it: it is a family matter.

"Why not allow the family unit to take care of the security and happiness and well-being of its members? You don't like to put the question in that fashion, do you? No, I think you prefer to play on the fringe of socialism without examining it and call one another 'brother' and 'sister' without meaning anything. There is something badly wrong. The revolution which socialism requires goes deeper than most of its supporters realize, and socialism meets reaction within its own ranks from those who are not prepared to see its primary nature: it is an alteration of the family, an enlargement of the family, an extension of the family to the universal brotherhood of man."

She had at first spoken, in part, extemporaneously, but now she was reading everything she said. The papers before her were handwritten.

"Allow me to paint a hurried picture of the family. The man is at the apex and the spouse may stand in various relationships to him, but she is always an expansion or extension of him, as are the children. The nature of the wife reflects credit on the husband, and the other way round. The wife's position in the world is that of her husband. The children are extensions of them. There may also be a maiden aunt, a young married couple, a set of elderly parents in the family. If the man at the apex engages in some questionable business activity, he does it to provide for the family. If he hoards wealth, he does it to leave money to his children after he is gone, for they are an extension of him.

"Tying together this unit are a number of powerful affections, positive and negative: love, jealously, lust, possessiveness, the maternal tendency, filial respect, filial adoration, selfish pride in one's own. Compared with these affections, the universal bond is weak. The union based on these affections is the groundwork of the institution of so-called private property, which is actually family property, and it is the groundwork of every kind of selfish acquisition. Until there is some adjustment of those affections, how can it be hoped that the universal affection can unite many people in one body for the common good? Water cannot flow two directions in the same stream. The question might be presented in this manner: How large shall the hearthstone be? Shall it be large enough for one man and his spouse and his nearest natural kin, or shall it be large enough for a much greater family?

"I only ask that we examine what we are doing and cease to pretend that the problem is easy. Matrimony is called 'holy' and mother love is called 'holy.' All the relations and affections of the family have the aura of holiness about them. To examine them is blasphemy. Yet if you believe that you will establish socialism now and take up the question of woman's position at some later date, you act in blind ignorance of the deeper and most crucial involvements. You must begin the adjustment of the human affections, or you have made no beginning at all. The progress of socialism will be a history of the rising expectations of the human spirit, seeking new alliances and wider horizons.

"I appreciate your attention. If I have offended anyone, I ask your pardon. I've only said what my deepest conscience has compelled me to say."

She glanced at us awkwardly. Obviously her speech was finished.

After a moment Dr. Valentin asked, "What's the point of it?"

"I don't know what you mean."

"Do you advocate celibacy or free love or that we abolish marriage, or what?"

"I've said what I advocate. This is not easy for me, and I've chosen my words carefully and deliberately. Do you wish me to read portions of it again?"

"No, I don't think so," he said.

Brother Adams nervously tapped his fingers on the table for a moment, then asked Brother Bossereau, "Did you wish to make any comment?"

"Well, it all seems irrelevant," he said. "I have an unmarried daughter over sixteen years of age and I have no intention of placing her back in the young women's barracks. I so state in all humility and goodwill. I have no intention.

"As for blindness, I have been aware of the arguments advanced by Sister Harriet Edwards for many years and do not agree with them. I believe that communal living requires an even more guarded sexual morality than has been evident in the past."

Brother Adams asked for a voice vote on the issue of compulsion, and Harriet Edwards stubbornly, still seeming determined not to be insulted, said "Aye," but no one voted with her. Brother Adams observed that the vote did not relate to the value of the young women's barracks, but to the issue of compulsion.

I brought up my idea of the need to begin storing firewood, and the assembly did not take long in agreeing with me. That was all the business we were able to handle in that session. I had the feeling that Harriet Edwards, while doubtless disappointed at the reception of her ideas, must have achieved some satisfaction in having had her say.

I felt a kind of uneasy admiration for her, as I did for Dr. Valentin. Each of them believed strongly in his own ideas, had stated them vigorously, and had endured rejection by their colleagues, or at least a lack of acceptance. In this they were in a position similar to that of Brother Bossereau. They, as he, faced the bland, slow-moving inefficiency of the assembly and its temporary chairman and its committees, with their opinions laid embarrassingly bare; yet each of the three displayed a balance of dignity and stubbornness and willingness to continue.

That night the big rain began. It came in with a kind of squall to which we were becoming accustomed, with gusty wind and lightning and thunder. But it was not a shower that came over us and passed on. It was still raining steadily the next morning. We waited in uncertainty about when we would begin the day's work or whether we would at all. The sky was overcast with low clouds out of which came the steady rain, but I think heavier banks of clouds came in over them, for in the middle of the morning a downpour began. Water came down in huge drops, fast—poured down. It flowed in streams down the footpaths in the compound and flooded all the lower end of the village. It came in a straight sheet off the slanting roofs, splattering mud against the log walls.

The heavy rain killed any thought that we might work outside on our regular work crews. It dwindled to a drizzle, and Jim and I sat in our room or in the small leaky pavilion in front of it, listening to the constant sputters and splats of dripping water. Out in the dim light of the outdoors every dull object carried a sheen of wetness—the logs, the dead plants of our garden, the fences, farther out the dying leaves on the trees, the dry grass, the rocks, all shining without much light. Once Jim said, "What do you think he does, off wandering around, when it gets like this?"

"I don't know," I said. "I guess he finds a dry place somewhere." We hardly ever talked about Andy.

The earth had a smooth, washed look about it. The colonists moved about the village, though the drizzle continued, doing what had to be done, and the washed look disappeared. It became not clean earth but mud. By noon the village had become a mire of tracks, like a pigpen. It balled on our shoes; we kicked our feet to sling it off. Every step added more. We stopped before the doors to hunt scraping sticks, cursed,

kicked our feet against the doorsills. In a few hours the floors
of the houses were like the ground outside, a muddy mess, and
there was no escape from it. The brooms were no match for it;
we gave up and stopped trying to clean our feet, except when
the accumulated mud made walking difficult.

The rain alternated between downpour and drizzle for
seven dreary days. We had better housing now than we had
had during the long spring rain, but this dampness was chilly,
and many of us caught colds in the head. After the rain
stopped and the ground dried enough so that we could return
to our regular work, I had a feeling that the balmy days of
autumn were gone. The sun looked smaller and more distant;
the air felt wintry.

Andy had been around the quarters all day. When I came
in from work in the afternoon, I noted that a small fire had
been built in front of our door and a little lead spilled. The
tin of powder and several pounds of bullet lead that we kept
in our quarters had belonged half to me and half to one of the
employees who had left. It irritated me that Andy used it
without permission or thanks, especially in view of his constant ill temper. When I went in the door, I said, "I hope my
powder and lead lasts through the winter. I may need it for
game."

He stared at me as if I were an animal or an inanimate
object.

I waited outside the door for Jim. When he came up, I
noticed that some men were already entering the dining hall,
and I asked him, "Are you about ready to eat?"

He grinned and said, "Some young people have changed to
the last table so they'll have time to talk. So I've changed too."

"By some young people, you mean Sister Jeannette Bossereau," I said.

"That could be," he said.

At that moment Andy came out the door. He said in a

voice full of harsh feeling, but constrained, "If you were a man, you'd seduce that girl and get her pregnant and then see if King Bossereau would give his permission." He had paused only briefly as he came out the door and, as he said it, passed between us and walked toward the gate that opened toward the creek.

Jim was stunned, then angry. I saw him uncertain as to whether to run after his brother. When he turned back to me, his face was creased with a frown of puzzlement and worry. "What's wrong with him?" he asked.

I don't know whether he expected any answer, but I could only shake my head.

He pressed me. "What can we do?"

"We can take it to the assembly about his not working," I said.

Jim pondered a minute and said, "Jeannette wanted to talk to him. She thinks it's just that he doesn't understand. But who can talk to him the way he is? I told her to stay away from him."

I made up my mind that when Andy returned, we would get something settled, that we did not have to bear his contempt. And there would not be a fight where his younger brother bore all the brunt. The situation was becoming intolerable.

Music sounded from up toward the assembly room that evening, but Jim came in early. He asked me, "I don't guess you've seen Jeannette since supper, have you?"

"She wasn't with you?"

"She was but she left." In a minute he said, somewhat mournfully, "I guess her father needed her for something."

CHAPTER

14

THE next morning I was awakened by a sound without knowing what the sound was. I remember being aware that I had heard something, doubting that it was the cooks' gong which usually woke us, noting that the light was too faint for it to be time to get up. I threw back the blanket and drew on my trousers. I opened the door and saw that no light was visible from the dining hall or kitchen.

Then the sound repeated, a call from the upper end of the compound: "Jeannette!" A figure stood in front of Brother Bossereau's quarters. It was undoubtedly the French leader. He called again, urgently, "Jeannette!" All I could think of was that the girl had gone to begin work in the kitchen and that he had decided that he needed her for something and that he was making a ridiculous fool of himself, calling so that everyone could hear.

I put on my shirt and shoes. Jim was getting up. He asked, "What is it?"

"I don't know. I guess it's Brother Bossereau."

"Isn't he calling Jeannette?"

"Yes."

"Maybe . . . I could help him. Or go after her for him."

I went back out the door and he followed me, both of us

standing in uncertainty. Brother Bossereau was still alternately calling and listening. Others had come out of their doors, half dressed. Can it be possible, I thought, that he doesn't realize what a spectacle he is making?

He seemed to be dressed in a nightshirt or gown of some kind and trousers, and to be barefoot. He walked over to the door of the young women's barracks and stood there calling "Jeannette!" and was beating with his hand on the door.

Low voices buzzed among those watching all along the compound, and I heard laughter. It was clear what some of them were thinking; remembering rumors about lax morals and remembering that he had taken his daughter out of the barracks, they believed some scandal might be coming to light.

His attitude at the barracks door indicated that he did not know where his daughter was, that he was not acting from absentmindedness nor from being oblivious to opinion, but from some well-based concern. It seemed that he pounded on the door for an interminable time before it opened a few inches and he asked, "Is my daughter Jeannette inside?"

"No, of course she's not." Sister Harriet Edwards sounded annoyed.

"Do you know where she is?"

"I do not. If you will recall, she was taken out of here against my advice. I'm no longer responsible for her whereabouts."

"Are you certain she's not inside, Sister Edwards?"

"Yes. What do you want me to do? Take an oath on it?"

He turned away from the door and called out with the same urgent pleading in his voice, "Jeannette!" He began to walk across the old garden toward the dining hall.

Jim and I started toward him, as did several others at the same time. I think it had smitten the conscience of many of us at once that here might be a serious matter. He looked at those converging on him and his eyes stopped on Jim. He half begged, half demanded, "Where's Jeannette? Do you know?"

"No, sir."

"You were with her last night."

"She left. I thought she went to you."

"Then where could she possibly be?"

I asked him, "Sir, when did you see her last?"

"Yesterday. I believe she did not sleep in her bed."

There seemed to be no obvious place to look. We crowded into the dining hall and kitchen, for no reason other than the fact that he had been going in that direction, and satisfied ourselves that she was not in the building. By now the early daylight had come. Some of the crowd who were half-dressed returned to their quarters, some others joined us, some left this way or that to search erratically. We were a confused, milling group. Various people were constantly asking: "What happened?" "Did she go to live in the barracks?" "What is supposed to have happened to her?" "When was she seen last?" It occurred to me that we were a thoroughly unorganized colony, incapable of handling any emergency.

When Dr. Sockwell and Dr. Valentin had asked enough questions to know the bare facts, they began getting together the work-crew leaders to organize a search. They told each leader to find three or four of his crew, and they assigned places to search. Every room in the village was to be entered. One crew was to go down to the springhouse. When she was found, the fact was to be reported back to the compound immediately, and the kitchen gong would be sounded.

The people had mixed attitudes about it. Some thought we should eat breakfast, that the girl would show up on her own. I heard one woman say, "The child has fallen to sleep somewhere." I heard another say, "What about Indians? Has anyone seen the Indians?"

I told Dr. Sockwell that Jim and I would go out around the stock pens and the wagons. As we crossed the compound fence and proceeded to our search, Jim appeared grim. "I don't like it," he said. "She doesn't wander off like a child."

I kept thinking, "It will make sense. An hour from now we'll laugh about it." But I could not put it into meaningful words to speak to Jim.

He said, "If she left to talk to Andy, why would she stay away all night? I know her. She wouldn't do that."

"Brother Bossereau didn't know for sure that she stayed away all night," I said.

We finished our search and went back to the compound. By this time those who had gone through the buildings were reporting back to Dr. Valentin or Dr. Sockwell. All of them were seeing it as a serious mystery, and many of them talked of foul play and the Indians. The leaders were beginning to plan a far-flung search using all the colonists. I saw that Brother Bossereau had dressed and was hovering around those who did the planning but saying nothing.

Jim and I headed for the place below the stock watering hole on the creek where our two hobbled horses might be found. If the search were to be extensive, it would be well to have some men mounted. He was not talking, and by now a feeling of dread had come over me.

We angled toward the creek bottoms and were not halfway there when a man came running toward the village, one of the group which had gone to look around the springhouse. We turned to intercept him. He was a middle-aged man, running heavily. His face was contorted from shortness of breath. He did not turn toward us, but slowed to a walk and gasped out, "She's killed by the Indians!"

We went in the direction from which he had come. In the edge of the trees four men stood together, some distance from the stream itself and near a small slough which held a little water. They looked at us as we came up, but did not speak nor even point. On the ground, ten steps from them, lay the body of Jeannette Bossereau.

Jim moved a few uncertain steps toward her. My reaction to the sight was horror, but not so strong that I could not sense the tumult that was in him and wonder whether he would go to her and whether I should restrain him if he did.

The girl's clothes had been completely ripped from her except for some shredded parts that hung from her neck and one shoulder. Pieces of clothing lay in the grass as if they had been torn away in handfuls. The white curves of her body were crisscrossed with scratches as if cut by tree branches. Her neck was thrust back and to the side, one cheek down on the ground, her hair flung up and forward. The back of her head carried an ugly wound, from which the blood was so dark as to be almost black. The arm which lay half under her was broken, for it bent backward at the elbow. Some of her hair was stuck with blood onto a flat area of exposed rock behind her, so that one could imagine that her head had been pounded against it. The position of her body and limbs gave no sense of tension or relaxation, but rather of lifelessness where life had been.

The half of her face which was visible was dirty, as if it had been cruelly ground into the dirt. Dirt was in the open eye and the parted lips. I saw it clearly for only a moment, could have borne seeing it no longer than that, for all the pity of it was well contained in that small part of it: the dirt in the lips and eye.

I did not need to pull Jim away from the sight. We drew close to the other four silent men. At that moment the cook's gong clanged out in the morning air, loud even at this distance.

In the following quietness we waited. I thought that we ought to be stunned, that this was an outrage beyond any calm acceptance, and it may be that we were, yet my senses seemed keenly awake. Perhaps it was to keep my eyes and attention off the awful presence in that spot that I put them on the natural things around us: the pool of stagnant water with leaves floating on top of it, the damp washed earth at its edge with bird tracks on it, the tall dry grass in bunches with a film on it from the recent high water, a drift, made of twigs and whitened wood chunks and dead weeds, caught against the base of a tree. Up toward the east, away from the creek, the rolling land lay indistinct, shimmery, because of the difficulty of looking into the sunlight through the damp air. I noted the incongruous fact that only now was the sun coming up into the sky; the day seemed ages old.

A crowd was spilling down toward us from the village. I took off my jacket and laid it over the naked body. Another of the men did the same with his.

Dr. Sockwell came in the lead, carrying his leather satchel, trotting clumsily, disheveled from the effort of hurrying. He came up puffing and went directly to the body, knelt by it, felt the hand that lay outstretched, turned the head up a little. He rose slowly and said, still out of breath, "This girl's been dead for hours."

The crowd had gone all around, each of them wanting to see, most of them reluctant to go near. I heard remarks, usually in a hushed tone. "God, have mercy!" "They are fiends!" "The poor girl!" "She wouldn't harm a fly and look what they've done to her!" And some of the women took their children away, saying, "Here, come on; this is no sight for you!"

I found myself near Sister Harriet Edwards, who was saying, not loud but in a determined manner, "What I want to know is why something wasn't done about these Indians. In the first place, by the American authorities. But even more so, why wasn't the Indian problem given a little thought by the planners of this enterprise? They set themselves up as leaders, then bring civilized people out here to live at the mercy of savages."

The man in front of her turned quickly. I'm sure she had not known it was Dr. Valentin. He was upset. As quietly as she, but even more forcefully, he said, "The leaders set themselves up? The leaders! Damn you! You are one of the leaders!"

She froze into silence. Seeing that she did not answer, he moved away from her.

The crowd parted and drew back somewhat as Brother Bossereau came. He went and knelt beside the body of his daughter and slowly took the lifeless hand. Tenderly he brushed at the dirt on her cheek. He rolled a bit of her out-flung hair between his fingers. What repulsed some and made them stand back did not seem to deter him, but I could see that he was shaking like the broad yellow leaves of the cotton-wood trees that grew over us.

Dr. Sockwell asked some of the nearest men to get blankets and cut some poles to make a litter. About this time, when we were doing nothing but waiting, I chanced to meet the eye of Jim York, who was standing some distance away from me in the crowd. His young face was haggard, but it was his eyes that spoke, almost as clearly as if he had said it: We know something that none of these people know. What are we going to do? What in the name of God . . . ?

As a few of them took care of making a litter and moving the body to the village, others began to search for tracks. They had decided that the girl might have been attacked by one Indian or a few or a large group and hoped to find tracks that would provide clues. Of course, the crowd had already obliterated any tracks in the immediate vicinity, and the men who proceeded to the unorganized search did the same to any tracks down toward the creek. Seeing that they all remained on the near side of the stream, I waded across it alone and walked down it, examining every place that might have served for a crossing. I found the tracks of deer and bear and wild cattle and in one place those of two horses, but I knew that wild horses ran in the area, and as well as I could tell these horses did not cross but only drank. After a half mile I turned back to my starting point and followed the main branch up-stream. I knew that the chances were slim that I would find anything definite. Tracks would not prove anything, nor would the absence of tracks. Indians could have approached the village from any direction. They could have come mounted or on foot. What I wanted was to find clear horse tracks crossing, more than one, so that I could say: This could be the answer. I found nothing except a crossing a half mile upstream where the bed was white limestone and I judged a band of horsemen might have crossed without leaving tracks. As I walked back toward the village, I considered how the Indians had always been obscure and contradictory, their nature, their intentions, and thought that I had been foolish to hope they would provide any flicker of light on any dark problem.

I found Jim in our quarters, sitting with his head down in his hands. As soon as he recognized me, he asked, "What are we going to do?"

"I don't know the answer to it, Jim."

"I don't consider him my brother."

"... if he did it, you mean... If he did it."

"Who else...?"

"Just exactly who they suspect. Look, they jump to conclusions. They think they know, without a bit of proof. But you and I are doing the same thing, without a bit of proof. The first thing we think of is Andy."

He said, "Don't you know?"

"No, I don't."

"You know it," he said, not contradicting, but as if he hadn't heard me.

I didn't want to admit I even thought it. In a moment I asked him, "You think he was capable of it then?"

"Nobody could have been capable of it... not her. An animal could..." He burst out with a rush of words, as if he had a sudden compulsion to explain. "She was the most innocent person I've known. I knew her real well. We talked about everything. She was very good-hearted. I can't explain. She was the prettiest girl, but that didn't matter to me at all.

You might not believe it . . . the way I thought of her . . . I thought I would be a better man because of her. We talked about everything, but I never heard her say a mean thought."

He had to stop for a minute, then he went on. "It doesn't seem like it could be her. It's like somebody else. Her old man . . . she was loyal. She wanted things to go right for him. She was that way. I guess he'll have to give her up now. . . . One thing, he had sense enough to love her."

Suddenly he said in a kind of nervous frenzy, "Isn't it crazy? Seems like something big and awful has happened, and I want to go and find Jeannette and talk to her about it!"

None of the colonists seemed to be doing my work, so I sat an hour with him. I tried to get him to agree to a few things: first, that we actually did not know what had happened; second, that the things we knew upon which we based our suspicions would be difficult to explain, therefore we should not go to the colony leaders immediately with any information or charge. If Andy returned, we should not deal with him separately, but both of us together confront him and demand any explanation or denials he could make; then, unless he could convince us that he was innocent, we could forcibly take him before the colony leaders.

Even as I urged these agreements, I was not sure that I was right. It was not only true that Jim was not considering Andy as his brother; the fact was that he was little concerned with the justice of anything that might be done now, rather he was overwhelmed with what had already been irretrievably done, this in spite of the fact that he did not moan and weep and agonize. The truth was that he only halfway agreed with me; he also halfway did not hear me. As for myself, I took different trains of thought and arrived at contradictory destinations. Andy's frustrations and his cruelty in the fight I had witnessed, and his vulgar suggestion of the night before and his absence did not necessarily add up to murder. What added up to murder were certain brief, illogical, unexplainable events, such as when I said something about the powder and lead and he said nothing, but looked at me as if I were an ass braying. I think my desire not to condemn too hastily came from the fact that the logical evidence was circumstantial and from a particular consideration of capability: that the easy-going, hard-working, friendly man I had once known could not possibly have changed so much, even though he seemed to; but the Indians, those obscure, unexplainable creatures—who knew what senseless mayhem or murder or rape or torture they were capable of doing?

We buried the girl on a ridge a quarter mile south of the village by a lone oak tree. They had pulled boards out of the floor of the laundry to make a coffin. Brother Adams, the Unitarian, read at length out of the Old Testament. His voice was monotonous, but it had sincerity and dignity in it, and the reading seemed proper.

Brother Bossereau stood through it, somehow isolated from the rest of us. From where I stood at the edge of the crowd, he appeared composed, standing stiff, as if it were a duty. The autumn light reflected from his bare forehead, and the glint from his spectacles hid his eyes. Many were watching him. I heard one whisper, "He's taking it well." And another, "He simply worshiped her, you know."

I could see all of our village from where I stood, the rectangle of buildings large and small tied together with the crooked worm fence, the whole laid over a rise and down it into the nearly flat land toward the creek. Outside the enclosure stood stumps of different heights, the trees having been cut by different workmen, interspersed with standing trees that were too small for logs or too crooked for rails, and all about on the ground chips and trimmings of branches and vines that were not substantial enough for fuel. Through this disorder paths wound away from the compound in every direction. In the buildings the logs were mixed sizes. Some of the ridge lines were crooked. I think the crudity of it all had been more acceptable as long as the green leaves held; it seemed evidence of man's good intentions. Now, in the bare autumn landscape, it looked messy, also lonely.

The ceremony was over and we trooped back to the village before noontime. Three families, all Germans, had packed their belongings that morning into one wagon and they set out east immediately. They had given no reason for their determination to leave us except that it was for the good of the children, of which they had a dozen or more. They believed in the colony and wished us good luck, but they could not stay.

That evening Dr. Sockwell asked me to take a tray of food to Brother Bossereau, who had not eaten enough during the past two days. "He likes you," the doctor said. "Just take it in to him." It was the same uninviting food that the rest of us had eaten except for a glass of sweet milk. One of the cooks spread a small cloth over the tray and I took it to Brother Bossereau in his quarters.

He asked me to come in and I found him at his table with notebook and pen and ink before him. I set the tray on the table and told him he had doctor's orders to eat it all. He pushed his chair back a little.

"Look at my hand, Brother Langly," he said. He ignored the food and held out his hand and looked at it with a small, peculiar smile. "It trembles so that I cannot write and so it has been for these two days. I question whether my hand and my heart will ever again cease to tremble."

His eyes shone intensely at me as he went on. "If I put my head down on my arms, I can hear her quiet step and her pure voice, even feel her gentle touch on my shoulder. But it intrudes—her bloody, ravished body! And the things that attend it—the anguish, the revulsion she must have felt! Is nothing sacred? Will iniquity permit no innocent virtue to exist? She asked so little of life!

"And the fiends still exist! Still breathe and think! And remember! I would hope their consciences would torment them every day of their lives, except that they can have no consciences, having been capable of destroying the most beautiful and pure and virtuous creature they ever met. Why can some crude men not allow the beautiful and pure to exist? I keep demanding it of God. Why? I wish there were a literal hell where they might be put to suffer physical torment throughout a literal eternity."

I pitied him that he had this compulsion to talk about it.

"The days are so uncertain now," he said. "When she went out of this room and was placed in that grave, how much the world altered! How it changed its hue! How questionable people came to appear! Why build Uterica now? For whom should I build it? You see, a time of judgment has come for me. I ask, 'What's the use?' and fate asks, 'Did you ever have an impersonal love for humanity and truly desire to aid humanity?' I make a feeble answer, 'Yes.' 'Did you really, though?' I answer, 'Yes.' It's a true answer. God knows it's true. But fate says, 'You are only Jean Charles Bossereau; take Jean Charles Bossereau and crush him and damn him and forget him, then Uterica means still the same. It is as bright as before. The people are what they have ever been.' What a puny instrument I seem now!

"When our plans are realized, when the colony is established, when children yet unborn are reaping the harvest, they must be made to comprehend what the price has been. They will not appreciate what they are heirs to unless they know this black page. They ought to worship at her grave as at a shrine, not to the rational and the competent in our efforts, but to the anguish that has gone hand in hand with what we have done.

"I will not have a young thought again nor expect any joy, but we will not be defeated by it. There is a kind of futility, you see, and it is the most difficult barrier. It is the great fight, I think. Fate has decreed that we were not to benefit from our labors, but were to face a tasteless, dry life, bereft of any comfort. It's a tragic test. I must remain aware. I am desperate to do that. I am no Moses—I comprehend it better today than before—but the example is there: he who led them to the Promised Land was not permitted to enter and taste the fruits. I mean to lead them in her memory and in justification of her faith in me.

"If I could just forget her dead eyes. How she must have screamed and implored! Cried out for my help! I could forget the blood on her white skin, but all of it seems to be contained in my image of her eyes. They are what they were years ago, clear and trusting and wondering, and at the same time they are like they must have been when she felt that savage attack, and still at the same time they are like the round eyes of a fish staring out of a fish head. Langly, the world shouldn't be the way it is! It shouldn't be this way! It's not right for it to be this way!"

He became silent but was not subsided. I waited a while and then asked him gently to eat the supper I had brought. He told me that it was good of me to listen to him and promised to eat the food.

As I went out, he said, seemingly as much to himself as to me, "Many of us desire to play Socrates, but few of us want to drink the hemlock."

Some of his words—"I mean to lead them"—had seemed almost as if he had forgotten that we had taken the position of director away from him. It may have been a lapse of memory, or a slip of the tongue, or it may have been a kind of desperate

intention to continue to feel responsibility for Uterica whether
he had any authority or not.

Out of my own emotional upheaval I wrote this rather dis-
connected essay in my journal:

On Cruel Intrusions

The death of Jeannette could never be the matter of
poetry for me. The thing itself could not be. I could not
dwell on it. It is like a wound that is painful, surprising, a
quick hurt, less immediately disturbing because it was not
anticipated. I contradict myself here, for in the pages of this
journal I have put down words that point to this foul murder.
The essence of them is that they are words. They are in the
world of words. There is a thing named "murder," and the
name and the thing are not the same. The name is a weak sign
and the thing a bare, brazen outrage beyond words. If a man
say to another, "You are going to be surprised," and the second man later is, there is no falsehood in it, but there is contradiction aplenty. Surprise cannot be anticipated, and yet it
was. Somehow it is a matter of there being two worlds, with
one trying diligently to merge with the other and always
finding that the rules are not the same. So, there is the wound
I speak of which is surprising and comes to hurt worse after
the first day. It becomes swollen and throbbing and deep,
spreading its effect over the whole body, becoming less a
wound than a sickness with a center where the sharp pain
first was. Then, if probed, it is agonizing, if agitated, it is
unbearable. To tell the truth, while I want to see the whole
range of human life as much as anyone, I wish I had not seen
her lying there.

But there is a kind of thing that happens, which should not
happen, and this is one of them. The kind is not defined by
its badness, but by the fact that it does not follow. (Here is
the contradiction again, but more of that later.) It is an irresponsible kind of event, so important as to be devastating,
yet not belonging, an illegitimate event falling down out of

nowhere, connected to nothing, intruding itself into a procession where it has no right, cruelly disrupting what has a right to be. If I can pursue this idea in the abstract, skirting the unbearable instigator of my thinking (Is thought a response to a wound?) working in the general and metaphorical, I might be led to some conclusion to ease my mind.

It is amazing what ideas, akin to these, come to one out of a less tragic context. We do not play gambling games here, but I remember well when I learned to play poker, or rather when I played poker and thought I had learned it, but had to learn more and more and more. A fascinating game of chance, possibility, probability, these mixed with the personalities of fellow players, mingled with a few known certainties, stirred up with expectation. It doesn't take long to learn the principles of the game, and it takes even less time to learn that those principles are superficial, erroneous. Let Lady Luck repeat some quirk three times dramatically before a learner, and he induces a principle, and it will cost him dearly. I might have learned most of what there is to know about poker during one long night if I had had a Solomon to stand behind my chair and say, "Remember that," "Forget that," "Remember that," "Ignore that." But there is no Solomon, only the Lady. She is the enemy of the learner. Let him be taught by experience to play cautiously, and, sure enough, some bold coup will strike him on his blind innocent side; let him reply in kind to this new experience, and he has left the other flank exposed.

The maddening thing seems to be that there is really a science to it. A person somehow learns all the exceptions to the exceptions so that he loses forty stakes and wins sixty, or contrives that the pots he wins, though less in number, are larger in value. It is not really a game of chance.

An old retired soldier played with us. He sometimes tended bar in a place his brother-in-law owned, but most of the time he played poker or occupied himself trying to arrange a game. He did not lose. If the game was short, he might break even; if long, he had always won, at least a little. I had progressed in my learning to this realization: there is a science or a skill and then there is luck. If one could learn the skill, then he is buffeted this way and that by luck, and these buffetings become equalized, and skill prevails. But playing with that old soldier—I could not do as well as he regardless of my theories—I began to have the dubious but persistent thought that something more was involved than skillful mastery of the principles and the unpredictable, disinterested Lady. Could the old soldier know some third factor? A way of influencing her? Perhaps he could grasp something subtle about her *modus operandi*. Maybe long-enough experience revealed an entirely new level of principles. The old man did not talk except for simple old-man's joking now and then, but I was interested in ideas, not so much to become a better gambler, for I truthfully played only for sport, but because the factors involved seemed to me suggestive of some unique importance. The opportunity came when he and I sat alone waiting for the other players, and I asked him straight out: "What, in your opinion, is the secret of it?" He frowned at me as if my question were an unexpected insult and opened his mouth and said, "Play to win." Naturally, I mentally accused him of holding back for his own profit. After that I used to look at him and wonder what shrewd ideas were contained in his wrinkled old head. Maybe there was nothing in it. I found out that he could neither read nor write. I don't give too much weight to his always winning. He could have been cheating us some way.

But there is an example in this commonplace game, though I am unsure of the moral or lesson. One might by right reason and hard-gained knowledge build up a stack of benefits, then lose it to chance.

It is not that I see no chain of cause and effect leading to the death of Jeannette Bossereau. I see the canker growing in Andy, even see that her own father made his small contribution. The total effect simply does not follow. It would be all right, in the sense that some private tragedy is sure to come, sometimes even a repulsive tragedy, if it were actually private. But this strikes at the heart of Uterica. It would be all right, in the sense that sad matters have their own merciless propriety, if, the corn having failed because socialists are poor farmers, she had slowly starved to death. But this strikes at the deepest reasoning and sentiment that produced Uterica.

Her death pushes something over us. It is no passive thing, but a penetrating thing. Her death is like a black light that sends its fingers into all the cracks and hidden places of our village, that bathes us with darkness, that blackens our best hopes.

It is as if a jealous god had seen us coming back to Eden and had scorned to oppose us in any fair and just manner, but with vast contempt had struck us in our most tender and vulnerable spot—a god like Lady Luck, who in some subtle way might conform to higher principles that are not to be discovered in human experience. It is enough to make one turn back toward superstition. I think the understanding of the colony is this, for all of us, I mean: We are crippled. What blow could have done it more surely and more beyond argument? So there is a question implied: Can we do it now? All that we do will have that darker cast, and behind it that question, Now?—meaning after Jeannette.

I cannot probe it any farther. There might be a time in the future, when the black light recedes.

CHAPTER

15

WINTER came on erratically. One afternoon a man might be comfortable outside in shirt sleeves, even find himself sweating under hard work; that night a freezing wind would whistle down out of the north, cutting through the cracks of our buildings, penetrating every kind of clothing, and putting us all to shivering. Our thin summer blood had no chance to slowly thicken. We suffered, even though the cold was not enough to make more than a thin rim of ice on the water in the creek.

We hauled four wagonloads of good clay from a hillside a mile from the village. This we pulverized and mixed, in a metal vat, with water and dry grass to make chinking for the buildings. At the same time we began to work on three additional fireplaces. Up until now it had been difficult to imagine a cold winter in this part of the country. The piercing north wind convinced us. I persuaded the leaders of the colony that we also needed log windbreaks on the north sides of the stock pens.

We dug about half of our turnip crop. They filled a large room which had been the sleeping quarters of a family that deserted us; we piled them in to the rafters and had to board up the bottom half of the door to keep them from spilling out.

We believed that those we left in the ground would keep, at least until the ground froze.

I don't know whether the young people of the colony continued the parties and outings which they had once held several times a week. At least Jim York took no part in them. He did his work wherever he was assigned and did not talk much. He was not sullen nor difficult to live with. He would answer questions politely, but never joked. Sometimes it seemed to me when he was sitting silently in our quarters that he was waiting for something, not for anything conclusive, but just waiting, perhaps for his brother to return.

Dr. Valentin asked me about Brother Andrew York, why it was that he was not taking care of his duties with the stock. I'm afraid that I did not provide much satisfaction; I refused to try to offer any explanation. He was simply absent.

"Did he take any colony property with him?" the doctor asked.

"Not that I know of," I said.

"When he returns, will you please inform the assembly? Surely we must stop this kind of irresponsibility."

I told him that I would.

One afternoon while I was supervising the building of the windbreaks for the livestock, Dr. Sockwell came down to talk to me. Bundled up in a heavy jacket, he looked like a bear walking on its hind legs, except that his nose and cheeks were red from the chill wind. We stepped aside out of the hearing of the others.

"I don't suppose," he said, "that you have any brandy, do you? . . . or any such spirits? Our medical supplies are all gone, now when we need them most with this foul weather."

"No, sir, I don't know of any."

"I was afraid of that," he said. "Mainly, I wanted to ask you to come to the assembly. I've talked to you about it before. I wish you would attend every time it meets . . . and vote."

"What's happening?"

"You know about the guard?"

I'd heard that a guard was to be formed. Evidently Dr. Valentin had now had his way about it. I remembered that Mr. Finch had once said that something of the kind was needed. "Not much," I said. "I thought it might be a good idea."

"It may be necessary, but it may be dangerous too. Langly, you can't be a leader, as you certainly are, and be nonpolitical. You're a member of the assembly whether you like it or not. They will accept you and accept your vote, which means that you have a responsibility, it seems to me."

It occurred to me in a flash that I was carrying a responsibility, that of Andrew York, and that here was a man with whom I wouldn't be afraid to share it. At the moment I could see no reason why I should not. I thought, with a sense of irony, that if he were going to saddle me with a new concern, I might surprise him with one he had not dreamed of.

"What about the guard?" I asked. "What's happening?"

"Well, what Valentin said a while ago stuck in my mind. About Deveraux. About the guard and Deveraux. They're selecting a guard of twenty men. They figure we have twenty guns in the colony, so one guard for each. But it's to be a new organization of the whole colony, as Valentin planned long ago. Each guard is at the head of a squad, and he's responsible for their safety in an emergency, or he tells them what to do. Some guard will have Deveraux in his squad. Valentin says it will be up to the guard to shut him up."

"Do you object to that?" I asked him.

"Not especially. The man's a troublemaker. It seems he's telling people they don't have to obey the instructions of the assembly. But it sets me thinking. The guard is to be not only a militia against the Indians, but also a police force and a political arm."

"Does Valentin have charge of the guard?"

"I guess so. Supposedly it's under the assembly, but a group can't take care of the details. The only job Valentin has is treasurer, and there's no money."

In the back of my mind I was wondering whether now was the time to tell him about Andrew York.

He went on: "Dammit, Langly, we are bound to have some changes here. That's my point. If that idiot Valentin wasn't about halfway right, he wouldn't be dangerous. We were silly to come out here the way we did, expecting everything to be simple. We're waking up, some of us are. But what's the next move? We are going to make decisions during the next few months that will determine our future, maybe our success or failure. You know a lot about the work here, and I say we need your point of view in the assembly."

"I don't exactly enjoy that kind of thing," I said.

"Who does?"

"Well, I'll attend," I said, "but I've got something to talk to you about. Could you come to my quarters this evening?"

"What's wrong with right now?"

"I want to talk to someone else about it first."

"Sounds like another damned intrigue to me," he said, but he agreed to be there. As he started away, he asked, "You said you don't know of anybody who might have any brandy?"

"No, sir."

"That idiot Valentin won't send for any. Says we can't afford it."

That evening I asked Jim York for permission to take the doctor into our confidence. I thought it an excellent idea myself; it would be a relief to have someone share it. But Jim said, "If you think you ought to." It was not that he felt reluctant, but rather that he had not been concerned with the ethics of keeping it secret. When Dr. Sockwell came around, we were sitting in front of the room, but Jim rose and went inside.

"I suppose it's a medical problem," the doctor said.

"No, sir, it's not," I said. "Let me try to start at the beginning, even though it may not seem important, and when I get to the end, you can draw your own conclusions."

He took a seat on the keg Jim had vacated, puffed his pipe, and eyed me with skepticism.

I told him a little about the background of the York brothers and then told him briefly every event I had seen that might relate to the question, being as factual as I could, not inserting my own opinion except where it was necessary to describe Andy's manner. It took the better part of an hour and I ended by telling Andy's words the last time I had seen him, the evening before the girl was found dead. The doctor followed my words with a deep frown.

"What do you think?" I asked him.

"I'm surprised, to say the least. Surprised that I had no idea of any such possibility."

After a moment he said, "The implications are clear enough."

"Was the girl raped?" I asked.

"I don't know. Her clothes were torn off, as you saw. It would hardly have been incidental."

"What do you say? Did he kill her?"

"Look here, this isn't some kind of hypothetical case, is it? Some kind of peculiar joke on your part?"

"No, sir, it's precisely true. As well as I can tell it. Do you think Andy killed her?"

He mused, "It's anybody's guess the way frustration and jealousy and loyalty, such things, may twist together to cause an act. The human mentality is not so simple as we sometimes assume. It occurred to me that Bossereau himself and the girl lived in an unhealthy relationship, about as near incest as two people can come, and that without suspecting anything about it. But I have no right to speculate about that."

"Do you think Andy did it?"

"Yes, accepting all you say, I think he did. But I would hardly convict him on the evidence I have."

"Does the assembly have a right to know?"

He pondered a minute and said, "Well, I'll ask you this: If we knew that young Andrew York did it, would you say then that the Indians are harmless?"

"No, sir. I know very little about the Indians, but I certainly wouldn't say that those out there now are harmless."

"Then from a practical standpoint we still need the guard."

"How about from the ethical standpoint? Do you and I and Jim have the right to withhold this from the assembly?"

"I'm inclined to say No," he said. "Who am I—who are you—to judge these matters privately? We ought to have some institution we can trust to handle these things. But I'm not at all sure that the assembly is such an institution. As I said this afternoon, we've got considerable adjustment to make in this colony."

We agreed finally, as I had with Jim, that the only way possible to get any conclusive evidence would be to wait until Andy returned and charge him with the crime and see what he answered. We would put off taking it to the assembly until that time.

The next morning I came back to my quarters after breakfast and as I was going out again to start to work Dr. Valentin approached. Two men carrying rifles walked behind him.

"Good morning," he said. "I have come for your rifle."

"My rifle?" I asked stupidly.

"Yes. If you will bring it to me, please."

"I don't understand." The truth was that I understood perfectly well but simply had not foreseen this eventuality.

"I fear that you are neglecting the notices on the bulletin board," he said with his humorless smile. "The assembly requires all firearms to be handed over at this time for use by the guard."

It occurred to me that he might not have expected to see me here, nor to ask me about it, but might have intended to enter without my permission and take the gun. I could not forget the search he had led, and I felt irritation. "Dr. Valentin," I said, "I am a member of the assembly, as you are, and I will account to them for the rifle this afternoon."

"That is not the issue," he said. "Every person must cooperate—unless you wish to be a member of the guard."

"I've been urged to attend the assembly regularly," I said, "and I intend to do so. I'll account to them today." I walked away from him. He could hardly fail to get my meaning, that if he entered my quarters and took the gun, I would make an issue of it. I did not look back but was pleased to find later that he had not taken it.

After the noon meal I went to the assembly meeting room and found Brother Adams trying to build a fire in the fireplace with punk and flint. I carried a shovelful of coals from the kitchen to help him and we soon had a roaring fire, but the flue did not draw properly, and frequently a puff of smoke licked out into the room. Brother Adams had found out before that it helped to leave the door ajar; we found it hard to do so as long as assemblymen were straggling in, but when they were all present, we propped it with a stick of wood.

Deveraux was present. I sensed that he had surprised most of them; they kept glancing at him. I believe that he had not attended a meeting since the one back in the summer. His hard, youthful face was an enigma.

They were finding seats. Harriet Edwards said, "It seems that we have our choice; we may sit down there and freeze, or sit over here and roast our backs and suffocate from the smoke." Several of the men chuckled and agreed.

She said to Brother Adams, "I thought we were going to have the fireplace cleaned out."

"It seems that it's not obstructed," he said. "I don't know

what it is. It doesn't draw right." He looked around the table, uncertain as to whether any other comments about the fireplace were forthcoming, a meek man for one who was supposed to be the chairman.

Brother Bossereau, looking haggard but alert, said quietly to the acting chairman, "I found Brother Deveraux discussing the problems of the colony with a group yesterday, and I took the liberty of inviting him to meet with us today."

Deveraux laughed. "Discussing? Inviting? *Pommade!* There's some of your hypocrisy. You gabble and whine and never say what you intend. He found me protesting and arguing. And I didn't attend to discuss; I came to deliver a message."

They were listening but did not react with the shock which I believe he expected.

He said rather slowly and plainly, "We don't swallow the *merde* of this guard."

Dr. Valentin asked, "What do you mean by 'we'?"

"That's what I mean. We won't permit it."

"Who is 'we'?"

"We, the people. Who in the hell do you think?"

"That's interesting. The assembly has presumed that we represent the people."

"Yes, it is! That's interesting, for certain!" He reared back in his chair and looked around at us. "Suppose you just retreat a little and regard the matter. Who in the hell ever gave you authority over the people?"

Brother Adams said, "I believe we serve by common consent," but Deveraux paid no attention.

"You possess the minds of goddamned petit-bourgeois officials. The assembly, so called, and work leaders, so called, are insult enough. We can slightly bear their meddling and blundering. But this guard we will not accept. Next you will order us when to go to bed, when to get up, when to go relieve ourselves. We came to this place to avoid regimentation, not to have old fools restrict us tighter than ever."

Dr. Valentin said, "Young man, do you realize how much contempt you are showing for this body and how seditious your talk has been ever since we established this colony?" He did not seem to be so much arguing as baiting the younger man.

"I certainly do. You receive the message. I have sufficient contempt for this body. You are soft, too timid to do the things you set out to do in the first place. When will you learn the simple principle: Don't manipulate us? You set up two or three institutions and they fail, so you proceed to set up a dozen more. Are you all so saturated with desire for power that you can't learn a thing so simple? Don't manipulate us! Goddammit! Don't manipulate us!"

Dr. Valentin asked, "Would you be willing to become a regular member of the assembly and keep your mouth shut outside of this room?"

Deveraux stared at him and laughed. *"Nom de Dieu!* Keep my mouth shut? I would be willing to burn this building and then all the assemblymen might attend their own business."

At this point Dr. Valentin rose and deliberately walked out. Deveraux was taken aback, but seemed to think it merely a rude act. He went on:

"You are not revolutionary, nor socialist! Every one of you tries desperately to return to the old methods, the old rules, the old morals, the old standards. You smell with old ideas, and now you have the fantastic idea that you are suitable to lead us. I would propose for the man who suggested the guard, he be shot between the eyes and then he be asked whether he has more suggestions for taking the people's liberty."

He continued in this vein for five minutes. I kept searching in his harangue for some proposal he might make or some concession he might demand, but found none. He was amazingly convinced of his own rightness, but his purpose seemed only to insult his listeners. Then Dr. Valentin jerked open the door and reentered, followed by two men carrying rifles.

The doctor pointed and said, "Don't let this man leave the room until you have orders."

I think most of us were not surprised, but Deveraux was. He said, "So this is it! Now you reveal your colors!"

The doctor said, "With the concurrence of the assembly, I propose to lock this man up."

None of them said anything. Brother Adams looked around at us, seemed uncertain whether to take a vote or ask for comments.

Dr. Valentin said, "Take him and put him in the room I showed you."

One of the guards, a red-faced German, said, "What if he resists?"

"Why do you have guns?" Dr. Valentin said. "Why are there two of you? Use whatever force you need to use. Take him out of here."

They took him, one on each arm. He did not resist but yelled at us, "I've been in jail before!" And again, as they went out the door, "I've been in jail before!"

After Dr. Valentin had resumed his seat, Brother Adams ventured, "To lock him up . . . I don't suppose it would violate our principle of no locks on any door?"

Dr. Valentin said dryly, "I don't see how that applies, but we don't have a lock. We'll put a bar across the outside of the door."

They took up the question of what to do about Deveraux, and all agreed that his insolence had been tolerated too long already; he must be kept restrained. Brother Bossereau said that the man was sincere but completely unreasonable. They agreed that it did not matter whether Deveraux deserved punishment, or whether his jailing amounted to punishment; the morale of the colonists was so crucial and he was such a threat to it that he must be restrained.

Dr. Sockwell said, "I don't like the guard. This handling of Deveraux is necessary and I agree to it, but we're setting up a dangerous system, and we'd better be alert to the possibilities."

"Perhaps you would explain that," Dr. Valentin said. "In fact, I insist that you explain it. You are very fond of making these insinuations."

"It's an instrument of force. We're putting too much force in the hands of one man."

"What is your alternative?"

"I merely say, my dear Doctor, that we need to be on the alert. You already had it decided. You already knew what you were going to do to Deveraux before he came in here today."

"Which is absolutely necessary for efficiency. I hereby suggest that you take control of the guard. Right now. Take it and do the things that must be done. We have allowed that anarchist to subvert this colony for months. Now, do you wish to head the guard, or not? I presume you trust yourself to direct all that force."

It seemed ludicrous to consider Dr. Sockwell, grizzled and sloppy as he was, as the head of such a force. He said, "I don't have time. I've handled the problems of drinking water and sanitation and all the sickness."

"If you didn't go around half inebriated all the time, perhaps you could take care of more duties."

"Well, you have medical training. Perhaps if you took some responsibility for the health of these people, I would have more time for other duties."

"Anyone here may assume the command of the guard with my blessings. I only wish to be free from your snide insinuations."

It was obvious that they were merely exchanging insults and that it would lead nowhere.

A bit later I addressed my problem about my rifle to Brother

Adams. I said that I didn't need any training in its use, that I would be available to obey the orders of the assembly in any emergency, and that I might find the chance to shoot some game for the kitchen, as I had already done several times; therefore, if there were no objections, I would keep the gun in my own possession. No one objected. I had the feeling that Dr. Valentin was satisfied that he was accepted as the head of the guard and did not wish to have any further argument about it in the assembly.

We discussed a rumor that another family was considering leaving the colony and going east. It was felt that we would eventually have a great influx of people desiring to join us, but that we could hardly afford to lose further oxen or wagons or supplies at this time. We passed a resolution stating that we had all joined together voluntarily to practice the sharing of property, therefore all property on colony land belonged to Uterica itself, and anyone who quit us might take nothing with him but the clothes on his back. To this we added the ruling that no one should be sent on a mission to Jones' Mill unless he left members of his immediate family behind. This latter stipulation we would keep secret, for though it seemed a necessary precaution, we did not want to insult colonists by showing a lack of trust in them.

In all the discussion Brother Bossereau took a humble part. They were much aware of him, ready to defer to him, but he did not clearly assert himself. If, when he had unburdened himself to me by saying things such as, "Why should I build Uterica now? ... I will lead them in her memory," if he had forgotten for the moment that he was no longer the director of the colony, he remembered it now. But I think that he had never forgotten it at all, that such words referred to the fact that in some peculiar sense he was our leader regardless of what we did. His humility was not so simple as it appeared at first glance, not that of a defeated man, but a kind of determined deference.

After the assembly had adjourned, I saw one of the guards sitting in front of the door at the end of the long building where Jim York and I had our quarters. They had put Deveraux in the room vacated by one of the families which left us.

The man was not so easily subdued as we had thought in the assembly that he could be. We kept him in the prison room a week; then two guards, at Dr. Valentin's orders, took him a mile east and turned him loose with a warning not to return to the colony but make his way eastward the best he was able. Deveraux laughed at the warning and returned straight to the village behind the guards. Then Dr. Valentin had the guards forge a leg iron and chain the man to a log at the corner of the building, outside of the room they had chosen for a jail. Here they kept him day and night at the mercy of the winter air, with a couple of blankets and a fire on the ground in front of him. Sometimes during the day he dozed, wrapped in his blankets, leaning against the log wall; but he would wake up to curse any colony leader that passed and sometimes would scream to the guards to bring more wood for his fire.

There was sympathy for him among the assemblymen, but at the same time they thought he had brought things on himself. As for the appearance it made before all the colony members, we had no doubt that all of them had discovered what an unreasonable troublemaker he was. After he had been held outside three days and nights, Dr. Valentin had the leg iron removed and had him placed back inside the prison. We did not intend that he should run loose in the village anymore.

One frosty morning the sheepherder and the boys who helped him went to the pen to drive out their charges and discovered wool and blood on the fence and scattered out across the prairie. They came after me. Some of them had already blamed it on the Indians, but I found tracks which clearly showed that the sheep had been attacked by a pack of wolves.

Sheep had been killed inside the pen, then dragged, in pieces or whole, under the fence, through it, and even over it. Hooves, bones, heads, wool, and marks where sheep had been dragged could be seen a quarter of a mile beyond the pen. I estimated that six or eight had been eaten, by probably twice that many wolves. One sheep lay dead in the pen; nine others were maimed.

I got the crew which did the butchering to catch and tie those which were injured. Though we did not usually kill so many at one time, it seemed best to save what we could, and the meat would keep in the cold weather. The rest of the flock we counted carefully as we released them for their daily grazing. There were two hundred and fifty-five adult sheep. I reported this number to Dr. Valentin, who was attempting to keep an accurate inventory of colony property, and also mentioned to him that six or eight had been eaten by the wolves.

After lunch that day I saw Dr. Valentin with a notebook in his hand, talking in an animated manner with one of the butchers. The doctor gestured wildly, and it was obvious that he was dissatisfied with the conversation. He gave some stern instructions or warnings to the butcher, pointing his finger in the man's face, then strode away.

He was not at the assembly meeting when it began. We engaged in tentative long-range planning in the areas of irrigation, factories, and publishing. The latter proved of particular interest to several members, who believed that when we were able to purchase printing equipment we might produce a weekly newspaper or journal, to be distributed widely over the country, which might be a cultural asset as well as profitable. Sister Edwards believed that publishing, at least on a small scale, should be the next colony project after a school was established. She was discussing the matter when Dr. Valentin entered.

He jerked the door closed with a bang, which through

some unexplainable chain of reaction caused the fire to flare up, then spout a puff of smoke into the room. He took his seat, threw the notebooks he carried onto the table in front of himself, and frowned at us through the smoke.

Sister Edwards finished what she was saying without much enthusiasm. Brother Adams said, "We've been considering some of the possible industries in the years to come."

"You're talking nonsense," Dr. Valentin said. "You'd better talk about the next few months to come. This place is disintegrating, rotting, falling apart! Gentlemen, we are on the clear route to failure!"

We waited for him to explain his unpleasant statements.

"Most flocks increase," he said. "Ours decrease. On February the fourth we bought eighteen milk cows and one bull. The bull was killed and two cows ran off. Now we have fifteen milk cows. Eighteen minus two leaves fifteen. No one knows where the other cow is. It's no one's business to know.

"No one knows how many chickens the Indians stole and how many they traded for and how many chickens ran away. Perhaps it's of no consequence, for no one knows how many we had to start with.

"Presumably we started with three hundred and two adult sheep. The butcher told me that we are eating these filthy creatures at the rate of four per week. I have the estimate that the wolves got six or eight last night. Figuring seven, my books show that we have two hundred and sixty-four as of now. But do you suppose we have that many? Uterica? No. We have nine less. Where are the nine sheep? No one knows. Now the idiot butcher tells me that sometimes he butchers two sheep on Monday and three on Thursday. That makes four a week!"

One could see that Dr. Valentin's anger did not lessen as he spoke. He slapped his hand on the notebooks and glared at us.

"This kind of mathematics is destroying us! Two plus two

does not make approximately four. It makes exactly four!"

No one said anything for a minute, then Dr. Sockwell asked, "Are you concerned about our flocks' decreasing or about the difficulty of bookkeeping?"

"Both! How can we possibly control anything if we cannot keep account of our property? This is an example of our slack, irresponsible methods. We need discipline!"

"Pardon me," I said. "I estimated that six or eight sheep were killed last night, but it's unreliable. I could be wrong. Perhaps a more official estimate might be made." I rather hoped that Dr. Valentin would take a delegation out and try to count heads and bones in the area south of the sheep pen and find out how difficult it was.

Brother Adams talked about the missing sheep in a worried, undecided manner a few minutes, then proposed that we resolve that the wolves had killed sixteen sheep and that they should be so accounted for. There were no objections. Dr. Valentin seemed to accept it as not particularly reasonable but the only way he could balance his books.

We set up a plan to guard the sheep through every night. This would involve a schedule of men to stay at the pen, two at a time, and the building of a shelter with one open side, wherein would be kept a fire to warm the men and frighten away the wolves. With this sheep guard and the regular guards, the work of herding, hauling wood, chopping wood, and hauling water, and with the slowly progressing job of winter plowing, no kind of new work project or construction would be possible. The winter and the land and the details of mere living would keep all our workers busy.

CHAPTER

16

IT came to the point where all our meals were the same—turnip-mutton stew—even for breakfast. There was nothing else. Our cows were drying up, and the three or four gallons of milk they gave daily was taken by Dr. Sockwell for the sick.

A person could imagine his meal before he went to the dining hall, close his eyes and smell it, even taste it—the brown chunks of cooked turnip with their bitter tang, the watery soup with a sprinkling of rye or millet in it and globules of yellow tallow, which would harden to a greasy coating on a spoon, the stringy pieces of boiled mutton, gamy and strong. Sometimes he would imagine it beforehand and would feel such disgust that he could not go at all. Or, going against his will, believing that he must keep up his strength, he might find his stomach turned.

The cooks defended it at first, until, eating it themselves, they could no longer. After that I think they did not try to do their best. One could find pieces of wool in it, also grit, also various suspicious-looking, unidentifiable bits. People stopped saying, "At least it's nourishing." It was impossible to feel any kind of gratitude about the concoction.

It seemed that a new north wind came down upon us every

week, as chill as if it blew off the ice fields of the arctic. Sometimes it came in with fine freezing rain or sleet, and the sky
would be full of broken, scurrying clouds. Walking out of
doors, we leaned into the rush of air, struggling not only
against its force but against its penetrating cold, so that we
panted, breathless, when we came out of the reach of the
wind. Out in it, one's clothes were constantly jerked at, pulled
at, rearranged; the forms of women showed through their
loose clothes; they held their hands down at their sides to
control their skirts and ran clumsily. Everyone frowned out
in it. At night one could hear it moaning around our log buildings and whistling through the bare branches along the creek.

Because of our poor clothing and the erratic weather and the
fact that we had no heat in most of our sleeping quarters, we
suffered from winter sicknesses: colds, sore throats, stuffed-up
heads and chests. One difficulty seemed to strike us all: our
eyes would water as we slept and we would find our eyelids
and lashes crusted up in the mornings, even stuck shut. It was
hard to wash one's face in the icy water. People went about
picking at their eyes.

One of our problems was lack of bedcovers. We used our
coats and pieces of canvas and paper along with our quilts and
blankets. Some of the men had dug a tanning vat and had been
experimenting with the tanning of sheepskins. They chipped
up oak and willow bark to make a mixture in which to soak
the hides. The resulting leather was stiff and it smelled, but
the wool on it made it a warm covering. Some of the women
sewed the skins together to make covers. Those who slept
under them said that it was a question whether it would be
better to throw them away and bear the cold or keep them
and bear the stench.

If the wind was blowing in the daytime, everyone stayed
inside as much as he could, not in his quarters, but wherever
he could get near a fire. They crowded into the kitchen, the
laundry house, the dining hall.

Jim York was reluctant to crowd in with people where it was necessary to show good humor. Often he sat alone in our cold quarters. He told me that he would leave the colony in the spring. He had no criticism to offer, but he was thinking about going to sea.

On our bulletin board the copy of "Goals of Our Common Faith," in Jeannette's beautiful script, remained like a part of the board itself. It must have been good-quality paper, for it endured the wind and the wet and remained clearly legible, though the paper turned yellow and the ink turned brown. I thought that it had been a wise idea to fix it there, so that we might be frequently reminded of the reasons for agreeing to our hardships.

Early in January a light snow fell. Though the weather was cold, the air was still, and it was not unpleasant out of doors. One morning I saddled a horse and set out with my rifle, giving myself the reasonable excuse that I should use the gun I had so jealously kept to get some game for the kitchen, but the truth probably was that I wanted to get away for a few hours from the monotonous troubles of the village.

Snow lay on every tree branch along the creek. The sky appeared dead gray, duller than the snow. The limbs of trees, even the smaller ones, looked black, and the line of snow that capped each one made a contrast so that each limb stood out distinctly. Looking into the distance down the creek, I could see an infinite maze of branches, each as if painted by a thin stroke of black and a thin stroke of white. The distinctness pointed up the intricacy of the maze and lent an aura of long, long extension. Snowflakes sifted down out of the gray sky thinly, so small that they were hard to see. The snow layer on the ground was thin. My horse's feet melted it and left dark tracks.

I went downstream and stayed on the east side of the creek. The ice was a quarter to a half inch thick and I was afraid of cutting my mount's feet and legs if I tried to cross. I had not thought of Harney Myers when I set out, but after riding a while I became aware that I was near his cabin; then I heard the sound of an ax on wood. I rode through the trees to the spot where he lived, overlooking the stream.

Smoke poured out of the cabin chimney. He was chopping wood in a leisurely manner thirty paces beyond. I think he did not see me until I was about to dismount, for he was startled momentarily.

"I thought you was an Injun," he said.

I said, "Hello, Mr. Myers." He did not offer to shake hands.

I asked him, "Are there some dangerous Indians around here now?"

"They's Injuns and then they's Injuns," he said. "I ain't saying if they're dangerous or not, but it 'pears to me like a bunch of socialist fellers, no more than they know about Injuns, is fixing to lose their hair."

"You think they're more dangerous than they were before?"

"I ain't saying that. I'll tell you one thing: I know when to stay in these parts and when to pack up and get out. I know that much."

He seemed somewhat antagonistic. Hoping to make him more friendly and get him to volunteer what he knew, I told him about the large band of Indians on horseback we had seen.

He did not seem surprised. He said, "The way it is now out yonder, you better trade with 'em if you aim to stay around. You can't just set like you all do. Trade or get out; that's my warning and my advice."

"Trade? With whom?"

"Well, now I reckon you would like for me to tell you that. If you ain't forgot it, you remember I put it up to you all once: You could put up a thousand dollars' worth of goods, and me and Louey would handle the rest of it. I reckon you remember that. That's still my price. I ain't playing Injun agent for a bunch of socialist fellers for nothing."

I laughed; I suppose it was to show that I was not offended. He set the ax into a chunk of wood and put on a bearskin coat which had been lying on the chips behind him.

"I might art to tell you," he said, "I know you're in with all them socialist fellers. I didn't know that at one time, but Andy set me straight on it and he give me the lowdown on how you all operate and everything about it. I ain't out to cut your throat, but I damned sure ain't going out of my way to do you no favors. No offense, but that's the way I am."

"Where is Andy?"

"Round and about."

"When did you say you saw him last?"

"I never said."

"His brother is worried about him."

"He never said nothing to me about no brother. The way I heard it, you all call everybody 'brother,' even if they ain't no kin."

"Do you know how a person could get in touch with Andy?"

"I ain't saying."

It was obvious that I could not get any information out of him. I bade him good day, and as I mounted, he removed his bearskin coat and shortly afterward I heard his leisurely chopping again. I had evidently forfeited his confidence by being one of the "socialist fellers," but I had the definite impression, too, that he did not know as much about the Indians or anything else hereabouts as he pretended.

I flushed a flock of turkeys but could not get a shot at any large enough to waste powder and lead on. I went back to the village empty-handed.

We sent a wagon with two men of the guard to Jones' Mill. There was not enough money to buy any food, but the assemblymen thought it important to post the letters they had written seeking donations and to allow all the colonists to send any similar letters. Also, it was necessary for Dr. Valentin to write to the officials of the New Socialist Colonization Company; they frequently demanded accountings of one kind or another, and since they owned title to our land could not be ignored.

About this time Deveraux began to cause trouble again. He found out from a guard that a wagon was going to Jones' Mill and demanded that he be allowed to write a letter. When this was refused him, he spent several hours screaming and cursing in his prison room. On the day after the wagon left, he again began to argue and protest wildly, saying that he did not have enough covers to keep warm at night.

Storage space where supplies could be kept out of the weather being scarce, several items had been carried into his prison room: a keg of horseshoes, a small crate of four windowpanes packed in sawdust, and about two hundred pounds of threshed millet sacked in burlap. The guards discovered that Deveraux, in his anger and spite, had smashed the keg, broken all of the glass, and scattered the millet over the dirt floor. At Dr. Valentin's orders the guard took the man out of the room and again chained him outside at the end of the building. We felt that supplies were so precious and storage room so scarce that he had forfeited any consideration he might have deserved as a human being.

The wagon came back from Jones' Mill just before noon one day, and we had an assembly meeting immediately after the noon meal. As we came into the meeting room, we found waiting Dr. Valentin, two guards with their rifles, and a prisoner they had just taken in the dining hall. I was pleased to see that someone had already built a fire in the smoky fireplace.

The prisoner was a man named Thomas, a tall, rawboned Englishman who was rather quiet. I believe that he had been a schoolteacher; at least there had been some kind of understanding that he would be one of the teachers when our school was established. He seemed awkward and ill at ease standing between the guards to one side of the fireplace.

When the assemblymen were present and seated, Brother Adams said to Dr. Valentin, "Did you . . . ? I believe. . . ."

Dr. Valentin took a sheaf of folded papers from his pocket and said, "This man has written a letter—Brother John Thomas —has written a letter to a person in England. I won't trouble you with the entire contents, but there are three sentences that the assembly will want to hear and act on."

"How did you come by this letter?" Dr. Sockwell asked.

"It was sent by the wagon to Jones' Mill. He admits that he wrote it."

"And how did you come by it?"

"The contents, which I will read to you, will justify any action I may have taken."

"Just a minute," Dr. Sockwell said. "Mr. Chairman, I would like a clear answer before we have any reading. Are you opening and reading all the letters that leave here?"

Dr. Valentin said, "The evidence is its own justification."

Brother Adams looked around at the rest of us for help.

Sister Harriet Edwards asked, "Are you searching my letters?"

Dr. Sockwell asked, "Are you reading my letters? Brother Bossereau's? Brother Langly's? That's a plain-enough question, isn't it?"

Dr. Valentin said, "Indeed, that's a plain-enough question. Now allow me to ask one: Are you writing any letters which would embarrass you if they came to the attention of this body?"

Brother Adams seemed to realize that he should make a ruling of some kind without knowing what the ruling should be. Brother Bossereau said quietly, "Perhaps it's not necessary to be so formal. Brother Valentin seems to believe that the excerpts he wants to read are a partial answer to your questions. We might allow him to read them, without compromising our right to question him later." His words, though not forcefully spoken, seemed to amount to the ruling that was needed, and all of us around the table accepted them at once.

Dr. Valentin searched the papers, then said in a dry voice: "To his friend, Brother Thomas writes, 'Do not take any stock in the New Socialist Colonization Company, nor make any other such investments or donations.' Then he writes this: 'I advise you, I implore you, do not come to Uterica.' Then, over here, he writes, 'The colony is a failure.'

"Now, we are in desperate financial straits," he went on. "We are struggling to raise additional capital and struggling to justify our acts to the Company. Meanwhile this man publishes these seditious statements abroad to the world."

Brother Adams asked, "Did he send this to be published?"

"Who knows? Who knows what this Hamilton person might have done with it? I might read one more thing. Here he says, 'If you pass my advice on to others, please attribute it to a trusted friend or some such indefinite source. You can understand that I don't wish my identity advertised.' He is certainly aware that his lies are deadly poison to the colony."

Brother Thomas stood quietly, looking at the floor. He alternated between clasping his hands behind him and folding his arms on his chest.

"Now let us take up the matter of searching letters," Dr. Sockwell said.

Dr. Valentin asked sharply, "Would you prefer that I search a few letters or that such damaging lies as these go out without our knowledge?"

"Mr. Chairman," Dr. Sockwell said, "the head of the Finance Committee obviously does not intend to answer our plain questions. Therefore I desire to make a motion. I move that he be clearly instructed that he is not to read the letters of the assembly members, nor cause them to be read, that, if such letters need to be searched, they be searched in open assembly meeting, his own letters as well as the others. Further, that the head of the Finance Committee be instructed that the guard is an arm of the assembly, and he is to form no policies nor take any action using the guard without the express consent of the assembly."

Brother Bossereau added that the instructions should include a prohibition against searching the letters of any colonist except in special cases where particular suspicion existed. Further discussion modified and expanded the motion, and finally Brother Adams called for a vote on it. It carried, but since it was not put into writing, I doubted that all of us understood it exactly the same.

It soon became clear that the assembly members wished to read the entire letter that Brother Thomas had written and were unwilling to take any further action until they had done so. Dr. Valentin called it a waste of time, but he could do nothing but pass it around. When it came my turn, I saw that it was written in a fine, legible hand. It read:

My dear Hamilton,

I hope that you will forgive me for so long hesitating to write this promised letter, as I believe you will when you understand the many uncertainties of our situation. Even at this late date I may not be able to satisfy you—with clear advice, yes, with full reason, no. But I would be unworthy of our long friendship did I not make the full and sincere attempt.

As to the advice, do not take any stock in the New Socialist Colonization Company nor make any other such investment or donations, at least until further knowledge about its success is available. Its prospects do not look favorable at this end. It may never pay the dividends which its founders assured us, the capital itself may never be recovered, and I hasten to add, knowing you, that all the money expended may never advance any worthwhile social cause. Further I advise you, I implore you, do not come to Uterica. In so

doing you would enter upon difficulties and frustrations beyond anything of which you have dreamed. If you pass my
advice on to others, please attribute it to a "trusted friend"
or some such indefinite source. You can understand that I
don't wish my identity advertised.

At this point I can almost hear you say, "Well, you have
certainly been disillusioned!" You are right. I have that.
Please don't charge me too quickly with being fainthearted
and disloyal. When I joined, I cast away all doubts and cyni-
cism and opened wide my arms to Socialist Association. But
then followed all the confusion and delay and put-off departure. When we sailed I thought, "At last! Here it is!" But
that Ocean is not the Channel or even the Mediterranean,
I assure you. We, none of us, ever spent a more wretched
period of our lives before, and all unbelievably because of a
lack of the most simple kind of planning. Their attitude was
this: "Don't worry, all is well, all is arranged for," but—
can you believe it?—we did not even have enough water to
drink, much less for bathing, and hardly enough room in our
quarters to sleep all at once. I was seasick forty-two straight
days and lost almost that many pounds. Well, we were expecting hardships, so persevered in our faith, and when I set
eyes on America I breathed a great sigh and said, "Lo,
Utopia!" But it was not. There followed a period of even
greater confusion, if that is possible, than had transpired in
Europe, with traveling here and there, much suffering from
the ague and fevers, living in inadequate housing, including
a barn, during which time we, the "pioneers" of Uterica,
gathered together and equipped ourselves. When we set out
west, I reaffirmed my faith to myself, thinking we had left
the troubles of civilization behind, and said once more, "Now,
at last! Surely now!" I don't have the space here to describe
that terrible trip. I can only say that everything we own at
this place which is of any value we dragged here through
hundreds of miles of mud and slime. The oxen did not carry
us; we carried them. And so we came to Uterica. You can
understand my disillusionment. As we approached it, our
dream has retreated, and now that we have no farther to

travel in space, it surely lies somewhere beyond the horizon of time, if it exists at all. The problems up to now would not of themselves damn the colony, but they have caused me to open my eyes and examine critically our situation, our leaders, and all our folly. We who have done what we have already done could not possibly turn face about now and establish a viable colony.

I'm not alone in criticizing, though not much is done here openly. The official policy is that all constructive criticism is welcomed. The truth is that any real expression of lack of faith in our methods or goals is as welcome as cursing of the Archbishop in the English Church. We are perfectly free to do anything we wish as long as we wish to do what they want.

A part of my promise to you was that I would try to estimate the people, according to their nationality and their adaptability to socialist association. You are more of an authority on the English character than I. As for the Americans, insofar as I have had the opportunity of observing them, they seem quite different from the English, hardly even an extension of them. They venerate their independence and their federal constitution but hardly allow those things to affect their ways of living. Surely this country will not furnish a model for republics of the future. I think the Americans have not been able to improvise a nationality at all. Though I do not deny previous observations that they are industrious materialists, they seem quite variable to me. I see two distinct types here. One (those we employed were of this type) goes around with a grin on his face and an empty head and has the curious faculty of being able to do well at any job he sets his hand to. The other is more complicated. He is from the East Coast and has contempt for his fellow Americans who originate inland, considering them backwoodsmen, louts, provincials. The ideas which this type holds are moralistic, though he believes them intellectual, and he supports them with self-righteous fervor.

Of the colonists generally, the Germans are the best workers. Given a practical plan and a clear idea of what they are to do, they would make a success of the producing portion of this colony. I have not seen in their thinking much of that strange marriage of the rational and the mystic for which they are known, but some of them sneak off to themselves and converse in the German language, which is against the rules.

Of the others, I shall note only a few things about the French, which things have become more clear to me in recent months. Of all people they are the most nationalistic. Paris is the center of the world, and if any matter has ever been worked out by a Frenchman, then that is the last word on it. They are all temperamental artists. If one of them raises a pig successfully, then he is a master pig raiser, who knows the proper way to do it; any other way is vulgar and improper; anyone who questions his method has insulted his sensibilities. Everything is black or white. You may think me too hard on such a civilized people, but I'm surprised that I have not seen it before. They are emotional about ideals, and they have the ability to hypnotize themselves with their own words. Words are very precious to a Frenchman if he has arranged them in some complicated way that pleases him. Perhaps it is well that a Frenchman leads us (if we are led at all), for the French would follow no other.

But, my dear Hamilton, such observations seem almost beside the point. Do you recall the emphasis on planning? Others had failed, yes! They had foolishly failed to foresee difficulties. But *this* would be planned. Carefully. Foreseeing everything! The best example was in the selection of colonists, especially us, the pioneer colonists. Oh, how carefully were we selected! The cream of two continents! You will be shocked to learn that at this time there is no evidence at all that any intelligent selection was made. We have professors aplenty, but no school. Writers aplenty, but no press. Artists, lawyers, architects, but not a one of them can do the skilled work that needs doing here. I would trade a gross of intellectuals out here for a dozen rail-splitters. It appears to me now that all the choosing and selecting actually had as a purpose to gather like-minded people, those who would agree, but that is the most ridiculous irony of all. They seemed somehow to agree, at least in criticizing civilization. Now it appears they do not at all. I think we have enough different ideas for a hundred colonies, and each opinionated fool secure in his own convictions, taking comfort in a few vague words they have in common, not yet seeing the impossible contradictions. Can you imagine it so bad? It is.

I hardly know how to explain it to you. Do you recall all the arithmetic and the manner in which the financial details clicked into place? I presume that we are now completely out of funds. Pennyless! Money has been flung hither and yon in every kind of impractical manner. Leaders accustomed to writing and speaking about financing of nations with millions of pounds have proved incapable of handling a few thousand in a practical manner. I don't believe anyone has been dishonest, but they have surely been stupid and incompetent. Notice that I *presume* we are pennyless. With the company authorities and the colony authorities and stockholders and donors scattered over two continents, and with no bookkeeping here worthy of the name, I do not believe that anyone on earth knows the status of our financing.

But the uncertainty about money and leadership, these seem small beside the uncertainty of the wilderness and the savage Indians. Has the news come back to you about the killing of Jeannette, the daughter of Jean Charles Bossereau, by the Indians? We have no idea why they did it. It seemed such a senseless thing. They seemed so simple and playful. Now I ask myself whether they might be a thousand times more complicated than we can imagine. What weird things do they say to one another about us? What shrewd plans might they have to use us for their own purposes? What madness led us to thrust ourselves such a far distance out into this unknown place? In the face of this wilderness and the curious animals and curious natives, I think of us as puny and audacious.

I do not know what else to tell you. The women do not vote here. No one votes here. I see no sign that we shall ever have any degree of democracy.

My dear old friend, you are asking how can all this be.

I do not know. Why is it not possible to do some of those things you and I used to talk about? I do not know. My heart is very heavy as I write this to you. Even after months of confusion and hardship, the words of our leader, M. Bossereau, had the power to kindle in me a spark of the old hope; but since his daughter was killed by the savage Indians, he is half dead himself and not what he was. And I know now that all hope is past. The colony is a failure.

I'm sorry that I brought my wife and son here. In a few months I shall leave and try to find work among the Americans. I hope to see you again but cannot say when it might be. I wish I were in your pleasant house this night, with my family, by your warm fire, able to feel your hospitality and able to sup at your bountiful board. I will not tell you about our vile meals here, for you would not believe it.

I must close.

Ever your obt. servant,

Jno. Thomas

The letter as a whole had an effect on me quite different from that of the excerpts Dr. Valentin had read. As the letter passed among us, we were quiet and thoughtful. The time it took for all of us to read it was painfully long, and I thought how uncomfortable the two guards and their tall, skinny prisoner must be standing through it.

When the sheets of paper had come back to him, Dr. Valentin said, "Now, Brother Thomas, will you state whether you wrote this letter or not?"

The man said without looking up, "I wrote it. For the private reading of my friend."

Dr. Sockwell said, "You were aware, of course, that it might go further than your friend. You mention that possibility."

Miss Harriet Edwards said, "He gives the friend permission to pass on his advice."

"I didn't know," the man said, "when we set out in the

first place that a man was to be restricted in his thinking and writing. I thought we could believe according to our conscience, freely, and write the same."

"No one is restricting your thinking!" Dr. Valentin said loudly. "No one is restricting your conscience. No one is restricting writing. No one threatened to restrict anything about you. It is you who have made this insidious, underhanded attack. Who are you to judge the bookkeeping of this project? This is a contemptible effort to have the Company sell our land out from under us and withdraw all support. We cannot tolerate this kind of writing!"

The accused man said nothing. Brother Bossereau had turned his chair toward the man and now he said, "Brother Thomas, you write to your friend that you are heavyhearted. You ask the question why is it not possible to do these things you have dreamed of. Be assured that we have dreamed of them, too. Be assured that we, too, are sometimes heavyhearted. The answer to the question is this: These things *can* be done.

"Your letter is a catalog of hardships. I do not deny them. But it does not follow that Uterica is a failure. We are human beings; we make errors; we fail to foresee what is to happen. Yet because we are human beings we have a deep reservoir of stamina and perseverance to draw from. If we could list twice as many hardships, these would not make a failure of Uterica, for our sacrifices must be compared with our goals. We are trying a fantastic and wonderful thing, to make a place where the evils of private ownership do not intrude and where men can live as brothers. We seek to bring to pass the ancient idea of a Kingdom of Heaven on earth, where man's old fears and anxieties will fade away, where we will have an abundance of all things, material and spiritual. And these are not mere words; they are practical possibilities; they require only the sincere intention of man to bring them to pass.

"Brother Thomas, one does not snap one's fingers and

accomplish great things. On the day we came into this valley I made a brief speech and I said that an ideal society is not easily established, that we faced problems and difficulties. These were not mere words; I meant them. And I remember wondering at that time how many of us really appreciated what I was saying. We still face difficulties and our goals are fully as precious as ever. Uterica is a failure to those who have become willing for it to fail, but for those who believe that the final accomplishment is superior to any sacrifice, for those it is imperfection moving toward perfection. We shall not fail. We shall see it come to pass."

He paused a moment. I was thinking that he sounded like the Bossereau of old. He asked Brother Thomas, "Do you understand what I am saying?"

"Yes, sir."

"You agree with me then?"

"No, I don't."

"Then please tell me why you don't. Argument is based on reasoning. Please explain why you do not agree."

The man was ill at ease, as he had been from the start. I expected some argument from him, but he finally said quietly, "I just don't."

We discussed the matter at length. Brother Thomas said that he wished to take his family and leave the colony, but Dr. Valentin objected strenuously to allowing anyone to leave who might "spread lies across the countryside." Most of the assembly members held it against the accused man that he might have gone quietly and peaceably, as several families had done, or he might have brought his complaints before the assembly rather than send them to an outsider.

When we voted to restrain Brother Thomas, all were in favor except Brother Bossereau, who abstained. I believe that I would have abstained also had the man offered reasons when Brother Bossereau asked for them. The refusal seemed to indicate stubbornness.

After he was taken from the room, Dr. Sockwell said to Dr. Valentin, "This is exactly the kind of thing I warned against. Now it's come to searching letters without consulting the assembly. What will it be next?"

"I think the results of the search and the action of this body vindicate my action."

"I don't think they do."

"Are you determined that this entire project shall commit suicide?"

"I'm determined that these matters shall be decided in the assembly."

"And by the action of the assembly alone, the letter would now be on its way to England. My God! Sockwell, I am as much in favor of the freedom of speech and conscience as you or anyone, but these freedoms are a luxury. We are fighting for the life of this colony now. Would you see all the good possibilities subverted because we are not willing to limit our freedom for the time being?"

Dr. Sockwell did not speak for a moment and then he answered in what was an unusually deliberate manner for him. "If you present us another *fait accompli* such as searching letters, I shall move that the assembly take action against you. I mean punitive action."

"I think we have settled the matter of letters," Dr. Valentin said, "and now we are haggling, wasting time."

Dr. Sockwell did not answer.

I had given no thought to what the restraining of Brother Thomas would amount to and so was surprised that afternoon to see the guards bring the man from the blacksmith shop with an iron on his leg and a chain fastened to it. They took him to the end of the building where Deveraux was kept, passed the chain around a log, and fastened it by clamping shut an open link with a pair of tongs.

Later I saw that his wife and boy had joined him. The woman was as skinny as Thomas and rather hollow-eyed and solemn. She wrapped a blanket around herself and sat beside him, leaning against the log wall as he did and as Deveraux did. The boy, eight to ten years old, hardly seemed to be the son of such parents. He was sturdy; his body even appeared fat in his heavy coat. Like all the children of the colony, he had a runny nose. He did not sit but stood quietly and very erect by the fire. I saw him standing, facing the compound as some people approached on the path by the building; as they passed, he turned his head and stared at the rail fence behind the building. One could not help wondering how well he understood the issues involved, whether he had listened at length to his parents' discussing the problems of the colony, how it all looked to him through his inexperienced eyes; in any case, he was not asking any questions. He kept his hands in his pockets.

They were not such a curiosity, since Deveraux had twice been chained there. All of us seemed to try to refrain from noticing them any more than necessary. I saw Dr. Valentin there, talking with the woman. Her voice, high and stubborn, carried better than his. She said, "I'll stay where I please!"

The boy was standing, as inscrutable as ever, his back to Valentin. Deveraux was laughing gleefully.

The woman said, "I'll sit where I please and stay as long as I please!"

Dr. Valentin argued with her, but obviously got no satisfaction out of it. He walked away, looking grim.

After supper the woman and boy returned to where Brother Thomas was chained, the woman sitting beside her husband, the boy standing a few feet away. They were somewhat out of the chill wind, having the building to break its direct force, but it whipped around the corner, making their open fire glow intensely. The last I saw of them that evening, they—the three sitting beside the building, the two chained men and the woman—were almost indiscernible in the winter dusk; the guard with his rifle stood on one side of the fire; the sturdy boy stood on the other side, diligently looking away from the guard.

The next day at breakfast, I became aware that several assembly members were arguing in low voices at a table behind me; as the clatter of eating passed and most of the workers cleared out, they could be clearly heard.

Brother Bossereau said, "I intend to sit the night with them. That's all."

"With the man we're punishing!" Dr. Valentin said harshly.

"No, with the woman and boy."

"The idiots!" Dr. Valentin said. "How is it possible to do anything with such people, who don't have plain common sense? They are the ones, not me! They insist on sitting out to catch pneumonia! Tell me what kind of decent colony we can establish when the people insist on acting in such an idiotic and stubborn manner!"

I joined them and soon afterward we agreed that we must have an emergency meeting of the assembly. Even Dr. Valentin was not satisfied with our present disposition of the Thomas family.

When we had gathered, we first argued as to whether he should be put inside the prison room, but it was clear that we would still have trouble with the wife and son. We finally concluded that there was no alternative: he must be allowed to leave the colony. Brother Bossereau and Brother Adams drew up a paper for Thomas to sign wherein he stated that he had had some disagreement with the leaders of the colony but now realized that he did not know as much about the affairs and prospects of the colony as did the leaders; further, he agreed to leave peaceably and make no public criticism of the colony. It was thought that such a paper might be sent to the Company officials if it ever seemed necessary. Thomas was brought before us and agreed to sign it. Almost as an afterthought, we had Deveraux brought in and told him that he might leave peaceably with the Thomas family, but if he stayed or returned, he would certainly be chained out in the weather without mercy. He told us that he would go, that we were all insane, that he would rather live under the hardest slave driver than in Uterica, and various other insults.

The following day they walked east—Deveraux, Thomas, the woman, and the boy. They carried light packs of their personal belongings and for food had stuffed their pockets with turnips and wild pecans. They faced about a three-day walk, which seemed a harsh prospect for the woman and boy, but all of us had become inured to disagreeable activity. The weather was cold, but the sky did not threaten rain or snow.

CHAPTER

17

I KEPT the horses penned at night so that they had the shelter of the shed and windbreak. In the daytime they ran free except for one which I kept penned or staked out. The band roved up or down the creek bottoms mostly, not far from the village, sometimes grazing out onto the higher prairies during warm afternoons. They came of themselves to their pen when the weather was cold.

Following one warm afternoon in late February, the horses did not come in. I whistled for them, then saddled the sorrel mare which had been staked near the creek and rode out looking, but found nothing. The next day I rode all day upstream and down and out into the hills to the east as far as five miles. West of the creek and up the smaller fork I went no farther than a mile and, finding no sign, turned back. The loss of the horses, all but one, was a severe blow, but I was not willing to ride farther west into what I had come to think of as Indian country.

That same day a wood-gathering crew saw the Indians. They saw a large group riding a mile distant, and a small number, which must have been about a dozen, broke away and came to a rise overlooking them and sat their horses, watching them. The wood gatherers were evidently greatly scared and came together at the wagon, but the dozen or so Indians reined away and left. Reports as to the total number of Indians seen varied greatly. One man said there were no more than fifty. Dominique Henri swore there were "hundreds."

We concluded that the wood wagon had to go out some distance, particularly to get the dead wood that we needed for starting fires, and that each one in the future would be protected by a contingent of the guard.

We were, about this time, seeing much evidence of bad feeling and willingness to argue among the colonists. One day two guards had a fight in the auxiliary kitchen over a turkey one of them had killed. One of them wanted to give it to Dr. Sockwell for the sick; the other was determined to have it for his own family. Neither of them won. The bird wound up in the turnip-mutton stew. This incident did not help the guards' reputation; many colonists were building resentment against them because they did no work.

Another argument, upon which nearly everyone took sides, concerned plowing the compound. Our first intention was to have a garden in the area in the coming spring, as we had the year before. But many began to rant against building such a mudhole in what was supposed to be the main street of the village. The plowing crew refused to bring their plow into the compound. They maintained that the guard should be put to work laying stone walks across our main street rather than plowing it up. In the assembly we agreed to plan stone walks all around the edges and use the middle for a garden, but the plowing crew still objected to bringing the plow out of the field, so we put the matter aside; that work crew was the only one doing work beyond the immediate needs of living.

One day Brother Adams approached me and asked whether he could speak confidentially with me. I could hardly say No, though I did not care to play father confessor to anyone, even dreaded possibly being loaded with troubles or problems beyond what I was already aware of. He seemed, as always, an extremely serious and polite little man. I told him that I would be happy to listen, but doubted that I would be of any aid. He said that he had a moral dilemma. He knew of a family that intended to leave us when the weather became dependable and he could not decide whether he was duty bound to inform the assembly. "This man must not be chained by his leg," he said. "His thinking is in error, but he must not be chained up. He has three small children."

"Wait a minute, Brother Adams," I said. "Surely the assembly would not allow Brother Valentin to chain a man up simply because he disagrees with us and wants to leave the colony."

"Well . . . I hope it's true," he said. "This man—forgive me for not specifying his name—also believes that he should have some property to take away, a wagon or something. And he says others want to leave also, but he won't tell names. I don't know. . . ."

"I don't think you have any moral obligation to tell the assembly his name," I said. "I know a man who intends to leave and I haven't told anyone."

He stood uncertain for a moment, then said, "I'm worried. How many want to leave? What should we do? I wish Brother Bossereau were the director."

It was a kind of pitiful complaint, but I liked him at that moment more than I ever had before. I realized that what I wanted more than anything else for our colony was that Brother Bossereau should be in charge and that he should set our course and lead us with the genius that such as Brother Adams believed he possessed. I told him that I felt certain that our disunity and the flagging determination of some colony members ought to be investigated in depth in the assembly. He agreed.

The assembly room that afternoon was chilly, but we decided to sit in our coats and do without a fire in the smoky fireplace. I soon found that other assembly members were thinking about the same problems that Brother Adams and I had discussed. Dr. Sockwell said that the primary problem was psychological, the result of a bleak and difficult winter, also a result of malnutrition and exposure and the chills and fevers; in short, the colonists' strength was sapped and this affected their wills.

Sister Harriet Edwards said she believed the problem was exactly what it had always been. "If it is not an advantage to practice socialism," she said, "why do it? I say we must develop a cultural life that is superior to what the colonists have given up. I, myself, didn't come out here to live like an animal; I came to live like a superior human being, to live the higher life. And on that point, I'd appreciate it if someone would explain to me why we located so far out here in such inhospitable surroundings."

An uncomfortable silence followed her speech. Brother Adams finally said, "I wonder whether we could have some indication . . . how many colonists intend to leave? How many of us know at least one person who is considering. . . ?"

Twelve of us sat at the table and each indicated briefly by raising the hand that he knew of some such person. Dr. Sockwell said, "I know of four families who intend to quit us."

Dr. Valentin said, "This is doom for our entire project if we permit it. When a person leaves here, we can be sure he will be asked questions, and we can be sure he will talk. This will ruin our hope for donations, which we must have to survive. Also, if half our people leave, the Company will surely know of it. One of these days they will sell this land right out from under us. I move that we do not permit anyone to leave until we are economically self-sufficient."

Brother Bossereau said, "I believe we cannot do that."

"We don't need to make it public policy," Dr. Valentin insisted, "but we can do it. Tell them to wait. Offer inducements to wait, perhaps colony property. But, finally, they should not be permitted to leave. They are in this as the rest of us are. Why should the ungrateful ones be allowed to destroy us?"

"I believe we cannot do it," Brother Bossereau said.

"Cannot? We can stop them with the guard if we must. Of course we can."

Dr. Sockwell said, "The guard is as much the reason as any other for dissatisfaction."

"I suppose," Dr. Valentin said, "you would disband the guard and leave us at the mercy of the savage Indians?"

"You were not speaking of using them against the savage Indians," Dr. Sockwell pointed out.

"If a dozen families leave here this spring, we are ruined!" Valentin paused, then went on with a desperate note in his voice. "It is maddening to know that you can do something if only people will be patient and submit themselves to reasonable discipline for a time! And yet the people you have to deal with! If only we could make them stay! They would see! Then later they could do as they wished!"

There was no talking for a minute. We all seemed to realize that the argument was leading nowhere. Finally Brother Adams cleared his throat and said, "Possibly at this time . . . I wonder whether Brother Bossereau would want to give us his assessment of the conditions or his thoughts on what might be done."

The old French leader seemed surprised at the request, also somewhat pleased. "The conditions are grave," he said, "but not hopeless. No one is defeated until he admits defeat." He cleaned his spectacles with his handkerchief, frowning, thinking, then said, "I believe I know what we must do, but I do not have any definite plan or specific program. It will require careful planning. What we must do is this: involve the people. Make them feel and know that they have responsibility for their own destiny."

"You mean hold an election?" Dr. Sockwell asked.

"Well, we should involve them deeply and continuously.

It might be that we should carefully select an issue and present it to the colonists at the beginning of the week, then present it as a referendum at the end of the week.

"We also require lectures to inform and inspire the people. This is not possible in cold weather, but as soon as it is feasible we should do it. Very soon. And regularly. These lectures should be carefully designed to raise the morale of the people. Then perhaps we could have discussion groups; these should be guided. Perhaps we could interest all the colony members in writing essays on subjects like these: Why I Am a Socialist, The Blessings of Equality, Living in Harmony, Man and Nature. The superior essays might be read before a general assembly of the colonists. These are not specific proposals, but these are the types of things we must do to involve all the people, and inspire them and educate them."

All of us were hanging onto his words. He went on. "I think of one other possibility. If we could find a way for colonists to express criticism... perhaps we could have supervised sessions of criticism in which they would criticize each other and their work leaders and the assemblymen."

Dr. Valentin said, "Jean Charles, in the name of God! What are you suggesting?"

Brother Bossereau was not taken aback. He said, "It is the nature of people that they are critical. They need an outlet. Shall we encourage criticism and guide it and limit it so that it is constructive, or shall we ignore it and allow it to rage unrecognized in private?"

"It rages," Dr. Sockwell put in. "When you see them talking in low voices with sour expressions, and when they stop at your approach, you may be sure they are not talking about the blessings of socialism."

Brother Bossereau said, "Morale is the crucial issue. We cannot be defeated if we are determined. I believe the people must be constantly inspired and educated. In a week or two weeks we will feel the first message of spring. I sense it already. We can have a new awakening, a new dedication."

It seemed that most of us at the table were in agreement with him, at least tentatively. Brother Adams obviously was. He said, eagerly but with his usual apologetic manner, "I wonder whether it would be in order... I propose that we elect Brother Bossereau the director of the colony and ask him to make plans along the lines he has indicated."

It appeared obvious that Brother Adams had not consulted with anyone about the proposition, though he must have been thinking about it privately for a long time. No one seemed much surprised. Several assemblymen spoke briefly, then we voted. Nine were in favor. Brother Bossereau and Sister Edwards abstained, and, to my amazement, Dr. Valentin did not vote against it, but also abstained.

Brother Bossereau walked over to the window and stood with his back to us for a minute. I thought that he might be weeping. From that window he could see the hill where the body of his daughter lay. In a minute he cleaned his spectacles with his handkerchief, came back and sat down, and began some further dignified discussion.

And so we reinstated the French leader in his old position, not, I think, with great confidence but because he had confidence. It was clear that we needed to do something to counteract the disunion and disillusionment that were descending upon us, and we grasped desperately at his proposals and his leadership.

The weather was such that no one could guess whether winter was done. The afternoons were warm enough for a person to go outside in shirt sleeves in comfort, but not much warmer than some afternoons had been in December and January. Spring was creeping upon us subtly. I had begun an agonized indecision about corn planting, anxious to get it into the ground at the earliest safe time, worried lest it be caught by a late freeze. I thought about Mr. Finch, who seemed to have been gone years rather than months, and how much I would have appreciated his help in making the decision. I asked Jim York his opinion, and he answered that he didn't think it mattered when it was planted.

On the second day of March the wood wagon went out to the west early in the morning with three axmen and five guards. I rode the sorrel mare out to watch the plow crew begin their work and to look at the condition of the soil. I had the mare saddled nearly every day now, because patches of spring grass were beginning to show, and the milk cows and the unused oxen loved to stray long distances to find it; I rode out once or twice a day to turn them back toward the village.

Looking over the fields, plowed and unplowed, I determined to get another plow crew to work even if I had to make a nuisance of myself or make some colony leaders angry. About the middle of the morning I rode back to where the one crew was plowing and dismounted to discuss with them whether the four of them would be willing to split up into two crews and take some less competent helpers. We were talking when one of the men said, "Look!" and pointed.

Away down past the village, a mile from us, the wood wagon was bouncing out of the trees near the creek. Three or four men flailed at the oxen to make them run. The other men, though their figures appeared small at this distance, moved as if they were excited, often looking back. They did not have as much as a half load of wood on the wagon. When they had come half the distance from the creek to the village, three of them, running together, pointed their rifles at the sky and fired them in quick succession.

"What in the world . . . ?" one of the plowmen said.

"Trouble of some kind," another said.

I mounted the mare and told them, "I guess you'd better unhook and come in."

I rode down to the village. The wagon had been brought into the compound, and men, women, and children milled about it. I tied the mare and asked the first man whose attention I could get what had happened.

"The Indians attacked," he said.

"Was anyone hurt?"

"I don't know."

A woman pulled at my sleeve and I saw that she was extremely frightened. "Brother Langly," she said, "we'll all be murdered!"

I saw Dr. Sockwell talking with one of the guards and went to him. He said to me, exasperated, "I can't even find out what happened!"

"I was up in the fields," I said. "I just got here."

The guard said, "There's Hale. He was with the wagon."

Dr. Sockwell and I pushed through the crowd to the man named Hale. Dr. Sockwell took him by the arm and said, "Would you come with us, please. We would like to get a clear report on what has happened." With the man's help, he picked out from the excited crowd two others who had been with the wood crew, and we took them aside. Dr. Valentin was talking with two guards over in front of the assembly room, and we joined them. As we came up, I heard one of them say, "That country west of the creek is swarming with them."

With five of the involved men together and out of the confusion, we pieced up a fairly clear account of the incident. The wagon had gone some distance past the creek and the men had spread out to gather wood. The guards had scattered, one remaining near the wagon to build a fire, two going some distance away hoping to shoot a turkey, and two going with the three axmen. A group of mounted Indians had appeared on a rise above the wood gatherers. One guard had fired a warning shot, then another had begun to fire at the Indians, who took cover and returned the fire with guns and arrows.

The men retreated to the wagon. The two turkey hunters had also seen Indians, riding their horses in a run. The men started the wagon for home as fast as they could, but encountered more Indian horsemen, who appeared to be trying to cut them off from the creek crossing. It was not clear whether this last group was one of the first two bunches seen. The men exchanged fire with them, hustled the wagon across the stream, and came to the village as fast as they could. No one had been hit unless it was one of the Indians, which a guard said he was sure he had hit in the early firing.

Dr. Valentin and Dr. Sockwell drew no conclusions as to the danger we faced, but they agreed that I should ride out and tell the sheepherders to bring their flock in near the village and also bring the milk cows and oxen to their pens. As I crossed the compound, I saw a woman holding a baby talking to Brother Bossereau. She said, "We must escape before it's too late!" and he answered with patience and gentleness, "It was our men who fired; the Indians did not fire." He seemed to be the only one of us all who still thought the Indians might be harmless.

I mounted the mare and rode south, studying frequently and carefully the country out to the west. It was a clear day with a light east wind. I could see no movement out there in the landscape beyond the creek; it had a patchy appearance, the lighter prairie alternating with darker spots of leafless trees. I fancied that over one hidden valley I could see a haze that might be smoke, but it was so thin that it might also be one of those sights that starts in the eye of the beholder. That I saw nothing definite lent no comfort; clearly there were places for a literal horde of savages to lie concealed out there. I told myself that I was filled with uncertainty rather than fear, that we really had no evidence that the Indians would act violently, but I wished that our men had not fired their guns.

I told the sheepherders as calmly as I could that some In-

dians had been sighted and they were to drive their flock back
and graze them between the village and the fields. From this
point I could see the milk cows and oxen, fortunately grazing
together, a half mile to the east. I rode out around them and
drove them back and, with some little trouble, penned them.

Back at the compound the people still milled in confusion.
They were all there, all outside, talking, asking questions of
one another. Some of the guards had climbed to the roofs of
the houses and were staring west. I heard that Brother Bossereau had proposed a peace mission to the Indians, but had not
yet persuaded anyone to go with him. The assembly would
meet immediately after the noon meal. Some kind of argument was going on among the kitchen workers; it came partly
because some of them wanted to stay outside with everyone
else, partly because the women from the auxiliary kitchen
protested that they needed water.

I got some men to help me, and we unloaded the little wood
from the wood wagon. We moved up to the auxiliary kitchen
and loaded two water barrels and headed for the springhouse.
I realized that it was only because I acted as if there were nothing to worry about that they were willing to go with me;
had they known my uncertainty, most of them would not
have gone. As we dipped water, one of the men said, "Wait!
Listen!"

We became quiet, probing with our ears and eyes into the
maze of trees across the creek. Nothing stirred. We started
again dipping and pouring, and the man said, "There! Listen!"

Again we heard nothing. Another man said, "Let's get the
water and get out of here."

We went back toward the village with our load, and I
sensed that all of them were as relieved as I to come back to
the company of all the people in the compound. We carried
the water in by the bucketfuls and had nearly completed this
task when I became aware that the guards on the roofs had
seen something. I had been through all the morning, as nerv-

ous as I was, without my gun. As I went to my quarters to get it, one of the guards yelled, "Someone is coming!"

I checked the load in the gun and this thought flashed in my mind: "Someone...one person...Andy York!" I had not thought of him for what seemed like weeks.

I ran around the end of the building to look toward the creek, as the others were doing. A horseman came up toward us, riding a large paint horse. By the rider's posture I knew that it was not Andy York, but he did not appear to be an Indian, either. He wore a battered felt hat. He had something familiar about him. It was hard to make him out because he carried a load across the saddle in front of him. He headed for an opening toward the lower part of the compound where the rails were down. Just as he passed out of my sight I realized that the load he carried was a body.

The crowd swarmed out to see the rider, not to get too near, but to see. It was the man, half-breed or whatever, named Louey. His dress was greasy buckskins, as it had been before, and I was impressed again with the incongruity of his red sun-bleached beard and his deep copper skin. He seemed again harsh and coarse and inscrutable. Some of the people had never seen him before; I heard their gasps and passionately whispered questions.

He reined up twenty feet from me, looking at us all. Then he raised his arms slightly, and the body he carried face down before him slid feet first, not thrown nor pushed, but released from its precarious balance, to the ground. It squatted grotesquely on lifeless legs and fell back face up, its scalped top shining furiously red.

Then Louey, contrary to my positive impression of him, spoke. I was surprised that he could speak English, and even, in the grasp of the whole excitement, I was startled by it. His voice was rough, fitting his appearance, but clear, so that in that quiet crowd none could have failed to hear him. He said, "They burn this place at sundown."

He pulled his horse around and kicked it in the sides. Our attention was half on him, half on the form he had dumped on the ground. I ran after his horse as it leaped into a trot and yelled, "Louey!"

He turned, not enough to look at me, and said something else without stopping his horse. I think he repeated the word "sundown." He went out of the compound fast and charged back down the slope toward the creek.

Some of them were bending over the body. Dr. Sockwell pushed them back, took one of the limp wrists, and felt for a pulse. He shook his head. The corpse wore buckskins and the vest was pierced in several places, around which the blood was still red and fresh.

A ragged beard grew out of the lower part of the face. I had to stare at it a long moment before I recognized the Andy York that I had known. This face was twisted and tortured, but it was he. The half-closed, squinted eyes looked at me. Then a pang, a surging heartache, fixed on me and I saw some glimpse of the soul of Andrew York the murderer, running in the winter wilderness alone, away from what he had done, fighting a battle between a peculiar righteous rage seeking justification and a desperate, contrite guilt seeking impossible mercy. A moment after I recognized the face, I saw the face of Jim in the crowd; the two faces were not much different.

They were horrified by the scalped head. The skin had been cut across the forehead and around above the ears to the rear and pulled off, leaving only a fringe of matted brown hair. The exposed tissue had oozed blood, bright red, and it was covered over with a clear glaze so that it was made more vivid. Someone brought a blanket to cover the sight.

They were saying, "That's two they've killed!" "Why did he go among them?" "The quicker we get out of this country, the better!"

It was clear that the temper of the colonists was not so much uncertainty now as it was fear. Here and there I saw them talking to, arguing with, the assembly members and the work-crew leaders. I saw Dr. Valentin and Dr. Sockwell evidently arguing passionately with Brother Bossereau. The noon meal had been forgotten. I thought that we would surely have an assembly meeting soon. I was trying to estimate the value of the defense we could mount in this sprawling village with the approximately two dozen guns we owned and with the half dozen good marksmen; I could give no answer, for I had no knowledge of what we must defend against. At one time I had seen with my own eyes a strong force of horse Indians out there. That some were out there now and were serious in their threat was plain; Andy York had been killed after the wood crew's skirmish.

Brother Dominique Henri approached me and grabbed me by the front of my jacket. "They won't listen!" he said. "Brother Langly, they won't listen!"

I firmly disengaged his hand from my clothes and asked him, "What is it?"

"They are mad! We'll all be dead tonight! It's the guns! The guns must be destroyed!"

I managed a confident look and told him, "The assembly will consider every pertinent fact. Please don't be so much concerned, Brother Henri."

I headed toward my quarters, for no purpose other than to get away from him. I almost bumped into the two doctors. Dr. Sockwell, in addition to being as slouchy as usual, appeared disheveled and somewhat breathless. Dr. Valentin seemed to brood darkly and nervously.

Dr. Sockwell had a pencil ready over a folded and dirty sheet of paper. "Langly, I want a quick vote. Do we stay here or do we pack up and get out?"

I didn't want to answer. I asked, "Aren't we going to meet?"

"No. Vote, man!"

"I don't know what to say. How do we know . . . ?"

"How does anyone know? We damned sure don't have

time to talk or think. You're an assembly member. Go or
stay?"

I looked at both of them. "How are you voting?"

Dr. Valentin said, his excitement as great but more contained than Sockwell's, "We want independent judgments.
None of us wants to vote, but we must."

"Goddammit! Will you tell me?" Dr. Sockwell said.

I said, "The people are scared; they want to leave."

They looked at me with fierce insistence.

"I vote to go," I said.

"That's seven," Dr. Valentin said, looking over the other's
shoulder. "And only Bossereau opposed. I think we'd better
proceed to get ready."

Dr. Sockwell said to me, "Could you get some men and
bring the wagons up into the compound? We'll go ahead and
poll all the assembly even though the matter is settled."

I agreed to get the wagons if they would see to it that a
crew took down all the rails of the fences connecting the
buildings so that we could have easy access. As I turned to go,
my eyes happened to fall on the covered body lying so lonely
amidst the hubbub of activity. We quickly agreed that it
must be buried in the compound and done without much
ceremony. They would arrange for it.

I began to search out men who could handle oxen and order
them to come with me. When I got my crew down to the
pen, I made a brief speech to them. "Don't get in too much
hurry," I told them. "Don't panic. Don't scare the animals.
There's plenty of time." When they had begun to catch the
oxen and lead them to the wagons, I thought about the penned
milk cows and realized, looking at the position of the sun,
that there was not actually plenty of time, that I could not
possibly poll the assembly on what to do. I turned them out
and their calves with them.

Then I thought of the sheepherders. I ran back to the end
of the compound where I had tied the sorrel mare, mounted,

and put her into a lope out toward the fields. Shortly, topping a rise, I saw the sheep, unattended. The herders had left them and come in long before.

That was a hectic afternoon. Our frantic haste slowed us up in spite of ourselves. Articles were loaded carefully into wagons only to be unloaded to make room for other things. We wanted light loads and so decided to take no furniture. In the confusion some self-appointed bosses decided that trunks full of personal belongings must be left behind; some time was required to straighten out this error. The people now had forgotten any idea of owning anything in common. It seemed that they were all concerned with two things: to get away as fast as possible and carry with them as much private property as possible. The guards gave orders and were cursed for it. Men with two wagons pulled out and tried to go ahead; they were persuaded to wait.

Of us all, the most calm and efficient in that confused time were Dr. Michel Valentin and, surprising to me, Miss Harriet Edwards. They must have been as excited as Dr. Sockwell and the others of us who were supposed to be leaders, but they revealed it less. Valentin studied the activity with a cool eye and passed among the people giving instructions as if he expected them to be obeyed. They did not always obey him, but it was probably a result of his leadership that we were able to do at all what we were trying to do. Harriet Edwards seemed to gravitate toward those women and children who were almost in a panic; she did not give them instructions, but began methodically to help them gather their belongings and load them.

Dr. Sockwell, his hair flying wildly, became progressively more agitated, until it was a wonder that he was able to care for his own family. We had got all the wagons out of the compound, and I think Valentin had told Sockwell to quickly check all the buildings to see that no person was left behind. Once he called toward the empty compound, "Sockwell!"

A man hurrying by me asked, "Did you see what that idiot Sockwell was doing?"

I said, "No, what?" but he did not pause to enlighten me.

The sun was no more than an hour high when we straightened all our wagons into a line and lumbered east. I rode the mare up and down the line, anxiously hoping that we would have no trouble, for it was too late to halt. Some of the wheels were squeaking from not having been greased in several months, and I decided that if one wagon broke down before dark, we should leave it and go on.

It was a sad caravan. There was no talking beyond what was necessary. In a middle wagon, standing up, lurching this way and that, nearly losing his balance at times, was Brother Bossereau. He rode there as if he had been placed there against his will and he had not yet found out what to do about it, as if it were a temporary thing. His face was pale. I tried not to meet his eyes as I rode past him. Brother Adams walked beside that wagon and sometimes said something to the French leader, but seemed to get no response.

In a wagon toward the rear a woman was sobbing, quietly, possibly about some keepsake or particularly treasured item she had left behind. She made little noise, but two children, a boy of about four and a girl of about seven, evidently her own, took it up; then our movement was accompanied by their prolonged wailing. It was not a loud sound but it penetrated even to the lead wagon, a peculiar, unpremeditated dirge.

We wound up past the fields, past the outcrops of white limestone, toward the highest land that overlooked the valley. Our shadows thrust away out ahead of us in the late light. Here and there the people were looking back. We had come to the highest rise and from my vantage on horseback I could see the shadowed land falling away to the east. Then, without a signal, but as if by common consent, the caravan slowed to a halt. I turned the mare. The sun split the horizon behind us.

The village lay dim and indistinct, a dark blotch, small against the immensity of the valley. I could not make out the individual buildings in it. From this distance it appeared to lie against the creek. I fancied that I could see a faint haze of smoke over it. The people had become quiet, all watching.

Then the sun was gone. For a moment I wondered whether it was all a mistake and we had fled for nothing, whether in that great darkening land we ourselves produced with our imaginations hidden and savage things to be feared. But I could not wonder long. Unmistakable points of flame began to show in the blotch, tiny, spreading, rising. The earth was dark and the sky was still light, and now we could see the smoke as it rose above the horizon. I fancied that I could hear a sound, minor and broken, and it was senseless, like the puny cries of baby birds in a nest.

The people had waited silently and had watched the rising flames without comment. Then they began to talk, as if a kind of nervous tension had been relieved. A man beside one of the wagons asked me whether there was too much play in one of the wagon wheels. I dismounted, tied the mare by one rein to the rod in the end of the wagon box, and went to the front wheel where he stood. I took hold of the wheel at the top and shook it on its axle. I was aware of a commotion at the end of the wagon a moment before I turned to look.

Brother Bossereau had untied the rein and was scrambling to mount the mare as she shied from him. He had the saddle-horn in one hand and the rein in the other, trying to mount on the off side.

Dr. Valentin and Dr. Sockwell were running from the front of the line of wagons. Dr. Valentin screamed, "Jean Charles! No! For the love of God!"

How he mounted I cannot say. I ran toward him, not even understanding at first, but thinking to control the mare and

prevent his being hurt. He got his leg over and got a precarious balance on the frightened horse, grabbing for the loose
rein.

Dr. Sockwell yelled breathlessly, "Stop him! Bossereau,
don't be a fool!"

No one was near enough to stop him. I was still ten steps
from the skittering horse when he got the rein and kicked her
into a run. Then he half turned in the saddle and shouted to
the three of us who ran after him, "I must talk to them!"

He turned her straight back for the village and she poured
her recent panic into hard running. He was crouched low,
but bouncing. The two loose stirrups flailed wildly at the
mare's sides. I heard both of the men who stopped beside me
choke off shouts that were useless.

He went over the first small rise and we saw him no more.

I don't know how long we waited and watched. People
were asking questions, exclaiming, speculating. But then they
ceased. I guess it came to us one by one, little by little, that
we could expect no message out of the west, no flaring of the
fires, no climax.

We got the wagons moving, over the high place from which
we could see the fires, and eastward into the darkness, making
silent, reasonable arguments to our consciences. We would,
seven days later, three others and I, ride back and find his
remains and bury them beside the remains of his daughter, in
sight of the great rectangle of ashes that had been for a time
Uterica. But it was over before that. The end of it was there
in the fading light as we paused on the hill, and that is the
way I best remember him. I hope that I may be excused for
moralizing, but a visual memory of an event and a meaning
may inextricably entwine themselves—I remember him thus:
a ridiculous figure bouncing on the horse, clutching the saddle-
horn, riding directly toward the holocaust and toward the
uncertain savagery of the wilderness valley, as foolish as Don
Quixote riding against the windmills. But he is also larger

than a man; he towers over the horse and the fire and the violence until his size matches the valley. He is not one going to defeat by reality, but himself a timeless, potent part of it, a stubborn part that intends to talk to savagery.

I cannot end this account without telling what Dr. Sockwell had done to delay us a minute before we fled, that fool doctor who had drunk up all the medical spirits, who had never given me any cause to suspect him of sentimentality. He slashed from the bulletin board the scroll which had been done in script by Jeannette and was titled "Goals of Our Common Faith." He rolled it up and put it inside his shirt. As if that were the only copy of those words...I had my copy and do not doubt that among those defeated pioneers, who took up life in various parts of the country, many copies were preserved. Some may even have been recopied, for the original printings were with rough type on cheap paper, somewhat like circus handbills.

AFTERWORD

$\mathbf{B}$ ENJAMIN CAPPS' fifth novel, *The Brothers of Uterica* (1967), added to his growing reputation as an important American novelist, perhaps the best in Texas, and set his feet firmly on the road he had chosen to follow. It was a straight and narrow road, limiting his choices as a writer and his chances at fame and fortune, but it suited him. Capps wanted to write historical novels about life in nineteenth-century Texas, and he intended that they should be taken seriously. He had written one formula western, *Hanging at Comanche Wells,* and that was enough. His characters might experience the transition to modern times but he had no intention of exploring the contemporary scene. He was attracted to the roots of life in his native state, leaving the branches to somebody else. Above all, he wanted to understand what went on a century ago—not to accuse, not to justify, just to show how things really were. He would have to deal with violence, but he would not pour on the gore. He would have to handle sex, but there would be no perversion, no explicit scenes. His people would talk the way real people talk, but there would be no overuse of the Anglo-Saxon monosyllables. In short, Ben Capps was not going to prostitute himself for popularity.

The sixties was not a good time for a man with these intentions. American writers were becoming liberated in many ways. Language taboos had crumbled, reticence about sexual matters was almost gone. In a hundred years the pendulum had swung all the way and the Indians were now seen as the civilized human beings and the pioneers as the savages. It has become almost impossible to take a balanced view of these matters, and most of us seem to have become passionate defenders of the Indians and their way of life. We have insisted loudly that we have used Indians badly and have tried to ease our consciences by handing them millions of dollars which they have not always known how to use. We have become accustomed to reading passages concerning the non-Indian settlers of the American West like this one from John Upton Terrell's 1972 volume, *Apache Chronicle*:

> It must be understood that almost every Spanish and Mexican *colono* and ordinary American who sought his or her fortune in the Apache country stood low on the social scale, a great many of them the dregs of their respective societies. There were among them very few persons of education, and an even smaller number with any type of professional training, and not very many possessed amenities that ranked above a bawdy-house waiting room. The vast majority were uncouth, ignorant, bigoted, and looking for something for nothing.

At the other extreme we have Geronimo, once (according to General George Crook) "the worst Indian who ever lived," now a symbol of heroic resistance to injustice and oppression, the Indian George Washington. In Forrest Carter's *Watch for Me on the Mountain* (1978) he is the Indian Messiah.

Ben Capps avoids these extremes and remains impartial, whether the reading public likes it or not. He is one of a distinguished minority of contemporary writers who can see the good and the bad in both sides. He is one of the few who maintain near-Victorian standards of respectability at a time when the phrase "good taste" has almost disappeared from the language. He has refused to pander to popular taste and has made his reputation almost in spite of it.

He does, however, have much to recommend him to today's readers. First of all he is an excellent writer, handling the tools of his trade with precision and ease. His prose flows, his dialogue is convincing, his word pictures bring his settings to life. He probes deeply into character, Indian or white, and shows sympathy and compassion toward his men and women. He knows that human beings do foolish things and is well aware that they can behave heroically in defense of an illusion. There are no stereotypes in Capps' books— just men and women trying to make the best of their situations according to their lights.

Capps is aware also that human beings cannot free themselves from their time, place, and culture. Cultural changes pose insoluble problems. Captured by Comanches, eleven-year-old Helen in *A Woman of the People* is old enough to resist acculturation. Her five-year-old sister, on the other hand, has no difficulty in becoming an Indian. Sam Chance, the cattle baron, is a product of open-range days and can't adjust to barbed wire and government regulation. Joe Cowbone in *The White Man's Road* is a reservation Indian who longs for the freedom of the old days and tries in vain to recapture it. The union of time, place, and character —whether for good or ill—is the bone and sinew of Capps' novels.

As a result the writer looks for situations which might be called crucibles of character, and *The Brothers of Uterica* gives him one of his finest opportunities. It is the story of a monumental failure and the catastrophe is the product of an unfortunate combination of time, place, and character. The colonists are mostly foreigners unprepared for life in the New World, ignorant of the skills needed to make a living on the land. They are idealists—socialists and dreamers—who hope to found a perfect society without counting the costs. The place is wrong for them—far from civilization, exposed to Indian attacks, plagued by all sorts of unforeseen difficulties. The York brothers, who are fitted for that particular time and place, could save the day, but they get no help from the other colonists. There is real steadfastness and even heroism in their leader, Jean Charles Bossereau, but his dedication and determination are not sufficient to rescue the colony from disaster. Time, place, and character simply do not come together in this situation.

The Brothers of Uterica has not fared as well with the critics as Capps' Indian novels. It is, however, a fresh and original work. It has the depth and grasp that characterize Capps at his best. It dramatizes the interplay of time, place, and character that made the American frontier the most interesting part of our historic record and laid the foundation for the life we lead today.

C. L. Sonnichsen
Tucson, Arizona

ABOUT THE AUTHOR

B ORN in Dundee, Texas, Benjamin Capps moved with his family at the age of eight to a ranch in Archer County, where he lived till he entered Texas Tech. In 1939, he joined the Civilian Conservation Corps in Colorado and later worked as a surveyor there and in his home state.

Capps was commissioned a second lieutenant in the Air Corps in 1944, subsequently flying forty bombing missions as navigator of a B-24 in the Pacific. At war's end, he completed his education at the University of Texas at Austin, graduating Phi Beta Kappa in 1948 and receiving his M.A. the following year.

Capps is the author of eight novels, of which *Sam Chance*, *The Trail to Ogallala*, and *The White Man's Road* have won the Spur Award as best western novel of the year from Western Writers of America. For the general contribution of his work to the body of western literature the same organization has honored Capps with its prestigious Levi Strauss Golden Saddleman Award, and he has also received two Wrangler Awards from The Cowboy Hall of Fame and Western Heritage Center.

Benjamin Capps lives now in Grand Prairie, Texas.